Forbidden Garden

Victoria Burks

WESTBOW
PRESS
A DIVISION OF THOMAS NELSON
& ZONDERVAN

WestBow Press books may be ordered through booksellers or by contacting:

WestBow Press
A Division of Thomas Nelson & Zondervan
1663 Liberty Drive
Bloomington, IN 47403
www.westbowpress.com
1 (866) 928-1240

ISBN: 978-1-4908-3120-6 (sc)
ISBN: 978-1-4908-3122-0 (hc)
ISBN: 978-1-4908-3121-3 (e)

Library of Congress Control Number: 2014905420

Printed in the United States of America.

WestBow Press rev. date: 4/9/2014

Acknowledgments

$\mathcal{I}$ would like to say thank you to my family and friends for their generous support and encouragement. Kay Standridge, my friend, I could never say enough to express my appreciation for your honest critique of my work and your belief in me as a writer. To my daughter, Roberta Palmer, thank you for your ongoing words of encouragement that help keep me on the path that God has carved for me in His vast kingdom.

To my pastors and friends, Darryl and Faith Wootton, thank you for your faith in me, both as an author and as a child of our King.

A special thank you to Dr. Jim Young for sharing medical expertise that helped advance the plot of Forbidden Garden.

To William, my husband and best friend, how I adore you for your confidence in me and your willingness to enable my career when and where you can.

"This is the Lord's doing; and it is marvelous in our eyes."
Psalm 118:23

Chapter 1

Mackenzie Adams sat straight up in bed, her heart pounding. An icy sensation gripped the back of her neck and then slithered down her spine. Trembling, she held her breath, blinking to rid the drowsiness from her eyes. Her body tense with anticipation, she balled her hands into fists, preparing to do battle. She quickly skimmed the perimeter of her room, the murky glow of the night-light her only ally in the search for the intruder.

A moment later, she tilted her head in confusion. Squinting, she again scrutinized each shadowy corner of the bedroom. But as before, she saw no sign that danger lurked nearby. She stacked her palms against her stomach. So what accounted for the knot of fear clenching her insides like jaws of steel?

A blast of air from the cooling system sliced across her clammy skin. Shivering, she reached to straighten the tangled bedclothes but stilled her intention, realizing the nightmare she'd had moments before she awoke, not a burglar, had instigated her fright. The memory plunged into her thoughts like a sudden avalanche. Mackenzie clamped her hand across her mouth, stifling the cry of alarm that leaped to her lips. Shrinking deep into the bed, she dragged the covers to her chin, the scenario repeating in her mind like the recollection of an appalling YouTube video.

Mackenzie had stood near a large oak tree, its branches swaying back and forth against a strong wind, the gale so fierce she'd found it difficult to keep her feet on the ground. All of a sudden, she'd spied a tornado whirling toward her, the raging tempest wrenching limbs from the tree and hurling them into space.

She'd reached out to hug the trunk of the tree for support but had cowered in terror when it cracked and split apart before her eyes. Covering her head with her arms, she'd tried to run, but her legs had seemed frozen to the earth like stalagmites bound to the floor of a cave.

Mackenzie threw back the bedding and stood. The implication of the vivid vision was crystal-clear: she had to get away—had to flee the constant reminders that held her captive beneath the southwestern sun. Wisdom spoke it—her sanity required it. If she stayed, she would become like that oak tree—twisted, mangled, and torn apart, her life destroyed by the oppressive storm that besieged her night and day.

She shuddered, the sense of urgency stripping away any thought of further slumber. With a glance at the bedside clock, she switched on her table lamp. Soon it would be daybreak.

She thrust her feet into a pair of slippers and hurried to the entryway of her room. She cracked open the door and stole a peek toward the bedroom at the end of the hall. Relief zipped through her. All was quiet. She eased the door shut and hurried to the shower. Dressed within a few minutes, she pulled suitcases from the closet. Within less than an hour, she had her clothing and personal belongings packed and loaded into her car.

Back inside the house, Mackenzie tiptoed down the hallway, breaking her stride when a sudden glow of light appeared beneath Steve and Reagan Adams's bedroom door. Her breath caught and held. Had she been longer in completing the task, her parents might have become aware of her plans much sooner than she desired. After slipping into her room, she leaned back against the door until her erratic heartbeat slowed to its normal pace.

She moved toward the window a moment later, opened the blinds, and gazed at the gorgeous sunrise glistening through the sheer curtains. Most people associated sunlight with hope. Did she dare believe a brighter future existed on the eastern slope of the continental divide? Mackenzie closed her eyes. She had to believe it. She just had to!

After pressing the back key on her iPhone, Mackenzie pocketed the device and then stepped into the hallway. She turned to take in the room she'd called her own for most of her life, her last two years of college the only exception. During that time, she'd had her own apartment close to the campus. As she glanced around the interior, nostalgia brushed a path across her thoughts. She and her friends had shared many happy moments in this room. Mackenzie's shoulders slumped forward. Would she ever be that carefree again? If only she could erase the last year from her life. She sighed. Destiny moved forward, never backward.

Again, she surveyed the room. The decor in shades of rich southwestern colors had been a high school graduation gift from her parents. She and her mother had planned and decorated the room together. It had been one of the few times she'd felt close to Reagan. Mackenzie's mouth curved downward. Days like that had been few. Her mother's devotion to her job as an elementary teacher was understandable, but Mackenzie had yet to condone the excessive hours Reagan devoted to community service, the various projects year after year taking a toll on her relationship with her husband and child.

Mackenzie's lips tightened. A quest for answers now would be like searching for water in a dry well. She shut the door to the sanctuary, closing off thoughts of her childhood at the same time. Without a backward glance, she walked toward the back of the house, grateful that she hadn't let this chance for freedom slip away. She took a deep breath. Her future beckoned—and she intended to make the best of it.

About to enter the kitchen, she hesitated at the doorway, taking a moment to observe her mother, who stood at the counter, measuring pancake mix into a bowl. Catching a glimpse of Mackenzie, Reagan pushed back a strand of her dark hair flecked with gray and smiled.

"Well, you're up early."

"Yes. A—a dream woke me, and I couldn't go back to sleep." Mackenzie poured herself a cup of coffee and stirred in a spoonful of sugar and a dollop of cream before she took her usual place at the table. She knew her mother would spurn an offer to help with breakfast. Reagan preferred to handle family meals in her own time and way. Mackenzie smiled inwardly. Her mother might not be the most nurturing of women, but the best chef in the world would have to work hard to compete with her mother's ability in the kitchen.

Mackenzie aimed a cautious glance toward her father, who sat at the other end of the breakfast nook, sipping coffee while he scanned the latest edition of the *Arizona Republic*. She took a drink of coffee. How would she ever be able to get her announcement past the bale of cotton in her mouth? She picked up a section of the paper from the table to read, but a glimpse at the scene outside the kitchen window diverted her attention.

The family cat crouched beneath the orange tree in their backyard, his gaze centered upon a robin splashing in the birdbath a few feet away. Just as the cat sprang to grasp its prey, the bird lifted its wings and flew to the top of the tree. A hint of a smile touched Mackenzie's lips. *Hooray for the robin,* she thought. The cat's tail moved back and forth as if daring the bird to budge from its lofty position. Sobering, she turned from the scenario, a sigh escaping her lips. She would miss the old fur ball. She closed her eyes. Like the bird, could she escape the enemy that stalked her?

Feeling her father's gaze on her, she directed a look his way. The lines at the corners of his warm brown eyes crinkled from his smile. "If you're going to read the newspaper that way, you'll have to stand on your head." All of a sudden his grin faded. "Is something wrong, Mackenzie?"

She righted the paper and laid it beside her plate. The sound of the whisk against the side of the mixing bowl ceased abruptly. Dead silence invaded the room. Her eyes downcast, Mackenzie observed her mother's movements from beneath her long eyelashes. Pulling a griddle from the cabinet beneath the counter, Reagan glanced at her husband before she fixed a gaze on her child.

Mackenzie cringed inside, aware that the next few moments were sure to be agonizing for the three of them. Sighing, she held her hands tightly against her lap. There was no sense in putting off the inevitable any longer. "Mom, Dad, I have something to tell you. I didn't want to say anything until after we'd eaten breakfast"—she pocketed her bottom lip between her teeth momentarily—"but I suppose now is just as good a time as any."

The worried look in Steve's eyes intensified. He leaned forward. "And that is?"

Mackenzie lifted her lashes to take in her father's features. It still amazed her that he'd never lost his Mississippi drawl, although he'd lived in the Southwest for many years. She swallowed hard. "I've accepted the offer from the Huntingtons. I e-mailed Mr. Huntington earlier to expect my arrival at their home on Thursday morning."

The griddle slid from Reagan's hand and landed on the floor, the clatter resonating in the sun-drenched room. Reagan stared at her daughter, her face clothed in disbelief.

"But that means—"

"Yes." Mackenzie turned away, guilt pricking her at seeing the incredulous looks in their eyes. She straightened her posture, bolstering her resolve. "I have to leave this morning. I'm packed and ready to go. In fact, I loaded my car while you were asleep."

Steve stood and walked away from the table. Bending, he picked up the griddle and placed it on the stove burner. Without a word, he left the room.

Mackenzie flicked a piece of lint off the tablecloth, her breathing ragged. She filched a glance at her mother, who stood stock-still, staring into space. A moment later, the smell of burning bacon filled the air. Reagan's nose wrinkled, her violet-blue eyes, the likes of which Mackenzie had inherited, widening. Reagan did an about-face and then resumed her task of preparing breakfast, her full mouth drawn tightly against her face.

Mackenzie waited, aware that any second, her mother would bare her thoughts without reservation. Mackenzie steadied her torso against the back of her chair as if steeling against a blow from an iron fist.

Her eyes acute with anger, Reagan faced her daughter. "Mackenzie Dawn Adams, do you realize how hard your father and I have worked all these years to see a college diploma in your hands? A master's degree, for heaven's sake! Or the sacrifices we made through the years to put aside money every month for your education?" Reagan's lips trembled. "Beginning the day you were born. Your father, eager to start saving for your college education right away, stopped by the bank that same afternoon to open an account. When he returned to the hospital, he waltzed into my room as proud as I've ever seen him." Reagan glared at Mackenzie. "How could you throw all that away to become a glorified *babysitter*? What's come over you?"

Mackenzie swallowed the retort that leaped to her lips, allowing the heat that singed her cheeks to cool before she spoke. "Mom, you know I appreciate what you and Dad have done for me. My grades should speak for that." Mackenzie's eyes snapped. "In case you don't remember, I wore a summa cum laude stole around my neck during graduation."

Mackenzie lowered her gaze. And what effort that had taken to accomplish this past semester! She drew a long breath, hating her brusqueness. "I'm sorry, Mother," she said, softening her voice. "You and Dad have given me much more than I'll ever deserve."

Reagan slammed a glass of orange juice down next to Mackenzie's plate, staring at the liquid when it mushroomed over the rim and dripped onto the tablecloth. She grabbed a nearby napkin and dabbed at the spill, halting the cleanup to peruse her daughter's face.

"You've changed. You used to be so animated, full of life. Does this decision of yours have something to do with your broken engagement? Surely you've ceased mourning over that. Believe me, there are plenty of other guys out there much more responsible than Zachary Gilbert."

Mackenzie flinched. *Mourning?* What an understatement! The mention of her former fiancé burned in her heart like salt poured into a wound. If only she hadn't listened to Zack or yielded to his scheme, hadn't believed the promise he'd later thrown to the wind.

Mackenzie's jaw tightened. She choked back angry tears. Why had she let herself be used? She grimaced as the answer swooped into her thoughts. Swayed by Zack's charm, she'd been blind to his true nature. Her eyes narrowed. She had meant nothing more to him than an easier ride to his doctorate, her love for him a mere pawn in his hands. Her mouth twisted. Oh, how he'd pleaded for her to understand that he wasn't yet ready for marriage. *And then to find out he'd been dating a college junior while I worked extra hours so he could devote his entire time to his education.* Mackenzie's cheeks burned. How could she have been so deceived?

With a slight shake of her head, Mackenzie tilted her chin to glimpse her mother, who now leaned against the sink counter, fanning her flushed face with a dish towel.

"Well, aren't you going to say anything?" Reagan said, pausing to take a deep breath.

A plea for understanding in her eyes, Mackenzie opened her mouth to speak but clamped it shut. No need to waste her breath expounding on all the courses she'd taken on the development of children in order to earn her MA in family relations and child development, not to mention all the hands-on experience she'd had in her teen years. The hardness in her mother's eyes told Mackenzie the attempt would be futile.

"Don't you think we've discussed it enough?" Mackenzie glanced away. The heated debates with her parents in the last two weeks about the subject of employment had been plenty of deliberation for her.

She glimpsed the hands on her wristwatch and then pushed her empty plate toward the middle of the table. All of a sudden, breakfast at a fast-food restaurant on her way out of town seemed much more apropos at the moment. Mackenzie stood.

"It's getting late. I should get on the road. I suppose Dad left for work?"

"No, I haven't. Not yet," Steve said, entering the kitchen.

At the sound of his voice, Mackenzie turned and smiled at her father. "I'm glad you're still here. I-I would have hated not being able to tell you good-bye."

"I called in to say I'd be late this morning."

"Good," Reagan said, tossing the towel onto the counter. "Maybe you can talk some sense into your daughter before she wanders off into God knows where."

Mackenzie rolled her eyes toward the ceiling. "Mom, you know exactly where I'm going—Little Rock, Arkansas." Seeing a flicker of sadness march across the ire lodged in her mother's eyes, Mackenzie softened her features.

"Mom!" Mackenzie darted a glance toward her father. "Dad! I know you don't understand, but this is something I have to do. I love you both very much, and I'm sorry I've hurt you, but you need to trust me on this one. And please—let's not argue about it anymore," she said, an appeal for their support in her eyes. "I intend to keep my word to the Huntingtons." She faced her father. "Dad, you've always taught me to follow through with my decisions if I believe in them."

Steve nodded. "Yes, that's true." His eyes misted. "But in this case— please forgive me—I don't comprehend this endeavor of yours at all." He swallowed hard, causing the Adam's apple in his long, slender neck to bob up and then down.

Unable to bear the sadness in his eyes, Mackenzie turned from his searching gaze. She reached out to give her mother a hug, but Reagan drew away from the embrace. Mackenzie gasped. Staggering backward, she turned toward the built-in desk in the corner of the kitchen, where she'd stowed her handbag the night before. She grabbed the purse and rushed out the back door.

Steve's words to his wife, insisting they see their daughter off, rang in Mackenzie's ears. A moment later, the couple stood on the driveway of their middle-class Phoenix, Arizona, home, a volley of emotions crisscrossing their features.

Steve cleared his throat. "Well, Mackenzie, I can see that you're determined to go through with this. Is there nothing we can say or do that will change your mind?"

Mackenzie shook her head. "I'm so sorry." She closed her eyes, unable to bear the despair in his eyes. When she opened them again, her father stood at her side. He slid his hand inside his sports coat, withdrew an envelope from the inside pocket, and placed it in Mackenzie's hand.

"For days, I've felt this moment would come. So I made sure this would be available."

Mackenzie opened the envelope and glanced inside, her eyes widening. "Dad, I have some money saved."

Steve shook his head when she started to hand back the envelope. "No. You may need some things before you get your first paycheck."

Mackenzie reached out and hugged her father. "Thanks, Dad. You know I'll pay you back."

"Yes." A slight grin lifted one side of his mouth. "Your mother often tells me how much we're alike. But this is a gift, Mackenzie, not a loan."

The image of her father blurred. She glanced toward Reagan, and a sharp pain twisted inside Mackenzie's chest. Her mother stood rigid, her face tight and unyielding. Mackenzie leaned her head on her father's chest, harboring the love she sensed in the tightness of his embrace. She opened her lips to speak, but the words she longed to utter stuck in her throat. After another quick hug, she unlocked her car.

Once settled behind the wheel, Mackenzie observed her parents through the windshield. Her stomach lurched at the sight of her father's grief. She found it odd that she hadn't noticed how much his dark brown hair had grayed in the last year.

In contrast, the hostility revealed on her mother's face seemed merciless like the heat of the sun striking the rocks in their desert-landscaped yard. Mackenzie could hold back the tears no longer, aware that she alone possessed the blame for their misery. She glanced at the envelope on the seat beside her. She didn't merit one ounce of her father's generosity.

Mackenzie tightened her grip on the key ring to steady her hand. At last able to feed the key into the ignition, she gave them a wobbly smile as the car sprang to life. Guilt surged through her. They deserved to know the reason behind her departure. Mackenzie's shoulders caved in at the notion. No. She could never share that part of her life—it would destroy their love for her altogether. Blinking back the tears, she slipped on her sunglasses and then shifted the car into reverse.

She backed the car down the driveway. *It's now or never,* she thought. Once on the street, she braked the car for a final wave. Only her father responded in return. A moment later, she pressed the accelerator, steering the eight-year-old Camry toward a new beginning filled with promise—a future she could only hope would somehow vanquish her heartbreak.

She glanced backward for one last look at her parents. If only she had never met Zack. Mackenzie pulled a tissue from a box beneath the dashboard and brushed away the rebellious tears that rolled down her cheeks. Would her parents someday forgive her? Maybe, but they would never understand how she could turn down the counselor's position she'd been offered at a prominent women's hospital in the Valley. Not in a million years.

If only she could find the courage to turn the car around and pour out her soul to them. She stilled the thought. The secret she lived with would have to remain hidden in her heart like an unattended, forbidden garden—a garden secluded from humanity and guarded by unspoken words.

Mackenzie's eyes widened when a pickup truck cut in front of her car. She slammed on the brakes. "Whew! That was close." Her shoulders shaking, she shifted her weight in the seat. If she wanted to reach her destination all in one piece, she needed to concentrate on her driving.

Later, when traffic thinned, Mackenzie relaxed her shoulders. Now able to cruise along the interstate, her thoughts drifted to the new employment waiting at the end of her ambiguous journey. A vague smile touched her lips. Had early explorers experienced similar uncertainty at the onset of their exploits into uncharted territory? But in spite of the turmoil within her, she sensed that she'd made the right choice. Mackenzie sighed. Someone had once said, "Time heals all wounds." Would time and distance mend the gap in the relationship with her parents or widen it? Still, she could hope for the best.

As she exited to travel north on Interstate 17, Mackenzie's heartbeat quickened. Once she made her home in Arkansas, would the agony that awoke with her each morning and wrecked any thought of peaceful rest at night vanish from her mind? The state carried the motto "The Land of Opportunity." Would it become a land of opportunity for her? She glanced around at the nearly lifeless desert terrain. *Please, please, let it be so!*

All of a sudden, the image of the church she'd attended in childhood stole into her thoughts, along with the memory of the pastor's often-spoken encouragement to his congregation to give their cares to God; he insisted that He was a safe harbor where all could anchor their hope and faith. A bitter laugh spilled from her throat. How could she dare fathom for a split second that God *or* her parents might forgive her sin?

Mackenzie pushed her hand tightly against her chest. Would she have to live with this ache in her heart for the rest of her life? Coiling one side of her hair behind her ear, she narrowed her eyes. She had to focus on her future, not the past. If not, she would be an emotional wreck by the time she landed on Mr. Huntington's doorstep.

Mackenzie jumped at the sound of her cell phone. She fumbled in her purse to retrieve the device and smiled when she saw a text from her best friend since her kindergarten days, Kari Wysong. Mackenzie glanced back and forth between the road and her phone, and her eyes widened as she scanned the message.

"Just met Brad Pitt. Will phone tonight with details. My heart still racing."

Pushing the back key on her phone, Mackenzie laughed, convinced that the evening ahead would prove entertaining.

Kari, who'd chosen to attend a prestigious nanny school in the Midwest instead of college, had, like Mackenzie, received a diploma a few weeks ago. The two friends hoped to embark on their careers before the end of summer. Mackenzie recalled the evening she had learned about Kari's job offers soon after her friend had returned to Arizona.

"So which position have you decided to take?" Mackenzie had asked while the girls enjoyed a meal at their favorite restaurant.

Lines distorting her brow, Kari had taken a sip of cola before she'd replied. "Well, they both offer good salaries and benefits, but I intend to accept the one in California. Los Angeles is just a short flight from Phoenix. I can visit my family often." Kari grinned. "And think about the celebrities I might get to meet." She rolled her eyes toward the ceiling. "Who would have thought I would become a nanny to the children of a Hollywood star?"

During the conversation, Mackenzie's eyes had lit up with inspiration. After a lengthy inquiry about the nanny post in Arkansas and the criteria needed for the job, Mackenzie had decided she would take advantage of the opportunity and apply for the position.

With that in mind, the girls had driven to the Southwest placement center for the nanny school the next day. A few days later, Sharon Breckenridge, the director of the center, had phoned Mackenzie to inform her that she would have a phone interview with the Huntingtons later that week. Unlike her parents, Kari, although surprised by Mackenzie's change in career options, had supported her friend without question. Mackenzie frowned. Her friend knew nothing of the true motive behind Mackenzie's desire to build a life so far from home. "And," Mackenzie muttered, "I intend to keep it that way." Her irreversible action several weeks ago had jeopardized her relationship with her parents, and she had no desire to lose her best friend as well.

Mackenzie adjusted the settings to the seat cushion for a more comfortable ride. The memory of her conversation with Mrs. Breckenridge just before the scheduled conference call filled her mind.

"You are aware, I'm sure, Miss Adams," the director had said, peering at Mackenzie over her glasses, "that your education and child-care experience far exceed the limit for a qualified nanny. And the reports from your references were"—Mrs. Breckenridge smiled—"well, glowing, to say the least. It's obvious you have a good rapport with children."

Mackenzie had reddened. "Yes, ma'am, I do love caring for them. That's one of the reasons I feel I'm right for this job. And it would help me better understand that type of family environment—a hands-on situation that I believe would aid a future career in family counseling."

Mrs. Breckenridge had taken a long moment to scrutinize Mackenzie's features. Shaking her head, she'd punched in the phone number. By the end of the conference call with Andrew and Jasmine Huntington, the couple and Mrs. Breckenridge had been convinced that Mackenzie Adams would be the ideal nanny for the couple's baby girl. However, when

Mackenzie had stopped by the agency a few days ago to pick up her copy of the contract, Mrs. Breckenridge's departing advice had shaken the core of Mackenzie's innermost being.

"Dear, please remember," the director had said as she'd laid her hand on Mackenzie's arm, "you can't run away from your problems forever. Sooner or later, you'll have to face that giant and stare him down. And God will help you if you ask Him."

Mackenzie's eyes had widened; the gentleness and compassion in the woman's gaze had been compelling. Mackenzie had been aware that if she didn't walk out the door that instant, the truth she held in her heart would spill from her lips, laid bare for the world to judge. Her cheeks flaming, she'd stammered something about being late for another appointment and hastened from the building. Had she stayed, Mrs. Breckenridge would have understood within moments just why God wanted nothing to do with Mackenzie Adams.

Mackenzie swerved the car to miss a piece of tire cap lying on the road, the movement jarring her attention back to the present. Another mile down the road, a rest-area sign caught her attention. A couple moments later, she drove onto the exit, believing some fresh air would clear her mind.

Feeling rejuvenated after a short walk, Mackenzie returned to her car. Excitement she hadn't experienced in some time stirred within her. Maybe she *could* find solace and relinquish the pain associated with the memory of Zack after all. If so, any sacrifice she'd have to make for that accomplishment would be worth it.

Close to an hour later, nearing Flagstaff, the snow bowl of Arizona, she glanced toward Humphrey's Peak. The past cold season hadn't produced enough snowfall to entice winter sports enthusiasts to the area, as in prior years. However, one mountaintop towering above all the other peaks around it seemed to defy the status quo with its fluffy white bonnet sparkling beneath the rays of sun. As the mountain shied away from her view, a rush of fortitude gripped Mackenzie. Just as the mountains rose from the nearly useless desert floor, somehow, someway, she would rise from the dregs of the last few months. Nonetheless, just as snow continued to blanket the mountaintop, she knew she would never get away from the remorse that shrouded her soul. She could only hope it would become less painful in the days to come.

Chapter 2

*T*hree days later, Mackenzie parked her car alongside the curb outside the Huntingtons' redbrick colonial revival home. The estate known as Park House stood in one of the original affluent Little Rock neighborhoods. She took in the structure through the side window of her car. Two large French-paned windows guarded by white wooden shutters graced the front of the house, and two sets of smaller windows similar in design designated the two additional floors of the house. *Mercy! That's some house.* She nodded. No doubt about it—the place oozed with early American charisma.

Mackenzie glanced at the holly shrubs adorning the perimeter of the front lawn. Their vibrant, shiny leaves sprinkled with dewdrops shimmered in the morning sun like emeralds. A three-foot carved swath in the greenery revealed steps next to the street and the paved walkway that led to the covered porch shading the entire width of the house. A few days ago, when she'd researched the area that was to become her new home, she had read on the web that the house was listed in the National Register of Historic Places.

All of a sudden, a sense of foreboding squeezed into her thoughts. Frowning, she shook off the shiver that rippled down her spine. Had she made a mistake? Or was the nostalgic scene a caustic reminder that just as history remained in the solid core of time, so did a person's past, in spite of his or her efforts to flee from it?

Refusing to contemplate the matter further, she pulled down the sun visor and glanced in the mirror. She plumped up her hair, admiring the new highlighted, just-below-chin-length hairstyle. Tilting her head, she studied her image, deciding the blonde streaks gave her a more sophisticated look. Satisfied, she glanced at the stately manor again, anticipating the meeting with her new employers.

On the two occasions she'd spoken with them on the phone, they'd seemed friendly and down-to-earth, considering Mr. Huntington owned a large real-estate and land-development corporation that had made millions according to Fortune 500. Glancing at the portfolio on the passenger seat, Mackenzie smiled. Mrs. Breckenridge had researched her clients well, assuring Mackenzie that all their clientele underwent the same scrutiny. The prestigious school desired and sought the best homes in the nation for their nannies. Mackenzie applied a coat of gloss to her lips and emerged from the car a moment later.

She smoothed her skirt over her hips, conscious of the additional curviness she felt beneath her hands. She blamed the extra ten pounds she'd gained on the stress she'd endured of late. Some people lost weight when dealing with anxiety, but the opposite had occurred in her case. Once she became established in her new job, perhaps a membership at a nearby gym would be a good way to occupy some of her free time.

Mackenzie strapped her handbag over her shoulder and climbed the steps. Halfway up the sidewalk, she paused to wipe away the sudden perspiration on her upper lip. Would meeting the Huntingtons in person go well? She stored the used tissue in her purse, breathing deeply to slow her heartbeat. If so, she would begin her nanny duties the following day, once she'd settled into her quarters. She eyed the hands on her wristwatch. *Right on time.* Lifting her shoulders, she planted a smile on her face and proceeded toward the door, eager now to begin her employment.

She had no more than pushed the doorbell, when the door swung open. A woman who looked close to retirement age and was dressed in a maid's uniform studied the newcomer a long moment before she spoke, her dark brown eyes filling with disapproval. "Miss Adams, I believe?"

Awed by the sharp contrast between her light skin and distinct African American features, Mackenzie lowered her eyes, desiring not to stare.

Seconds later, a slight frown capped Mackenzie's brow. She hoped her reception from the Huntingtons would be more congenial.

All at once, Mackenzie's heart leaped. Had she been in err about the time of the meeting? *No,* Mackenzie thought. The instructions from Mrs. Breckenridge had stated ten o'clock. Then why the icy demeanor?

Mackenzie widened her smile, opting to forget the woman's rudeness. Perhaps something beforehand had upset the lady. "Yes, ma'am. Mr. and Mrs. Huntington are expecting me."

The woman bent her head and then stepped aside, beckoning Mackenzie inside the house. "Mr. Huntington told me to bring you to him right away. I'm Mrs. Slater, the house manager. The interview will be different than you expected, but I'm sure Mr. Huntington will explain all that."

Mackenzie tensed. Did she still have a job? Her heartbeat quickened. Had she made the trip to Arkansas in vain? But wouldn't the Huntingtons have notified her or Mrs. Breckenridge if they'd engaged another caretaker for their child?

At that moment, an infant's scream tore through the house. Mrs. Slater threw a glance toward Mackenzie. "I offered to feed the child, but Mr. Huntington insisted he could do it while he ate his breakfast." Mrs. Slater's expression hardened. "Her mother is unavailable at present."

Mackenzie's eyes widened. What did Mrs. Slater mean? The introductory meeting was to be with both parents. Mackenzie's mind raced. Perhaps unexpected circumstances had called Mrs. Huntington out of town. A look of sympathy crossed Mackenzie's features. Or maybe the woman had become ill. A moment later, when Mackenzie walked through the doorway of the spacious dining room, her chin dropped at the scenario that greeted her. All questions subsided as she struggled to rein in the chuckle teasing her throat.

The baby sat in a high chair, half of her blonde curls drenched with liquid that Mackenzie guessed to be milk by the look of the upturned bowl and soggy cereal scattered across the tray and on the floor. She drew within reach of the sobbing child, darting a glance toward the distinguished-looking gentleman standing nearby, whose gray designer business attire accented the streaks of gray visible at his hairline.

Assuming he was Mr. Huntington, Mackenzie felt startled by how his facial features belied the image his clothes portrayed. His swarthy complexion haggard and drawn, his dark eyes sunken deep into his face, he looked as if he hadn't slept in days. Mackenzie eyed his efforts to rid his coat and tie of the milk splatters with a cloth napkin. He looked up, a wan smile lifting the corners of his mouth.

"I do apologize, Miss Adams." He glanced at his watch. "You are Miss Adams, I presume?"

Mackenzie nodded and smiled. "That would be correct, sir."

Placing the linen napkin next to a plate filled with an adult's breakfast now grown cold, he stepped forward to shake her hand.

"I'm Andrew Huntington." He glanced at Mrs. Slater, who stood staring at the catastrophe before them as if she couldn't believe what had just happened. "You can tell Angie to clear the table."

Mr. Huntington smiled at Mackenzie. "I thought I could feed my daughter with no problem." His smile broadened. "But as you can see, I didn't quite pull it off to perfection."

Mackenzie laughed. "No, sir. I'm afraid I have to agree with you."

Mr. Huntington eyed the house manager, who seemed rooted to the floor. "Mrs. Slater?"

She started at the sound of her name, a tinge of red staining her cheeks. She blinked and then turned to Mackenzie. "I beg your pardon, sir. This is Miss Adams, the new nanny."

Mr. Huntington grew to his full height, a frown replacing his smile. "Yes, Mrs. Slater, we've met. You seem troubled. Is something wrong?"

The house manager turned her gaze toward Mackenzie, disapproval again clouding her expression. "Not at all, sir. I'm just not used to the child creating such a disturbance."

"I see. Well, I'm sure our house is not the first home that has had to deal with an overturned bowl of cereal."

Mrs. Slater lowered her eyelashes. "No, sir. I would think not."

While her new employer conversed with the house manager, Mackenzie appraised the infant whose sobs had quieted during the interchange between the adults, although tears still trickled down her red cheeks. When the room grew quiet, Mackenzie stepped closer to the child.

"Now, now, little one," Mackenzie cooed. "It's okay. Just an accident. We'll have you cleaned up in a jiffy."

3

Mr. Huntington and Mrs. Slater turned toward Mackenzie and the child. The baby lifted her crystal-blue eyes to behold the stranger. Mackenzie picked up the napkin discarded by the father and began to wipe the tears from the baby's face. "There. That's better, don't you think? Now, let's see what we can do about this mess."

She glanced toward the house manager, smiling. "Perhaps Mrs. Slater could bring us a wet cloth to make the chore a bit easier."

Mrs. Slater grew rigid, a look of displeasure leaping into her eyes. However, at Mr. Huntington's nod, she pivoted on her heel and left the room, returning moments later with a dampened washcloth and a roll of paper towels that she presented to Mackenzie. Mrs. Slater then stood off to the side, her gaze fixed on the new nanny's attempt to make the child presentable again, not once offering to assist with the cleanup.

Mackenzie smiled within. Mrs. Breckenridge had warned her that other household employees often took offense at requests from a nanny. Although her status in the house would be closer to that of a family member, the rest of the staff would consider her just another employee. Could that have been the reason for the instant dislike she'd sensed earlier from Mrs. Slater? Mackenzie sighed. Would the other employees treat her likewise? She hoped not. She'd much rather find friends among them.

The sound of the doorbell drew their attention. Mrs. Slater hurried from the room.

Mr. Huntington surveyed Mackenzie's efforts for a moment and then reached for the paper towels. Bending, he tackled the spill on the floor while Mackenzie mopped up the debris on the tray. Once finished, she set the tray aside and began to swab goo from the baby's clothes, realizing that only a bath and a change of clothing could rectify the situation. After a few minutes, Mackenzie held her hands out to the angelic-looking child, who eyed the gesture momentarily and then reached for Mackenzie.

"What's your name, little one?" Mackenzie said, ignoring the moistness collecting on the new outfit she'd purchased for her arrival at the Huntingtons. She thumbed away a last stray tear that had seeped onto the baby's cheek. The child grinned, hiding her face in Mackenzie's shoulder. Mackenzie glanced up at her employer, wondering just how much Mr. Huntington knew about caring for an infant. She buried her cheek against the top of the baby's head to hide her grin. *Not much,* she thought, the perplexed look on his face a good sign her opinion had value.

He cleared his throat. "Elise—her name is Elise. I'm sorry, Miss Adams, that you were exposed to this. Things are a little unsettling here." Both Mackenzie and Mr. Huntington glanced up as Mrs. Slater and a tall, brawny gentleman entered the room. Mackenzie's eyes widened when he held up his identity badge.

Without waiting for an introduction, the police officer spoke. "Mr. Huntington? I'm Captain Wallace Sprinsky. Just after dawn this morning, a woman's body was discovered by a fisherman near the edge of the Arkansas River. From the description and the photograph you presented to us two days ago ..." The captain paused. "I'm sorry, Mr. Huntington. We believe the body is that of your missing wife." At the sound of the gasp escaping Mackenzie's throat, the officer glanced in her direction briefly before he riveted his attention back to Mr. Huntington. "If at all possible, sir, I need you to accompany me to the morgue in order to make a positive identification."

Mackenzie's legs buckled. Afraid she might drop the baby, Mackenzie sat down quickly in one of the dining room chairs. Too stunned to move, she stared at the officer as he whipped by her to steady Mr. Huntington, who now gripped the edge of the table with his hands, his knuckles stark white. She swept her gaze toward him, wincing at the emotions that waltzed across his features—shock, disbelief, and then a look of intense pain she assumed had to do with the knowledge that his wife could be dead.

"Of course, Captain. Just give me a moment. Please," he said, straightening his shoulders.

Captain Sprinsky's stern expression softened. A look of sympathy flashed in his blue eyes. "Anything I can do, Mr. Huntington?"

"No, but thank you anyway." His eyes darted back and forth as if the action would help him collect his thoughts. Seeming to regain control again, he turned to Mackenzie. "Miss Adams, would you mind starting your post a day early? I need you to care for my daughter while I accompany the captain to the precinct. I'm sorry, but we'll have to postpone our meeting until later. In the meantime, if you have any questions before I return, Mrs. Slater should be able to answer them." He glanced at his child cuddled in Mackenzie's arms, a skeleton of a smile touching his lips. "I believe you and Elise will get along fine."

Mr. Huntington started to walk away but broke his stride. "Excuse me, Captain," he said, motioning toward Mackenzie. "This is my daughter's new nanny, Miss Mackenzie Adams. She arrived this morning from Arizona. Of course, you've already met Mrs. Slater."

The captain nodded. Stepping forward, he held out his hand to Mackenzie, a lock of his sandy-colored hair sliding onto his brow. A pleasant smile touching his eyes, he pushed the hair back in place, his focus again on Mr. Huntington.

His professional demeanor reincarnated, Mr. Huntington turned to Mrs. Slater. "Please show Miss Adams the nursery and the room she will occupy. Tell Gregory to unload her belongings from her car and take them to the nursery wing."

Mrs. Slater bowed her head. "Yes, sir. Everything will be taken care of promptly." She moved forward, compassion filling her eyes. "Anything else, sir?"

Mr. Huntington shook his head. "No. Carry on as usual." After bending to give Elise a quick kiss, he joined the officer, who now stood just inside the doorway. "I'm ready now, Captain. Shall we go?"

When the men left the dining room, the two women became absorbed in their own thoughts, each of their faces bathed in shock. Elise stirred in Mackenzie's arms, the movement breaking the spell.

Mrs. Slater glanced at the new employee, her expression cool. "If you're ready, Miss Adams, I'll take you to the nursery. I believe you'll find it adequate for the care of the child."

Mackenzie's lips curved upward. *Of that, I have no doubt, Mrs. Slater,* Mackenzie thought, taking in her surroundings. Hoisting Elise into a carrying position, Mackenzie followed a pace behind the house manager.

Awe mixed with appreciation filled Mackenzie's eyes when she glanced up at the turn-of-the-century chandelier above her head. Its crystal beauty sparkled in the glow of sunlight cascading through the dining room window. Would her parents be pleased when she told them about this charming place?

Entering the hallway, she studied the floor-to-ceiling inlaid walnut panels ensconced deep in thick, ornate moldings that lined each wall, the rich-looking crown molding next to the ceiling stained to match the paneling. Noting the shadowy corners of the corridor, Mackenzie wrinkled her nose. *Just a tad too dark and gloomy for my taste,* she decided.

At that moment, a touch of homesickness for the brightness of the desert struck her. She swallowed the lump in her throat. Would she live to regret her decision to forsake the only home she'd known? She'd been at Park House for less than an hour, and without a clue as to how, she'd made an enemy of a woman she'd hardly spoken to—not to mention the fact that she'd stumbled into a family tragedy. Mackenzie shuddered.

Frowning, she glared at Mrs. Slater's rigid spine. *What is her problem?* Mackenzie stopped midstride. Her breath caught. *What if ...?* Had the house manager, at first glance, discerned Mackenzie's secret and deemed her unfit to care for Elise? Did the woman have some type of mental telepathy? What if she expressed the knowledge to Mr. Huntington? Mackenzie frowned. She didn't have to work at Cape Canaveral to access the answer to that. Most likely, her job would be terminated within moments.

She caught up with Mrs. Slater, throwing a cautious glance her way when the woman paused at the bottom of the staircase. Turning, the house manager stepped toward the foyer window, which overlooked the front lawn. She pulled back the curtain to better view what had drawn her attention.

Mackenzie moved forward to stand alongside Mrs. Slater. For the second time that morning, Mrs. Slater seemed to have forgotten the new nanny existed. Mackenzie looked out the window to see what had captured Mrs. Slater's interest. The two women stood in silence, observing yet another episode of the drama that had begun to unfold a few days prior to Mackenzie's influx upon the household.

Mackenzie cringed. Landing in the middle of an appalling situation hadn't been on her agenda at all—peace and tranquility had been her goals. But still, how sad for Mr. Huntington if the dead woman proved to be his wife. Mackenzie glanced down at the baby in her arms—the accident would be such a loss for the child.

All at once, a thought struck Mackenzie. What if it hadn't been an accident—she shivered—but, instead, a suicide? Or, worse, a homicide? At her sharp intake of breath, Mrs. Slater frowned at Mackenzie. After a quick scrutiny of the nanny's face, Mrs. Slater again viewed the scene outside the window.

The plain-clothed police captain opened the passenger side of his unmarked sedan to assist Mr. Huntington into the vehicle. Mackenzie turned her gaze toward her own car parked across the street. Would it be best to hand Elise to Mrs. Slater, walk out the door, and drive away, forsaking her new career? Mackenzie kissed the top of Elise's head. The child's hair tickled Mackenzie's nose. But how could she desert this precious baby?

And maybe this present adversity, as horrible as it might turn out to be, could be just the diversion she needed from her own troubles. Heaven knew she could stand a reprieve. At that moment, Mrs. Slater adjusted the curtain back to its original position, the police car no longer in sight. She motioned Mackenzie toward the stairs. Catching Elise's toothless grin, Mackenzie abandoned the notion of ditching her new job.

She smiled at the touch of a small hand on her cheek. Her priority at present was this child who needed someone to love and care for her, especially if her mother had died. Shifting Elise so she'd have a more comfortable ride, Mackenzie followed Mrs. Slater up the stairs. Once they reached the second level of the house, Mackenzie glimpsed around, savoring her good fortune.

This magnificent house would be her home for the next year—or longer if Mr. Huntington offered another contract at the end of her term. But would the job be enough to bring the inner healing she yearned to achieve? If her expectations didn't pan out the way she intended, what then?

Mrs. Breckenridge's parting words pelted her thoughts. Where could she run to next? With a slight shake of her head, she smiled at Elise. There was no time to think about that now. She had a child in her arms who needed a bath, a different breakfast more suited to her young palette, and then hopefully a nap while Mackenzie unpacked her belongings.

Once she had bathed and fed Elise, Mackenzie played with the baby. The child's laugh was a delightful sound. When Elise's eyelids began to droop, Mackenzie searched for a bottle and a can of formula while the baby played on a blanket spread on the floor. *This is going well,* Mackenzie thought, *in spite of Mrs. Breckenridge's concern.* The director had cautioned Mackenzie that the child might not accept a new nanny right away if there had been a strong bond with the former caretaker. Mackenzie smiled and glanced toward Elise. The odds seemed to be mounting that the two would connect sooner than expected.

Mackenzie had wanted to question Mrs. Breckenridge about the termination of the former nanny. But the Privacy Act would prevent a response, even if the agency was aware of the circumstances. Mackenzie smiled. She'd contended many times with her fervent inquisitiveness, curiosity second nature to her as far back as she could remember. She'd been reprimanded often in childhood for her continual bombardment of questions to anyone willing to give answers.

However, her need to understand different facets of life and how they worked had won the blue ribbons pinned to her science fair projects in junior high school. Mackenzie flinched. But she had to admit she'd more than once paid a far different price for her curious nature. The time her parents had taken her camping at an Arizona state park was just one example of her regrets.

Told to stay near the campsite while her parents prepared the evening meal, Mackenzie had become enthralled with the antics of a jackrabbit scrapping for food on the desert plain near their trailer. She'd trailed the rabbit from a safe distance, following its staccato movements for several minutes until the rabbit discovered her presence and ran away. She'd turned to retrace her steps but realized the campsite no longer remained in sight.

Mackenzie had walked in the direction she thought would take her back to safety, but within minutes, she'd known she was lost. Tired and thirsty from her long trek in the desert, she'd crawled beneath a large rock that jutted out from its stone companions and soon fallen asleep.

Early the next day, shivering from the cold of a desert night, she'd spotted a large rattlesnake coiled on a rock a few yards from where she huddled. Afraid to move, Mackenzie hadn't been able to stop crying after a crew of park rangers rescued her later that morning.

A cold chill bathed the back of Mackenzie's neck. She would never forget the awful sound of those rattles at the rangers' approach. One of them had hooked the snake on the end of the long rod he carried and then transported his dangerous cargo several hundred feet in the distance before releasing it onto the desert floor. Parental punishment and some bits of wisdom she'd gained in her adolescent years had protected her— Mackenzie's face darkened—at least until ... Mackenzie measured the powder into the bottle and replaced the cap. Her lips drawn in a thin line, she shook the bottle hard.

Mackenzie jumped at the touch on her leg, surprised to see that Elise had managed to scoot herself across the room. She lifted the infant from the carpeted playground and carried her to the rocking chair. As she observed Elise gripping the bottle with her tiny hands, a surge of love for her enveloped Mackenzie. Tears filled her eyes and rolled down her cheeks. All of a sudden, she felt powerless to stop them. Would she ever be able to hold and feed her own child? The doctor had stated there was a slim chance but no guarantee when she'd questioned him after ... after ... *Oh God, oh dear God! Will I never forget?*

After tucking Elise into the crib a short time later, Mackenzie removed her cosmetics bag from her purse and entered the bathroom off the nursery to apply fresh makeup. Satisfied that no trace of tears showed on her face, she began to explore her surroundings.

Mackenzie examined several of the colorful educational toys, games, puzzles, and books hovering on the shelves, waiting in patient expectation until each would have a turn to divulge secrets of knowledge to its dainty owner. Once Mackenzie had circled the room, she glanced around again and nodded. Yes, educating this child in the wonders of her young world would be a delightful experience.

Mackenzie smiled. She had no doubt Mr. Huntington would do everything in his power to ensure his daughter had proper and well-rounded growth through each stage of her journey to adulthood. Mackenzie sighed. But his prosperity and influence were useless in providing the one thing Elise needed the most—her mother's love. Mackenzie glanced toward the crib. And now the child might be deprived of that love for the rest of her life.

An image of Mackenzie's mother appeared in her mind. Reagan hadn't given her daughter a major portion of herself; her career and community life had always been more important to her than motherhood. But her father had tried to make up for her mother's lack of time for her in his own way. He had been the one to attend her sports games and tournaments, school functions, and other outside activities that required parent participation. And how she loved him for it!

But in spite of Reagan's inattentiveness, Mackenzie didn't doubt her mother's love. She'd shown it in other ways—always making sure Mackenzie had everything they could afford to give her, helping her with homework, and, of late, keeping her informed about various scholarship opportunities that had helped fund her education. As much as Reagan seemed incapable of giving the affection required for a child, Mackenzie could never argue that Reagan desired a prosperous and fulfilled future for her daughter.

Standing next to the baby bed a moment later, Mackenzie kicked back the temptation to smooth a lock of silky hair from Elise's brow. After draping a light blanket over the baby, Mackenzie slipped away to give the child her rest, desiring above all that the body found beside the Arkansas River proved to be someone other than Jasmine Huntington.

Chapter 3

*T*he nursery straightened, Mackenzie set out items to prepare a snack for Elise for when she awoke from her nap. All at once, Mackenzie realized she had yet to check out her own lodging. She tiptoed toward the entryway between the two rooms Mrs. Slater had indicated earlier would open into Mackenzie's accommodations.

Mackenzie stepped across the threshold, her eyes rounding as she glimpsed the oversized room arranged similar to a studio apartment. To her right. a large picture window adorned with designer drapes enriched the cozy sitting area, which included a fashionable love seat and matching recliner. In the corner stood a square side table sporting a decorative lamp, a small flat-screened television with DVD player, and a basket of artificial vines that softened the contemporary display.

Crossing the room, Mackenzie ran her hand along the smooth granite countertop of the kitchenette. She took in the microwave, the coffeepot, the dorm-sized refrigerator, and the small dinette set that completed the galley. She shook her head. The Huntingtons had provided well for their child's nanny. She again studied her surroundings, marveling at the generosity of her employers.

Mackenzie strode toward the window, curious to see what lay within its scope. Taking in the plush back lawn, she eyed the large patio and swimming pool below; the sparkling blue water that lapped against the edges looked as if it were lying in wait, ready to entice the first person who walked by to engage in a long, leisurely swim.

A garage large enough to house six vehicles stood to the left of the backyard, with living quarters built above it. While similar in construction to Park House, the building had been constructed at a much later date. Off to the right, she saw an older but well-maintained structure stationed near the house. *Most likely, in early years, a carriage house that was converted into the original garage,* she thought.

She leaned forward to catch a better view of the picturesque backyard sprinkled with native trees and an array of other plants. *Exquisite,* she thought, noting that the ornate lawn furniture and potted flowers had been placed in strategic locations to enhance the beauty of the landscape. She smiled. It would take some time for her to get used to such lush foliage. The desert had been her habitat from the day she'd been born.

Mackenzie kicked off her sandals to scrunch the deep, soft carpet between her toes and then shuffled across the floor to check out the bedroom side of the small apartment; the decorative bed cover and pillows coordinated with the window hangings in the living area. Turning to investigate the private bath, she paused at the sound of a knock on the door leading to the hallway. About to grasp the doorknob, Mackenzie jumped back as the door swung inward. She grabbed at her chest with both hands, gulping back the scream that leaped to her lips.

Powerless momentarily to remove her feet from the spot where she stood, Mackenzie stared at the good-looking man about her own age standing in the doorway, a startled look on his face. After a few seconds, a grin tweaked the corners of his soft-looking, full lips, the expression in his dark eyes—framed with curling eyelashes any girl would die for—much too bold. Her cheeks grew warm at his slow, raking glance that trailed from her head to her toes.

"Sorry," he said. "Thought you were in the nursery." His raised his eyebrows. "My, what lovely, big blue eyes you have, Miss Adams."

Mackenzie's lips tightened, but she held her tongue. She had one household member against her already—there was no use doubling the score. Brushing the remark aside, she checked out her luggage within his grasp. He'd strapped the two smaller cases to his broad shoulders, the handle of her large rolling bag clenched in his left hand. Without waiting for an invitation, he moved forward and deposited all three bags on the large, round rug that divided the sleeping area from the rest of the suite. As he stood upright once again, the corners of his lips tilted.

"Really, Miss Adams. I promise I'm not the big bad wolf. No need to look at me as if I might devour you any second."

Mackenzie gasped. *What impertinence!* The spots of warmth on her face began to blaze. Momentarily, she'd been mesmerized by the muscles bulging in his chest and arms, along with his deep tan shown off to perfection in a sleeveless, tight-fitting T-shirt. Seeing the look tucked in his eyes that said he'd noted her interest in his physique, she flashed him a look of anger. He laughed out loud.

With a sigh of exasperation, she pivoted on her heel to return to the nursery. In doing so, Mackenzie glimpsed the image of the coiled rattlesnake tattooed on his upper right arm. She shuddered. *Just what I need,* she thought, gritting her teeth. *A fellow employee around who will be a reminder of my terror of reptiles.* Not even twenty-three years of desert living had been enough to squelch that fear.

Sighing, she pulled a fresh determination to be cordial from within her. "Thank you, uh, Mr. Gregory, I believe? For bringing up my luggage."

"You're welcome, Miss Adams. My name is Martin—Gregory Martin, to be exact. But most people call me Greg." Without waiting for her to respond, he turned, speaking to her over his shoulder. "I'll be back in a jiffy with the rest of your gear." He snapped the fingers of his left hand and then did an about-face. "By the way, Mrs. Slater said to tell you that lunch will be brought to you soon. Also, she would like for you to check the nursery supplies. If you need anything, make a list, and she'll pick up the items this afternoon when she goes to the grocery store." Greg looked as though he needed to recall something. "Oh yeah. Angie said she'd help you unpack after lunch."

Mackenzie frowned. "Angie?"

He nodded. "She does most of the cleaning here at Park House."

"I see. Please inform Mrs. Slater that the supplies in the nursery are sufficient for now. And tell Angie thanks, but I can handle it. Kind of her to offer, though."

Greg shrugged. "Suit yourself." He pulled a set of keys from his jeans pocket and tossed them to her—the set she'd handed Mrs. Slater earlier. "I drove your Camry around to the back and parked it in the garage."

He grinned at her look of surprise, again lifting his shoulders. "Mr. Huntington's orders. Don't worry—there's a spot for your car. When you have some free time, I'll give you a tour of the house and grounds so you can see for yourself. I'm the official chauffeur, gardener, handyman"—he paused and stared into space, his eyes darkening—"and anything else Mr. Huntington desires me to do." A sudden grin tumbled onto his lips. "Can't argue about the pay, though."

Mackenzie wrestled with her feelings. Perhaps she'd misjudged him. "Thank you. I would like that. With our employer's approval, of course?"

Greg shrugged. "Can't think of a reason for him to object. And besides, you know what they say: 'When the cat's away ...'"

She bridled. *Well, Mackenzie, you can scratch that misconceived notion!* "Thanks, but I prefer to have his permission, if you don't mind."

Greg scowled momentarily before a look of admiration stole into his eyes. "You've got grit. I like that in a woman. And you've got Lacey Carmichael's looks beat by miles. Yeah. A lot prettier."

Again, heat glowed in her cheeks. She looked away, annoyed that the compliment pleased her in spite of his obnoxiousness. "Who is Lacey?"

"The last nanny who worked here. She didn't last long. Seems she had a yen for Jasmine's—I mean Mrs. Huntington's—jewelry. Mr. Huntington came home early one day and caught Lacey pilfering in his wife's jewelry case. Lacey explained that she'd only been admiring the pieces. Mr. Huntington let it drop then, but later, when a diamond necklace turned up missing and was found a few days later in a corner of the nursery, he fired her. She swore she never took it. Said it must have fallen off Mrs. Huntington's neck on one of her visits to the nursery. But they wouldn't listen to Lacey."

A cloud of disgust covered his face. "It upset her a great deal. She may not be the smartest chick around, but no one can make me believe she's a thief. Besides, she wouldn't take that chance. She cared a lot for their baby."

A look touching upon risqué filled his eyes. "Later, I did my best to soothe her anger at losing her job."

I just bet you did. Mackenzie stared at him, her face like stone. "That's too bad."

Greg smiled a slow smile. "She didn't seem to mind."

Mackenzie shot him a look that bordered on contempt. "I was referring to her job loss."

He shrugged. "Yeah, a bummer."

At that moment, sounds from the nursery interrupted their conversation. She swallowed a sigh of relief, thankful she'd held back the fiery words she desired to let flow from her thoughts.

"Pardon me—Elise is awake and needs my attention." Mackenzie hesitated a moment to offer him a weak smile. "Again, thanks. I'll probably be in the nursery when you return. Just place the other items on the floor next to my bags. I'll put it all away later."

Mackenzie watched his shoulders lift and retreat, thinking he ought to patent and sell the gesture, the perfected movement so in sync with the rest of his demeanor.

"No thanks necessary. Like I said earlier, just following orders, Miss Adams. After you've worked here awhile, you'll learn that when Mr. Huntington speaks, everyone tunes in to hear what he has to say. Unless they desire short-term employment, that is." He smiled. "Jas—I mean Mrs. Huntington, however, didn't pay much attention to his rules. Pretty much did her own thing. It's too bad about her unfortunate demise."

Mackenzie's eyes widened. "Is Mr. Huntington back from the police station? Was it truly his wife's body they found?"

A strange look appeared in Greg's eyes, as though he wished he could take back his last statement. "Not sure. Just going by what Mrs. Slater told me. I apologize, Miss Adams," he said with a slight bow of his head. "Didn't mean to assume that she's dead."

Mackenzie sighed. "No problem. I guess we'll all know one way or the other soon enough. Now, if you'll excuse me, I need to do my job and let you get on with yours." Casting another disapproving look toward his back, Mackenzie shook her head.

"Hey, what about the tour?" he said, peering at her from around the edge of the door.

"I'll get back with you about it." Even if Mr. Huntington gave his okay, Greg Martin would be the last person she'd choose from a list of possible escorts.

Greg lifted an eyebrow, a hint of a sneer curling his lips, as if he'd read her mind. "Sure. Whatever you like. See you later."

Sighing, Mackenzie entered the nursery. She seemed to be batting a thousand in making enemies today. She had two thus far, and the day was less than half finished. With her present score, she'd be kicked off the team before she could play another round.

Taking a seat in the rocking chair, she mulled over her conversation with the estate caretaker. She found it strange that he'd alluded to Mrs. Huntington by her first name. *Twice,* she recalled. Since when did employees refer to employers by their given names? Somehow she knew without instruction that Mrs. Slater wouldn't approve of the action. Mackenzie frowned. Well, Greg had intimated that Mrs. Huntington lived by her own code of behavior. So maybe she allowed the informality. Mackenzie shook off the entire issue. After all, it might not be important anyway if the woman was deceased.

A few hours later, she'd stored the things she'd brought from Arizona, finding plenty of space in both the closet and dresser. Seated at the small desk across from her bed, Mackenzie laid down the writing pen to tear off the top sheet of the notepad she'd found in the drawer. After taking a moment to inspect the list, she then slipped it inside her purse. She decided her first day off duty would be soon enough to purchase the items. She smiled. What fun it would be to explore the shopping opportunities her new surroundings had to offer.

Looking around, Mackenzie grinned. Her future looked brighter by the moment. A glimpse at the framed photograph of her parents atop the bedside table caused her smile to crumble. Would it be too much to hope they'd accepted her decision by now? Mackenzie groaned. She'd know soon enough when she called them tonight to tell of her safe arrival.

Mackenzie turned away from their smiling faces. She made her way to the refrigerator, where she plucked a bottle of water from the supply she'd found there earlier. She held the bottle to her cheek to cool the sudden guilty flush that stole across her features. She hadn't seen her parents look that pleasant for weeks. Maybe it would be best to wait another day or two before she phoned them. What was that old cliché? Oh yes, something about absence causing the heart to grow in love—or something like that?

Drawing a long breath, Mackenzie took a seat on the sofa, grateful that she could relax for a while before Elise awoke from her nap. After downing the last of the water from the bottle, she parked the empty container on the side table and then leaned back against the soft cushion.

A short while later, Mackenzie jumped from the sofa, steadying her balance while she looked around to collect her bearings. Had she just heard a gunshot? Panic seized her. She rushed into the nursery. As she glanced into the crib, Mackenzie's chest caved inward, the constrained air in her lungs gushing forward. She mouthed the words of gratitude that tumbled to her lips.

At that moment, she heard a loud knock on the door to her room. She eased the nursery door closed and retraced her steps to answer the insistent request for her attention, realizing now what had jarred her from a restful doze. She peeked into the mirror on the wall beside the entryway and quickly finger-combed her hair, but she could do nothing about the drowsiness still visible in her eyes. She opened the door. Mrs. Slater stood in the hallway, her expression oozing impatience.

"Sorry to disturb your nap, Miss Adams," she said after a moment. "But Mr. Huntington would like to see you downstairs right away. After I show you to his office, I will sit with Elise until you return to the nursery."

Mackenzie looked away, her cheeks blazing. Was she destined to live in the shadow of Mrs. Slater's scorn? "O-of course. I'll just look in on Elise to make sure she's still asleep."

A couple minutes later, Mackenzie followed Mrs. Slater down the stairs. She did her best to ignore the sinking sensation in her chest. She held the distinct notion that whatever Mr. Huntington had to say wasn't going to be pleasant.

Once inside his office and seated, Mackenzie listened intently as Mr. Huntington, in faltering words, explained that the fisherman's discovery that morning had indeed been the body of his wife.

Mackenzie moved her head back and forth, her face contorted with sympathy. "Oh, sir. I'm so sorry. I …" Words seemed to escape her. She gave him an apologetic look.

Mr. Huntington held up his hand. "I understand, Miss Adams. I'm sure this must be a shock to you."

She nodded. "Sir, may I ask how she died?"

Mr. Huntington closed his eyes momentarily before he spoke. "The police say she died from strangulation after suffering a trauma to her head. They believe the electric cord they found attached to her neck to be the weapon that caused her death, the wire having been ripped or cut from some type of hair appliance."

Mackenzie moistened her lips. "I-I see."

"Also, during the police investigation of the master suite earlier today, Jasmine's hair dryer could not be found. Captain Sprinsky said it's possible the murderer could have wielded the blow to her head with the missing device and then strangled her with its cord, but at this point, it's only speculation. And to complicate things further, thus far, they haven't unearthed any evidence that the crime took place at Park House."

His professional countenance wilting, Mr. Huntington crumpled into his chair. He scrubbed his face with his hand and then raked his fingers through his hair, his gaze centered on nothing in particular. "Captain Sprinsky said he will return to investigate the nursery wing after Elise wakes from her nap. But he didn't seem hopeful they would find any evidence of her murder there either."

While waiting for Mr. Huntington to regain his composure, Mackenzie tried to assimilate the news that had fallen on her ears. She glanced to her left. Her breath caught at the realization that another gentleman stood at the back of the room, near a window. Too concerned with what her employer had to say, she'd failed to notice his presence. Catching his eye, she nodded a greeting. He gave a brief smile in return and then flashed a concerned look toward Mr. Huntington.

Mackenzie focused her attention on her clasped hands resting in her lap. Assessing the stranger from the corners of her eyes, Mackenzie concluded his height to be nearly six feet one or two and his age to be late twenties or early thirties, and he was not what she would consider drop-dead handsome but had nice features. A look of strength penetrated his jawline, and his dark blond hair was styled to accentuate his professional attire. Mackenzie decided some women might find him attractive—at least those who were interested in men. At the sound of Mr. Huntington's voice, she raised her eyelashes, forgetting the gentleman for the moment as she leaned forward to better concentrate on what her employer had to say.

"Now, about ..." Mr. Huntington glanced around the room and then stood, his expression apologetic.

"I'm sorry, Miss Adams. Please forgive my lack of manners," he said, nodding toward the other gentleman as he stepped forward. "This is my nephew, Trace Patterson. He's also the vice president of Huntington Incorporated. Trace, meet Mackenzie Adams, Elise's new nanny. He paused. "I ..."

Noting the sudden loss of color in her employer's pallor, Mackenzie jumped to her feet, her eyes wide. "Sir, are you okay?" She frowned. *Of course the man's not okay. He looks like he's going to keel over any second.* "Should I phone for a doctor?" Mackenzie turned to Mr. Patterson, an appeal for help in her eyes.

Mr. Huntington's nephew hurried to his uncle's side. "Uncle Drew, Miss Adams is right. You're quite pale."

"No, please. I'll be fine in a moment," Mr. Huntington said, pulling a handkerchief from inside his suit coat to wipe away the drops of perspiration that had formed on his forehead. He sat down as if a great weight pushed him into the chair. "I just keep envisioning Jasmine's body on that cold slab in the morgue." He picked up a stack of papers on his desk and shuffled them into a neat pile, waving Mr. Patterson toward the other chair in front of his desk. Trace waited until Mackenzie was seated once again before he sat down.

Mr. Huntington knit his fingers together and placed his woven hands atop his desk. He drew a long breath and cleared his throat before he continued.

"The other reason I wanted to speak with you, Miss Adams"—he paused momentarily, disappointment darkening his eyes—"is because although Elise responds well to you, I am willing to release you from your contract. The situation being what it is, I don't want you to feel obligated to stay in my employee should you feel endangered in any way. My wife's murder must be frightening to you, and although I don't relish searching for another nanny, you are free to return to Arizona.

"I will pay all the expenses for your return trip and give you a month's salary, as well as inform Mrs. Breckenridge of the situation, assuring her that the termination of your employment has nothing to do with your ability as a caretaker." A weak smile appeared on his face. "Right away this morning, I realized you are quite capable of caring for my daughter. But the decision is yours, Miss Adams."

Mackenzie ran her tongue across her lips. It seemed as if she'd been cursed with options for months. And now she had to decide whether to accept her employer's generous offer or remain in the volatile setting she'd walked into just hours ago. He'd given her this one chance to escape. Should she accept the offer? But where would she go? She had no intention of returning to Arizona—not for some time, if ever. Her jaw set with a new determination, Mackenzie smiled.

"Sir, if it's okay with you, I'd like to stay. You're correct. Elise does need me." *Not nearly as much as I need her.* Mackenzie felt her stomach lurch. Where had that thought come from? She bit her lip to hold back a grin. "Forgive me, but from what I observed this morning, my staying would be of benefit to you as well."

A vague smile touched Mr. Huntington's lips. "I do love my daughter. However, I don't expect to receive the Mr. Mom award anytime soon. I'm afraid my experience with children is limited at best." He glanced at his nephew. "Trace is my one exception," Mr. Huntington said, the sadness in his eyes overshadowed momentarily by the look of love and pride he showered on his nephew. "But Trace was half grown when he came to live with me." Seeming to sense he'd offered too much family information to a new employee, Mr. Huntington grew quiet.

"Well, sir, I believe that's why you hired me." She smiled. "To offset your issue regarding the care of children, I mean." She stood, and the two men did likewise. "And now, sir, if you have no further need of me, I should return to the nursery. Elise is probably awake by now." She extended her hand to Mr. Patterson. "It's nice to have met you."

When Trace took her hand, Mackenzie's heart skipped a beat and then seemed to skitter across the inside of her chest. The earlier summation she'd held regarding his looks toppled when she saw his smile. It was as if the sun had been held hostage in his deep-set green eyes and was now free to shed its magnificent rays into the room, spreading light and warmth to all four corners of the office. She tried to turn away from him, but the life-giving energy in his gaze captivated her. Steadying herself against the sinking sensation in the pit of her stomach, she realized her nonchalant attitude toward him had disappeared.

Trace seemed to share her reaction. He looked similar to a person who'd just had his breath knocked out of him. As he looked into her eyes, his face gleamed with understanding. He smiled. "It's a pleasure to meet you too, Miss Adams." He squeezed her hand. "I'm sure we'll see each other often. I'm a regular at Park House."

She lowered her eyelashes to study the hand he'd placed over hers—his left hand, which, to her surprise, bore no sign that a marriage contract existed among his legal documents.

All of a sudden, the temperature in the room seemed to rise at least ten degrees, the heat spreading throughout her whole body and coming to rest in her cheeks. She needed air—the cooler the better.

She quickly removed her hand from his clasp, ignoring the twinkle in his eyes. No matter the attraction she felt at the moment, she wanted nothing to do with him. Her last experience with romance had been enough to last her a lifetime. Mr. Huntington's voice seemed to come from far away. If he'd noticed his nephew's effect on his new employee, he gave no sign.

"Thank you, Miss Adams. Given the circumstances, I'm sure it was a difficult decision for you. In fact"—he cleared his throat—"until the police find a motive for Jasmine's death, the whole household could be in peril." His eyes bored into hers. "I want Elise in someone's care at all times. Do you understand what I'm saying?"

As she glimpsed Mr. Huntington's tortured features, perception dawned in her mind. Elise in danger? But who would want to harm her? Mackenzie pulled her body to its full height of five feet four inches. "Yes, sir. I understand."

Leaning forward, Mr. Huntington gripped the edge of his desk, his gaze locked on Mackenzie's face. "Yes, Miss Adams, I can see you do comprehend. Elise is all I have of Jasmine now."

Although he was not a tall man—five feet ten or eleven at best—his commandeering presence couldn't be argued regardless of the situation at hand. She sensed a hardness beneath his gentlemanly, caring manner. Greg hadn't exaggerated. Mr. Huntington wasn't a man to be crossed. If she deterred one step from his wishes, her days at Park House would come to an abrupt end.

Mackenzie's thoughts swirled. Could it be he'd made an enemy in his business or otherwise who'd murdered his wife for revenge—someone who wouldn't hesitate to take the life of his innocent child as well? Clasping and unclasping her fingers, she swallowed hard.

"Anything else, sir?" she said, her voice cracking. How could anyone want to injure that beautiful child?

"No, Miss Adams. You may return to the nursery."

"Thank you, sir."

With a nod toward Mr. Patterson, she quickened her pace to the door, but she stopped short when she started to turn the door handle. Her breath quickened. She turned around to stare at the men, her eyes wide.

"Is something wrong, Miss Adams?" Mr. Huntington said.

"Uh—no, sir." Apparently, neither he nor Mr. Patterson had heard the footsteps rushing away from outside the office door. When she stepped into the hall, Mackenzie glanced up and down the corridor but saw no one. She frowned. Had she imagined it after all the talk of murder? No, absolutely not. Someone had stood outside the closed entryway, listening to the conversation in the office, departing quickly before he could be spotted. Closing the door behind her, Mackenzie put her hand to her throat, glimpsing the length of the hallway once again. A familiar coldness trailed down the length of her back. She shivered. Who had it been? And why?

Chapter 4

*M*ackenzie rushed up the stairs two at a time. Pausing outside the door of her room, she pressed her hand against her chest, her heartbeat throbbing against her fingers. Could she be mistaken? She shook her head. A man, she guessed, from the heavy tread of the hasty retreat, had stood just beyond the office door. About to turn the latch to her room, she hesitated. Was it possible Greg had desired to see Mr. Huntington about some matter and then hurried away, not wanting to intrude when he realized his employer wasn't alone? She relaxed. That sounded more credible than a spying interloper.

Entering the room, she glanced around, noting that everything remained the same. *Well, what did you expect to see, Mackenzie? The murderer of Jasmine Huntington staring you in the face with a gun pointed at your head?* Mackenzie shuddered. *Get a grip, girl.* As she started toward the nursery, all at once, an icy blast of fear pelted her stomach. Her eyes widened. *What if …? Oh no, not that!*

She hurried across the room to peer into the nursery. Her eyes widened. Seated in the rocker with Elise on her lap, Mrs. Slater laughed at the baby's attempt to play peek-a-boo. Mackenzie wilted against the doorframe. *The child is safe!*

Mackenzie studied the antics between adult and baby while waiting for the trembling in her arms and legs to cease. The house manager's face looked soft and loving, as if she truly cared for Elise. Mackenzie smiled. Who could not love such a sweet child?

The sparkle in Mrs. Slater's eyes vanished when Mackenzie entered the room. "Oh, you're back, Miss Adams. I suppose Mr. Huntington told you the news about his wife's demise."

"Yes, he did, although difficult for him. I could see how much he loved her."

"That he did, I'm afraid." Mrs. Slater's full eyebrows arched. "Is there a problem, Miss Adams?"

Mackenzie ran her fingers through her hair. "No—no, I just ..." Mackenzie straightened. "Well, actually, yes, there is something bothering me. What have I done to justify your dislike for me, Mrs. Slater?"

The house manager placed Elise on the floor amid an array of toys. Upright again, she faced Mackenzie.

"Miss Adams, what possible reason could I have for not liking you? We only met a few hours ago."

"My precise thoughts. You *don't* know me. And that's why I fail to understand your attitude toward me. It's obvious you disapprove of my presence here."

Mrs. Slater strode across the floor, hesitating a moment beside the hall door. Turning, she stared at Mackenzie, the look in her eyes hard as iron. "Miss Adams, you're an attractive young woman. Beautiful women and trouble seem to walk hand in hand in this house." Without another word or backward glance, the woman snapped the door shut behind her.

Her face numb, Mackenzie gaped at the closed door and then sank into the vacated rocker. She shook her head. Could the statement she'd just heard from Mrs. Slater have been a backdoor complement? A mirthless laugh leaped to Mackenzie's lips. *Yeah. Just like birds fly north in the winter.* Mackenzie's eyes narrowed. Once an opportunity presented itself, she would insist that Mrs. Slater explain her cryptic remark.

Leaning forward to roll a rubber ball toward Elise, Mackenzie grew still. Did Mrs. Slater's proclamation somehow tie in with Mrs. Huntington's murder? Was it a warning in disguise? Mackenzie's lips flattened. Or just a subtle attempt to rid the household of its new nanny? Giving the ball to Elise, Mackenzie massaged her forehead, the pressure behind her eyes mounting. Whatever the purpose, she wouldn't let it affect her decision to stay at Park House. Mackenzie lifted Elise from the floor and hugged her tightly.

A glance at the clock reminded Mackenzie it was time to feed Elise. After buckling the baby into the high chair, Mackenzie kissed the baby's cheek and then handed her a toy. Shortly thereafter, Mackenzie spooned warm food onto a child's plate, the simple task bearing witness that life went on regardless of tragedy. Mackenzie curled her hair behind her ears. She understood that firsthand—maybe held a monopoly on it. The move to Arkansas might have won a battle, but the war inside her soul still raged. If Mr. Huntington knew what had brought her halfway across the United States, would he have hired her as his daughter's nanny?

Mackenzie frowned. Like a cowboy roping a steer, she reined in her oppressive thoughts. Her job description called for the care and protection of Mr. Huntington's daughter, not instructions to unravel the house manager's psyche. Mackenzie winced. She had her own demons to fight.

Mackenzie chuckled when Elise screwed up her tiny nose after a bite of pureed vegetables, her rosebud lips widening into a smile when the next bite of fruit proved tastier. A bucket of love seemed to pour into Mackenzie's whole being. She couldn't explain how it had happened, but after less than a day, her heart now rested in the hands of this child. She smoothed Elise's hair back from her face.

"I can never take the place of your mother, little one, but I will nurture and love you to the best of my ability."

That's what I did for you—gave you all my love, my agape love personified, when my Son died for you. He bore all your sins on that cross so that you might not suffer eternal punishment but have life everlasting.

The baby's spoon fell from Mackenzie's hand. She threw a look over her shoulder, but no one stood behind her. *But the voice ...* She frowned. *Just a trick of my subconscious*, she thought. God didn't talk to those He'd abandoned. Mackenzie stared at the spoon on the floor. It had been different when she'd been in her teens—before she'd rebelled from Christ's teachings. But that was then, not now.

Oh yes, she knew all those Scriptures in the Bible that talked about God's grace and how He removes a person's "sins as far as the east is from the west" and "casts them into the sea of forgetfulness to be remembered no more." She knew that when a person "is in Christ, he becomes a new creation; the old is gone, the new has come," that God has "called his people out of darkness into his marvelous light." She'd quoted those verses many times in her youth.

During her travels to competitions with her church's Bible quiz team, few among her youthful peers had been able to outwit her ability to memorize Scripture. Their team had won the state championship many times. Mackenzie sighed. But neither those verses nor any other Scripture would apply to her now—her sin was unforgiveable.

She retrieved the utensil from the floor and carried it to the sink. Elise had finished anyway. Removing the bib from around the baby's neck, Mackenzie frowned. She'd more than had enough of reminiscing in the last three days.

Mackenzie closed her eyes. She had to find a way to forget. "Come on, little girl. Let's get you cleaned up." Mackenzie glanced at her watch. "Afterward, I'll read you a story while we wait for my dinner."

After laying the storybook aside a short time later, she sat on the floor, playing with Elise, laughing at her frustration as she attempted to raise her little body to a creeping position. "You'll crawl soon, little one."

At that moment, someone tapped on the nursery door. Mackenzie looked up, presuming her meal had arrived. "Come in."

She jumped to her feet when Mr. Huntington entered the room. "Come in, sir. Elise is entertaining me with her determination to crawl, but she hasn't gotten the hang of it yet."

He laughed. "So I see." He reached down, picked up his daughter, and held her close to his heart. "Miss Adams, I opted to forego dinner this evening. I thought you might want to take your meal with the staff. I'll stay with Elise."

Compassion filled Mackenzie's eyes as she beheld the haunted look in his eyes. "Are you sure, sir? I don't mind having dinner here."

He waved her toward the door. "No, Miss Adams, you go ahead. It will give you a chance to get acquainted with the rest of the staff."

"That's kind of you, sir. I would like that." She started toward the door but paused, turning on her heel. "Elise has been fed and changed. I'll get her ready for bed when I return."

Mr. Huntington hugged Elise, giving her a kiss. "Sounds good. Now run along, Miss Adams. Enjoy yourself. And take your time. I always spend an hour or more with Elise in the evenings."

"Is there anything I can get for you before I leave?"

"No, thank you. We'll be just fine," he said, tickling his daughter under her chin.

Mackenzie smiled at the sound of the baby's laughter. She watched Mr. Huntington toss his child into the air and then catch her in his arms, cuddling her close. Assured that Elise was in good hands, Mackenzie made her way downstairs.

When she entered the kitchen, she found Greg and a young woman seated at a pedestal table made of oak. They glanced up, their eyes filling with surprise. Mrs. Slater, standing near the stove, placed the tray she held in her hands on the countertop.

"Why, Miss Adams, I was just about to send up your tray. Is there something you need?"

"No, Mr. Huntington opted to spend the dinner hour with Elise, so he suggested I take my meal in the kitchen. I do hope that's okay."

Mrs. Slater abandoned her task, a frown squeezing her full eyebrows together. "He should have mentioned that you would be joining us." She started pulling dishes from cabinets and drawers. "Take a seat. I'll have a place set for you momentarily."

"Not a problem." Mackenzie sat down in one of the vacant chairs, wondering at the sudden quietness. Had they been discussing the new nanny? She glanced at them, believing their flushed cheeks a sure giveaway her suspicions were correct.

The young woman broke the silence. "Hello, Miss Adams. I'm Angela Valencia. But Angie works for me. Is it all right if we call you Mackenzie?" A teasing glint appeared in the young woman's eyes. "Miss Adams is a mite stilted, don't you think?"

Mackenzie laughed. "I agree." She turned to Mrs. Slater and saw that the look on her face was far from approval for Angie's lack in protocol. "I hope I haven't inconvenienced you, Mrs. Slater."

Before she could answer, Angie spoke, her dark brown eyes sparkling with warmth and friendliness. "It was nice of Mr. Huntington to give us a chance to welcome you to Park House. And to get to know you."

"I believe that's what he had in mind," Mackenzie quipped. She smiled at Angie before cutting a glance in Mrs. Slater's direction. Did the others know the woman's assessment of the new nanny? If not, they would soon detect it.

Finally sending a half smile toward Greg, Mackenzie grew rigid at his audacious perusal of her—for the third time that day. Lifting her chin slightly, she sent him a look that would have made Hades desire heat. She ignored the smirk in his grin.

Her eyes widened when she turned to thank Mrs. Slater for the glass of iced tea she placed in front of Mackenzie. The house manager was glaring at Greg, her full lips thin and tight against her face. Catching the look, he squirmed in his chair and directed his gaze toward his plate.

Mackenzie glanced away, smiling within. Apparently, Mr. Huntington wasn't the only authority in the house Greg needed to obey. Eyeing them from beneath her eyelashes, she couldn't help but believe the unspoken dialogue between Mrs. Slater and Greg pertained to more than just a censure for his actions at the table.

Most girls would have thought themselves lucky to have him glance their way, including herself had it been a few years ago. Nevertheless, she and romance had nothing in common of late. She'd found it to be too painful a trip, the scars from her relationship with Zack forever etched on the walls of her heart.

The image of Trace Patterson's smile careened into her mind. She took a drink of her tea, hoping the cold liquid would calm the fluttering in her stomach. Twice in one day, her body had betrayed her at the thought of his name. Well, it had to stop. Mackenzie blinked at the sound of her name.

"Yes, Angie?"

"Are you all right, Mackenzie? You looked a little feverish for a moment."

Mackenzie pasted a smile on her face. "Perfectly fine. Just hungry." She reached for the meat platter that Mrs. Slater passed her way and forked a piece of fried chicken onto her plate.

"So, Mackenzie, what brought you to Arkansas? Greg said your car carried an Arizona license plate."

Mackenzie laid aside her fork and then lifted the linen napkin from her lap to dab at the corners of her mouth. The sudden silence in the room grew loud in her ears. "Well, Angie, not much to it, really. After graduation from my master's program—"

"You have a master's degree?" Angie's eyes widened. "Oh, wow! What I'd give ..." She frowned. "Excuse me, but with that kind of education, why would you choose to become a nanny?"

Mackenzie shrugged. "I couldn't pass up the opportunity. Since I've never been out of the state of Arizona, this employment provided me a chance to see more of the good ole US of A. And the job is good experience for me. My degree centers on family relations and child development." She smiled, again lifting her shoulders. "And here I am." She glanced at Greg, wondering if he would approve of the gesture.

Swallowing a bite of mashed potatoes, Mackenzie took in their expressions. She realized at once that the three didn't believe her for one second. And to make matters worse, the look on Greg's face told her he planned to explore the matter further. She glanced at her watch.

"Oh my goodness! I promised Mr. Huntington I wouldn't be gone too long."

"But, Miss Adams, you haven't finished your dinner," Mrs. Slater said, eyeing the half-eaten portions of food on Mackenzie's plate.

"Sorry. I guess I wasn't as hungry as I thought. Thank you, though. It was delicious." Pushing her chair against the table, she hoped she had a meal bar in her purse.

Once in the corridor, Mackenzie paused at the sound of Greg's voice. "Nice little fairy tale, if you ask me. Talk about shades of gray."

"Even if I agree, it's none of our business. So lay off, Greg."

He laughed. "Sure, Angie, you know I will."

Mackenzie placed her hand on her stomach. It churned like hornets preparing to attack an unsuspecting trespasser approaching their hive. She raced up the stairs.

Taking deep breaths, she paused outside the nursery door to mold her features into a cheery countenance. Entering the room, she realized the role-play had been unnecessary. Mr. Huntington sat in the rocking chair snoring, his sleeping child draped over his shoulder.

Mackenzie gave his arm a gentle shake. He opened his eyes, careful not to wake his daughter once he grew alert. Seeing that he'd dressed Elise in her nightclothes, Mackenzie lifted the child and placed her in the nearby crib, the aroma from her hair evidence her father had bathed her. After Mackenzie tucked a light blanket around Elise, she turned to thank Mr.

Huntington for his help, but he was tiptoeing through the doorway into the hall.

Mackenzie followed him, pulling the door shut behind her. "I'm sorry, sir. Time got away from me. Thank you for getting Elise ready for bed."

He held up his hand and then glanced at his watch. "No, no, Miss Adams. You weren't too long at all. And I didn't mind the task. I guess we both were tired. It's been an exhausting day for all of us."

Mackenzie glanced at the dark circles beneath his eyes. After a moment she risked laying her hand on his arm. "Sir, try to get some rest tonight. You need to keep your strength up for Elise."

"Thank you, Miss Adams, for your concern. Good night." With a slight nod of his head, he turned and made his way to the opposite end of the house.

Mackenzie eyed his retreat, the sag in his shoulders heartbreaking. After a moment, she stole back into the nursery. Assured that Elise still slept, Mackenzie left her at peace and entered her room. She sat down in the recliner and tried to read, but her eyelids wouldn't cooperate. Deciding to call it a night, she headed for her shower. Soon dressed in pajamas, she checked on Elise once more before she crawled into bed.

Unable to fall asleep right away, Mackenzie reflected on the events of the day. It seemed as if she'd lived a lifetime in the last twelve hours. Just before sleep impaired her musings, the inaudible words she'd heard in her heart while she fed Elise that evening flickered into her thoughts. Could she be wrong? Had God spoken those words to her after all? Or as she'd suspicioned, had her imagination been playing a cruel joke? Before she could decipher an answer, sleep overtook her.

Returning from her first walk with Elise the next morning, Mackenzie eyed the police car pulling away from the front of Park House. She lifted her hand in response to the officers' waves. Her feather-like eyebrows pinched together, she maneuvered the baby stroller close to the curb. Had the investigation of the premises the previous day uncovered a link to Jasmine's murder?

Tilting the stroller so she could ease Elise up the steps onto the sidewalk, Mackenzie started at the sound of footsteps. She glanced upward to see Mr. Huntington walking toward them. He stood next to her seconds later, a twinkle appearing in his eyes.

"Sorry, Miss Adams. I didn't intend to frighten you."

"That's okay, sir." She laughed. "I guess I'm a little skittish since our talk yesterday."

A smile touched his lips. "So I noticed. Here, let me help you with that contraption," he said, lifting the stroller onto the sidewalk.

"Thank you, sir."

"Think nothing of it. I'm glad I noted your approach. Now I can spend a few minutes with my daughter before I have to leave for Huntington Incorporated," he said, bending to release Elise from her restraints. A moment later, he held her in his arms.

"Elise and I had a nice stroll around the park. I wanted to take her out before it got too hot."

He nodded, glancing toward the sun. "We've had some unseasonably warm temperatures for June. And the weathermen are predicting a sweltering summer."

Mackenzie groaned. "Just what I wanted to hear." Chuckling, she wiped the perspiration from her brow with the back of her hand. "I'm used to heat, but I have to tell you, this humidity is a bit much for me."

Mr. Huntington laughed and then lowered his eyes, his brow creasing. "Are you okay, Miss Adams? You look, as we say around here, a little peaked around the edges."

"Excuse me?"

Mr. Huntington smiled. "In other words, you look pale."

"I'm fine, really. Just need some time to get used to the climate."

As he glanced at his daughter, who bounced in his arms, all of a sudden, Mr. Huntington's expression changed from cordiality to concern.

Mackenzie's eyes widened. "Is something wrong, sir?"

"No. But in the future, I'd rather you didn't take Elise out of the house unless you have another adult with you, considering the situation at present."

"Yes, sir, I understand," she said, recalling his apprehension for Elise's welfare the previous afternoon. Mackenzie's breath caught and held. Never would she forget the heart-stopping moment she'd became aware that someone had listened to their conversation in a devious manner—a puzzle she had yet to solve.

Mackenzie chewed on her lower lip. What if her theory about Greg proved incorrect and he'd eavesdropped on purpose? What could he gain? He seemed to be in the know about the happenings at Park House already. She could ask him, of course, but that would mean she would have to engage in conversation with him. Mackenzie shuddered. She'd rather spend the time hanging from a cliff while holding on to nothing more than a tiny branch jutting out from the rock wall.

Should she mention the incident to Mr. Huntington? But what could she say? That she heard footsteps rushing away from outside his office? With the house staff and policemen coming and going in every part of Park House the day before, he would probably think she'd lost her mind.

Bending to retrieve the diaper bag from the back of the stroller, Mackenzie tried to dodge the memory that popped into her mind—her introduction to Mr. Huntington's nephew. As she thought about his smile, the bag slipped from her fingers. She snatched it up, gripping the handle of the stroller until the trembling in her fingers grew still. Warmth filled her insides and crept upward to flare in her cheeks. She closed her eyes. Had Mr. Huntington noticed? Sliding a glance his way, she let out a slow breath. Elise held her father's full attention.

A moment later, he turned to Mackenzie. "I believe I have the perfect solution. I'll notify Gregory to accompany you on your daily outings with my daughter."

Mackenzie moaned within. *Oh no! Anyone but Greg Martin.* "Yes, sir. Whatever you think is best." Mackenzie cleared her throat and spoke just above a whisper. "Perhaps Angie could go with us on occasion as well?"

Mr. Huntington studied Mackenzie. "I'll inform Mrs. Slater to schedule Angie's time just for that purpose two or three mornings per week."

Mackenzie kept her shoulders straight. "Thank you, sir. Angie gave me a warm welcome last evening, and I'd like to get to know her."

"Yes, Miss Valencia is an asset to our household." A look of pain flickered across his brow. "Jasmine often remarked about her lively and caring personality."

Mr. Huntington blinked several times and then smiled at his daughter, whose interest had turned to a bird perched on a shrub nearby. When it flew away, she clapped her hands in delight. Smiling, her father tweaked her nose and then walked toward the house.

"Come along, Miss Adams," he said, laughing when Elise began to rub her eyes. "Let's get this little minx inside before she falls asleep in my arms." After closing the door behind them, he handed the child to Mackenzie, bent to fold up the stroller, and tucked it inside the foyer closet a moment later.

Mackenzie grew thoughtful. "Sir, I noticed a police car drive away earlier. I thought they finished their investigation of the house yesterday."

Mr. Huntington nodded. "Yes, they did. These officers were from an extra task force ordered by Captain Sprinsky to patrol the neighborhood until a motive can be established for Jasmine's death." He leaned forward and kissed Elise. "See you later, sweetie. Daddy has to go to work now. Have a good day, Miss Adams."

"Yes, sir, I will," Mackenzie said, bracing Elise for the climb to the second floor. Shaking her head, Mackenzie eyed her employer as he exited down the hall and through the dining room door. Had he even heard her response?

At that moment, a loud gasp from the living room across the hall startled her. She peeked inside the doorway to see Angie drop the dustcloth in her hand and pick up a vase from the floor. She turned it in her hands, examining it with a critical eye before placing it on top of the ebony baby grand piano stationed near the window. She glanced up at the sound of Mackenzie's entrance into the room, a look of fear in her eyes. Her shoulders falling forward, she expelled a long sigh when she saw Mackenzie.

"Oh, I thought you were Mrs. Slater. I'm so glad she didn't see me drop this vase. I know it's expensive. Thank goodness for thick carpet." Angie glanced toward the painting above the fireplace. "Mrs. Huntington brought it back from Europe on her last trip abroad."

Mackenzie lifted her lashes to follow Angie's gaze. Her eyes widened.

Observing Mackenzie's expression, Angie laughed. "Yeah, I know. Drop-dead gorgeous. To be honest, I don't think the painting does—I mean did—her justice." Angie's eyes filled with sadness. "She always had a kind word for me."

Mackenzie couldn't seem to tear her gaze from the portrait. Jasmine's thick dark brown hair hung in waves past her shoulders, the casual style framing a flawless, heart-shaped ivory complexion. Her sapphire-colored eyes reminded Mackenzie of the gems she'd glimpsed beneath the jeweler's spotless showcase when she and Zack had picked out her engagement ring. Mackenzie's throat constricted.

She blinked away the mist forming in her eyes, concentrating instead on the chic blue off-the-shoulder evening gown Mrs. Huntington had worn for the sitting. The color of her eyes and the shade of the dress were a perfect match—whether in reality or by the touch of the artist's brush, Mackenzie would never know. As she studied the painting, Mackenzie saw how the artist had captured a hint of laughter in Jasmine's eyes, as if she alone protected a secret unknown to anyone around her. "Wow! Like you said—gorgeous. When was this portrait painted?"

Angie continued her task of dusting the furniture. "About five years ago, not long after I came to work for the Huntingtons."

"She seems to have been several years younger than Mr. Huntington."

"Yes. Twenty years, in fact. But they seemed to get along well." Angie paused to glance toward the ceiling. "At least until lately."

Mackenzie scrutinized the portrait again. "Mrs. Huntington must have been the envy of every woman who met her."

Angie shrugged. "Maybe. She didn't seem to have many women friends, though, but men flocked to her like bears to honey."

Mackenzie laughed. "Imagine that!" At that moment, something stirred inside her. Before she could reflect on the sudden urge, Elise whimpered. Mackenzie glanced at her charge. "Good grief—I need to get this baby upstairs, changed, and into her crib." Mackenzie's eyes brightened. "Say, Angie. Why don't you join me for lunch in the nursery? We can talk more then."

Angie shook her head. "Sorry, I need to run an errand during my lunch break. May I have a rain check?"

"Sure, no problem. We'll do it another day," Mackenzie said, masking her disappointment behind a smile. With a last quick glimpse at Mrs. Huntington's likeness, she darted from the room. As Mackenzie climbed the stairs, she deliberated her sudden twofold desire: one, to learn more—much more—about the beautiful Jasmine and two, to uncover the identity of the person responsible for snuffing out her life.

Chapter 5

*S*eated at the table in her kitchenette, Mackenzie typed answers to her friends' e-mails on her laptop, diverting her gaze now and then to keep a sharp eye on the time. Soon Angie would be at Park House—not to work but to collect Mackenzie for a trip to a nearby mall. *Yeah,* she thought, relishing the idea, *the perfect way to spend my first day off since arriving at Park House.* Not that she regretted forfeiting the previous weekend in order to get to know her duties and Elise—Mackenzie smiled. Bonding with the precious child had been more than worth the miniscule sacrifice.

"We need to get away from the gloom and doom for a while," Angie had stated when she'd invited Mackenzie to a day of shopping the previous evening. She had to agree with Angie's sentiment. Waves of sadness and fear had drenched every nook and corner of the house—so much so that they seemed tangible. Elise's lively personality was the one beam of joy in the shadow of grief.

Deciding she had just enough time to scan her Facebook page, Mackenzie clicked open the social-networking site that helped her keep up with family and friends. She smiled at a message from Kari, who seemed happy and content with her job on the West Coast.

Mackenzie grappled with melancholy momentarily. She missed her friends. But like her, they'd moved on in separate directions since their graduations from formal education, each hoping to make a difference that would last a lifetime in his or her chosen career.

Choice! How she detested that word. One single decision had changed her life forever. But she'd loved Zack so much she hadn't been able to bear the thought of losing him. With her fingertips, Mackenzie blotted the moisture that seeped from the corners of her eyes. She gritted her teeth. But she'd lost him anyway, and she despised him for it.

As she started to click out of the site, her eye caught the notation sign that announced a new message on her profile page. Seeing that her father had sent the post, Mackenzie felt her stomach roll like waves on a stormy sea.

> Hope you had a safe journey. I miss you. Your mother—well, you know your mother. Please let us know how you're doing from time to time. Love you.

The screen blurred. Yes, she knew her mother all too well. But at least her father desired to keep in touch, a possible thread that would help bind up the wound in his heart. Guilt enveloped Mackenzie. She'd been away from Arizona ten days and had yet to find the courage to contact them. Her hands shaking, Mackenzie began to type.

> No problems on the trip. Enjoyed the drive. Hot and humid in central Arkansas, but I like the abundance of trees and greenery that grows here. Elise (the child I nanny) is a doll and sweet, too. Love caring for her. I'll post pictures later. And, Dad, I miss you too. Tell Mom I love her. Have to go now. It's my day off, and I'm going shopping with Angie, a girl about my age who works at Park House also. And thank you, Dad, for at least trying to understand my decision. Maybe someday I can explain. I love you.

Mackenzie hit the enter button on her keyboard to send the reply and then closed out of the Internet. *Perhaps I should phone them*, she thought as she shut down the PC. It would be nice to hear their voices.

She glanced toward the door. "Come in."

Mackenzie smiled. "Good morning, Mrs. Slater. Thank you for taking my place today. Elise is still asleep. I noticed last night that the tooth she's been cutting has finally appeared. She should feel much better today."

"That's good to know. I'll make sure Mr. Huntington is aware of it."

"I left my phone number on the table if you should need me."

"Miss Adams," Mrs. Slater said, her spine rigid. "I've been taking care of Miss Elise now and again since she was born. You have nothing to fear. In fact, I served as a nanny in this house years ago."

Mackenzie lowered her eyelashes. "I didn't mean to imply that you weren't capable of watching over her. I just thought ..." Mackenzie grabbed her purse from the table. "Anyway, my phone number is available if you need it. Good day, Mrs. Slater. I'll wait downstairs for Angie."

"That woman is the most infuriating person I've ever met," Mackenzie muttered as she descended the stairs. Glancing out the foyer window, she decided the wicker settee on the porch would be the best place to await Angie's arrival. *Besides, a little fresh air might be just the thing to temper my temper,* she thought, smiling.

Mackenzie sighed. Trying to develop a civil understanding with Mrs. Slater had been difficult, but even the Romans hadn't built their empire in a short time. Brushing off a couple leaves and a twig that had settled onto the cushion, Mackenzie shrugged. *Tomorrow is another day.* She just needed to come up with a different stratagem. Mackenzie set her jaw—she would win or die trying. Her eyes narrowed. And when she held the trophy in her hand, she intended to discover why the house manager believed Mackenzie would bring trouble to Park House.

At that moment, Mackenzie spied Angie's car at the end of the block. Before Angie could park, Mackenzie darted onto the street, reaching the passenger side of the economy compact vehicle just as Angie drew to a stop. Seated in the car a moment later, Mackenzie threw off her frustration, deciding she would let nothing spoil the day with her new friend.

"Thanks again, Angie, for asking me to go with you today," Mackenzie said once they'd greeted each other. "I haven't had a chance to do any kind of shopping since I arrived in Arkansas."

Angie laughed. "Well, you have been a little busy."

Mackenzie touched her forefinger to her chin and gazed toward the headliner, grinning. "You think so? Elise is a delight, but I'm glad she got that tooth through."

The baby had awoken on Thursday morning with a temperature, which the doctor at the emergency room of the hospital had attributed to teething, since nothing else seemed wrong with her. Mackenzie smiled within. She had to admit the past two days cooped up with a fretful child had been a mite stressful, although a blessing in disguise as well. Their daily walks to the park postponed until Elise felt better, Mackenzie had been able to avoid Greg. She grinned. *Guess when one is in turbulent water, life does favor with a rainbow now and then.*

Angie glanced at Mackenzie. "You're quiet this morning. Everything okay?"

"Yes. Just thinking about Elise. Granted, her fever prevented our outings, but I think she missed her morning walks. Did Mrs. Slater mention that you would be joining us a few days a week, at least until they find Mrs. Huntington's murderer?"

"Yes, she did. I'm to go with you every other day. Mr. Huntington is concerned that someone might try to harm his daughter—even kidnap her. Can you believe that?"

"Given the circumstances, his caution is understandable. Thanks for aiding the cause. I try to leave around nine thirty." Not familiar enough with Angie to know how she felt about Greg, Mackenzie decided not to mention that the so-called cause had to do with avoiding him as much as possible.

"Say, Angie, have you given much thought as to why Mrs. Huntington was killed? Or who might have wanted her dead?"

Angie rolled her eyes. "Only every spare moment."

"Got any suspects in mind?"

"No, not really. Unless ..."

Mackenzie's eyes widened. "Unless what?"

Angie's brow puckered. "Mrs. Huntington and I got along fine, but she did have some enemies. You saw how stunning she was. When I helped at her bashes, it wasn't unusual to hear a cutting remark about her. Mostly it had to do with her refusal to give someone a loan. From what I picked up from her guests, she had money. Old money—a lot of it from generations back. The source of her finances was a manufacturing conglomerate in the Northeast, I believe. I don't know why, but she seemed reluctant to part with much of it. In fact …" Angie tensed, a guilty flush stealing across her face. "I'm sorry, Mackenzie. I shouldn't say any more. Like I said, she treated me great."

"That's okay. I can't help but be curious about the whole thing. It's so—"

"Well, here we are," Angie said as she drove into the parking lot of a large mall. "I hope we find some good sales today."

Grasping that Angie wanted to drop the subject, Mackenzie slid from the car, strapping the handle of her oversized purse over her shoulder. "Yeah, me too. I could use some new shorts, and tops to go with them. As bad as I hate to admit it, I've gained a few pounds, and the clothes I brought with me are a little snug. By the way, do you know of a good fitness center close to Park House?"

"Not right offhand. But you might check in the phone book or go online."

Mackenzie nodded. "I had the same idea. Just haven't taken the time to do it."

Angie grew thoughtful. "Hey, you might ask Greg. He works out all the time."

Mackenzie looked away. "Sure thing. First chance I get. Oh, look." Mackenzie pointed to the junior section in the popular clothing store they entered. "I see a twenty-five-percent-off sign. Let's check it out."

Late that afternoon, Angie parked her packages in a mall restaurant booth alongside Mackenzie's purchases. "I know just how a prowling lion feels the moment he spots an antelope."

Mackenzie laughed. "Yeah, starved and ready to chow down." She opened her menu. "Let's see—one of everything will work for an appetizer."

Angie chuckled. "Hey, what do you say to taking in a movie after dinner? I don't know about you, but my feet would love it."

"Sounds good to me. What's playing?"

As they enjoyed their meal moments later, their conversation turned to the happenings at Park House. Mackenzie was not surprised to learn that Captain Sprinsky had questioned the staff about the murder. "I'll probably be next," she said, frowning.

Angie shook her head. "I don't think so. When Mrs. Slater asked the captain if he'd like to speak with you, he declined. He believed you wouldn't have anything to contribute to the case since you arrived after the discovery of Mrs. Huntington's body."

"He's right. I'm clueless." A wry smile touched Mackenzie's lips. "I can't say I'm disappointed about missing one of his question sessions. After my introduction to Captain Sprinsky, something about him reminded me of Bates, a bulldog that belongs to a friend of mine in Arizona."

Angie looked aghast. "You think the captain resembles a bulldog?"

Mackenzie laughed. "No. I was referring to Bates's habit of nosing into every room of the house when we would tease him by hiding his treats. I swear that dog would not rest until he had sniffed out his prize."

"Oh, I see. Poor Bates." Angie propped her elbow on the table and rested her chin in her hand. She stared off into space momentarily, her eyes filling with mirth. "Come to think of it, the captain does look a mite pugged around the eyes."

Mackenzie pursed her lips and then smiled. "Maybe. Although he seemed nice when I met him, something about him intrigued me—a look in his eyes that told me he could be a bit overpowering if he desired to be. I can't help but wonder, with his size and all, if he's the type you hear about or see on television—you know, the kind of police officer who's skilled at coercing an individual. For instance, like questioning someone in such a way to get a signed confession, the criminal swearing by all that's in heaven he committed the crime, when he might not be guilty at all." Mackenzie's eyes twinkled at the look of disbelief on Angie's countenance. "Just kidding, Angie. However, you have to admit the size of the man would be intimidating to anyone he interrogated."

Angie grinned. "He is tall—and those biceps. Not even Greg's muscles compare to the captain's build." Angie tapped her finger against her chin, her eyes glistening with laughter. "I wonder if he's married."

Mackenzie scrunched up her face. "You can't be serious. He's at least twenty years our senior. Besides, he's not my type—too tall and too old, and for heaven's sake, did you notice the size of his feet? I'd be scared to step anywhere close to him, afraid he'd crush me. Where do you suppose he finds shoes large enough to fit him?"

At that moment, an image of Trace Patterson's smile flashed in her mind, a strong sensation sidling alongside that she might enjoy becoming more acquainted with him. She shook off the feeling, her lips thinning. "No, not interested at all."

Angie grew sober, a puzzled look in her eyes. "I didn't mean to upset you."

Mackenzie shook her head. "Oh, you didn't upset me. Our discussion just reminded me of something else. Sorry."

"That's okay." Angie smiled. "Captain Sprinsky really wasn't the kind of officer you described; in fact, his visit proved friendly but professional. He kept his inquiry centered on the investigation." Angie grinned. "However, you might have a point about the man."

Mackenzie's eyes twinkled. "How so?"

"Though not to the extreme that you described a moment ago, I did have the notion that Captain Sprinsky wouldn't condone any evasiveness in my answers. When he asked about any arguments I might have seen or heard between my employers"—Angie shrank against the back of the booth—"the way his eyes bored into mine, I knew I'd best not be elusive about the quarrels I'd overheard between them. I had the distinct feeling he'd discerned what I intended to say before I did, like he could read my mind or something." Angie grimaced. "I hope I don't have to give another statement. Already I feel as if I've been disloyal to the Huntingtons."

Mackenzie studied Angie's features. That must have been why Angie had cut off their earlier conversation about Mrs. Huntington's murder.

While they were sharing a dessert, a friend of Angie's entered the restaurant and spotted Angie soon afterward. After introducing Mackenzie to Shellie, Angie invited her friend to join them. Accepting the invitation without hesitation, Shellie slid into the booth next to Angie.

While glad to meet the young woman, Mackenzie hid the twinge of disappointment nettling her. Now she'd have to wait to hear more about the Huntingtons—Jasmine in particular. If Angie knew the motive behind the quest for information, would she think her new friend a prime candidate for asylum row?

The next morning, following breakfast with Elise, Mackenzie relinquished the baby to her father's care for the day, and then made her way downstairs. Mackenzie glanced at the scrap of paper in her hand, glad the directions to a local water park she'd written down earlier seemed simple. She hurried to her car, smiling. A day with nothing to do but swim, read, and get some sun—how lucky could a girl get?

Mackenzie took in her surroundings as she drove toward her destination. She squinted at the bright sun keeping pace with time in the eastern sky. A few months ago, she and a girlfriend or two would have been embarking on a similar journey, looking forward to a day of enjoyment in each other's company.

Mackenzie's fingers tightened on the steering wheel. Afraid that her friends would guess the secret of her turmoil, she'd drawn away from them, using her breakup with Zack as her excuse for refusing social invitations. However, she'd hung on to Kari like a life support, desiring to confide in her best friend several times. But she'd bypassed each chance to do so. She'd paid a high price that mounted daily for her mistake, and she couldn't risk losing Kari's friendship. Mackenzie grimaced, remembering the words to an old proverb: "Oh, what a tangled web we weave, when first we practice to deceive."

Recalling the Facebook message from her father earlier, Mackenzie cringed. She didn't know which she hated the most—the breach in her relationship with her parents, herself for her betrayal of their trust, or Zack.

With a slight shake of her head, Mackenzie tightened her jaw. Catching a glimpse of a Walmart sign, she slowed her car and pulled into the parking lot. A moment later, she climbed out of the vehicle, balling her hands into fists. "No," she said. "I won't think about it today."

Mackenzie ignored the curious stares from the couple who stood in the next parking space, loading sacks of groceries into their car. Within a short time, the glint of resolve still visible in her eyes, Mackenzie emerged from the store; her cart contained a small ice chest, food items for a picnic-style lunch, and a lightweight folding lawn chair she could easily tote and store in the trunk of her car.

At her destination within a short time, Mackenzie picked out a vacant spot near the swimming pool and settled in for the rest of the day, bent on making the most of the activities provided by the park.

Later, after a vigorous swim and ready for lunch, she dried off and then tossed her towel aside to retrieve her ringing iPhone from inside her beach bag. Glancing at the number on the screen, she wrestled with mixed feelings. "Hey, Dad, how are you?"

Mackenzie closed her eyes, a wave of homesickness torturing her. "Yes. I'm doing fine. At a water park right now, enjoying some sun. Say, is Mom around? I'd like to say hi. Sure, no hurry—I can wait."

Mackenzie tightened her hold on the phone, her grip so taut she wondered if it might crush beneath her fingers. Several moments passed before she again heard her father's voice. "I see. Tell her we'll talk another time. Oh, sorry, Dad," she said, her voice constricting. "I need to go. You take care too. I love you. Talk to you soon." The phone dropped from her fingers. Her mother had refused to speak to her! Her phone peeled again, but Mackenzie didn't notice; the echo of heart break in her ears obviated all other sounds around her.

Mackenzie ignored the looks of sympathy from a couple a few feet away. She brushed away her tears with the back of her hand and began to pack up her things.

"Pardon me. I couldn't help but notice how upset you are. Is there anything I can do?"

Putting on her sunglasses, Mackenzie glanced upward to see the young woman had left her companion and stood within reach. Tears flowed beneath Mackenzie's glasses. "No. Nothing. Nor can anyone else, for that matter. But thank you for asking. Excuse me—I need to leave now."

Mackenzie parked her car in the garage at Park House and pasted a smile on her lips. She couldn't let anyone see the turmoil twisting knots inside her. She drew a long sigh. The day so filled with promise had bombed for her. Would she never be free of the monkey that clung to her back?

Moisture glistened in her eyes, threatening her fragile composure. She grabbed the sack containing her Chinese takeout meal and hurried inside the house. The silence on the lower floor felt a bit eerie. Just as she entered the hallway and started toward the stairway, she paused, startled by a swooshing sound at the far end of the hall, followed by a distinct click. She felt a cold chill cross from one shoulder blade to the other. She whipped around but saw nothing.

Feeling a touch of cool air on her cheeks, Mackenzie laughed, her heart rate slowing. *Only the cooling system coming to life,* she thought as she began to ascend the stairs. She looked back at the long corridor, the look in her eyes wary. If it were the air system, then why did she have this uncanny feeling that a person, not an object, had caused the sinister noise?

The next morning, Mackenzie pulled back the drapes to examine the sky from the window in her room. The weatherman had forecast a tornado-watch alert for central Arkansas. She sighed. It was not the best day for relatives and friends to pay their final respects to Jasmine Huntington. She eyed the ominous-looking black thunderheads hovering over the suburban horizon and inching their way upward with each passing moment. She shuddered. The air in the room was so heavy she thought that if she cupped her hands, moisture would dribble through her fingers onto the carpet.

She turned away from the scene. To her, the atmosphere in Park House mirrored the darkness of the approaching clouds. Soon after the police had released Jasmine's body, Mr. Huntington had announced the arrangements for his wife's burial. Since that moment, the staff had crept about the house, doing their work in silence, only speaking when necessary. Mr. Huntington had spent most of each day closed inside his office. Mackenzie shook her head. *So sad.* According to Angie, she'd delivered his meals to him there only to remove trays of untouched food later. And for the past few days, he'd even foregone his nightly visits with Elise.

Mackenzie stole into the nursery so as not to awaken her charge. She reached inside the crib to straighten Elise's blanket. Mackenzie had grieved for the baby, experiencing her loss each time she looked toward the door when they heard footsteps in the hall. Mackenzie frowned. As the child's nanny, she had a responsibility toward Elise's well-being. She decided she must speak to Mr. Huntington about his absences from the nursery. It wasn't that she didn't sympathize with the man. Yes, he'd lost his wife in an unconventional way—Mackenzie's eyes narrowed—but Elise had lost her mother; the child didn't deserve the additional loss of a father.

Mackenzie jumped at the knock on the nursery door. She tossed a look toward the crib, glad the sound hadn't disturbed the child. Putting aside her musings, she hurried to open the door.

Mackenzie put her fingers to her lips and then motioned her visitor toward Mackenzie's room. "Yes, Mrs. Slater?" At the look on the house manager's face, Mackenzie's eyes filled with compassion. No matter how much she disliked Mrs. Slater, the woman must have cared deeply for Mrs. Huntington.

"Miss Adams, Mr. Huntington prefers that you keep Elise here and not attend the funeral. However, once people arrive at the house later on, he would like you to bring her downstairs to be introduced to everyone. I or Angie will let you know when he's ready for you. Probably around four, I would guess."

"That would be a good time. Elise usually wakes from her nap around three thirty."

"Very good. I'll inform Mr. Huntington of the schedule."

Mackenzie reached out and touched the woman's arm. "Mrs. Slater, I'm sorry about Mrs. Huntington. I didn't know her, of course, but Angie said she was kind. I can see you cared much for her."

Mrs. Slater grew to her full height, jerking her arm away from Mackenzie's hand. "You're wrong, Miss Adams. I didn't care for the woman at all. In fact, I despised the witch. Mr. Huntington is the one I'm mourning for this day. He deserved a much better wife than"—she spat out the name—"Jasmine Grace Huntington."

Mackenzie drew back her hand, her fingers burning as if she'd just touched a hot stove burner. "I'm sorry. I didn't mean to offend you, Mrs. Slater."

"No offense taken, Miss Adams. Now, if you'll excuse me, I must see to things below."

Following Mrs. Slater's retreat from the suite, Mackenzie stood motionless. She'd never seen so much hate portrayed in a person. Mackenzie's curiosity rose to a higher tier in her mind. What had Jasmine done to provoke the house manager to such revulsion? Mackenzie couldn't get away from her yearning to know and understand the deceased woman, nor could she quench the desire to discover who had killed her and why.

Mackenzie halted in her stride to the kitchenette to brew herself a cup of tea. Was this why she'd had such a compulsion to take this job? Had it been fate that had compelled her to flee hearth and home? And now that she resided at Park House, had Jasmine somehow spoken beyond the grave to incite Mackenzie's help in exposing the killer?

Mackenzie shook her head. *Mackenzie Adams, what is wrong with you? You know that notion is ridiculous. And besides, you have no business interfering in matters that don't concern you. What difference does it make anyway? The woman is dead and will be buried this afternoon. And*—a smile tugged at Mackenzie's mouth—*if I recall correctly, my studies in family relations and child development had little to do with solving crime.* She adjusted the thermostat on the wall, hoping the air conditioner would drive the oppressiveness from the room.

Nevertheless, she couldn't deny that something had drawn her to Arkansas—a deep impression that she would find the desire of her heart in this geographical location known for its natural wonders. But what? And how did the ugliness of Jasmine Huntington's murder fit into the picture?

She recalled her plea to her mother to try to understand her decision to leave family and friends. Mackenzie slipped into the recliner, taking a sip of her tea. How could she possibly expect her parents to grasp something she herself couldn't explain in full?

Elise's jabbering roused Mackenzie from her troubling meditation. She set her cup and saucer down on the side table. She'd work on analyzing the situation later. Mackenzie's eyes widened. She tried to extinguish the horrible thought slithering into her mind. But she couldn't discard the notion. She would not soon forget the vivid, callous hatred she'd witnessed on Mrs. Slater's face. Mackenzie shuddered. Could Mrs. Slater be responsible for Mrs. Huntington's death? Had her animosity toward Mrs. Huntington been brutal enough to commit murder?

Chapter 6

ate that afternoon, following the funeral and interment ceremony, Mackenzie carried Elise around the formal living area so that Mr. Huntington could introduce his daughter to the guests he'd invited to Park House to celebrate his wife's life. Mackenzie glanced out the window, thankful the heavy rains that had plastered sheets of water against the panes earlier had decreased to a light summer rain.

Mackenzie had spent most of the day comforting Elise; the loud, ferocious thunder had brought tears to the child's eyes each time the sky crackled and moaned. Attempting to keep a tight rein on her own trepidation, Mackenzie had huddled with her charge when the golf-ball-sized hail beat against the house, sounding like miniature bombs exploding on the roof. Now that she thought about it, perhaps in the final moments before Jasmine's burial, the heavens had in their own way cried out for justice.

At that moment, Elise reached for her father. Smiling, he took her from Mackenzie's arms and made his way around the room, introducing his daughter to business associates and friends. Mackenzie, glad for a bit of freedom, surveyed the guests, having an intense notion that someone held her in his scrutiny. Glancing about the room, she caught the eye of a man who stood near the fireplace, assessing her, a look of curiosity stamped on his features.

She shied away, her breath sharpening when, in her peripheral vision, she saw him sauntering toward her. She viewed him from beneath her eyelashes, his pale blond hair, mustache, and eyebrows a stark contrast against a tan that seemed too perfect. *No doubt purchased at a local tanning salon,* she thought. When he drew close, he held out his hand, smiling.

"Hello. I've been told you are Miss Adams, Elise's new nanny. I'm Jason Crane, one of Mr. Huntington's associates." His gaze seemed to hold her captive—a look so bold it made her face radiate heat as if she were standing too close to a lighted torch.

As Mackenzie reached to shake his hand, it struck her as odd that he seemed familiar. However, as she had never been in this part of the country, a chance that they had met on some occasion seemed remote. Before she could utter a greeting, Mr. Huntington stepped up beside them.

"Actually, he's—" Mr. Huntington cleared his throat. "He was my wife's attorney. I'm sorry, Crane, but I can't recall sending you an invitation to this event. I can only trust that you're here to pay your respects and now are about to take your leave?"

Mackenzie's eyes widened. All of a sudden, the air seemed to spark with deadly electricity. She glanced about the room, desiring to be standing anywhere but where she stood. She held her breath, her gaze dancing back and forth between her employer and Mr. Crane.

"Great to see you too, Drew." All of a sudden, the smirk in his eyes changed to a look of sadness. "I truly am sorry about Jasmine."

Mr. Huntington sighed. "Yes, I suppose you are. You knew her a long time. My wife will be missed by all those who knew and loved her."

Mr. Crane lowered his gaze, a tinge of red darkening his face. He reached out to stroke one of Elise's blonde curls, a smile in his deep-set blue eyes. "She will be striking once she's grown—as exquisite as her mother." Mr. Crane turned toward the portrait of Jasmine at the opposite end of the room and held the goblet in his hand toward the painting. "To dear Jasmine, may she be at rest."

When Mr. Huntington offered no response, Mr. Crane again took in Elise, placing her small hand in his palm. Her smile of delight captured the eyes of several guests gathered around them, and several expressions of *ah* and *oh* broke the sudden silence in the room.

Releasing her dainty fingers, Mr. Crane reached to shake Mr. Huntington's hand. "You're a fortunate man, Drew."

Ignoring the gesture, Mr. Huntington straightened to his full height. "Yes, I am. Jasmine left me both her beauty and soul in our daughter."

His eyes narrowing, Mr. Crane dropped his arm to his side, the skin around his lips paling. At that moment, Trace Patterson stepped up alongside his uncle. "Good afternoon, Jason. Kind of you to stop by to share your condolences."

Mackenzie felt her stomach grow weak. She clasped her hands together to still her trembling fingers. The scent of his woodsy aftershave in her nostrils, she looked around for a way to escape unnoticed, but to no avail. Too many guests surrounded them.

She glanced upward to find Trace looking at her. The gleam in his eyes revealed he suspected her dilemma. A slow smile caressed his lips.

Mr. Crane cleared his throat. "Yes, well, I did want to stop by and express my thoughts." He slid a look toward Mr. Huntington. "Again, you have my greatest sympathy, Drew. Jasmine was a great friend. I hope the police find her killer real soon."

Mr. Huntington glared at the man. "As do I. Now, if you'll pardon me, I have other guests to attend."

The crowd parted at his words, and he moved forward a pace, but a whimper from Elise halted his departure. She leaned toward Mackenzie. Mr. Huntington obliged his daughter and then moved toward a group of four selecting canapés from the tray Angie held in her hands.

Mr. Patterson extended his arm to Mr. Crane, who shook Trace's hand before moving toward the entrance of the room. "Since I've worn out my welcome here, guess I'll be on my way."

Trace's lips tilted slightly. "Probably a good idea, Jason. Thanks for coming anyway. I'm sure Uncle Drew will appreciate it in days to come."

Mackenzie watched Mr. Patterson escort Mr. Crane from Park House, questions whirling in her mind. What had caused the discord she'd witnessed between the two men? Just before Mr. Crane stepped into the hall, he turned, as though aware of her inspection. Mackenzie ducked her head, her cheeks turning crimson. He lifted his hand in a brief wave before he followed Mr. Patterson to the entrance of the house. She bit her lip. Where and when had she seen this man before today? The lines in her brow smoothed at the sound of Angie's voice. Mackenzie cocked her head to hear what her friend had to say.

"I promised Mrs. Slater I'd help with the cleanup this evening. When we're finished, I'll come up for a visit before I drive home," Angie whispered.

"Sounds great. See you then." Shifting Elise to a more comfortable position, Mackenzie turned aside, her heart fluttering like butterfly wings when she caught a glimpse of Mr. Patterson heading in her direction. Before she could move away, he stood at her side.

"Good afternoon, Miss Adams. I hope this is not too unsettling for you."

"No, although I feel much sorrow for Mr. Huntington. No one should have to go through something like this." She looked down at Elise, who smiled up at Mr. Patterson, her one tooth shining in triumph. "But as someone once said, 'Life gives, life takes away.'"

"All too true, Miss Adams. I experienced it firsthand. I'd just turned nine when my sister died in her teens. My mother, grief stricken over my sister's death, passed a short time later. That's when Uncle Drew brought me to Park House."

As she observed the pain in his eyes, Mackenzie's heart filled with compassion, untying the knot that had formed in her chest at his nearness. "I'm sorry for your loss."

Mr. Patterson stared off into space as though recalling the events. "Thank you. For years, I blamed myself for their deaths. I thought if only I had come home earlier … But later on, I started attending a small church with a buddy of mine from high school. With some wise counsel from our youth leader, I soon realized that although tragic, I couldn't have prevented their deaths. But freedom from the guilt that I might have saved my sister's life had I not stayed out past my curfew didn't happen overnight. Only when—"

At that moment, Mr. Huntington beckoned to them. "I believe Uncle Drew desires our presence at his side," Trace said, nodding toward the piano.

Once they stood near Mr. Huntington, he introduced Elise and her nanny to a gentleman and his wife, explaining to Mackenzie that Mr. Compton held the position as top Realtor at Huntington Incorporated. The three gentlemen conversed a few moments while Mr. Compton's wife played with Elise and made polite conversation with Mackenzie.

Soon afterward, Elise started to fuss. *No doubt disgruntled from all the tweaks on her cheeks and her need for a diaper change,* Mackenzie thought, smiling within. Mr. Huntington gave Elise a kiss and then excused Mackenzie to take his daughter to the nursery.

Mackenzie climbed the stairs a moment later, her thoughts in a jumble. Trace Patterson's smile just before she left the group had left her shaken. How could she halt her growing attraction for the young executive? She mulled over their conversation. And what had caused his sister's death?

"Whew. That was some wake," Angie said once she and Mackenzie had settled down in her apartment for a chat later that evening. "I thought we were going to have to shovel out the last of the guests. But I guess Mr. Patterson realized his uncle had had enough sympathy for one day, because he began to steer the herd of mourners out the door not long after you left with Elise. I'm not sure what he said to each of them, but within a few moments, the living room had been cleared."

Mackenzie's eyes widened. "Did anyone get upset?"

Angie laughed. "No. From the bits and pieces of conversation I overheard, Mr. Patterson used a good deal of diplomacy. In fact, you would have thought the guests departed the house by their own decision. One time, I heard Mrs. Huntington tell a visitor to Park House, 'Mr. Huntington allows his nephew to negotiate their larger contracts because of his winning and credible personality.'" Angie laughed. "That's understandable after seeing Mr. Patterson in action today."

Angie kicked off her shoes and curled her legs onto the sofa. "I'm glad this day is over. Maybe things will get back to normal soon. It's been like working in a mausoleum since Mrs. Huntington disappeared."

"Yeah, I know what you mean," Mackenzie said once she'd settled into the recliner. "Poor Mr. Huntington. Did you notice how his clothes just seemed to hang on him today?"

Angie nodded. "He looked so sad."

"I wonder if Mrs. Huntington realized how much her husband loved her."

Angie rested her elbow on the arm of the love seat and cupped her chin in her hand. "I think so"—she shrugged—"but who knows? I can say, though, that when at home, she livened up the place." Angie leaned forward, her eyes twinkling. "Although much to Mrs. Slater's disapproval. The two didn't get along at all."

Mackenzie nodded. "I discovered that just this morning. When Mrs. Slater came upstairs to give me a message from Mr. Huntington, I noticed how sad she looked. Believing her sorrow due to Mrs. Huntington's death, I offered my sympathy. Mrs. Slater let me know in an instant that her grief was for her employer, not his wife. Angie, that woman spoke as if she hated Mrs. Huntington."

"Can't say for sure about that, but I do know she disliked Mrs. Huntington's impromptu entertaining. Mrs. Huntington liked gaiety and laughter, less formality. Often when her husband had to be away on business, she would invite several people to Park House for an evening of fun. It did, of course, make extra work on the staff, but I didn't mind. I enjoyed the vivacity she brought to the staunch atmosphere of Park House.

"I suppose Mrs. Slater must have complained to Mr. Huntington about the situation, because I overheard him confront his wife about her gatherings, declaring it caused too much of a workload for the staff. Mrs. Huntington insisted that he replace Mrs. Slater, but he refused, stating that she'd been with the family for decades, that in fact, she'd been employed as his nanny soon after his birth."

"Really! Mrs. Slater mentioned that she'd once been a nanny, but she never said to whom. How interesting. That explains the nurturing attitude toward Mr. Huntington that I've noted."

Turning her ear toward the nursery, Mackenzie slid from her chair. "Excuse me, Angie. I think Elise is awake." Mackenzie returned shortly, shaking her head at the question in Angie's eyes. "Still asleep. She must have been dreaming." Mackenzie closed the door with care and took a seat on the sofa next to Angie.

"I'm glad Mr. Huntington chose to play with Elise a few minutes before he retired. I told him how much she'd missed him. And after surveying their interaction before I left them alone, I believe he'd had similar feelings."

Mackenzie lifted her eyes toward the ceiling and tapped her forefinger against her chin. "Say, Angie—about this afternoon. What do you know about that Mr. Crane, who came to the house uninvited? Mr. Huntington introduced him as Jasmine's attorney prior to her death. I don't think Mr. Huntington considers him a friend."

"You're right. From what I've heard, Mr. Crane's father was Mrs. Huntington's parents' attorney before they died. And when the elder Mr. Crane retired, Jason and his brother took over the practice."

"I see. Did he come to Park House often?"

Angie pursed her lips, nodding. "More than Mr. Huntington desired—that's for sure."

Mackenzie tilted her head, her eyes full of questions. "And the reason?"

"Mrs. Huntington decided to take up golf, and Mr. Crane volunteered to be her instructor, often escorting her to and from the country club."

"From your tone of voice, I take it Mr. Huntington disapproved of the game?"

Angie smiled. "Not the sport, just the time she spent with Mr. Crane. One morning while mopping the hallway"—Angie cut a glance toward Mackenzie and then shrank further into the sofa—"I heard them fighting in the library about Mr. Crane. I wasn't eavesdropping, but they were shouting so loudly that it was impossible to ignore the argument. When Mr. Huntington demanded that she find a real instructor, Mrs. Huntington just laughed at him, stating that he'd overreacted to an innocent relationship, that she'd been friends with Jason since they were children." Angie grew thoughtful. "But I'm not convinced about the innocence of the relationship."

Mackenzie's eyes widened. "What do you mean?"

"About two years ago, while Mr. Huntington was out of town on business, I saw Mrs. Huntington and Mr. Crane together at a restaurant in one of the five-star hotels downtown. My boyfriend at the time had taken me there to celebrate my birthday."

Mackenzie moved to the edge of the sofa, turning to better observe her new friend. "And?"

Angie grimaced. "I shouldn't speak about her this way. It's like taking the kindness she showed me and tossing it in a trash can."

"Look, I respect your loyalty, but really, Angie, it's not like you can hurt her now."

"I know, I know."

"So they had dinner together. It doesn't mean they were having an affair."

"Maybe. When they stood up to leave their table, he put his arm around her to guide her out of the restaurant. Normally, I wouldn't think much about that. But at that moment, she smiled up at him as if no other person in the world existed except him."

"Did they see you there?"

"No, Kevin and I sat several tables away from them. Besides, they were too engrossed in each other to notice anyone else in the restaurant.

"And then"—Angie brushed her hair back from her face—"a couple of days later, I entered the living room to clear away the debris from a gathering the Huntingtons had hosted the previous night. To my surprise, I discovered Mrs. Huntington seated at the piano, just staring out the window, a look of deep sadness on her face.

"When she turned and noticed my presence, she said, 'Angela, when you find that special someone whom you love with all your heart and soul and you know without a shadow of doubt he loves you too, don't let a silly disagreement cause you to settle for second best.' Stunned by the passion in her voice, I couldn't move or utter a sound. Without another word, she closed the piano lid and left the room. Later, I couldn't help but wonder if Mr. Crane had been on her mind at that moment."

"I see your point." Mackenzie chewed her bottom lip. "I have this strange feeling I've met Mr. Crane before today. But that's impossible since I've never been in Arkansas." She shrugged. "He probably just resembles someone I'm acquainted with in Arizona." Mackenzie frowned. "But I just can't think who it is."

Angie nodded. "That would be my guess. To tell the truth, I don't like the guy. He's attractive but too self-assured, too free with his attentions, and too conscious of every appealing female within his eyesight." Angie chuckled. "And did I mention shallow?"

Mackenzie laughed. "Yeah. Believe me, I know the kind—good looking, charming, sharp dresser, but nothing on his mind except the next conquest he can add to his repertoire of disenchanted women who became victims of his magnetism." Mackenzie swallowed hard as the image of Zack barreled its way into her thoughts. Oh yes, she knew one man who fit that description to a tee. She blinked and stood from the chair. "Would you like something to drink?"

Angie straightened and moved toward the edge of the love seat. "Is something wrong, Mackenzie?"

"No," she said, her voice strained. "I just remembered I broke a rule of hospitality. I have bottled water or hot tea. What would you like?"

"Water would be great."

"So other than the fact that she looked like a goddess," Mackenzie said when seated again, "we've established the possibility that Mrs. Huntington might have been an unfaithful wife, but what about her maternal qualities? Did she spend a lot of time with Elise?"

Studying Mackenzie's expression, Angie frowned. "Do you mind if I ask why you're so interested in Mrs. Huntington? Forgive me if I'm wrong, but your interest seems a bit past simple curiosity."

Mackenzie laughed. "Not at all. For the past few days, I've had this inexplicable urgency to learn as much as I can about Jasmine and the details of her demise. Call me weird, if you must, but I have to know who and why. And this is even more eerie." Mackenzie leaned forward. "I think Mrs. Huntington would approve of my quest."

Angie stared at Mackenzie, openmouthed. "Are you trying to tell me that you believe Mrs. Huntington has spoken to you from her grave?"

"Good heavens, no. I don't believe in that type of supernatural. I just feel drawn to her tragic circumstances and need to understand them."

Angie's lighter-than-usual complexion darkened to its natural tone. "Thank God. You had me worried."

"Sorry, Angie. Didn't mean to scare you."

She waved away the apology. "I would like to see her murderer caught and convicted as well. Do you think there's a way we could help the police solve the crime?"

Mackenzie grinned. "Thought you would never ask. Seriously, though, I suppose we could try, if by nothing more than keeping our ears and eyes open." Her eyes narrowed in thought. "Since you knew her better than me, do you think the late Mrs. Huntington would sanction our involvement in the case?"

Angie nodded. "Yeah, I believe so. If it were possible, I'm sure she would appreciate additional aides in her corner. And you're right. By paying more attention to what goes on at Park House, perhaps we can aid the investigation."

"Thanks, Angie. I appreciate your willingness to help. Now, what about Jasmine's mothering skills?"

"Mrs. Huntington didn't spend as much time with Elise as she should have, in my opinion—no more than an hour or so on any given day. It's inconceivable to me that a mother could neglect her child that way."

"But I suppose as the wife of Mr. Huntington, Jasmine had numerous obligations that required her time and attention."

"Yeah, sure," Angie said, her eyes narrowing. "All her appointments at the beauty salon, the gym, and the spa, and don't forget those important golf lessons." Angie sighed, her shoulders slumping forward. "That wasn't quite fair. There were business functions she had to attend, and she did have to travel back east often to handle the affairs of her own company. It's just that among my kin, family is priority."

Mackenzie looked away, pressing her suddenly cold hands against her hot cheeks. After a moment, she lifted the corners of her mouth into a smile that didn't quite connect with her eyes. "There was a time I didn't comprehend that like I do now."

Angie's eyebrows grew together momentarily, as if trying to make sense of Mackenzie's statement. With a look of concern in her eyes, Angie took in her friend, who stared into space. Brightening at Mackenzie's smile a moment later, Angie continued.

"I do realize that no one is perfect. And I don't have any right to judge the woman. As I mentioned earlier, she treated me with respect, even defended me a time or two when Mrs. Slater grew upset with me." Angie raised the back of her hand to her lips to stifle a yawn and then glanced at her watch. "Oh my goodness! Guess I'd better call it a night. Five o'clock in the morning comes early."

Mackenzie stood. "Wow, you must live farther away from here than I thought."

Angie shook her head. "Not that far. However, I get up early to help my mom conquer the breakfast hour for our hungry crew. My parents and I leave the house about the same time to drive to our respective jobs.

My brother, a few years younger than me, is in charge of getting himself, another brother, and two sisters to school on time."

"I see. You must count yourself lucky to be from a large family. I'm an only child." Mackenzie smiled at the look that passed across Angie's face. "Oh, don't feel sorry for me. I had several friends that helped fill the void of not having brothers and sisters."

"Being the oldest, I've always had to help out at home—not much time to make friends. The kids are older now, though, and share more responsibilities." Angie smiled at Mackenzie. "To my joy, I believe I might have discovered a good friend just this week."

Mackenzie laughed. "That you have, dear Angie. Now off with you. I don't want Mrs. Slater accusing me of stealing your rest." Mackenzie grew serious. "Good night, Angie. And thanks for the visit. On occasion, I feel a little isolated up here."

Angie smiled as Mackenzie walked her to the door. "Sure, anytime. We'll get together again soon."

After locking the door behind Angie, Mackenzie slipped into the nursery. Noting that Elise slept—Mackenzie grinned—like a baby, she checked the dead bolt on the nursery door opening into the hallway. Satisfied, she eased back into her room and prepared for bed.

Once in bed, she adjusted her pillow to a more comfortable position, thinking that once she closed her eyes, she'd fall fast asleep. But she couldn't rid her mind of Jasmine. No matter her lifestyle, she hadn't deserved a violent death. Had she been unfaithful to Mr. Huntington with Jason Crane? And had her husband suspected they were involved, or had he just been jealous of the time she spent with the man?

Although miffed at herself for her reaction to Mr. Patterson, she'd been glad that he'd interfered to smooth the volatility mounting between Mr. Crane and her employer. "Trace Patterson," she whispered, liking the sound of his name on her lips. She turned on her side and struck the pillow with her fist. *No. No. No!* She would not be fooled again.

Returning to thoughts of Jasmine, Mackenzie recalled Angie's revelation of the friction between Mrs. Slater and the mistress of Park House. Could her earlier notion about Mrs. Slater—that she'd murdered Jasmine—have worth? Mackenzie shook her head. Mrs. Slater needed some training in people skills, yes, but Mackenzie just couldn't visualize the woman as a cold-blooded killer, no matter how often hatred proved a motive for murder. Mackenzie narrowed her eyes. *What about my loathing toward Zack? He still breathes in spite of my desire to squeeze the life from his body with my bare hands.*

Mackenzie glanced around her dimly lit room. Maybe she should discuss her knowledge about the house manager with Captain Sprinsky after all. Mackenzie sighed, jerking the covers up to her chin. *No. Not a good idea.* He'd probably mention her report to Mr. Huntington, and they would laugh her all the way back to Arizona.

Mackenzie sat straight up in bed, perspiration drenching her skin. A person could be classified as a murderer in more ways than one. Lying down again, she tightened her fist against her lips. In some people's eyes, she'd be just that—a killer. Moreover—Mackenzie buried her face in the pillow—they would be correct.

Chapter 7

*C*lose to nine thirty the next morning, Mackenzie juggled Elise on one hip and the diaper bag on her opposite shoulder, ready to descend the stairs for their morning walk. Engrossed in her thankfulness that the child showed no signs of illness, she glanced upward at the sound of a low chuckle. Her eyes widened. She'd been within a stair step of bumping into Greg Martin.

"Oh, hi, Mr. Martin."

Holding out his hands as though to steady her, he lifted the corners of his mouth in a cautious smile. "Hello, Miss Adams. Mr. Huntington told me you planned to resume your walks with Elise today. And that I'm to go with you."

"Yes. He informed me that either you or Angie will accompany us on our excursions." She sighed. "I guess it must be your turn today."

A trace of scorn glowed in Greg's eyes. "No need to fear, Miss Adams. You and"—he chucked Elise under the chin—"the baby are quite safe with me." As he observed Elise's wide grin, a smile purged the scowl from his features.

Mackenzie pulled the stroller from the closet. "I don't doubt that for a moment, Mr. Martin." Ignoring the mirthless chortle that escaped from his lips, she opened the door and rolled Elise onto the porch. She lifted her face toward the sky, the slight breeze cooling her irritation. Since she couldn't go against her employer's orders, she would adapt to the situation. *Best to just keep my mouth shut and put on a happy face,* she thought. Eyeing the hostile look on his face, she wondered how long she could keep her vow. Above all, she hoped the next hour would pass quickly.

Greg stepped past his charges, reaching the steps at the end of the walkway ahead of them. Before Mackenzie could protest, Greg lifted the stroller and placed it onto the street. Bowing, he relinquished the handle to Mackenzie.

"Look, Miss Adams, I don't want to be here no more than you want me here. But neither of us can alter the fact, so don't you think we could at least try to be civil to each other?"

She stepped backward and stared down at her feet. *All right. So the guy has a few dislikeable quirks in his personality, but that doesn't excuse discourteous behavior on my part.* She pulled back her shoulders and gave him an apologetic smile. "Shall we start over? My name is Mackenzie Adams," she said, extending her arm for a handshake.

Taking her hand, he grinned. "Greg Martin. Glad to make your acquaintance. And like Angie, may I call you Mackenzie?"

She laughed. "Only if I can call you Greg."

"Most people do."

A moment later, Mackenzie again gripped the handle of the stroller and pushed it toward their destination. She studied her companion from the corners of her eyes. "So, Greg, you know my story—what brought you to Park House?" She ignored the dubious look that leaped into his eyes.

"I came with the territory."

Mackenzie lifted an eyebrow. "Excuse me?"

"I spent a lot of time at Park House in my childhood. Both my mother and grandmother worked on the estate. I became a part of the establishment after I graduated from our local tech school—not long after some friends and I got into a scrape with the law. My mother decided a job at Park House might keep me from hanging out with those guys. She kept telling me they were nothing but trouble." He shrugged. "Guess she was right. After I received probation from the court system, Mother talked Mr. Huntington into hiring me as a full-time handyman slash chauffeur for Park House. The pay is good, so I stay. Been here just over five years now."

"Your mother?"

"Yes, you know her as Lois Slater. I was born late in her childbearing years."

Mackenzie's jaw dropped. "Mrs. Slater is your mother?"

Greg drew back, his lips curling into a sneer. "Yeah, I'm black. Is that a problem with you?"

A look of shock overrode the confusion written on Mackenzie's face. "No. Of course not. Included in my list of friends are African Americans"—an image of a smiling Kari dropped into Mackenzie's mind—"and, FYI, Asians as well."

A look of penance leaped into his eyes. "Sorry. It does make a difference with some people."

Mackenzie smiled to soften her features. "It's just that you don't ... I mean, I would never have believed it if you hadn't told me."

"I suppose you're trying to say I don't look the part. My father and"—anger flashed in Greg's eyes—"grandfather were white."

"I see," Mackenzie said, drawing back to stare at him. *Now, what was that all about?* "Look, Greg. Why be on the defensive about your biracial ancestry? It's not that uncommon today for people to marry out of their culture. I admit in generations past marrying outside one's race wasn't accepted too well. For instance, when men married Indian women in the old west. Nonetheless, think about the grit it took for your parents and grandparents to go against the norm."

She paused to take in the old wooden-sided church across from the park. The picturesque scene provoked the memory of a Bible story she'd heard in childhood. "And if I recall, even Moses of the Bible married an Ethiopian. True, he received a lot of criticism from his fellow Israelites, but he must have thought love would conquer whatever problems they might face. Don't you think your relatives may have felt the same way?"

Greg grew quiet, a strange look that seemed to be a mixture of anger and sadness enveloping his features. He opened his mouth as though to speak but snapped it shut. Mackenzie sucked in a breath, a feeling of regret stealing over her. What had she said that had caused him to react that way?

He kicked a small rock to the side of the street. "Sorry, not acquainted with the guy."

She broke her stride. "You've never heard ...? You know. The man who wrote the Ten Commandments in the Bible and the person who led the Israelites to freedom from the Egyptians."

Greg held up his hand. "Oh, that guy. Saw a movie about him once."

Mackenzie turned into the park entrance, shaking her head. Obviously, Greg hadn't been reared in church. Elise's squeal of delight when Mackenzie placed her in the baby swing a few moments later swept her thoughts aside. But once she had the swing moving back and forth in a rhythm conducive to Elise's enjoyment, Mackenzie again sought to abate her curiosity about Greg's family.

"So do you have other relatives residing in Little Rock?"

His face hardened. "My mother has a half brother in the vicinity, but he refuses to acknowledge kinship with us. Wouldn't be good for business is my guess." He lifted his shoulders. "We've learned to live with it. Mother's other sibling, a half sister, lives in North Carolina. Aunt Greta never married."

Greg seemed to take a sudden interest in the grass surrounding his feet. He bent toward the ground, broke off a blade, and popped it between his teeth. "And I have some cousins on my dad's side sprinkled around the South, but we aren't close."

"So Mrs. Slater's given name is Lois?"

Greg laughed. "Yes, but you'd best not call her that. She'd be livid. She has a real issue about the younger generation having respect for their elders."

Mackenzie's eyes narrowed. "You don't think that's important?"

"Okay for some people, I guess. To be honest, I've not known many people deserving of the prize. I've always heard that respect has to be earned."

"That's true. But it's not an excuse to be disrespectful in any situation."

Greg threw her an appalling look before he wandered over to the slide. Discarding the mauled stem of grass from his lips, he pulled a pack of cigarettes from his shirt pocket and was blowing smoke rings into the air soon afterward.

Mackenzie shook her head. *What is it with this guy anyway?* And what had made her think she could become friends with him? She sighed. His on-again, off-again insolence was more than she cared to cope with on a day-to-day basis. But until things at Park House settled down, she supposed she'd have to endure him.

Perhaps you could show him the way to the cross of salvation.

Mackenzie dropped her hands to her sides, the swing beginning to go amok from its course.

Hearing Elise's frightened cry, Mackenzie grabbed the chains and steadied the swing. A moment later, she stared into space, pondering the words she'd heard in her heart. After a few seconds, she shook her head, smothering the ridiculous thought. She, of all people, had no right to speak of salvation to anyone. She'd forfeited that right when she'd succumbed to Zack's demands. Mackenzie subdued the nausea creeping up her throat. Shuddering, she threw a glance toward Greg. *I need to be careful,* she thought. *No sense in adding fuel to his suspicions about me.*

After a moment, she turned to find Greg at her side. "What's wrong?" he said, scanning Mackenzie's face. "You look as if you're about to lose your breakfast."

Surprised at his sudden change of mood, Mackenzie brushed back her damp hair. "I'll be fine in a moment. This stifling humidity is hard on a desert girl." Mackenzie slid her gaze away from his probing eyes. She glanced toward the wooden bridge spanning the width of the brook that trickled through the length of the park.

All at once, she noted the presence of a young woman with dark, spiked hair looking their way. Dressed to her toes in black, she stared back at Mackenzie. Turning back to Greg, Mackenzie smiled. "But thanks for asking." She looked at her watch and then glanced toward the woman again. The knot in her chest tightened. "Guess we should head back now. It's almost time for Elise's bottle and morning nap." Without another word, Mackenzie lifted the baby from the swing and settled her into the stroller. At hearing Greg's muttered expletive, she glanced upward to see the woman in question walking toward them. Greg curled his fists and stepped toward her.

"Lacey, I told you last night not to come here." He glanced toward the street. Wariness infiltrated the anger exploding in his eyes. "If Mr. Huntington should happen by and see you here, we could all be in a lot of trouble. You can't have forgotten his promise to have you arrested should you come near Elise."

The young woman's mouth turned downward. "I just wanted to see the baby," she said, her face reddening at the sight of Mackenzie's lifted eyebrows. Rolling her shoulders back, she stepped closer to Mackenzie. "You must be Mackenzie Adams, the new nanny."

"Yes. And I assume you're Elise's former caretaker."

Anger sparked in the woman's eyes. "Yeah. But not by my choice. You're right. I'm Lacey Carmichael. And I didn't steal Mrs. Huntington's diamond necklace. I don't know how it got into the toy basket."

Lacey cut a sideways glance toward Greg. "My guess is that someone in the household wanted to get rid of me and stashed it there, hoping I'd be accused of taking it." She faced Greg. "Your mother maybe? You know she hated the fact that you and I were going out."

Lacey lifted her chin and brushed past him, the look on her face daring Greg to stop her. She crouched beside the stroller. Elise stared at the newcomer and then smiled, lifting her arms to Lacey, but she ignored the gesture, her eyes filling with sadness. "Sorry, sweetie pie. I'd better not take you."

Lacey rose from her position and stepped backward, her focus on Mackenzie.

"Greg told me you came here all the way from Arizona. To expand your horizons, I believe he said." The newcomer's eyes dimmed with wariness. "Interesting."

Mackenzie lowered her eyes. "Not so much. Just needed some meaningful experience away from home." She ran her fingers through her hair, thankful that Lacey once again turned her attention to Elise.

"I miss taking care of her, you know. She's so sweet."

Mackenzie reached out and touched the girl's arm. "I'm sure you do." She glanced at Greg, who bored his narrowed gaze into his girlfriend's back. Mackenzie grabbed the handle of the stroller. "Now, if you'll excuse us, we must leave." Elise rubbed her eyes with the backs of her tiny hands. "This child needs a nap." Mackenzie turned to Greg. "Shall we go, Mr. Martin?"

"Sure, Miss Adams, whatever you say." Greg stepped past Lacey, throwing her a look over his shoulder. "We'll talk about this later."

Once they were out of the girl's hearing, Mackenzie turned to Greg. "Why are you so upset with Lacey?" Mackenzie bent forward to smooth Elise's windblown hair from her eyes. "I can think of worse crimes than your girlfriend's desire to see this lovely child."

He shrugged. "Like I said earlier, my job pays well." Greg doubled his fists. "And if I should get fired over someone else's stupidity, that someone will regret it."

Mackenzie's eyes widened. She swallowed the grin she'd intended to soften her next words. "Don't you think you're overreacting just a little? Really, Greg, what harm did it do?"

Greg paused in his stride to glare at Mackenzie. "The point is, I told her not to come when she suggested it. Let's just drop it, okay?"

Mackenzie lifted her head skyward, her jaws clenched. "Whatever. You should realize, though, we don't live in the dark ages anymore. In this country, women now have the right to come and go as they please in this generation."

Greg opened his mouth to speak but instead sent her a look that would have deadened a freshly cut rose.

"Okay, Mr. Macho Man, the subject is closed." Slapping her lips together, she quickened her pace. They had covered half the distance to the house before she spoke again. "It's a shame Elise lost her mother to such cruel injustice. From our conversation the day I arrived at Park House, you seemed to know Mrs. Huntington well. Do you have any idea who might have murdered her or why?"

Greg lit a cigarette and took a few puffs before settling a detached gaze on Mackenzie. "Can't say that I do. But Mr. Huntington's wife lived life the way she pleased, and there were those who hated her for it." Greg shrugged. "But she had enough money to not let it bother her. Funny thing is, a lot of people wanted her to finance one cause or another, but she kept a tight rein on her funds. Even Mr. Huntington couldn't get her to part with much of it."

Mackenzie frowned. "And how do you know all this?"

Greg laughed. "She would tell me things when I chauffeured her around town. She used to say I was the only real friend she had."

Mackenzie lifted an eyebrow, skepticism stealing into her eyes. "And were you? A true friend, I mean."

Again he lifted his shoulders. "I suppose as much as anyone could be with her."

Mackenzie studied Greg's features. Why did she have the feeling he knew more than he desired to reveal?

Arriving at Park House a few moments later, she realized she would have to table further questions about the late Mrs. Huntington until another day.

Once inside, Greg helped her store the stroller and then turned toward the kitchen. He pivoted on his heel and clipped a wave to Mackenzie, the familiar smirk perched on his lips. "See you later. Hope you feel better soon."

Mackenzie opened her mouth to give him an answer he deserved, but before she could say anything, Trace Patterson stepped into the foyer from the living room.

"Hello, Miss Adams. I've been waiting for you. Uncle Drew said you should return soon from your trip to the park. I wanted to see Elise before heading back to the office." He glanced at Greg, nodded, and then turned his attention back to Mackenzie, his eyes full of concern and something else that made Mackenzie's knees grow weak. "I do hope you haven't taken ill, Miss Adams."

Mackenzie's heart began to flutter. "Really, sir. It's nothing. I'm just not yet used to this climate." She tried to laugh, but it sounded a bit stilted. She resisted the urge to clasp her tightening throat. "Air-conditioning is the best prescription for me right now."

With a nod of understanding, he allowed his gaze to linger a moment on Mackenzie's face. Seemingly satisfied that Mackenzie's well-being remained intact, Trace reached for Elise, who lurched into his arms. He gave her a hug. "And how is my little cousin today?" Elise smiled and then placed her tiny hands on each side of his face, leaning in to place a wet kiss on his cheek.

His eyes dancing with both laughter and pleasure, Trace eyed her wide smile. "Aha. I see you've sprouted another tooth since I last saw you." Elise giggled as he tickled her tummy.

A whiff of his cologne wafted toward Mackenzie. Her breaths became shallow. She clasped her trembling hands behind her back, her insides seeming to turn cartwheels. Mackenzie backed toward the staircase. If she didn't put distance between them, she'd faint at his feet.

"If you don't mind, Mr. Patterson, I'd best get Elise ready for her nap." She reached for the child. Detecting a movement in the hall, she turned, surprised to see that Greg still stood at the dining room entrance, the look of anger in his eyes centered on Trace. Her eyes widened. What did Greg have against Mr. Huntington's nephew? When he realized that she'd noted his presence, Greg turned and made his way toward the back of the house, his heavy tread echoing in her ears.

Trace turned and glanced down the hall, his brow wrinkling momentarily before Elise's laughter regained his attention. He gave her a kiss and then handed the child to Mackenzie. "Sorry I detained you, Miss Adams, but I do enjoy my young cousin." He reached to shake Mackenzie's hand.

Although reluctant to do so, she extended her arm, and warmth filled her when he took her hand. She fought the inclination to jerk her fingers from his grip. His smile deepened.

"Such a pleasure to see you again, Miss Adams. I look forward to another visit soon." A shiver ran through Mackenzie as he held her gaze momentarily. Releasing her hand, he grinned and then strode toward the door. He paused and slowly faced her, looking as if a sudden idea had struck him. "Miss Adams, I'd like to take Elise to the zoo. Would you mind coming along?" He laughed. "I'm afraid I'm not too familiar with the care of a baby, but I think she would enjoy the outing. What do you say?"

Mackenzie moistened her lips. Inside her head, she heard, *Can't do that.* But that was not what sprang forth from her lips. "Well, I suppose I could—that is, if Mr. Huntington is okay with it."

"I can't see him not approving of the adventure. Tell you what, I'll mention it to him and see what he says. Well, good-bye, Miss Adams. Hope to see you soon."

Once he'd closed the door, Mackenzie marched up the stairs, the banister aiding her trek while she fought the wave of dizziness that threatened to send both her and Elise plummeting down the staircase. She pulled her lips into a thin line.

Come on, Mackenzie. You know men can't be trusted. They use you, abuse you, and then go along their merry way, no longer needing you in their lives. They could care less what tragedies you suffer after the fact. Mackenzie tightened her hold on Elise. *No! They care not at all.* At all costs, she decided she must avoid an entanglement with Trace Patterson. No way did she want to be at the mercy of another failed romance—the cost was too high a price to pay.

Once she had tucked Elise in for a nap, Mackenzie took a quick shower, which seemed to put the emotional events of the morning into perspective. Later, relaxing on the love seat, she recalled Greg's earlier fierceness toward Trace. She frowned. The look on Greg's face had bordered more on hatred than just dislike. Mackenzie rubbed her temples. She'd definitely stumbled into a house full of mysteries. Perhaps in time, she'd be able to unravel a few of them, her first and foremost interest exposing Jasmine's killer. How well she could aid the police in that endeavor, she had no idea.

Transporting a load of laundry to the utility room while Angie kept an eye on Elise the following day, Mackenzie heard the sound of a car door just as she reached the foyer. Glancing out the window, her eyes widened at the site of Captain Sprinsky. Realizing it was the perfect opportunity to speak to him, she set the laundry basket on the hall floor and, with a glance over her shoulder, opened the door before the officer had a chance to ring the doorbell.

"Hello, Captain. I saw your arrival from the window. I hope you don't mind my answering the door."

"Good afternoon—Miss Adams, I believe?"

Mackenzie smiled. "Yes, sir." Waving him into the foyer, she pointed toward the wooden bench stationed nearby. "Sir, do you mind if we sit here so I can talk to you a few minutes?"

A smile mingled with curiosity lit up his blue-gray eyes. "Certainly not. How can I help you?"

"Well"—she gazed at her hands in her lap momentarily—"to begin with …" Mackenzie straightened her spine. "Sir, have you any idea who might have killed Mrs. Huntington? I feel so sorry for her baby—and Mr. Huntington too, of course. But the child seems so sad sometimes, and I can't help but think she misses her mother."

The officer's eyes filled with sympathy. "No doubt you're right, Miss Adams." He shook his head. "And no, we don't have any suspects thus far. Only a person of interest or two—and I'm not at liberty to reveal their identity."

Mackenzie failed to hide her disappointment. "I see. So I suppose that means you don't have a motive in mind either."

Captain Sprinsky studied Mackenzie. "Pardon me, Miss Adams, but you seem to have an interest in the case other than just concern for the child. May I ask what that might be?"

Mackenzie glanced away from his probing gaze. "To tell the truth, sir"—her mouth curved upward into a wan smile—"I do hope you don't think me strange, but soon after I learned of Mrs. Huntington's death, I've had this strange overwhelming urge to discover all I can about the deceased and who might have wanted her dead." She shuddered. "You could almost say it's creepy."

"Don't you think you should leave the particulars of the case to me and my staff?" A grin touched his lips. "After all, crime solving *is* what the city pays us to do." He placed his hand lightly on her shoulder. "In all seriousness, Miss Adams, I suggest you curb that curiosity of yours and do what *you're* paid to do—just nanny the child—and leave the detective work to us." His eyes filled with concern. "Not to mention the danger you could face should you pursue those thoughts." He reached inside his sports coat and pulled out a business card. "If you do by chance come across any information you deem useful to the case, by all means, give me a call."

Mackenzie frowned. Should she mention Mrs. Slater's hatred of Jasmine? She opened her mouth to share the information, but approaching footsteps, followed by the sound of Mr. Huntington's voice, startled Mackenzie, rendering her speechless. They stood at his approach, both eyeing his look of curiosity. She rushed to move the basket from his pathway.

"Sorry, Mr. Huntington. I was on my way to the utility room, when I observed Captain Sprinsky's arrival and took the liberty to invite him inside."

Mr. Huntington smiled. "I thought I heard voices," he said, reaching out his arm for a more formal greeting. "Hello, Captain. What brings you to Park House today? I hope it's to tell me you've found Jasmine's killer."

"I wish that were true, sir. However, I do need to speak with you about the investigation."

"Shall we proceed to my office?" Mr. Huntington nodded a dismissal to Mackenzie. "We can discuss the matter there without interruption."

Mackenzie turned toward the back of the house, hugging the basket to her chest as she quickened her pace toward the laundry room. What she'd give to listen in on that conversation.

As she neared the doorway that led to the back of the house, Captain Sprinsky called out to her. "Nice to have seen you again, Miss Adams. Do think about what I said."

Mackenzie shot him a look over her shoulder. "Yes, sir, I will." Giving both men a quick smile, she hastened to her task, less than pleased at how Mr. Huntington's eyebrows had lifted at the captain's words. His eyes narrowing, he studied her. Her stomach seemed to drop from the top of a tall building. Once she stepped into the dining room and could no longer be seen, she paused, her eyes wide. *Oh, please, Captain, don't mention our conversation to Mr. Huntington.* Her heartbeat picked up speed. Would she be reprimanded for her conversation with the officer? Or, worse, fired from her job?

Chapter 8

Close to dusk, Mackenzie scooped Elise up from the floor, where she'd been absorbed in the new toy her father had bought for her, and hurried to answer the door to her suite. Smiling, she grabbed Angie's arm with her free hand, drawing her inside. Mackenzie motioned her friend toward the love seat and sat next to Angie momentarily. Elise, cozy in her nanny's arms, greeted Angie with a smile.

"I just have a few minutes, Mackenzie, but I wanted to stop by and invite you to come to my house tomorrow night for dinner so you can meet my family. I spoke to Mr. Huntington about it, and he offered to watch Elise a few hours. Mom would like to cook a special meal for my new friend." Angie giggled. "I hope you like Hispanic food."

"Actually, it's my favorite. I'd love to come. Thank you"—Mackenzie laughed—"and your mom." Mackenzie's forehead puckered. "Are you sure he didn't mind? I'm not off duty until Saturday morning."

"I explained that my mom had tomorrow off but would have to work Friday and through the weekend. He understood, saying he would love to spend the extra time with Elise."

Mackenzie laughed. "Well then, it looks like you'll have a guest for dinner."

"That's wonderful." Angie fumbled in the pocket of her uniform and withdrew a folded paper. "I wrote down the directions to my house. It's not hard to find, only about fifteen minutes from here. And come early.

Maybe I can teach you a thing or two about preparing authentic Mexican cuisine while I help Mom with dinner."

"I'll plan on leaving just as soon as Mr. Huntington comes to collect Elise." Mackenzie's smiled faded. "Say, Angie, did you know that Captain Sprinsky came to Park House this afternoon to speak with Mr. Huntington?"

Angie clapped her hands against her cheeks. "Oh my goodness. I almost forgot." Angie looked around and then leaned forward, lowering her voice. "Yes, I did know that. I was tidying up the living room when Mr. Huntington escorted the captain to the door. I could hardly wait until my shift ended so I could rush up here and tell you what I overheard."

Mackenzie's eyes widened. "Did they say something about Mrs. Huntington's death?"

"At least in a manner of speaking. I heard Captain Sprinsky tell Mr. Huntington that once the men on the list had been investigated, a report would be sent to him.

"But get this. I couldn't believe my ears when I heard Mr. Huntington's response. He told the captain that he wasn't indifferent to Jasmine's little flirtations by any means and that she knew how he felt, but that's all they were—harmless little flirtations that meant nothing to her. He never once doubted her faithfulness." Angie paused to take a deep breath. "And then he indicated that not all the men she dallied with accepted her loss of interest in them with clemency. He said, 'Jasmine never let them down easy. Once she tired of the individual, it was as if he no longer existed. But she never took their threats of harm seriously. She just laughed them off and moved on with her life.'"

Mackenzie looked stunned. "Are you saying that Mr. Huntington accepted his wife's indiscretions?"

Angie shook her head. "No way. I overheard the two argue about them several times. And believe me, Mr. Huntington's nonchalant attitude toward his wife's improprieties this afternoon falls far short of the fiery encounters they had over her men friends."

"Maybe he wanted to paint a less-than-true picture of their problems for Jasmine's sake. You know how it is—once a person is dead, people tend to forget his faults and focus on the good memories. Did the captain seem shocked by Mr. Huntington's statement?"

"No. More like sympathetic. He said he realized how difficult it had been for Mr. Huntington to reveal this important information and would give it his full attention."

One arm draped around Elise, Mackenzie strummed her fingers on the sofa cushion. "I know you liked Mrs. Huntington, but I think it's terrible how she treated her devotees. Just a game with her. Didn't she realize what could come of it? I can understand she deserved some type of retribution for her actions, but not *murder*."

"I agree," Angie said, brightening. "Maybe this is the lead that will help the police find the killer. I'm sure Mr. Huntington desires closure to the case. It must be horrible not knowing who killed his wife." Angie stood, placing the strap of her handbag on her shoulder. "I hate to rush off like this, but I have to pick up my brother from his after-school job. We'll talk more tomorrow." Angie bent and kissed Elise on her cheek. "See you, pumpkin."

Later that evening, after Mr. Huntington had rocked Elise to sleep and tucked her into the crib, he turned to Mackenzie, who'd entered the nursery when she heard him preparing to take his leave. He glanced at his sleeping daughter and then spoke in a low voice.

"Miss Adams, would you mind stepping into the hallway? I need to speak with you a moment."

"Yes, sir," she said, clasping her hands tightly behind her back. She followed him through the doorway. Had her fear come true—Captain Sprinsky informing Mr. Huntington of their conversation? Closing the door behind her, she pulled in a deep breath. How could she possibly say good-bye to Elise? Mackenzie waited, her gaze focused on the pattern of the inlaid floor.

"Miss Adams, when I spoke with Captain Sprinsky this afternoon, he related your concern that my wife's killer is still at large. I just want you to understand that the police and I are doing everything possible to see that my family and employees stay safe."

Mackenzie lifted her eyelashes to stare at her employer. She shook her head slightly. A few seconds ago, she'd believed her unemployment a breath away from Mr. Huntington's lips. Had she mistaken his words?

Mr. Huntington frowned. "If you're still concerned, I can speak to the captain about stepping up the patrol of our neighborhood."

"No, sir. That won't be necessary. Really. I'm sure the police are doing their best to protect us," she said, smiling, her eyes bright with gratefulness.

"I do hope you're not planning to leave my employ. Elise has flourished in your care. It's a joy to know I don't have to worry about her in that regard."

Mackenzie's eyes widened. "Oh, no, sir. Not at all. I admit the whole situation is unnerving. It's hard to imagine that Elise could be in danger—that someone might want to harm her. But you can rest assured, sir, that I will do my utmost to keep her safe."

"I don't think I would be responsible for my actions should she be taken from me," Mr. Huntington said, his voice low. He lowered his gaze.

Mackenzie lifted her eyes to stare at her employer. "I'm sorry. I didn't quite catch what you said. I still had Elise on my mind."

He shook his head. "Nothing to cause you worry. Just thinking out loud." He smiled. "However, I am glad that we had this little talk. Thank you for setting me at ease about my daughter. Now I will bid you good night." He started to walk away and then did an about-face. "Oh, Miss Adams, Trace plans to take Elise to the zoo tomorrow and has requested that you accompany them. He thought she would enjoy the experience more with her nanny beside her." Mr. Huntington's smile deepened. "His lack of expertise in changing diapers may also have been a motive for the request as well."

Mackenzie hoped the dim light in the hallway hid the color rising in her cheeks. "Of course." She bit her lip. "I'll be delighted to go with them." *Liar, liar!* Just what she needed—hours of devising ways to fight off her attraction to a man she barely knew. "What time do I need to have Elise ready?"

"I believe Trace said nine a.m. He has a full day of activities planned for Elise—the zoo in the morning, lunch, and then an indoor playground in the afternoon. So go prepared, Miss Adams."

Oh, great. Not just a few hours, but a whole day of enduring the roller coaster in her stomach that launched each time she stood near Trace Patterson. *Merciful heavens!* By the end of the day, she'd probably be able to write a book entitled *Fifty Ways to Sidestep Romance.* A tremor in her hand, Mackenzie wiped away the sheen of moisture that had crept onto her brow. "Yes, sir. Elise will have a wonderful time."

"I hope you'll enjoy the day too."

"I'm sure I will." Mackenzie turned an ear toward the nursery door. "Excuse me, sir, but I believe Elise may have awakened."

"By all means. Have a good night, Miss Adams."

"Thank you," Mackenzie said over her shoulder. In the nursery, she leaned back against the door after a glance at the crib revealed Elise still slept. She closed her eyes, breathed deeply, and exhaled slowly. Calmer now, she moved forward and peeked over the top of the baby's bed. At this moment, she could have been packing to leave Park House, yet providence had stepped in and saved her.

Mackenzie smiled. *Bless Captain Sprinsky.* She must declare her gratitude to him the next time she saw him. She blew a kiss toward the sleeping cherub. "Oh little darling, now that you've stolen my heart, how could I let you go?" Mackenzie whispered.

All at once, Mackenzie stood upright, her hand on her chest. Something Mr. Huntington had said earlier had bothered her at the time, but caught up in the realization she still had employment, she'd let it slip past her. Mackenzie strode toward her room. What was it? Her brow knitted together. They'd been discussing the safety of the household, and she'd voiced the incredibility of Elise's endangerment.

Mackenzie snapped her fingers. Mr. Huntington's remark had intimated revenge toward anyone who would dare take Elise from him.

Mackenzie's breath caught and held. Did he know a person who might kidnap his daughter? Although he'd claimed his remark unimportant, the cloud of anger that had traipsed across his features at that moment told a different story. Why hadn't she paid more attention and questioned him further? She tapped her finger on her chin. Should she ask him about it later?

Once in her room, Mackenzie stood at the window, taking in the twinkling lights on the horizon that outlined one sector of the city, while she contemplated Angie's declaration. Had Mr. Huntington been thinking about his conversation with Captain Sprinsky when he'd uttered the threatening statement? Did he suspect one of Jasmine's former "friends" capable of kidnapping Elise for revenge? Did he suspect one of them of murdering Jasmine? Mackenzie shook her head. So many questions danced in her head, but so few answers.

Angie's statements about seeing Jasmine and Jason Crane together at a restaurant trickled into Mackenzie's thoughts. Could the perpetrator be the prestigious lawyer? Had he tired of the late Mrs. Huntington's blasé treatment of his affections and, in a fit of passion, killed her? If so, had Mr. Crane been the eavesdropper in the hallway, hoping to discover how much her employer knew about Jasmine's death?

Mackenzie turned away from the view and gathered her nightclothes. Had Mr. Crane's name been on the list given to Captain Sprinsky? All of a sudden, an idea struck Mackenzie. If given a chance, she would cultivate a friendship with Mr. Crane on the off chance she might learn something that would indicate his guilt. Smiling, Mackenzie entered her bathroom. At once, her face straightened at the thought of the captain's warning. But surely an innocent chat with Mr. Crane wouldn't be considered dangerous. She'd just have to choose her questions with care.

Mackenzie awoke the next morning to the sound of Elise's playful jabbering. Groggy, she pulled the pillow over her head, wishing she could do anything but be with Trace Patterson the entire day. Unable to sleep for worrying about how she could keep her feelings at bay after spending a whole day with him, she had yet to come up with a solution. Glancing at the clock on the side table, she roused from her bed. Hurrying into her clothes after a quick shower, she greeted Elise with a smile and cheery words, determined to make her day a fun and educational experience. After all, her job demanded it; any personal conflict or sentiments about the proposed trip were irrelevant to the situation.

"There you go, pretty one," Mackenzie said once she had Elise dressed. Slipping on her shoes a minute later, Mackenzie called, "Come in," at the knock on the nursery door.

Angie sashayed through the doorway, a silly grin on her face. "Mr. Patterson is waiting for you in the living room. Wow! A date with Trace Patterson. Some girls have all the luck."

Mackenzie shook her head. "You've got it all wrong. Elise is his *date*, not me. He's taking her to the zoo and asked me to tag along to see to her needs."

Angie's eyes twinkled. "Yeah, sure. And monkeys never have fleas. You should have seen how his face lit up when I offered to run upstairs and announce his arrival." She glanced heavenward. "I'd be glad to take your place. Just say the word."

All of a sudden, Mackenzie's knees seemed to liquefy like hot jelly. "Believe me, if I could choose, I'd make the trade in a heartbeat." Mackenzie rubbed her clammy hands down the length of her new shorts.

"You can't be serious." Angie gaped at Mackenzie as if she'd just lost her mind.

Mackenzie grabbed the large tote bag she'd filled earlier with items she and Elise would need for the day and followed Angie, who carried Elise down the stairs. Just before the girls stepped into the living room, Angie grabbed Mackenzie's arm and propelled her into the foyer. "I expect a full report this evening—every detail of your day."

Mackenzie heaved a disgruntled sigh and then stepped away from her friend. Bracing her shoulders, she entered the living room with Angie and Elise in tow and greeted Trace with a tight smile.

"Good morning, Miss Adams." He glanced at her tote bag. "It looks like you're ready for our outing. The weatherman has forecast lower temperatures, the break in the heat making it a perfect day for what I have in mind for this little munchkin." He took Elise from Angie's arms.

"Yes, Mr. Patterson, I'm ready."

"Great. Uncle Drew assisted me in loading the stroller and car seat into my car before he left for work. Shall we be off?"

Mackenzie glanced at Angie, who turned away to hide the smile breaking onto her face. "Sure." She reached for Elise.

"No, no. You go ahead. I can strap Elise in her seat." He grinned. "I've had *some* practice." He turned to Angie. "Thanks for your help. Have a good day."

Mackenzie hoisted the bag onto her shoulder. She turned to face Angie with narrowed eyes. "Yeah, Angie. You have a marvelous day."

Angie responded with a coy grin. Mackenzie ducked her head. How could she take out her frustration on one who had a friend's best interest at heart? She lifted her lashes and smiled. "Truly, Angie. See you later."

"Have fun, and remember what I said." Chuckling, she entered the hallway and made her way to the back of the house, humming a popular love song.

Mackenzie rolled her eyes toward the ceiling before she turned and followed Trace out the door. What would Mr. Patterson think of that exhibition? When they reached his Lexus, she started to climb into the backseat next to Elise, but Trace waved a no and pointed to the string of toys attached to the car seat. "Elise has plenty to occupy her for now. You can sit up front with me."

Mackenzie turned her gaze toward the pavement, gritting her teeth. *Time to outline the rules in that book. Number one rule to discourage the attention of a prospective admirer: sit as close to car door as possible, keeping your head turned toward the side window so your heart won't leap into high gear when accosted by your companion's infectious smile.*

"It is a lovely neighborhood, isn't it?" Trace said, driving down the street a moment later.

Mackenzie glimpsed her clasped hands stationed in her lap. "Yes. Quite charming."

They rode for a few minutes in silence, and then Trace cleared his throat. "Look, Miss Adams, you don't have to be nervous with me. My uncle is your employer, yes, but when you get to know me, you'll discover that I don't hold with the old tradition of an upstairs, downstairs attitude toward employees of prominent households. So I'd like a shot at becoming your friend, if it's okay with you. For starters, do you think we could call each other by our given names? Mackenzie is such a pretty name." He laughed. "And when you say Mr. Patterson, it sounds so formal and *old*."

Mackenzie didn't dare breathe. When he'd said her name, it had sounded more like a caress than a word. *Rule number two: don't ever agree to a first-name basis, as it could lead to friendship, which later might turn into a more intimate relationship.* She glanced his way, the corners of her mouth lifting. "I suppose that's permissible, Mr.—I mean Trace." She centered her gaze toward the windshield. What was wrong with her? She hadn't meant to say that at all. *Be safe, Mackenzie. Don't get caught up in his appeal.*

Trace smiled. "Now may I suggest you move away from the door? If it should happen to open when I go around that curve just ahead, I'd lose you for sure."

Her jaw dropping, she sent him a startled look and then shifted in the seat to accommodate his suggestion. A moment later, her eyes shimmered with amusement. "I wouldn't want to be a driving hazard."

He chuckled and then grew serious. "Mackenzie, you don't have to be afraid of me."

Mackenzie turned away from his gaze, tears gathering in her eyes. She blinked several times. *Rule number three: never believe a soft-spoken man whose words tinged with hope of a brighter tomorrow dip right into your soul.*

Trace glanced over his shoulder. "Isn't that right, munchkin?"

Elise gurgled a stream of baby jabber. Mackenzie and Trace broke into laughter. She glanced at Trace from the corners of her eyes. Friends—yeah, she could handle that. She'd just have to make sure their relationship didn't go any further. He smiled at her, his eyes saying things she didn't want to hear. Mackenzie glanced out the window at the countryside, taking in the trees and dense underbrush as they left suburbia behind them. *Yeah, right. Friends.* Who did she think she was kidding?

Trace again glanced at Elise. "We're almost there, little one." A short distance ahead, they saw a sign that read City Zoo pointing to the left, and soon Trace drove onto the exit ramp.

After enjoying several of the exhibits, Mackenzie and Trace sat on a park bench, cooling themselves with a soda from a nearby vendor stand while Elise napped. Mackenzie eyed his movements as he adjusted the canopy on the stroller to better protect Elise from the sun.

"You seem to like children," she said when he again sat next to her.

"Yes. When I decide to marry, I hope to have a house full of them. And since you've chosen a career in child care, I have to assume you have similar feelings about them."

Mackenzie lowered her eyelashes, her gaze fixed on the pebble she moved about with the toe of her sandal. "I love children." *Just not sure I'll ever have them.* "I started babysitting when I turned thirteen and have been caring for kids since then. In fact, my love for children is what influenced my choice of a college degree and then again for my master's program."

"Uncle Drew told me about your educational background. I'm impressed. I have to wonder, though, what made you decide to come all the way to Arkansas to start your career. And to begin as a nanny. Your

BA in elementary education alone qualifies you for a much higher position in the workforce."

She turned her gaze toward the monkeys swinging from limb to limb in their man-made habitat, her thoughts in tune with their antics. "I needed a break from desert life, and when my friend Kari, who trained as a nanny, turned down Mr. Huntington's offer for a position in California, I decided it would be a good chance for me to enhance my education with hands-on experience."

"But with your background, I would have thought you'd had plenty of hands-on experience," Trace said, his eyes shining with laughter.

"Yes, but not in this area of child care."

"So how do you like being a nanny thus far?"

Mackenzie's eyes lit up. "I love taking care of Elise. She's such a joy."

He laughed. "That she is. I've spent considerable time with Elise since her birth. I couldn't love her more if she were my own child."

Mackenzie tilted her head to study her companion. "Do you mind if I ask why you're not married?"

Trace shrugged. "Friends seem to think I'll be like Uncle Drew and marry later in life. While business took up most of his time in earlier years, it's not so much with me. Yes, I enjoy my work, but I like to volunteer for projects in my church as well as be available to go on occasional mission trips. To be candid, I just haven't found the right person who desires what I have to offer. What about you? Did you leave a string of broken hearts behind when you left Arizona?"

She stood from the bench to attend to Elise, who'd begun to stir from her sleep. So her suspicions had been right. The day she'd met him in Mr. Huntington's office, she'd noted a difference in him. She eyed his peaceful countenance from beneath her eyelashes. No, his interest in religious matters hadn't surprised her at all. Studying him momentarily, she realized he expected an answer from her. She turned aside. Her voice just above a whisper, she said, "Only one. Mine." She cringed. When had she begun to speak her thoughts?

Trace stood beside her within seconds. He reached out, cupped her chin, and turned her to face him. "If you ever desire to share the reason for the sadness I've seen in your eyes from the day we met, I'm a good listener."

Rule number four: never confide in a man who causes your breath to quicken when he stands close to you, his touch causing you to forget your self-imposed promise to renounce all temptations to love another man for the rest of your life.

Mackenzie pulled away from Trace. Looking around, she noted restroom facilities nearby. After removing Elise from the stroller, Mackenzie picked up the tote bag and started toward her destination, tossing a look over her shoulder. "I'll be right back." She hadn't meant to hurt his feelings, but the wounded look in his eyes proved she had. How could she talk about her mutilated heart? Every word spoken would be like peeling skin from her body inch by inch.

Upon her return, she glanced toward a food vender a few yards away, thinking she could ask an attendant to warm the baby food she pulled from the bag, but she realized the heat from the sun had sufficed. After breaking the seal on the jar, she spooned the mixed beef and vegetables into Elise's mouth, unsure of what to say to Trace.

Observing the ritual, he broke the silence a few minutes later. "Since it's still a little early for our lunch, I thought we'd take Elise on the park train and then head off to a fifties diner down the road that's got great burgers and shakes. I've known the proprietors for years. Uncle Drew used to take me there after our trips to the zoo when I was a boy. Everything is the real stuff—no ice cream mixes or burgers stuffed with soy meal."

Mackenzie sent him a smile, hoping he would see the apology in her eyes. "Sounds wonderful. We have a place like that back home."

By the time they reached the restaurant, Elise had fallen asleep. Rather than wake her, Trace unstrapped the car seat, carried it inside the diner, and placed it in a booth. Mackenzie sat next to Elise. They scanned the menus the hostess had set before them. Within a short time, she and Trace were enjoying their meal and a smattering of conversation, the tension between them earlier canned for now.

"You're right. These are great," she said, preparing to indulge in another bite of her burger.

He laughed. "I told you. Best comfort food in all of Little Rock."

Later, after Elise had awoken and Mackenzie had given her a bottle of formula, Trace drove them to an indoor fun center for small children. Their time taken with entertaining the child, they had little opportunity to converse with each other. Mackenzie found it comforting. It left no room for reminders of her past or questions from Trace about it.

However, the touches on her arms and back as Trace guided her about the play dome *were* a matter for concern. Each time he laid his hand on her, she felt as if heat from an incinerator engulfed her. *Rule number five: always carry a wet towel filled with ice to cool your neck and arms when in the presence of an attractive man who looks at you like you're the most beautiful woman in the world, his glimpses causing you to tremble and your face to light up like LED lights on a Christmas tree.*

Her emotions spent, Mackenzie couldn't wait to get back to the nursery when Trace drove them to Park House late that afternoon. Although she'd enjoyed the day tremendously, with the exception of a discussion or two, she needed to prioritize her feelings. She eyed Trace's profile from beneath her eyelashes. *Rule number six: don't give in to your feelings; keep your distance, and try to avoid further excursions with a man who could steal your heart at any given moment—should you allow it.*

*I*nside the house, following their arrival at Park House, Trace stowed the stroller and handed Mackenzie her tote bag just before she mounted the stairs to take a fussy, hungry Elise to the nursery for a cooling bath and dinner. When she reached the second floor landing, Trace called to Mackenzie. She jumped at the sound of his voice. Turning, her breath caught and held. Rays from the late-afternoon sun danced through the foyer window, intensifying the ardent glow in his eyes as he held her in his gaze. She felt as if her knees would buckle any second.

"Oh, Mr. Patter—Trace, I didn't know you were still here."

His smile radiant, he crossed his arms and rested them on top of the newel post supporting the staircase bannister. "I just wanted to say thank you for making my time with Elise special. And I would like to repay you by taking you out to dinner tonight. I'm sure Uncle Drew would take care of my cousin for a couple of hours. Especially if I asked him."

Mackenzie shook her head. "Sorry, I already have a dinner date this evening."

"Oh, I see. Perhaps another time then."

Compassion swept through her at his crestfallen expression, consideration for his feelings warring with her appreciation of Angie's invitation. "Yes, perhaps." *Rule number seven: don't give in, even if every breath inside your body is whispering, "Yes, just name the time and place."* She watched his shoulders slump forward momentarily and then bounce back to their former position.

He lifted his hand in a farewell gesture. "Well, so long then. Enjoy your date. I'm sure we'll see each other soon."

Mackenzie observed his exit and then turned aside, closing her eyes. *Oh Trace …* If he looked at her that way in the future, she knew she'd lose in her struggle with fate no matter how many stratagems she could come up with to avoid his allure. She had to do her best to keep that from happening; her heart was too fragile to take the chance.

If only he didn't seem to be everything she'd desired in a man—caring, considerate, attractive, filled with a yearning for home and family, established in a good career, and the one trait she admired the most—a man who, she now believed, loved and served God passionately. However, her right to such a mate had been severed the moment she'd agreed to Zack's plan for their future. Oh, why hadn't she been strong enough to refuse his ultimatum?

Tears blurred Mackenzie's steps to the nursery. Each footfall seemed to scream, "Fool! Fool! Fool!"

Later, following a light tap on the nursery door, Angie whizzed into the room and parked her tiny frame next to Mackenzie, who stood at the sink, cleaning Elise's dinner utensils.

"Okay, I have to know before I go home—how did it go today?"

Mackenzie shrugged. "Elise had a great time. We saw lots of animals and birds. In between, I fed her, changed her diapers, and did my best to keep her cool." Mackenzie smiled at the bewilderment clouding Angie's expression.

Catching the teasing glint in her friend's eyes, Angie grinned. "That's not what I meant, and you know it. How did things go with you and Mr. Patterson?"

Mackenzie reached out and touched Angie's shoulder. "Mr. Patterson is a very nice, kind man. And I enjoyed talking with him when we weren't busy amusing Elise."

"Oh," Angie said, her expression changing from hopeful to bleak. "He really seemed taken with you this morning. I thought you might—you know—feel the same way about him by the end of the day."

Mackenzie walked over to take Elise out of her high chair, throwing Angie a glance over her shoulder. "He did ask to be friends with me, desiring that we use our first names with each other."

Angie's face lit up like a diamond in sunlight. She snapped her fingers. "Now you're talking." She raised her arm to glance at her watch. "Hey, I've got to go. See you about six thirty." At the door, she paused and faced Mackenzie, a look of compassion emblazoned across her features. "Although you haven't said anything, I know some guy hurt you badly. Call it woman's intuition or whatever." She moved forward to give her friend a quick hug and then stepped back, clasping Mackenzie's hand. "Please don't close your mind to a new relationship—you're too warmhearted and too cute to let that jerk, whoever he was, destroy your chance for real happiness." Turning, Angie rushed out the door, throwing a good-bye wave over her shoulder. "See you soon," she called from the hallway.

Mackenzie crossed the room to close the door, staring openmouthed after her friend for a long moment, and then eased the door shut. She withdrew a children's book from the bookcase and sat down in the rocker, settling Elise in her lap for story time. Mackenzie glanced toward the door. How could she explain to Angie that there were occasions when people lost their right to true happiness?

On the following Monday morning, with Elise tucked in her arms, Mackenzie strode down the second-story corridor. Recalling the past weekend, she smiled. The dinner with Angie's family on Thursday evening had been great fun. They were a lively group and had welcomed her with open arms. Nevertheless, after promising to visit again soon, she'd hurried home following the cleanup, desiring not to take advantage of Mr. Huntington's generosity.

And then the next morning, to everyone's surprise, Mr. Huntington had dismissed the entire staff for the weekend, explaining his plan to take Elise with him on a trip to visit some relatives in another part of the state. Gathering Elise into his arms a short time later, he'd assured Mackenzie that his cousin would help him take good care of his daughter. Just before they left the nursery, he'd leaned Elise forward to receive a good-bye kiss from her nanny, urging Mackenzie to enjoy her break.

With Park House to herself, she'd hung out by the pool, read a new novel, done a bit of shopping, and even had an encouraging phone conversation with her father. Mackenzie's mouth turned downward. The only blight on the weekend had been Reagan's stubborn refusal to talk to her daughter. "Give her time," Steve had said. "She'll come around."

Mackenzie stepped up her pace. "That old weatherman said to expect rain around noon, so we'd best hurry to the park," Mackenzie informed Elise, tweaking her nose. "We don't want to miss out on the fun, now, do we?" Just before they reached the staircase, the sound of voices drifted upward from the foyer. Hearing her name, Mackenzie stopped short, inclining her ear. All at once, she clutched her chest, her eyes narrowing into thin slits. How dare Greg Martin brag to another individual his intention to win the heart of the new nanny! *Of all the nerve.* Mackenzie stood motionless, waiting to identify the recipient of Greg's words.

"I thought you and Lacey were together," a man said, his voice low.

Mackenzie's eyes widened. Could it be? She inched closer to the end of the hallway.

"Nah. She claims she has someone else now. You know how it is—you win some, lose some."

Mackenzie leaned against the wall, cringing. In her mind, she could see Greg's lifted shoulder. Heat coursed through her from the top of her head to her feet. She glanced at Elise, praying she wouldn't disclose their presence.

"You talk as if it's a done deal—that no one else would stand a chance at capturing Miss Adams's interest. May I ask on what you base your assumption?"

Oh, merciful heavens! It is him, Mackenzie thought. She looked toward the floor. If only it were possible for her to will the oak flooring to open so that she could slip through the cracks into nothingness. She peeked around the corner of the wall. Trace stood near the door. She couldn't determine whether he'd just arrived or was leaving the house.

Mackenzie held her fist against her mouth. She started to back up out of view, but Elise's cry of joy caused both men to glance upward to see the baby holding her arms out to Trace, her wide-eyed nanny, in the meantime, looking as if she could commit murder any second.

Trace stepped forward, a bright smile lighting up his eyes. "Good morning, Mackenzie."

Her heart seemed to leap into her throat, blocking a response. Holding her head high, she proceeded down the steps one at a time, a tight clasp on the railing. She had to get out the door now. She held her breath, her gaze straight ahead. If she looked at either one of them, she couldn't account for what she might say or do, but whatever it was, she had a distinct feeling she'd regret it.

She'd just reached the closet to pull out the stroller, when she felt a hand on her shoulder. She squashed the urge to yank free of the touch, afraid she'd frighten Elise.

"Mackenzie, on my way out from an early conference with Uncle Drew, I met up with Greg in the foyer. He explained his mission."

She lifted her chin, a defiant look in her eyes. "So I heard."

Trace raised his hands chest high, palms facing outward. "What I'm talking about is Greg's arrangement with Uncle Drew to escort you on your walk today." Trace paused to take a breath. "I hope you don't mind, but I told Greg I would take his place, assuring him Uncle Drew wouldn't be displeased with the change in plans. He knows my fondness for Elise. Since I don't have any appointments this morning, I decided I wouldn't pass up the chance to spend a couple of hours with her."

Mackenzie turned to face him, her eyes narrowing. "Really? But then you two"—she glanced at Greg, her lips melding into a straight line—"couldn't finish your discussion." Oh, what she'd give to slap that smugness off Greg's face! She pivoted her glare toward Trace. "While you're at it, be sure to inform Mr. Martin that he needn't bother with his scheme, because the party in question is not interested—with a capital *I*. Now, if you'll excuse me, Elise is ready for her walk."

The two men watched her movements as if in a trance. When she had a bit of difficulty maneuvering the stroller out the door, Trace shook his head slightly and then stepped forward to assist her. Once outside, she thanked him through scrunched teeth and then rolled the stroller toward the street without a backward glance. He caught up with her, taking her arm.

"You know you can't go alone, Mackenzie. Uncle Drew would be outraged. I'm coming whether you like it or not," Trace said, his voice low but firm.

She lifted an eyebrow. "Sure you want to take the risk?"

"Come on, Mackenzie—be fair. I know it looked bad, and you deserve to be upset, but just before you made your appearance"—he grinned from the side of his mouth—"boy, were you furious! I thought flames would burst from those gorgeous eyes any moment."

She gave him a look that washed the grin off his face.

He sighed. "I was about to tell Greg to back off, when Elise alerted us of your presence on the landing." Trace reached out as though to stroke her cheek. Tilting her face away from him, she backed up a step. He dropped his arm. "Greg has a lot of growing up to do. I do hope someday he'll be deserving of a woman like you."

All at once, her shoulders crumpled forward. Unable to speak past the lump in her throat, she faced Trace, an apology in her eyes. Why should she let Greg Martin and his stupid ego spoil her day? Men like him existed by the dozens, and here a man whom she believed had integrity and worth walked by her side—a gentle man who had expressed an unpretentious desire to become better acquainted with her. She looked away from his endearing gaze. Her heart said yes, but her soul said no, it could never be. At the least, she could be cordial, although she might pay the consequences later. Her heart jolted within her. Would she never stop paying for her crime?

She glanced toward the picturesque wooden-sided church she'd noted on each of her treks to the park. But today, the flowering bushes of various colors that bordered its sides and steps seemed to beckon to her, calling for her to experience the peace that its sanctuary offered—a haven, no doubt, to those who worshipped there each week. She choked back a sob. In her middle teens, she'd been a recipient of the "peace that passes all understanding"—a time in her life that now seemed like eons ago. Would she ever have harmony in her soul again? She jumped at the sound of Trace's voice.

"Mackenzie, would you like to talk about it?"

"No." She shook her head. "No. I mean—I'm sorry, Trace. It's not your fault that Greg is such a cad. I thought once or twice when he accompanied Elise and me on our walks that he and I might become friends, but he has a large chip on his shoulder and won't let anyone close to him"—she looked away—"except for the wrong reasons."

Trace nodded. "I understand. He's been that way since he turned old enough to grasp his situation in life."

"So you've known him a long time?"

"Since a few weeks after he came into this world. I had been living at Park House a few months by that time. Mrs. Slater would bring him to work with her."

"Come to think of it, he did mention that his mother had worked at Park House most of her life—and a grandmother as well."

Wariness etched a path across Trace's features. "Did he mention anything else about his family history?"

"Just that both his father and grandfather were white and that he had an aunt who lived in another state." Her brow puckered. "I got the impression he isn't close to his father. But he indicated he had an uncle who lived in this area, although he didn't mention his name."

Trace nodded. "His father, Tom Martin, took off for parts unknown not long after Greg's birth. That's when Mrs. Slater moved into the apartment over the garage. A few years later, she married again, but her husband, Robert Slater, the former caretaker of the estate, died from a heart attack about six years ago."

"That's too bad on both counts. It's a shame Greg didn't get a chance to know his father." Turning into the park, Mackenzie smiled at Trace. "When Greg spoke of his African American descent, it took me a moment to process the fact. I would never have guessed." She slowed her pace. "Italian maybe—if I had taken time to think about it."

Trace grinned. "You were quite adamant earlier about his not appealing to you as a suitor. May I ask why?"

"Sure. He's just not my type. To be honest, he's too arrogant for my taste, and his attitude is rotten most days. We have nothing in common at all." She frowned. "Now it's my turn to ask you something. A moment ago, you seemed annoyed that Greg had spoken to me about his heritage. Why?"

Without waiting for him to answer, Mackenzie secured Elise in the baby swing. Trace observed the activity, laughing at the baby's squeals of delight before he moved to stand beside Mackenzie.

Not understanding what she read in his eyes, she lowered her eyelashes. "Sorry, Trace. I didn't mean to pry—just curious."

"I hesitate to say anything, because Greg's family history is not pleasant. But since it involves my family as well, I suppose I can tell you." He reached out and touched her arm. "You can't reside in a community for several generations like the Huntington family and expect their ancestral skeletons to remain hidden from the public. Several in our circle of friends and business associates are aware of our family history. And since you'll probably be asked to bring Elise to intermingle with guests when Uncle Drew is ready to entertain again at Park House, I would rather you hear about it from me than from a gossip."

Mackenzie's eyes widened, her curiosity rising to peak level. She held her breath, waiting. Feeling she needed to give him an out, she held the swing still. "Look, Trace, you really don't have to tell me. After all, I'm just an employee."

He ran the back of his hand down her cheek. "Not to me. Mackenzie, I know that we met just days ago, but there's a chemistry between us that is special, no matter how much you try to fight it. That's why it's important for you to discover who I am, including my background."

Mackenzie lowered her gaze. If she continued to stare into his eyes, she would melt like ice and fall at his feet, staining the leather of his pricey shoes now dusty from their walk through the park. She slowly pushed the swing back and forth. Did he feel the same way about her history? Did he expect her to be open and candid with him about the skeleton in her closet? And if he did, could she disclose it? Never!

She doused her thoughts with a smile. "So what are these big secrets that apply to both yours and Greg's family?" she said, her tone light and teasing. Observing his somber expression, she dropped her smile. "Sorry."

"To begin, it's not Greg's family or my family—it's our family."

All humor evaporated from Mackenzie's face. "Excuse me?"

He nodded. "It's true. I guess I should start at the beginning."

"Please do."

"My great-great-grandfather Reuben Huntington came to Little Rock from the East Coast in his twenties. Desiring to become an entrepreneur in this part of the country, he bought up numerous parcels of land, later developing the properties"—Trace swept his arm wide—"turning acreage such as this area into estates for the more prosperous of the city—thus the beginning of Huntington Incorporated."

"Interesting. Go on."

"Needless to say, Reuben became one of the wealthiest men in the state of Arkansas at that time. He had been close to seeing his own estate, Park House, completed when he developed pneumonia and died, leaving both the estate and company to his son, James, my great-grandfather. James's hope for a bright future died due to the stock market crash in 1929 and the Great Depression that followed—his only assets the titles to his landholdings that no one could afford to buy."

Mackenzie nodded. "A very desolate time for America. Was James able to compensate in some way for his losses?"

"Yes. But not in a conventional way. Having inherited his father's drive for financial gain, he took advantage of the nation's war on Prohibition, soon creating an illegal entity to deliver alcohol known as corn squeezins— or, the more familiar term, *moonshine*—to those thirsty for whiskey from Canada to the Gulf of Mexico."

Mackenzie shuddered. "He took quite a risk. Where did he get his supply?"

"From hidden distilleries in the hills of the South. The owners of the crude whiskey stills would bottle the brew in Mason jars, and then send the cargo to their distributors. James stored his jars in a secret underground room beneath Park House. Once he received an order for the whiskey through a coded message, a runner would put the moonshine in a hidden compartment in the back of a truck and deliver his load."

Mackenzie's mind began to whirl. "Secret room? Did you ever see it?"

"Yes, in my early teens, when Uncle Drew related this story to me. At the time, he intended to close it off, but if he did, he never told me."

"So did your great-grandfather get caught by the authorities?"

Trace laughed. "How he kept from it, no one knows for sure. Uncle Drew thinks he bribed the revenuers, as they were known to the people of the hills. By the end of the Depression, James had built up a sizable fortune, reinstating his father's real estate company to become bigger and better during his lifetime.

Not long thereafter, and the construction on Park House complete, the estate became a popular place of entertainment for the upper echelon of the city."

The wind started to pick up, and Mackenzie gazed upward, surveying the dark clouds. "I think we'd better head back to the house," she said, unstrapping Elise from the swing.

Following her gaze, Trace nodded. "I agree. I hope we get back before it starts raining."

"I think we have plenty of time," Mackenzie said as she settled the baby into the stroller and rolled her slowly toward the street. "What you've been sharing is fascinating, but how does it affect Greg?"

"I'm about to get to that," Trace said, smiling at Mackenzie's rapt attention.

"In James's lifetime, Park House had a large staff to oversee the place. One such staff member, a fifteen-year-old housekeeper's assistant, was newly hired by my great-grandmother. The same year the young African American came to work at Park House, Uncle Drew's father, John Huntington, graduated from a well-known boarding school and returned home to work in the family business until he ventured off to college in the fall.

"Intrigued by the striking young housemaid, my grandfather forced her into an intimate relationship. By the time he left for college, the girl was pregnant with his child."

"I'm beginning to understand. How awful for her," Mackenzie said, shaking her head.

"Yes. When she approached James about the matter, he laughed it off, saying something like 'Any boy worth his salt would sow some wild wheat before he settled down.' However, my great-grandfather did permit her to stay on at Park House, allowing her to raise the baby in the servants' quarters, which were torn down a generation later." Trace drew a long sigh. "That young woman was Mrs. Slater's mother."

Mackenzie's chin dropped. She slowed her pace and came to a complete stop. Her hands tightened on the stroller handle. "No wonder Greg has that log strapped to his back."

"Yes, some would say he's rightful of his attitude, but do you remember that youth leader I mentioned the day we talked at the house following Jasmine's funeral? Something he told me changed my life. He said I should never let the past dictate my future—that the future holds all kinds of promise to those who will let go of their past and seek to obtain God-given opportunities. I shared those words with Greg, but he sloughed them off, stating he didn't need me to tell him what to do. I know that Uncle Drew offered to send Greg to college, but he refused, said he wanted to stay around and look after his mother."

"At least he showed decency in that."

Trace's face darkened. "But that was only an excuse. It was Jasmine that kept him here. Greg became infatuated with her. And to make matters worse, she encouraged it. Not sure if Uncle Drew picked up on it—" Trace raked his hand across his face. "Mackenzie, please forgive me. I shouldn't have told you that."

She laid her hand on his arm. "I think I knew it already. Greg has a way of saying things without too many words." Mackenzie's eyes widened. "Oh my goodness, you—" Her expression glowed with understanding. "You and Greg are cousins, and Mr. Huntington is the uncle Greg mentioned."

Trace nodded. "Yes, that's right."

"I assume Mr. Huntington included the details about Mrs. Slater's connection to the family when he shared about your grandfather's exploits during the thirties?"

"Actually, no. That information I learned by accident. I had just turned sixteen and had my first car. All I needed was an excuse to drive somewhere. So when Mrs. Slater asked me to drive Greg to school one morning, I gladly agreed. But once we were in the car, I remembered I hadn't asked Uncle Drew for gas money. I hurried inside and was about to knock on his office door, when I heard an argument between Mrs. Slater and my uncle. Mrs. Slater was accusing him of giving me preferential treatment over Greg. And she said that she, as Uncle Drew's half sister, deserved to demand equal rights for her son.

"Needless to say, the news shocked me—so much so that we ended up late for school. When Uncle Drew arrived home from work that evening, I asked him about what I'd overheard, and he told me the whole sordid story. I suppose Mrs. Slater told Greg about it, because he told me some time ago that he knew about his relationship to the family."

Mackenzie lowered her head. It all made sense now—the harsh treatment she'd received from Mrs. Slater, her hatred of Jasmine, Greg's first-name basis with the deceased, and the stern look Greg had received from his mother when Mackenzie had joined the staff for dinner her first night as Elise's nanny. Mackenzie lifted her chin and pushed the stroller forward, increasing the pace when a bolt of lightning zigzagged across the sky. *Yes, perfect sense—and all because a mother desired to protect her son?* Evidently, the house manager believed any woman associated with Park House was off limits to Greg. She turned to Trace. "Is your being related the reason Greg seems to dislike you so much?"

Trace tilted his head, pursing his lips. "Maybe, but I think it has more to do with my uncle's failure to acknowledge publicly that Mrs. Slater is his sister and that Greg is his nephew."

"I guess that would be tough for Greg since he knows how Mr. Huntington feels about you."

"When we were boys, we had some good times together. And now that he's grown, I've tried to be a good friend to Greg, but he resents it."

Just before they reached the house, Mackenzie noticed an unfamiliar car parked next to the curb. She glanced at Trace to see if he'd noticed the vehicle as well. A dark scowl overshadowed his features. "Trace, do you know whose car that is?"

"Yeah. It belongs to Jason Crane. And it's my guess the visit is not friendly. Uncle Drew despises the man. For what reason, I've yet to learn."

At that moment, large drops of rain began to fall. They hustled to get Elise inside, just entering the foyer when a downpour burst from the clouds. Mackenzie, preparing to take Elise upstairs a few minutes later, paused when Trace touched her shoulder.

"Mackenzie, would you like to go out to dinner with me this Saturday?" He grinned. "That was wicked of you to make me think you had a real date last Thursday, when you actually had dinner with Angie and her family."

Mackenzie's face grew hot. "Who told you?"

"Angie mentioned it when I saw her a few minutes after I arrived this morning. Also, she related how much her family enjoyed meeting you."

"Oh," Mackenzie said, looking downward.

"So shall I plan on picking you up about six on Saturday?"

"Trace, I—"

At that moment, shouts from Mr. Huntington's office drew their attention. Trace immediately started walking toward the sound. But before he could enter the office, the door opened and slammed against the wall. His complexion beet red, Jason Crane hurled himself from the room, knocking Trace to the floor. Mr. Huntington, following close behind Jason, grabbed his shoulder and spun him around, bringing their faces just inches apart.

Grasping Jason around his throat, Mr. Huntington shouted, "If you ever come near Park House again, I swear I'll kill you!" Releasing his hold on the man, Mr. Huntington opened the door and pushed Jason onto the porch. Glaring at his adversary, Jason straightened his posture and opened his mouth to speak, but Mr. Huntington slammed the door in his face before Jason could utter a word.

Mackenzie stared at the lawyer through the foyer window. Mr. Crane ran to his car and fell against it, his Hollywood facade now drenched by the pounding rain. At hearing Trace shout his uncle's name, she focused on the situation at hand. Glancing up, she saw Mrs. Slater, her hand clamped over her mouth, enter from the hallway behind Trace, who now stood in front of his uncle. "Uncle Drew, have you gone crazy? What happened?"

Mackenzie stood motionless. She pulled Elise close when she began to cry, the sound drawing the attention of her father. He turned, remorse gripping his expression when he saw Mackenzie standing halfway up the staircase.

"Miss Adams, please take Elise to the nursery. I'm sorry you had to witness that encounter." He turned to Trace. "Just forget it, will you? It's my affair."

Mackenzie watched the two men walk to her employer's office, their weighty tread reminding her of the heaviness that hung over Park House. What had Mr. Crane done or said to trigger Mr. Huntington's violence? Turning, she started up the stairs to carry the whimpering child to her room. She had managed only a couple of steps, when she looked up and saw the reflection of her own fear in the ebony eyes of her new friend. Angie stood rooted to the second-floor landing, gripping the dustcloth in her hand as if it held the key to restore the sanity of all who inhabited Park House. When Mackenzie reached the top floor, she shook her head. Angie nodded, her eyes revealing she understood that it wasn't the time or place for conversation.

Chapter 10

*A*fter putting a fretful Elise down for her nap later than usual, Mackenzie beckoned Angie into the nanny suite, taking the tray from her hand and placing it on the table, elated to see the tray held enough for both their lunches. Mackenzie helped transfer the food to the table.

"So glad you brought up lunch early, Angie. I could hardly wait to talk to you about what happened this morning. I had a hard time getting Elise asleep. I think Mr. Huntington's anger frightened her."

"I understand completely. As you know, I've heard some of his battles with his wife, but they were nothing compared with what I witnessed earlier. I shook so hard it's a wonder I didn't tumble down the stairs. What do you think took place between Mr. Crane and Mr. Huntington? He's such a good employer. I couldn't believe I heard the word *kill* come out of his mouth." Angie shuddered. "*Murder*—that seems to be a household word lately."

"I agree. Mr. Huntington—a killer? Ludicrous, of course. He's been the epitome of kindness to me. When we got back from Elise's outing and saw Mr. Crane's car, Trace stated his doubt about the friendliness of the lawyer's visit. That didn't surprise me after Mr. Crane and Mr. Huntington all but collided during the celebration of Jasmine. But the volatility we witnessed, I just can't imagine—" Mackenzie gasped. "Unless …"

Angie lifted her sandwich and held it in midair, focusing on her friend. "Unless what?"

"If your suspicion about Jasmine and Mr. Crane is correct and Mr. Huntington discovered their affair, he could have invited Mr. Crane here for a confrontation. If so, maybe Mr. Crane admitted their guilt and that's what caused Mr. Huntington to erupt like a volcano."

"But had he known about an affair, don't you think he would have dealt with the knowledge before now?" Angie took a bite and then returned the sandwich to her plate, her expression thoughtful. "Do you think Mr. Huntington would carry out his threat?"

Mackenzie waved away the implication. "No. He's too intelligent for something like that. Just because you're angry enough with a person to see him dead doesn't mean you could actually kill him." Mackenzie glanced toward the window, a faraway look in her eyes.

"That's true." Angie took a sip of water. "Speaking of murder, have you come up with any ideas of who might have killed Mrs. Huntington? I'm sorry that we couldn't get together last weekend to thrash it out. However, Mr. Huntington's surprise of the weekend off worked out great for me. It was my grandmother's eightieth birthday celebration. There were relatives everywhere in Grandma's little house; we could hardly breathe." Angie giggled. "The place looked like a crowd at a Black Friday sale. I think I even saw a few young cousins hanging like monkeys from the light fixtures now and then. But we had a great time."

Mackenzie laughed. "Sounds like it. And no, I haven't come up with a name. I tried to discuss the murder with Mrs. Slater, but she just turned and walked away without saying a word. And Greg evades the issue like a cat running from a turned-on water sprinkler."

"They probably think it's none of your business since you came after the fact."

"Touché. They are right." Mackenzie grinned. "But I guess you could say I'm making it my business. Also, as much as the thought repels me, I need to get better acquainted with Mr. Crane away from Park House." Mackenzie ignored Angie's lifted eyebrows. "For information purposes only." Mackenzie poured a small pool of ranch dressing onto the side of her plate and dipped a carrot into it. "Got any ideas on how I might accomplish a meeting with the man?"

Angie shook her head. "I've seldom had opportunities to speak to him, other than the few times I've answered the door when he would pay Mrs.

Huntington a visit. Just like I did when he came to see Mr. Huntington the day you arrived at Park House"—Angie shuddered—"the day we learned Mrs. Huntington had been murdered." Angie's eyes lit up with inspiration. "Hey! Why don't you call his office and make an appointment to see him?"

Mackenzie held up her hand to give Angie a high five. "Brilliant idea. I'll phone right after lunch—" Mackenzie's eyes widened. "Wait—back up a minute. Did you say Mr. Crane came to Park House the day the police discovered Jasmine's body? Do you remember what time he arrived?"

Angie smiled. "Yes, and yes. About three in the afternoon—during the time you and Mr. Patterson were in conference with Mr. Huntington. I seated Mr. Crane in the living room, saying I would announce his arrival to Mr. Huntington just as soon as his meeting had ended. When I checked later and saw his office door open, I told Mr. Huntington that Mr. Crane desired to see him. But when I entered the living room to escort Mr. Crane to the study, he wasn't there—and neither was his car parked in front of the house. I guess he decided not to wait."

The skin around Mackenzie's mouth whitened. Had she been wrong about Greg? Had Mr. Crane been the person who'd stood in the hallway and listened in on their meeting that day? If so, he must have ducked into the living room when she started to leave the office, exiting the premises after he'd heard her trip to the upper floor. Mackenzie frowned. What would have been his interest in the meeting? To get answers, a talk with her two suspects would be a given. Could she muster up enough courage to approach them?

Angie chuckled. "Mackenzie, where did you go in that head of yours?"

"Oh, sorry. About to leave the office that afternoon, I heard a noise outside the door—that of a person scurrying away, as if he'd been listening at the closed door and wanted to escape without detection. Until now, I thought Greg had been the snoop; the footsteps I heard were a man's tread. Since the time of the meeting coincides with the arrival of Mr. Crane, the eavesdropper could have been the overfriendly attorney."

Angie's eyes widened and then grew narrow with thought. "Maybe he wasn't spying at all but had to get to another appointment and decided to interrupt the meeting to speak with Mr. Huntington, changing his mind after he approached the office."

Mackenzie tapped the back of her hand against her chin. "Or heard something that upset him." She sighed. "Oh, you're probably right. I may be reading more into the situation than the actual truth."

"Let's hope so." After a moment, Angie grinned. "Now that we've laid that to rest for now, let's talk about your outing this morning with Elise *and* Mr. Patterson. Did you discuss Mrs. Huntington's murder with him?" Angie tilted her head and smiled, a teasing glint in her eyes. "Or did you speak about more important things—like a date with the dashing executive, for instance?"

Mackenzie waved away Angie's comment. "How did you know that Trace accompanied me today?"

"Simple. I was getting some extra cleaning instructions from Mrs. Slater, when Greg walked into the kitchen, angry that Mr. Patterson had volunteered to walk you and Elise to the park. His displeasure surprised me, considering he's always complaining about the treks to the park. He claims they take him away from his other work."

Mackenzie's disbelieving laugh ended in a snort. "I wonder when he changed his mind."

A blank look crossed Angie's features. "Huh?"

Mackenzie held up her hand. "Never mind. It's not worth the time to discuss it." At that moment, they heard Elise rousing from her nap.

Angie gathered up the remains of their lunch and picked up the tray. "We'll finish our talk later."

"Okay. Once I get a free moment, I'll phone Mr. Crane's office and let you know the day of the appointment."

"I'm curious. Do you plan to tell him straight up why you want to see him?"

Mackenzie laughed. "You're kidding, right? I don't want to scare him away. Don't worry—I'll think of something legit before I give him a call."

"Okay. See you later."

With Elise dry and ready to play soon after Angie's departure, Mackenzie sat on the floor and helped the child fit shapes into a plastic box with designs cut into it to match the three-dimensional ones she poured from the container. When Elise tired of the game, Mackenzie started to pick a book from the shelf but put it back when a thought struck her. Searching through the chest of drawers, she found what she wanted.

A few minutes later, Mackenzie carried Elise through the dining room, a romp with her in the shallow end of the swimming pool the intended purpose. After taking a moment to make Mrs. Slater aware of her plan in case Mr. Huntington desired time with his daughter, Mackenzie soon enjoyed the baby's shrieks of joy as she splashed her way even more so into her nanny's heart.

Mackenzie looked up at the bright blue sky; not a cloud was in sight. The earlier rainstorm had passed through quickly. As she gazed at the trail of smoke that surged from the tail of a jet plane, somehow the ominous events that had encroached Park House seemed far away.

The feeling, however, didn't last long, as all of a sudden, she had the inclination that someone nearby watched their activity. She steered the plastic doughnut that held Elise back toward the steps allowing entrance to the pool. She turned to find Greg watching them from behind a bench stationed beneath a large rose arbor, a pair of garden clippers in his hand. He gave her a nod, his half smile not traveling any further than his lips.

"Afternoon, Miss Adams. Looks like you're enjoying one of the amenities of the estate."

"Yes. Mr. Huntington gave me permission to use the pool, and I quote, 'anytime you so desire.'"

Greg raked a gaze over her. "Did you also enjoy the morning with Trace? As I recall, he *desired* to spend time with Elise. So percentage wise, how did that work? Twenty-five percent Mackenzie and seventy-five percent Elise, or the other way around? From the way he looked at you this morning, if Elise got any of his attention at all, it would surprise me."

"Good ole Trace, the man with the Midas touch—a winner every time. Perhaps I need to ask him his secret." He paused as if in deep thought. "But then, it never hurts to set one's sight on the heir apparent, now, does it, Miss Adams? From what I understood earlier, in your eyes"—he held up the shears—"a gardener wouldn't make the cut."

Mackenzie felt heat surge through her, a redness that a gallon of sunscreen couldn't have prevented. Her eyes narrowed. "Not that it's any of your business, but Elise had a great time with both of us." Mackenzie lifted Elise from the baby protector and carried her up the steps. Mackenzie's body pimpled from the cold chills racing up and down her skin—not from the hot breeze blowing across her, she decided, but from Greg's blistering stare.

She wrapped the baby and herself in a large beach towel. After slipping on her flip-flops, she walked toward the house without a backward look. The *gardener* could put the doughnut and the arm floaties back inside the pool house. *After all, he got paid to do that, right?* And she had a phone call to make just as soon as she put Elise down for her nap.

Late that evening, Mackenzie crawled into her bed, ready for sleep to overtake her. She sighed. When Mr. Huntington had entered the nursery for his visit with Elise, he had again apologized for the episode that morning with Mr. Crane. Mackenzie had assured him that she'd recovered just fine. But oh, how she'd wanted to question Mr. Huntington about the struggle. Nevertheless, by the time his visit had ended, Mackenzie hadn't found the courage to express her inquisitiveness.

Perhaps she'd be more enlightened on Friday after her appointment with Mr. Crane. Angie had promised to keep an eye on Elise during Mackenzie's time away from the house. Although she'd gained Mr. Huntington's permission to do an important *errand*, Mackenzie hoped he would be too busy to question Angie about the details. Mackenzie groaned. If he did, Angie wouldn't be able to hide the truth from him. Mackenzie winced at the thought of the consequences she might suffer.

An image of Trace floated into her mind. Once he'd entered Mr. Huntington's office following the incident, had his uncle explained the situation? Would Trace tell her if she asked him about it? Mackenzie's eyes brightened. If she accepted his dinner invitation, that would be the perfect occasion to quiz him. And should he prove to be open with her, would he be willing to discuss Jasmine, including her friends and activities, along with her relationship with Jason Crane?

A sense of shame washed over her. No way could she use Trace like that. She had plenty of wrongdoing to her credit in her short lifetime, and she didn't intend to add another victim to the list of people she'd deceived. She'd just have to find another way to satisfy her curiosity. Perhaps he would accompany her and Elise on their morning ritual again soon. She could question him then.

And besides, if she agreed to go to dinner with him, he would misinterpret her action. Mackenzie flipped onto her side, her skin tingling at the mere thought of being that close to him. Just one whiff of his spicy cologne and her emotions would be in a tailspin, the interrogation becoming a complete bust. She yawned, her thoughts turning in a different direction. She needed a good excuse for her meeting with Mr. Crane. But she'd have to think about that later. Sleep called to her now.

"I wonder if the police have made any progress in solving Jasmine's murder," Angie said to Mackenzie, as they walked toward the park the next day.

Mackenzie stopped to tighten the seat belt around Elise and then pushed the stroller forward. "If so, I'm sure Mr. Huntington would have made us aware of it. I hope they come up with something soon. It's only been a couple of weeks, but the waiting makes it seem longer. I wish I had more time to play detective"—Mackenzie glanced at Angie's nod of understanding—"but the care of Elise requires most of each day." Mackenzie lowered her lashes to take in the baby, smiling at the rays of sunlight bouncing off her golden curls. "Not that I mind. After all, she *is* my job."

As they started to turn into a paved pathway on the park grounds, the sound of squealing tires caught their attention. Mackenzie and Angie turned toward the street, their eyes widening. A black sedan stopped abruptly at the curb, not ten feet from where they stood. A slender, young woman wearing a large pair of sunglasses, her blonde hair falling about her shoulders, stepped out of the car and ran toward them, an aerosol can in her outstretched hand.

Sensing danger, Mackenzie gripped the handle of the stroller and whirled it around, ready to run. But Angie's pain-filled cry stopped her. Turning her head, she saw Angie on the ground, moaning, her hands splayed across her face. At that moment, the woman pointed the container toward Mackenzie and sprayed. Her vision blurred, the burning in her eyes

excruciating. Shoving Mackenzie backward, the woman ripped the stroller from Mackenzie's hands, and then pushed Mackenzie to the ground.

Mackenzie tried to rise, but another shot of the spray forced her back down, her vision now blinded. She heard the hurried unfastening of the seat belt and Elise being lifted from the stroller. The baby's frightened cry just before a car door slammed seemed to leave a painful, gaping gash in Mackenzie's heart. Again, tires squealed. Uncontrollable sobs spilled from Mackenzie. Oh, how could she have let Elise be taken from her?

At that moment, she heard someone shouting. Her vision a bit clearer, she looked up, able to see the forms of two women running toward them, a child in each of their arms. Mackenzie reached out toward them. "Please phone the police. Elise has been kidnapped."

An hour later, Mackenzie lay on a table in a hospital emergency room. Angie was in the next cubicle. They were being treated for the burns they'd received from the pepper spray the woman had used to keep them from preventing the abduction. Tears rolled from Mackenzie's eyes onto the pillow. Although her pain had lessened, the flame of guilt in her soul continued to burn like dried grass. Elise was gone. How could she face Mr. Huntington? She could hear him talking with Captain Sprinsky just outside the curtained room.

Mackenzie looked up at the nurse. "How is my friend Angie?"

The nurse smiled. "You both will be fine. Whoever did this made sure you two couldn't stop them from taking the child." The nurse's angry expression turned to compassion when fresh tears gushed from Mackenzie's eyes. "No need to blame yourself, honey. It wasn't your fault." The nurse cleared away the items she'd used to clean the pepper spray from Mackenzie's eyes and face. "You have visitors. I'll tell them you can see them now."

Mackenzie shrank back against the bed, her heart pounding. A moment later, Mr. Huntington and the captain stood beside the bed. She lifted her hand toward her employer. "I'm so sorry, sir. I tried to get Elise away from that woman, but she blinded me before I could stop her."

Mr. Huntington, his face ashen, took hold of Mackenzie's hand. "Miss Adams, I understand. According to Miss Valencia, it happened so fast you couldn't have prevented it. I'm the one who should apologize. I should have taken more precaution. Never did I dream that Elise could be kidnapped with so many people around to see it." His voice broke.

Captain Sprinsky stepped forward. "I have your statement from the policemen who initially arrived on the scene. Have you thought of anything else that might aid our search for the child?"

Mackenzie moved her head back and forth across the pillow. "Like Angie said, things happened so fast. And the windows of the car were tinted too dark for me to see the driver."

"Yes, I recall that in the report," the captain said, nodding. "If you do happen to remember something, please don't hesitate to phone me. Do you still have my business card I gave you the other day?"

"Yes."

He nodded. "Good."

They glanced toward the opening in the curtain at the doctor's entrance. He nodded at the two men and then turned his gaze on Mackenzie, a smile lighting up his eyes. "Miss Adams, you and your friend are free to go. If you have any more burning sensation, just apply a cold cloth to the area." He picked up her chart and made a few notations. "A nurse will be in shortly to escort you to your vehicle." Giving them each another nod, he departed.

A few minutes later, when she stepped out into the floor space dividing the two rows of cubicles, Mackenzie saw Angie and her mother standing near the detective and her employer. Both women rushed forward to give Mackenzie a hug.

"Dear, you are more than welcome to come home with us." Mrs. Valencia looked up at Mr. Huntington as though seeking his approval. He looked at Mackenzie and then nodded.

Mackenzie reached for the older woman's hand. "Thank you for your kindness, but I believe I should return to Park House so that I can be there"— she glanced at the captain—"in case Elise is found tonight. She'll need me."

Mr. Huntington placed his hand on her shoulder. "Are you sure?"

Mackenzie straightened to her full height. "Yes, sir. Very sure."

Captain Sprinsky and her employer nodded their assent, looks of admiration and respect in their eyes.

The captain faced Mr. Huntington. "An Amber Alert has been issued throughout the United States. Also, we have undercover men posted at all travel terminals. But I have to be honest—I suspect they are driving toward the state line by now. And since neither Miss Adams nor Miss Valencia"—he smiled at Angie—"could identify the make or model of the car in question, it may be days before your daughter is located. If there is a demand for money, a phone call usually occurs within twenty-four hours."

Mr. Huntington cleared his throat. "Is there not anything we can do in the meantime?"

Captain Sprinsky's eyes filled with compassion. "Nothing except wait. There are already officers at your house, setting up technology to hopefully locate the origin of a call, should the kidnapper phone you."

Mr. Huntington turned to Mackenzie. "Miss Adams, would you like me to notify your parents?"

Mackenzie's eyes widened, the splotches of red on her face deepening in color. "Oh no, please. I don't want to worry them. It's not like I've suffered real harm and won't be okay."

Mr. Huntington glanced at Captain Sprinsky. "Do you think it's necessary?"

He shrugged and then smiled. "She's a grown woman."

"Very well then, Miss Adams. I'll leave it up to you to speak to them about this in your own time."

At that moment, a nurse came over to them, ready to escort the patients to their vehicles.

When they reached the entryway, the captain slowed his pace, turned, and addressed Mr. Huntington. "There is one more thing you could do."

Mr. Huntington's eyes lit up. "And that is?"

"You could pray, sir."

Mr. Huntington lowered his lashes, disappointment shading his expression. "That's something I can't recall ever writing on my agenda. But I will certainly try for my daughter's sake."

When they reached the parking lot, Angie hugged Mackenzie. "I'll see you tomorrow."

Mackenzie nodded, returning the embrace.

Once Mr. Huntington drove into the garage and they'd entered the kitchen, they were surprised to find Mrs. Slater, Greg, and Trace seated at the table, awaiting their arrival. After giving Mr. Huntington her condolences, Mrs. Slater turned to Mackenzie, glaring.

"This is all your fault, Miss Adams. You should have tried harder to stop them from taking our Elise. I knew you would bring trouble to this house the moment I first saw you."

A look of shock overtook Mackenzie. She wanted to run from the chilling stare in the house manager's eyes but couldn't seem to lift her feet. At that moment, Trace stood from the table.

"Mrs. Slater, you have no right to blame either Miss Adams or Miss Valencia. I escorted Miss Adams yesterday when she took Elise to the park, and she took great care of my cousin. No one could have done a better job. I think your remark is uncalled for, and you should apologize to her." Trace looked at his uncle.

"He's absolutely right, Mrs. Slater. If anyone deserves blame, it's me. I should have insisted that Greg go on my daughter's outings every day. But it's too late to think about that now. According to Captain Sprinsky, all we can do is wait until we hear from the kidnappers—if we hear from them—before we decide the next step in finding my daughter."

At that moment, Mr. Huntington began to tremble. He slumped toward Trace, who led his uncle to one of the kitchen chairs. After waiting until his uncle seemed settled and better composed, Trace moved to stand alongside Mackenzie, his gaze directed at the house manager.

"Well, Mrs. Slater. You heard my uncle."

She grew rigid and then turned toward Mackenzie. "Very well, Miss Adams. I apologize. Now I have lunch to finish"—she glanced at the other occupants of the room—"if anyone would care to eat."

Mackenzie moved forward to stand near the house manager. "Mrs. Slater, believe me, I understand. You can't feel any worse about this than I do. I know I haven't been here long, but I've come to love Elise very much." A tear slid down Mackenzie's cheek. For a split second, she thought she saw a hint of something less hostile in Mrs. Slater's expression.

"Like I said, Miss Adams. I have lunch to prepare. Now, if you'll excuse me, I'll go about my business and let you go about yours."

Mackenzie stepped backward a couple paces. *Guess I was wrong. Didn't hear any sympathy in that statement.*

Taking Mackenzie's arm, Trace drew a handkerchief from a back pocket of his trousers and handed it to Mackenzie. "Shall we step outside for a while?"

Patting her face dry, she nodded. She let him guide her through the French doors to a bench beneath a large maple tree. Once they were seated, she glanced up at him; the compassion she read in his eyes brought a sob to her throat. She swallowed the impulse to break into tears again. Bowing her head, she twisted Trace's handkerchief in her hands.

"Oh Trace. After that woman sprayed me the first time and pushed me down, I could see just enough to try and jerk the stroller from her hands, but she turned the nozzle toward me again, the spray blinding me completely. By the time I could stand to my feet, I heard the car drive away." Mackenzie, no longer able to keep her composure, sobbed into her hands. The feel of Trace's arm around her shoulders offered little comfort to her aching soul.

When her crying subsided, she tilted her head sideways to look up at Trace, a wobbly smile curving her mouth. "Thank you for not abandoning me." She looked toward the house. "I suppose lunch is ready, but I can't eat a bite." She started to move away from Trace, but he tightened his hold on her.

"I'm sure we all feel the same way." He shifted his weight and then cupped Mackenzie's chin in his free hand. "I don't know how, but the police will find Elise. When Uncle Drew called the office to inform me of her disappearance, I prayed all the way to Park House. I have a peace that God is watching over her and"—he raked his fingers through his hair—"I have to believe that He will bring her safely home soon." Trace swallowed hard, his Adam's apple jumping in response. At that moment, Greg called to Trace.

"You're needed inside. Captain Sprinsky is here and wants to see us," Greg said, giving them a come-hither motion.

When Trace stood from the bench, Mackenzie started to hang back, but he took her hand and pulled her upright. "Come on. They may have news about Elise."

Keeping stride with Trace, she viewed the structure of Park House, the tile roof baking in the summer sun. Even though the place looked as if it were destined to stand forever, one day it would crumble and fall, much like the hearts of its occupants, should Captain Sprinsky's tidings be opposite of all they still dared to believe.

Chapter 11

ntering the house, Greg led them to a room next to the kitchen. Mackenzie knew it was the family den, although she'd never had cause to be within its walls. Once inside, she noted that Captain Sprinsky stood near the fireplace, seemingly waiting for the threesome to sit before he shared what had brought him to Park House.

Mackenzie glanced around. Two policemen sat at the antique library table across the room, checking to see if the equipment they had wired to the phone and a laptop computer was working properly. Mr. Huntington sat on the edge of the sofa, folding and refolding his hands. In the meantime, Greg sat—or, rather, slouched, Mackenzie thought—in a chair near the fireplace, while his mother eyed his actions from the sofa, displeasure written on her face. Catching Trace's eye, Mackenzie grimaced at him and then sat down on the love seat. Trace seated himself next to her and reached for her hand a moment later.

She knew she should pull away, but the warmth of his touch helped to abate the tremors in her stomach. Feeling Greg's gaze on her, she looked his way. She recoiled from the anger registered in his eyes. Trace, noting her reaction, followed her gaze. Turning away from the malicious stare, she shuddered at the chills streaking down her arms when she saw the look that passed between the cousins—their expressions stated they would hash out the situation between them later. Trace turned to Mackenzie. Smiling, he squeezed her hand. At the sound of the captain's greeting, they glanced upward to give him their full attention.

Captain Sprinsky focused his gaze on Mr. Huntington. "I know it's only been a few hours since your daughter's kidnapping, but I wanted to stop by"—the captain reached inside his sports coat pocket and pulled out some folded papers—"to give you a copy of the judge's order that allows the wiretap. Although you've already given us permission to connect the trap and trace equipment to your phone, you need to sign this consent form to keep everything legal. Also, I wanted to let you know there's a new development in the case."

Mr. Huntington returned the form and pocketed his pen. He glanced toward the detective. "Please say you've found Elise."

"No, I'm sorry to say, but what we do know is pertinent."

"Go on," Mr. Huntington said, loosening his tie.

Mackenzie scooted to the edge of the sofa, refusing to think of any possibility for Elise other than her safe return.

Captain Sprinsky laid his arm across the top of the fireplace mantel. "About an hour ago, someone from a neighborhood south of the city reported seeing a dark-haired man and a young blonde-haired woman with a baby in her arms get out of a black car with dark windows. They quickly entered a dark blue minivan and sped away. The older woman who reported the incident said that she just didn't feel right about what she'd seen and decided to phone the police."

"Did she get a good look at the child?" Mr. Huntington said, his eyes glowing with hope.

"No, sir. She said she just caught enough of a glimpse to see that the baby looked to be about six or seven months old."

Air gushed from Mr. Huntington's lips like a deflating balloon. He sank to the back of the sofa, his body growing limp. Brushing first one hand and then the other through his hair, he drew a long sigh, nodding to the captain for him to continue.

"When the dispatched team of officers arrived at the location, they found a 2013 Chrysler 300 parked in the woman's neighborhood. They discovered it to be a rental car that had been rented early this morning to a young woman. The description of her reported by the rental agency employee matched the one from the woman who reported the abandoned car, as well as the descriptions given by Miss Valencia and Miss Adams.

"However, when we checked out the identification details given to the rental agency, we found that they belonged to a deceased woman who was killed in a hit-and-run accident last week. No handbag or other personal papers were found at the scene of the accident to identify the woman, leading us to conclude that the person causing the accident or someone who happened along before the police arrived stole them. All we had to go on was the registration found inside the glove compartment that showed the car belonged to a man out of the country on business. Once we got in contact with him, we found that the victim had been his daughter."

Mr. Huntington cleared his throat. "So I assume the person who rented the vehicle either wore a disguise to resemble the driver's-license picture of the deceased or looked enough like her that no questions were raised when she rented the car. Or that the rental agent didn't pay enough attention to the driver's-license picture to make a positive identification."

Captain Sprinsky nodded. "That's our theory exactly. As to how the kidnappers got the personal information, it's my guess the items found their way to the street and were sold to the individuals taking your child. The sale of identity, no matter how it's obtained, is common practice within the criminal culture."

Trace stood and began to pace back and forth. "Whoever kidnapped Elise had to know that Miss Adams took my cousin to the park most mornings *and* that she used the same path to the swings each time. How else could they have succeeded in their plot so quickly?"

"You're right. This wasn't a spur-of-the-moment operation. It had been well planned. The kidnappers had to have also known that most of the people in the neighborhood where they found the abandoned car are at work during the day. The woman who reported the incident was a visiting relative who had just stepped out of her son's house to take a walk." He turned his gaze on Mackenzie. "Miss Adams, can you recall anyone on your daily walks or at the park who might have been watching your activities with the baby—someone with more than just a passing interest?"

Mackenzie thought for a moment and then started to shake her head but stilled the action. "Actually"—she darted a glance toward Greg—"one day, when Mr. Martin accompanied us on our walk, I noticed a woman about my age observing us from the wooden bridge in the center of the park. Knowing that Mr. Huntington had been concerned that the killer of his wife might try to harm Elise, I started to leave the park. That's when Greg noted the woman's presence. He informed me that her name was Lacey Carmichael, Elise's former nanny. When she saw that we had noticed her, she walked over to talk to us."

Greg jumped to his feet, his face darkening. "Lacey wouldn't kidnap Elise. She just wanted to see her."

Mackenzie's eyes widened. Did Greg really care for Lacey?

Mr. Huntington stood, anger flashing in his eyes. "I told you to keep your girlfriend away from Elise."

Mackenzie stood. "Sir, Mr. Martin didn't know that she was there. It upset him so much that he tried to get Lacey to leave the park, but she insisted on staying, giving the reason that she missed Elise and just wanted to say hi to her. We left the park right away. And I haven't seen Lacey since that day."

Greg slunk back into the chair, his expression hard as steel. "She's not my girlfriend any longer. We broke up last week. It seems she has a new interest—someone who can give her everything she wants in life, according to her."

Captain Sprinsky stepped forward. "Mr. Huntington, considering the circumstances that surrounded Miss Carmichael's dismissal from your employment, we checked her out as a person of interest in your wife's death. Our efforts proved the young lady had an ironclad alibi for the night Mrs. Huntington died.

"Just before I came here, I stopped by Miss Carmichael's residence to inquire if she had noticed anyone outside the family taking an unusual interest in your daughter while employed as her nanny. Not finding her at home, I spoke with the landlady of the rooming house, discovering that Miss Carmichael moved to Tennessee a few days ago to live with relatives."

"Did she leave a forwarding address?" Trace asked.

"No, and the elderly landlady couldn't remember Miss Carmichael mentioning where in Tennessee she would be residing."

Mr. Huntington resumed his position on the sofa. "Have you had any luck locating the minivan the kidnappers were driving?"

"Not at this time. Since we don't have an accurate description of the make and model of the vehicle, it will take a miracle to find it. Our best bet is the Amber Alert, which makes people all across the United States aware that a child is missing, and most will pay more attention to what's happening around them. Hopefully, we will hear something soon from either a watchful citizen or a call from the kidnappers, demanding money for the return of the child."

At that moment, as if on cue, the house phone began to peal.

Each of the occupants in the room darted a glance toward the seated policemen. Mackenzie's arms tingled and then seemed to grow numb. Was the call from the kidnappers? Would they allow Mr. Huntington or her to speak to Elise? Mackenzie clutched her chest. If only she could pray, as Captain Sprinsky had suggested when they were leaving the hospital. Would God hear from a sin-sick soul a prayer for an innocent child? She had to try. *Oh God in heaven, please bring Elise back to us safe and sound!*

Mr. Huntington stood from the sofa and hurried to the phone. When he reached toward the receiver, one of the officers held up one finger, pushed a button on his recording device, and then motioned for Mr. Huntington to answer the call.

A couple minutes later, Mr. Huntington hung up the phone, disappointment clouding his features. He took in the anxious faces surrounding him. "Only a neighbor," he said, wiping his forehead with a handkerchief from his trousers. "Mrs. Baxter saw the police car out front and offered her assistance if we needed her. I'm afraid she feels the neighborhood-watch education she took some years ago qualifies her to intervene in the happenings on our street." A slight smile broke the sternness of his jawline. "Personally, I think she saw the crime-alert program as a means to authorize her meddling nature. The homeowners in this vicinity have endured her nosiness for years." Mr. Huntington sighed. "But I suppose she means well."

Captain Sprinsky smiled. "Granted, busybodies can be irksome, but information given by that type of person is often valuable in crime solving. For instance, the woman this morning noticing the possible kidnappers of your daughter—a perfect example. I remember one case—"

Again, the phone rang. After the signal from Officer Kelly, Mr. Huntington lifted the receiver of the house phone and held it a short distance from his ear so that the captain could hear the words of the caller. "Hello. Yes, this is Andrew Huntington. How can I help you?" He paused to listen. After a moment, his nostrils flared. "There is no way I can come up with one million dollars cash by tonight. I need at least a couple of days. Please, is my daughter okay?" After a moment, he replaced the phone in its stand.

For a moment, Mr. Huntington stared at the floor before he spoke. "The man assured me that Elise is in good hands. He said if I don't have the money within forty-eight hours, though, I will never see my daughter again." Amid the gasps in the room, Mr. Huntington stumbled to the sofa and fell into it. He leaned forward and covered his face with his hands, his low moans reverberating throughout the room.

Mackenzie glanced around, and Greg's impassive features caused her to frown. Did he not care for the child? Had the attention he'd shown to Elise on their walks been just to impress her nanny? Mackenzie swallowed the bile that rose to her throat. How could he be so indifferent? She looked away, biting back the words of reproof that rose to her lips.

Captain Sprinsky laid a hand on Mr. Huntington's shoulder briefly and then turned to address the others in the room, eyeing their expressions. "We must not give up hope. If we can find the child within seventy-two hours, there is a sixty percent chance she will still be alive. Even at this moment, Elise's picture has been posted on all social networks and nationwide media. Within twenty-four hours, her photograph will be on the bulletin boards of major stores."

"Excuse me, Captain," said one of the police officers. "The call came from a cell phone, but it didn't show to have a GPS system on the device. We'll have to wait to see which cell tower picked up the strongest signal before we can get an approximate location of the caller. You should get a call in thirty minutes or so."

"Good work, Kelly."

The detective turned to Mr. Huntington. "Sir, I doubt you hear from the kidnappers before the forty-eight hours is up, but if you do, you know how to reach me. The officers and I are finished here for now, so we'll head back to the station. As soon as we have a locale from where the call was made, I'll phone you. In the meantime, we'll keep searching for that minivan." The captain shook Mr. Huntington's hand. "Also, I'll make sure officers are available at a moment's notice to stage the ransom drop-off point once we know the location."

Trace stood and escorted the captain and the officers from the room. Meanwhile, Mr. Huntington rose slowly from the sofa and scrutinized his household staff. "I know this is hard on all of us, but please try to go about as usual." He centered his attention on Mackenzie. "Miss Adams, when Miss Valencia returns tomorrow, why don't the two of you take in a movie, go to the mall"—a hint of a smile tugged at the corners of his mouth—"whatever young women do these days. You deserve it after what you two suffered this morning. Also, it would help take your minds off things here for a while."

Mackenzie glanced at Mrs. Slater, who looked at Mr. Huntington as if he'd lost his mind. *If a pleasant brain wave ever comes into contact with her mind, I swear her face will shatter into a million dust particles,* Mackenzie thought, turning toward Greg. Whatever his opinion about the proposal, he hid it well behind his bland expression. At her look of protest, Mr. Huntington held up his hand.

"No, Miss Adams, I insist. It would do us all good to keep busy"—he lowered his voice—"or else how will we survive?"

At that moment, Trace reentered the room. He glanced around the den and then settled a look on his uncle. "Did I miss something?"

"Mr. Huntington suggested an afternoon out for Angie and me." Mackenzie smiled at her employer. "Thank you, sir, for your generosity. I don't know about Angie, but I think I'll take a rain check, if that's okay with you."

Mr. Huntington nodded. "Whatever you wish." he said, turning toward Trace. "I will be in the office." His face darkened. "If I'm to have a million dollars in two days, I need to start making phone calls."

Eyeing the droop in Mr. Huntington's shoulders, Mackenzie felt compassion sweep through her. *First his wife's death and now his—* Mackenzie shook her head. *No! I will not entertain that scenario.* She hardly noticed when the other two employees left the den. *It would be too much like … Oh, please, God, not Elise.*

"Mackenzie, is something wrong?" Trace moved to stand close to her and placed his hands on her shoulders. She sensed an inner strength in him that far exceeded his average-sized frame. All of a sudden, he seemed a shelter to which she could escape from all the chaos she'd endured of late. All she had to do was take one step forward. She curled her fists and slammed them against his chest.

"Wrong?" she asked, her eyes flashing. "Of course there's something wrong. Elise is missing and may be—"

"Stop, Mackenzie," Trace said, grabbing her arms. "Don't say it." She tried to wriggle out of his grasp, but he pulled her tightly against him. All at once, uncontrollable sobs that seemed to come from the deepest part of her soul wrecked her composure, her tears streaming onto his tie and shirt.

When her crying abated a few minutes later, Mackenzie slipped out of his arms and looked around. She walked over to one of the bookshelves next to the fireplace and withdrew several tissues from a box sitting on one of the shelves. Drying her eyes and nose, she turned from Trace's concerned expression, ignoring the statement she read in his eyes—*There is more to this than you care to disclose.* Who said women were the intuitive species of the human race?

A wan smile touched her lips. "Since I'm such a water bucket, it's a good thing someone has the sense to keep tissues in strategic locations."

He nodded toward his wadded handkerchief lying on the sofa beside where Mackenzie had sat. "It looks like I need to purchase additional handkerchiefs as well."

She couldn't help but grin. "Might be a good idea. In the meantime, I believe I shall go give the nursery a thorough cleaning. I don't know how long it's been since the toys were sanitized, and to follow your uncle's advice, this will keep me busy."

"I understand. I have similar thoughts about some paperwork I need to tackle at the office. Uncle Drew is right. Keeping active is the best antidote for our sanity until Elise is back with us. I think I'll check on Uncle Drew before I leave. I'll be back in time for dinner. I hope you plan to eat with us."

Shaking her head, Mackenzie opened her mouth to turn down the invitation. Trace shook his finger at her.

"No ifs, ands, or buts, please. We need to support one another. It makes the waiting easier." All of a sudden, the light in Trace's eyes dimmed. "I pray that Elise is not suffering in any way."

Before she had time to think about her action, Mackenzie reached out and gave him a hug. "I'm so sorry, Trace. I know how much you love Elise. And yes, I'll come downstairs to dinner"—she smiled—"no matter how many looks of disapproval I receive from Mrs. Slater." Mackenzie's eyes grew wide. She clapped her hand across her lips, scrunching her face. "Sorry."

Trace grinned. "No problem. I don't think she's that fond of me either." He brushed a finger across her cheek. "Just one more thing we have in common, Miss Adams. Perhaps after dinner, we can discover a few more."

The look in his eyes captivated her. What was it that drew her to him? Yes, the chemistry he'd referred to a few days ago was definitely there, but something else about him held her spellbound—something much more endearing that just physical attraction. With a slight shake of her head, she turned aside, biting her lip. *Remember, Mackenzie, men can't be trusted. Whatever his magnetism, you have to stay clear of it.*

A moment later, she heard him step into the hallway. The silence in the room pounded against her ears. Of all the mistakes she had made in life, suddenly, she felt as if she'd just made the biggest error of all. She drew a deep breath and let it slip through her lips slowly. Shaking off the notion, she left the room, the nursery a priority for now. As for the other mystery, she'd ponder that later.

When she stepped across the threshold of the dining room into the front hallway, she heard shouting from Mr. Huntington's office. She paused outside the door, noticing that it hadn't been closed all the way. She started to continue to the staircase, but the frustration in Trace's voice locked her feet to the floor.

"Uncle Drew, how could you do that after what happened the other day?"

"I don't have a choice, thanks to the housing market fiasco of late. There just hasn't been enough business in the last two years to give us that much cash flow. In fact, if the economy doesn't have an upturn soon, Huntington Incorporated will be in danger of bankruptcy."

Mackenzie jumped at the sound of Mr. Huntington's fist slamming against his desk.

"So help me, I will do everything in my power to make sure that doesn't happen. I owe it to my father, my grandfather, and his father to keep this company alive no matter what I have to do. I would think you, of all people, would understand, since you are next in line to acquire the family business."

"But not at the expense of taking a loan from a sleazebag like him."

"I phoned George at the bank, but he wouldn't loan me that much money without the board's approval. And he couldn't call an emergency meeting, because some of the members are out of town on vacation. I don't have time to cash in some of our stocks. So tell me, Trace. How would you have handled it?"

"I don't know at the moment. But Jason Crane, of all people. How could you think he would help after you nearly choked him to death?"

"Oh, he'll help. Trust me. I have an ace in my pocket where he's concerned. Now, go on to the office. I want that contract on the McDuggin property in our hands by tomorrow morning. The sale of that prime location is crucial to putting the company on a more solid foundation." Mr. Huntington grew quite momentarily. "Look, Trace, I appreciate the offer of your savings, but I can't take that from you. This is my problem, and I'll handle it my way. Now, run along. Jason should be returning my phone call any moment."

Mackenzie moved toward the stairs as quietly and quickly as possible. She climbed a few steps and then backed up against the wall, believing Trace would leave by way of the kitchen since he'd parked his car at the back of the house. When she heard his retreating footsteps, she let out her breath.

A sense of shame penetrated her thoughts. Her parents would be so disappointed to learn that she'd stood eavesdropping outside her employer's office—Mackenzie's breath caught—just like the unidentified individual she'd heard on her first afternoon at Park House. She cringed. Mrs. Slater's opinion of the new nanny might have weight after all.

But she couldn't get the conversation out of her mind. What did it all mean? What kind of ace did Mr. Huntington have that assured him of Jason's cooperation? Could anything she'd overheard be connected with Jasmine's murder or Elise's kidnapping? And furthermore, where could she get answers?

Mackenzie turned to climb the rest of the stairs. She had a lot to process. A movement outside the foyer window caught her eye. She glanced toward the sight, descending the stairs to stand next to the window. At the house across the street, a woman stood on her porch, sizing up Park House. Could that be the nosy neighbor Mr. Huntington had spoken about when they were all gathered in the den? Mackenzie tried to recall her name, but it eluded her. She turned at the sound of footsteps. Mrs. Slater came into view.

"Oh, Mrs. Slater. I didn't get the chance to tell you earlier that until Elise is returned, I would be glad to help out in the house or kitchen. My mother is a culinary artist, and she taught me a great deal."

The house manager, lifting her eyebrows, backed up a step. "Really. Well, Miss Adams, I've been the cook at Park House close to forty years, and I think I can handle the meals here. I suggest you stick to your other nursery duties. However, I do appreciate you sticking up for Greg earlier. I'm quite fond of the boy."

Mackenzie straightened her spine until she stood at her full height. "I couldn't let him be accused of something he tried to prevent. And, Mrs. Slater, I apologize for my offer. I thought we might help each other cope with the dire circumstances we're facing, but I guess I was mistaken. If you will tell me the name of that lady"—Mackenzie pointed toward the window—"who seems so interested in Park House, I won't bother you anymore."

The house manager took in Mackenzie's expression and then moved to view the person Mackenzie had a desire to know. "That's Mrs. Baxter, the woman Mr. Huntington received the phone call from earlier." Mrs. Slater sighed. "I suppose she feels it's her duty to keep an eye on the place since the police have gone."

"Oh, I see. Thank you, Mrs. Slater. If you do decide you need me, I'll be in the nursery."

"Before you go, I need to tell you that dinner will be at seven. Mr. Patterson informed me that you will be dining with him and Mr. Huntington this evening." She took in Mackenzie's casual attire. "They will be dressed appropriately for the dining room. Thought you would like to know."

"Thank you. I shall dress accordingly."

With a slight lift at the corners of her mouth, Mrs. Slater turned on her heel and strode down the hall. *Remember, Mackenzie, one brick at a time builds the house.* At least Mrs. Slater had been thankful about Greg. Apparently, she hadn't been informed that Mackenzie knew the true relationship between house manager and chauffeur.

Turning back to the window, Mackenzie looked to see if Mrs. Baxter still had her gaze glued to Park House. She now observed from her porch swing. Mackenzie lifted her arm in a wave. The woman immediately returned the gesture. Mackenzie laughed, her curiosity getting its prize. Now that they had met, so to speak, tomorrow she would pay the woman a visit.

Had she been just as watchful the night Jasmine died? There was only one way to find out. True, the police would have already spoken with the lady, but a chance remained she might recall something she hadn't thought of when questioned by Captain Sprinsky. Mackenzie hurried up the stairs. If she planned to get any cleaning done before it was time for her—she smiled wanly—"dinner date," she'd best hustle.

Following dinner, Mackenzie and Trace passed the rest of the evening on the front porch, the sun sneaking from their view. Observing the sky from the wicker sofa, she became entranced; the shades of red and purple stretching across the sky were breathtaking. "What a panoramic view. You can bet there's a photo artist snapping pictures at this moment."

Looking up at her from his position on the porch steps, he smiled. "I know a scene that's just as striking."

Realizing he eyed her rather than the sunset, Mackenzie smoothed her stylish sundress over her knees, keeping her gaze on her sandals. She searched for something to say. "I'm afraid Mrs. Slater's efforts in the kitchen tonight were a waste. The dinner looked delicious, but the few bites I swallowed seemed to taste more like sawdust than food." She grinned. "Not that I've ever eaten wood chips. But you get the idea." Her smile faded. "I kept wondering if Elise had been fed."

"I questioned that too. Perhaps thoughts of that nature accounted for Uncle Drew's sudden exit from the table soon after Mrs. Slater put the meal on the table." Trace shook his head. "He's had more than his share to cope with of late."

Mackenzie shuddered. "I can just imagine what horrible images float through his head. But we have to believe for the best. Do you think the kidnappers will harm Elise?"

Trace hung his head. "With all that is within me, I pray they don't."

Chapter 12

*E*arly the next morning, just past dawn, Mackenzie, dressed in jogging attire, peered out the foyer window, brightening at once. Mrs. Baxter stood with a hose in her hand, watering the flowers along the length of her porch. Mackenzie smiled. She'd intended to stop by the woman's house after her run, but this was better. Tilting her head slightly, Mackenzie listened for any sounds in the house, but hearing none, she slipped out the front door.

She ran across the street and stepped onto a sidewalk similar to the one in front of Park House. Although Mrs. Baxter's home had been built later than the Huntington residence—during the latter years of the Victorian Era, Mackenzie guessed, eyeing the gingerbread trim and turret at the side of the house—it had been well maintained akin to the other older affluent homes in the neighborhood.

"Hello," Mackenzie said. "You have lovely flowers. Those red petunias in the window boxes are eye-catching, to say the least."

The woman turned toward Mackenzie, frowning. "Thank you." Mrs. Baxter's green eyes faded by age grew brighter. Smiling, she said, "Oh, you're the young lady who waved to me from the window across the street. You and your friends take the Huntingtons' baby on her daily outings."

Mackenzie smiled. "Yes, ma'am. I'm Mackenzie Adams, Elise Huntington's nanny."

"I'm Estelle Baxter." She reached out and shook Mackenzie's hand. "Nice to make your acquaintance."

Mrs. Baxter moved her head back and forth. "Poor Mr. Huntington. A double tragedy for him—his wife murdered, and now the child in the hands of kidnappers. How that man must be suffering. Is there any news about the baby's whereabouts?"

"No. But we're all hoping for the best."

"My prayers are with the family."

"Thank you. Did you happen to see anything unusual around Park House yesterday morning?"

"That nice policeman who visited me following Mrs. Huntington's death—Captain Sprinsky, I believe is his name—stopped by yesterday afternoon and asked me the same question." Mrs. Baxter leaned forward as if to share a secret. "The police count on me, you know, to keep my eyes open. I'm a certified member of Neighborhood Watch, an organization designed to aid law enforcement in controlling crime." She straightened. "But like I told the officer, I haven't noticed any strangers in the neighborhood of late."

Mackenzie cleared her throat to stifle a laugh. "I believe Mr. Huntington mentioned your conscientious effort to keep the vicinity free of criminals. Speaking of Mrs. Huntington's death ... I mean ... Did you know her well?"

Mrs. Baxter reached down, turned off the water spigot hidden by a flowering bush at the end of the porch, and began rolling the hose onto a portable holder. "Not more than a friendly wave now and then. She didn't seem to be home much, except when she hosted one of those noisy parties."

"Did you happen to notice anything out of the ordinary around the time she disappeared?"

"Nothing except what I saw the night she vanished. The policeman didn't seem to give it much credit, though."

Mackenzie moved a step closer to the woman. "Please forgive my curiosity. What did you see?"

"Mr. Huntington's car. I thought it strange that his limousine should be leaving the house so late that night. Awakened by a brewing storm, I got up to let my cat in the house." Mrs. Baxter laughed. "Talk about a fraidycat. She's as nervous as a trout in a shark tank when it comes to thunder and lightning. Anyway, when I opened the door to let Mimsy inside, I saw the limousine pull onto the street."

"I see. Did you inform Mr. Huntington of this?"

"I thought about saying something to him about it the next morning when he and I came out of our houses at the same time to collect our newspapers. Seeing me, he stepped across the street to chat a bit. During the conversation, he inquired after my children. I told him that my daughter who lives in Nashville would be coming for a visit soon. He then mentioned his intention to fly to Nashville that day to meet with commercial investors interested in purchasing property in our city. From the way he talked, he would be gone two or three days.

"So caught up in our conversation, I forgot to mention what I'd seen. I thought about it later in the day, but Mr. Huntington had already left on his trip by then. I purposed to tell him on his return from Nashville, but I haven't talked to him since that morning. Normally, it wouldn't have bothered me, but his car seldom moves from the residence, except when their chauffeur drives Mr. Huntington to work and back or takes the limo to have it washed. He drove Mrs. Huntington around in a regular car."

Mackenzie's eyebrows drew together. "I see." Had their neighbor been referring to the red Lincoln Town Car that hadn't been moved from the garage since she'd arrived at Park House? "Mrs. Baxter, do you recall the time you saw the limousine leave the neighborhood?"

"Yes. Just before I returned to bed, I glanced at the clock. It read 2:20 a.m."

Clasping her hand against her cheek, Mrs. Baxter drew in a sharp breath. "Oh my. Now why didn't I think of that when the captain came by today?"

"What did you forget, Mrs. Baxter?"

"Yesterday morning, not long after you and Miss Valencia strolled the baby down the street … She's a nice young woman. I met her one day when she came to see her mother, who works at the nursing home where my husband now resides. I was surprised to learn that Angela worked right across the street from me. Small world, huh?"

Mrs. Baxter stared into space. "I kept my husband with me until a year ago, but his dementia became so bad that I could no longer see to his needs. If I didn't keep a close eye on him, he'd wander away." She smiled.

"I don't worry so much now. He's well cared for at the home. Especially by Mrs. Valencia—such a dear woman."

Mackenzie glanced over her shoulder toward Park House and then shuffled from one foot to the other. "She is, at that. I'm sorry to hear about your husband. Uh, Mrs. Baxter, you started to tell me about yesterday morning?"

The look in Mrs. Baxter's eyes dulled. "I did? Oh, mercy yes. Talking about the limousine made me think about the other car."

Her hands resting behind her back, Mackenzie curved her fingers into a choking circle. *Speaking of murder.* "A car?"

"Yes. Having just finished making a batch of jelly, I decided to take a rest in the porch swing. That's when I noticed you and Angela on your way to the park with the baby. Isn't it nice that we have such a place nearby?"

Mackenzie groaned inside. "Yes. The park is lovely. Please continue, Mrs. Baxter."

"As I started to say, you couldn't have been at the play area more than a few minutes, when a black car came whizzing up the street"—Mrs. Baxter pointed toward the intersection—"its tires squalling when the driver turned the corner yonder."

Mackenzie's eyes widened. *The kidnapper's car!* "Did you get a good look at the occupants inside the vehicle?"

Mrs. Baxter shook her head. "The windows were too dark." She stepped toward her porch. "If you'll excuse me, dear, I must notify Captain Sprinsky about my recollection. I promised I would phone him should I remember anything that might help him find that precious child."

Mackenzie nodded. "By all means." Evidently, Mrs. Baxter hadn't heard about the police locating the car. Mackenzie backed toward the street. But it wasn't her place to tell the woman. She'd most likely hear it from Captain Sprinsky. "It's great to have met you, Mrs. Baxter. Maybe we can talk again."

"I'd like that. Until another day then."

Mackenzie glanced at her watch. *Good.* She still had time for a short jog around the park. If her luck held out, she'd be back at Park House before anyone knew she'd been away.

At that moment, Mackenzie's optimism sank to the asphalt beneath her feet. Trace, dressed in running shorts and a T-shirt, walked out the front door of Park House. Had he seen her talking with Mrs. Baxter? Mackenzie shrugged. But what would it matter if he had? She'd done nothing wrong; she'd just had a friendly conversation with a neighbor. Mackenzie slowed her steps. Should she tell Trace about Mrs. Baxter's early morning observation?

"Well, good morning," he said, catching up to her. "I see I'm not the only early riser abiding at Park House. Do you mind if I accompany you on your run?"

She smiled. "Not at all." She ignored the skip in her heartbeat. *No harm in a friendly jog together.*

Within a short time, they arrived at the park. Mackenzie was out of breath, and moisture glistened on her skin. She glanced at Trace—not a sweat bead in sight. She laughed. "I guess we know which of us has avoided all marathons lately."

He chuckled. "Did you participate in running events in Arizona?"

"Just one or two during college days. But I did jog a few days a week just to rid the fuzz from my brain after long nights of study. At least before ..." Her face deepening in color that had nothing to do with exertion, she bent down to retie her shoe. When she straightened, Trace reached out and touched her face.

"There it is again," he said, running his finger along her cheekbone.

Mackenzie backed away, frowning. "What?"

He stepped forward, taking her hand. "That deep sadness I often see in your eyes. Won't you let me try to help you? I may not have the right words to say to take away your pain, but I know One who does. God is a life preserver to those drowning in heartbreak."

Mackenzie freed her hand and sped down the jogging trail, throwing her reply to the wind. "Don't you understand, Trace? No one can help me now." A moment later, she glanced over to see him beside her, his long strides slowing to keep pace with her. She eyed him from the corners of her eyes. *What am I to do about you, Trace Patterson?*

After a couple laps around the park, they headed back to the house, slowing to a walk. She wiped her face with the sleeve of her oversized T-shirt. "I'd forgotten how exhilarating a good run could be," she said between breaths.

Trace nodded. "I see you had a visit with Mrs. Baxter this morning."

Mackenzie cut a glance toward him but read nothing more than friendly inquisitiveness in his eyes. "Yes. I saw her watering flowers and decided to introduce myself. She's quite a conversationalist."

Trace laughed. "That's putting it mildly. She tends to go on and on, but she does have a kind heart. She used to bake cookies for me after I came to live with Uncle Drew. She was like a surrogate grandmother until my years at the university distanced our relationship. But I still check on her now and then."

"I think she's lonely. It's too bad about her husband."

"Yes. He used to toss practice balls to me when I played in Little League." Sadness crept onto Trace's face. "Now he doesn't even know who I am."

"Has Mrs. Baxter talked with you about Mrs. Huntington's murder?"

Trace stopped abruptly. "No. Why?"

Mackenzie backed up a step. "Well, she said she told the police that she saw the limousine leave the estate about two thirty in the morning during the time Mrs. Huntington vanished. She intended to tell Mr. Huntington about it when they visited the morning of his business trip to Tennessee, but she forgot to mention it, and she hasn't spoken with him since then."

"She must be referring to Uncle Drew's trip to Nashville to meet with potential investment buyers. In fact, Mrs. Slater had to be away at the same time."

"Who became aware that Mrs. Huntington was missing?"

"No one at first. It wasn't unusual for her to stay over with friends when Uncle Drew had to be away. But when the chairman of the board of directors for her companies back east hadn't been able to contact her, he phoned the office to speak to Uncle Drew. I took the call and afterward tried to reach her by phone but couldn't. I phoned a few of her friends I knew, but they hadn't seen or heard from her."

"I guess that's when you grew concerned about her safety?"

"Not then. Only after I had spoken with Jason Crane. I decided if anyone knew her whereabouts, it would be him, considering their friendship. He said they'd had a golf game scheduled, but she hadn't shown. He'd tried to phone and remind her about it, but she didn't answer his call.

"I went to Park House, hoping I would find her there. Angie reported that she'd spoken to Jasmine the day before Uncle Drew left on his trip but hadn't seen her since then. Greg said she left in her car for a hair appointment before he drove Uncle Drew to the airport. But when I phoned the salon, her hairdresser said she didn't come in and hadn't phoned to reschedule an appointment. Her car has never turned up either. When I realized close to forty-eight hours had passed without anyone having seen or heard from her, I notified the police and Uncle Drew. He cut short his meeting that morning and took the first available flight home. You know the rest since you arrived the next day."

Mackenzie nodded. "I never dreamed I'd be walking into so great a tragedy."

"Have you regretted your decision to stay?"

She shook her head. "No."

Trace picked up her hand and brought it to his lips. "I, for one, am glad that you did."

Mackenzie closed her eyes at his gentle caress. Her heart seemed to flip a 360-degree turn in her chest. Still, she couldn't give in to the pull on her heartstrings. Slipping her hand from his, she moved forward, refusing to acknowledge the hurt in his eyes. "I wonder if Captain Sprinsky informed your uncle about Mrs. Baxter's experience." She heard him draw a long breath.

"If Uncle Drew knew, he would be livid about it. He doesn't allow anyone the use of the limo. He takes great pride in it. His father purchased the vehicle a few months before he passed."

"I take it the two were close."

"Almost inseparable—they lived and breathed Huntington Inc. Uncle Drew grieved his father's death for months. His depression became severe when the real estate market all but collapsed soon after my grandfather died. The company took a hard hit. In the midst of doing everything in his power to keep Huntington Inc. intact, he met Jasmine. And as they say, he fell madly in love. After they married, he turned a lot of the business over to me." Trace lowered his head. "He's been through enough grief to last a lifetime. His mother died less than a year ago, his wife has been murdered, and maybe his daughter too."

Mackenzie gasped and then held up her hand. "No, Trace, you can't think that. We have to keep on believing that she will be found alive."

Trace nodded. "You're right. Even though Captain Sprinsky isn't too hopeful. He didn't express that, but his body language said it all when he briefed us in the family room yesterday afternoon."

Mackenzie's mouth hardened. "I refuse to give up hope. Once the kidnappers get their money, they will return Elise to her father." Mackenzie's voice broke. "You just wait and see."

Trace blinked a couple times and then looked toward the sky. "If perchance you're wrong, Uncle Drew and all who love her will suffer great pain." Trace reached out and cupped Mackenzie's chin in his hand. "But I'm with you on this, Mackenzie. We will not accept anything less than her safe return.

"The Bible tells us that all things are possible with God. As humans, we sometimes let circumstances hide that truth—for instance, yours truly a moment ago." Smiling, he dropped his arm to clasp Mackenzie's fingers. "Come on. It's heating up out here. Maybe a long shower will clear our minds of unpleasant thoughts, making room for more expectant hope."

The following day, her eyes shimmering with tears, Mackenzie stood by Elise's crib, folding and refolding the soft multicolored blanket she finally draped over the side railing. She jumped at the sound of Mr. Huntington's voice, realizing he stood next to her.

"My mother knitted that blanket just before she passed away last year. Thrilled to be having a grandchild at last, Mom wanted the baby to have something she'd made by her own hands. But cancer took her before Elise was born." He studied Mackenzie's face. "Miss Adams, are you okay?"

Mackenzie broke into sobs. She covered her face with her hands and slumped into the rocker. After a moment, she grabbed a handful of tissues and dried her face. "About as okay as everyone else in the house," she said, eyeing the large, dark circles under his eyes. "Is there still no word about the kidnappers?"

Mr. Huntington shook his head. "Our forty-eight-hour window is about to close. Gregory, in less than an hour, will take the ransom money to the bus station designated as the drop-off point. All I can do is hope and pray that Elise will be back in the nursery by the end of the day.

"Captain Sprinsky assures me that undercover officers will be at strategic locations both in and outside the terminal, ready to follow the person who picks up the bag." Mr. Huntington placed his hand on Mackenzie's shoulder. "Miss Adams, you must come downstairs and eat some lunch. Mrs. Slater sent me to fetch you. She's concerned that you've hardly touched your meals these past two days."

Mackenzie gaped at her employer. *Mrs. Slater worried about the nanny?* Surely Mr. Huntington had misinterpreted her words. Hearing a sound, they looked up to see Angie walk through the nursery door.

She grinned. "Thought Mr. Huntington might need a bit of reinforcement. Come along, *mi amiga*," Angie said, taking hold of Mackenzie's arm. "You have to eat. Or you won't have the strength to care for Elise when she's returned to us." Angie gave Mackenzie a once-over. "If this new habit of missing meals continues, you'll have no need for a membership at a gym." Angie guided Mackenzie to the hall. "Mrs. Slater has prepared her special chicken pasta salad. You'll love it."

Following the meal, Makenzie placed her knife and fork across the top of her plate. The salad and the fresh-from-the-oven hard rolls had tasted great, but the few bites she'd taken seemed to be stuck in her esophagus. She'd bypassed the dessert—strawberry shortcake, her favorite.

Mr. Huntington and Trace chose to eat with the staff, and she caught the silent exchange among the three men. Greg rose from the table a moment later. Without a word, he picked up the bag packed with the ransom money from the floor. Eyeing the suitcase, Mackenzie recalled the conversation she'd overheard between Trace and her employer the day the kidnappers took Elise. Had Mr. Crane loaned Mr. Huntington the ransom money? Or had the president of the bank decided to okay a loan without the board's consent?

All at the table observed Greg's exit through the back door. His Mustang roared to life a moment later. Mackenzie sighed. They had the money. That was all that mattered. If things developed as the police desired, Elise would be back in her arms in a few hours. *Oh, please, God, let it be so. For her—please!*

Later, in her room, Mackenzie clicked on an e-mail from Kari. After reading about her friend's experiences as a nanny in Hollywood, Mackenzie left her laptop on the table and moved to stand at the window. What she'd give to share her adventures with her friend. But she didn't dare. She couldn't take the chance of her parents discovering the circumstances that surrounded their daughter. She'd caused them enough heartache.

Hearing a car motor, she craned her neck to better see the garage area. Greg had returned. Mackenzie glanced at her watch. He'd been gone just short of an hour. Following his departure earlier with the ransom money in tow, Mr. Huntington had dismissed the staff to their duties while he convened with Trace in his office. Would their topics of discussion include the information Mrs. Baxter had revealed?

Her duties scrubbed for who knew how long, Mackenzie curled up on the sofa and reached for the book on the side table. She tried to concentrate on the story but tossed the book aside. *Oh Elise, please be okay!*

The sound of a knock startled Makenzie. Opening her door, she invited Mrs. Slater inside, surprised that the house manager's demeanor was less scornful than usual. *Maybe she's starting to realize I'm not the ogre she's believed me to be,* Mackenzie thought.

"Miss Adams, Captain Sprinsky has just arrived, and Mr. Huntington has sent me to ask that you meet with the rest of us in the family room."

Mackenzie's eyes widened. "Does the captain have news about Elise? Is she coming home?"

The house manager lowered her eyelashes. "I don't know. Let's not tarry, Miss Adams. We don't want to keep the officer waiting."

Mackenzie saw the dislike for her anew in Mrs. Slater's eyes. Mr. Huntington was wrong. This woman had no amiability for his newest household employee whatsoever. "No, we don't." Her lips tightening, Mackenzie extended her arm toward the doorway. "Shall we go?" Were her efforts to win Mrs. Slater's friendship a waste of time?

Her eyes wide with anticipation, Mackenzie followed Mrs. Slater down the stairs. Entering the den, all of a sudden, Mackenzie experienced a déjà vu feeling when she noted the captain's expression. He stood next to the fireplace in much the same way as he had the day before, his arm draped across the top of the mantel. If his countenance held a clue, what he planned to tell them would not be good news. Trace motioned to the two of them to sit on the sofa next to him. Once she and Mrs. Slater were seated, the occupants in the room turned their eyes toward the captain.

"Mr. Huntington, before I give you an update on the kidnapping, I need to brief you in regard to your wife's murder. To date, we've investigated the individuals on the list of possible suspects you provided the other day, and all have a solid alibi for the night your wife was killed."

"Including her attorney, Jason Crane?" Mr. Huntington said, pushing himself forward to sit on the edge of his chair.

"Yes, sir."

Mackenzie and Angie exchanged looks. The list the captain had referred to must have been the one spoken of in the conversation Angie had overheard between their employer and the officer.

"And just this morning, we located your deceased wife's car." Not a sound could be heard in the den.

"Where?" Mr. Huntington said, his look suspicious. "I would have thought a chop shop would have dismantled it by now or driven it to Old Mexico for a sizable cash sale."

The captain nodded. "Having not located the vehicle by now, those of us investigating the murder had come to similar conclusions. However, that all changed this morning."

"How so, Captain?" Greg said, shifting his body to a straighter position in his chair.

"A couple of Arkansas Highway Patrol divers were testing new sonar equipment and discovered the Mercedes on the bottom of the Arkansas River, the detection near a boat ramp about a mile upstream from where the fisherman found your wife's body. A company we use in these types of situations pulled the vehicle from the river about an hour ago. I just came from the recovery site. Officers are there doing a thorough search of the car."

Trace stood from the sofa. "Have they found anything significant that will help locate the killer?"

Captain Sprinsky shook his head. "Once a car is subjected to a body of water, it would be unusual to find any useful evidence. One of the back passenger doors had been opened, possibly by a strong underwater current, or it hadn't been closed properly and opened on impact. It's our theory

Mrs. Huntington's body became dislodged from the vehicle and floated to the surface, the river carrying her downstream to the discovery location."

"So technically, you're not any closer to finding Jasmine's murderer than before you dragged her car from the river," Mr. Huntington said, his voice tight with emotion.

"We now have two additional suppositions we can investigate. Either your wife died violently in her car, or the killer strangled her in another location, loaded her body into the back seat, and then drove to the boat ramp, where he shoved the car into the river."

Mackenzie glanced at Mr. Huntington and then frowned. She nudged Trace and nodded toward her employer, whose complexion had grown pasty, the dark circles under his eyes more prominent than usual.

"Do you think the killer had an accomplice?" Trace said, moving to the love seat to sit beside his uncle.

"Yes. It's my belief someone picked him up after he deposited the car into the water."

Captain Sprinsky's cell phone jangled a lively tune. "Excuse me," he said. He stepped to the other side of the room. After a couple minutes, he stood before them again. "Officer Kelly phoned to let me know they've found something of importance." The captain eyed the occupants of the room one at a time. He turned to Mr. Huntington. "Sir, your billfold was found lodged in between the seat and the console, your driver's license and a couple of credit cards still in their slots."

Everyone stared at the proprietor of Park House. Angie and Mackenzie exchanged looks a second time. Mackenzie swallowed hard. What did it mean? She watched as Mr. Huntington's face grew paler.

"My wallet?" He breathed deeply and then exhaled slowly. All at once, a slight smile touched his mouth. "So that's where I lost it. I thought sure it had slipped out of my pocket at the restaurant where Jasmine and I dined the night before I left for Nashville. I phoned and spoke to the manager, but he stated that no one had turned in a wallet. It was quite a hassle for me the next morning. I had to go to the tag agency to get a new license before I could leave on my business trip."

"So you drove to the restaurant in your wife's car," Captain Sprinsky said, pulling his mini iPad from his blazer pocket.

Mr. Huntington nodded. "Yes. She picked me up from the office and drove us to the restaurant."

"That's correct, Captain," Trace said. "Uncle Drew and I were just leaving the office when she arrived to pick him up. The statement I gave after I reported Jasmine's disappearance included that information."

The captain nodded. Yes, I have that in my notes. He turned to Mr. Huntington. "Sir, I may have more questions for you later, but let me bring you up to date concerning the kidnapping of your daughter. After Mr. Martin entered the waiting area of the terminal, he put the bag where the kidnappers had specified—next to the last chair in the back row of seats.

"Following Mr. Martin's departure from the bus station, a young woman carrying an oversized handbag and fitting the description of the female suspect sat down near the suitcase that contained the money and thumbed through the magazine she carried with her." Captain Sprinsky looked down at his notes.

"Shortly thereafter, she glanced around the terminal and then placed the magazine in the side pocket of the suitcase. After a moment, she stood, collected her purse, along with the suitcase, and then proceeded to the ladies' room. While waiting for her to emerge from the restroom, the undercover officers stationed in the area observed that several women toting luggage of various sizes entered and exited the ladies' room. Twenty minutes later, neither the suspect nor the money bag had reappeared.

"Sensing a breach in our stratagem, the officer in charge phoned me, and I dispatched a female officer to the scene. Upon her arrival, she checked the facility but saw no sign of the suspect or the money. During the officer's search, she found hidden in the baby-changing station a blonde wig, the clothes the suspect had worn, and the empty collapsible suitcase that had held the money, all the articles wiped clean of fingerprints. It was as if the suspect had worn gloves when she'd dressed that day and later, when she'd changed her disguise."

Mr. Huntington jumped from his chair, his face red. "Are you saying the woman came out of that restroom with a million dollars in her possession and walked past a team of police officers without an ounce of detection?"

"Yes, sir. As much as it grieves me to say so, I'm afraid that's exactly what happened."

Mr. Huntington shook his head. "And we pay good tax dollars for infractions such as this!"

"Uncle Drew," Trace said, standing. "I'm sure Captain Sprinsky and the other officers are beside themselves wondering how this could have happened."

"That's correct, Mr. Patterson," the officer said, an appreciative look in his eyes. He held up an eight-by-ten photo. "This is an image of the woman who carried the money bag into the ladies' room. One of the officers at the bus terminal snapped the picture with his cell phone. Do any of you recognize this person?"

The inhabitants of Park House shook their heads. Captain Sprinsky's face showed his disappointment. "I'd hoped the opposite would be true."

Mr. Huntington sat down again and motioned for his nephew to do the same. "So, Captain, since your officers bungled the opportunity to follow the kidnappers to the location of my child, what is your plan of action now?"

The captain's face colored. "With due respect, sir, we are still following up on leads from the Amber Alert. Also, the department sent officers to question shop owners in the area from where the kidnapper made his ransom call, but nothing came of it. And we've shown pictures of various blue minivans to the woman who reported seeing the alleged kidnappers. But no luck so far. She says the vehicles look too much alike for her to identify the exact make and model of the vehicle she saw. Again, the Amber Alert is our best hope at this point."

The residents of Park House sat as if in a daze. After a moment, Greg stood, his eyes focused on Mr. Huntington. "If I may be excused, sir, I need to finish cleaning the pool."

Standing, Mr. Huntington waved the gardener toward the doorway. "Go on with your work, Gregory. We're finished here anyway. Trace, I'll see you when you return from the office." Mr. Huntington glanced upward, the look in his eyes hard as steel. "I'll walk you to the door, Captain."

Exchanging a bittersweet smile with Trace, Mackenzie lagged behind to speak with Angie, who plumped pillows on the vacated furniture. "Come to my room when you get off work, if you can."

Angie nodded. "Okay. This is Mom's day off, so I don't have to pick up my brother from his job."

"Good. See you in a while."

Mackenzie climbed the stairs, every bone in her body feeling the pain in her heart. Trace's smile a few minutes ago had been to encourage her—she'd read the message in his eyes, but hopelessness had struck and hung like a cloud of doom over the residents of Park House. Elise had brought such joy in the midst of the agony Mackenzie had tried to flee. How would she endure another loss so soon if Elise were lost to them forever? As she stepped onto the second-floor landing, Mackenzie's chest tightened. She hurried to her room. After closing the door behind her, she fell onto the bed. *Oh God, if only I could find you again!*

Chapter 13

"*M*ackenzie, you can't be serious," Angie said that evening, staring openmouthed at her friend.

"I can be, and I am."

Seated on the sofa in Mackenzie's room, Angie pulled a drink from her water bottle. "Look, I understand how you might come to that conclusion from all that Mrs. Baxter and Mr. Patterson told you. And I know he's not the most congenial person in town. In fact, his attitude stinks most of the time. But a murderer? Sorry, Mackenzie—I'm not sure I can buy that."

"Think about it. Who else has even the smidgen of motive that he does?"

Angie placed her elbow on the sofa arm and cupped her chin in her hand, creasing her brow. After a moment, she shot a glance toward her friend. "If you are right"—Angie lifted her gaze toward the ceiling—"*que Dios lo perdone*—may God have mercy on him. Still, there's that burden of proof. What evidence is available to prove Greg killed Mrs. Huntington?"

Mackenzie sighed. "Not a drop so far. But if we take what we've learned and examine it piece by piece, maybe we can come up with an item or two. Let's go back to when Jasmine vanished. Trace said that none of you were concerned about the first night she didn't come home following Mr. Huntington's trip to Nashville."

"That's correct. When she partied late on the days Mr. Huntington was away on business, she would stay with friends, always returning by noon the next day. Then she would shower and spend some time with Elise before she went out again."

"Did she follow her normal itinerary the day Mr. Huntington left town?"

"I'm not sure. Except I know she didn't come to the nursery."

Mackenzie raised her brows. "Oh?"

"When I arrived for work that morning, I found Mr. Huntington waiting for me in the kitchen. He informed me that Mrs. Slater had left town the night before to tend to her ill sister for a few days and asked if I would care for Elise until Mrs. Slater's return to Park House."

"Such a tough decision," Mackenzie said, grinning. She lifted her palms, moving them up and down as if they were a set of balancing scales. "Play with Elise, clean house, play with Elise, clean house." Mackenzie lowered one palm below the other and held her hands in place. "It's my opinion that nursery duty won over polishing furniture."

Angie laughed. "Ah, what perception!" She waved away Mackenzie's playfulness. "After I assured Mr. Huntington I'd be glad to watch over Elise, he said he'd be flying out that afternoon on a business trip. He told me he'd arranged for a caterer and a temporary cleaning service so that I could give his daughter my full attention. So if Mrs. Huntington had visited Elise on either of those two days, I would have known it."

Mackenzie narrowed her eyes. "With you and Elise in the nursery, that leaves only Jasmine in the house, if she stayed here, and Greg in the garage apartment. According to Trace, Greg was infatuated with Jasmine." Mackenzie grimaced. "I'd come to that conclusion already from bits of conversation I've had with him."

Angie rolled her eyes toward the ceiling. "Along with me and his mother." Angie took in a deep breath, her expression submerged in regret, as if she'd just betrayed a confidence.

Mackenzie laughed. "Don't worry, Angie. I know about the relationship between Mrs. Slater and Greg. I'm surprised you haven't mentioned it."

Angie grinned. "You didn't ask. Who told you?"

"The first day Trace accompanied Elise and me to the park, he shared a good deal of his Huntington ancestry, including the sordid details surrounding Mrs. Slater's birth. He said he didn't want me to hear the tale from a gossip. May I ask how you knew?"

"Sure. When I first came to work here, Greg asked me out, and I agreed. During our conversation over dinner, we talked about ethnic backgrounds, and he revealed his. He tried to hide it, but I could sense his anger about the situation."

Mackenzie's eyes lit up. "You just suggested his first motive—anger. I caught a glimpse of a similar ire in Greg the other day while he observed Trace incognito from the dining room entryway. Both incidents establish the fact that Greg has antagonism toward the Huntingtons. And who can blame him? According to Trace, Mr. Huntington refuses to claim Greg as his nephew, although he allows him to work and live on the estate. And I can imagine how it must grieve Greg to see his mother regarded as nothing more than a servant. That along with the knowledge Jasmine would never consider him more than a friend at most—yeah, I can understand his infuriation. Not that I condone it, but maybe that anger issue played a role in Jasmine's death."

Angie scooted forward, her eyes full of doubt. "What do you mean?"

Mackenzie held up her hands. "Come on, Angie—don't look at me that way." Mackenzie laughed. "Okay. So maybe I'm a little crazy. Just hear me out. Suppose that Jasmine has gone out for the evening like she usually does when hubby's away, but she decides to come home—"

"And leave one of those fabulous get-togethers she likes so much? What possible reason would drag her away?"

Mackenzie frowned at her friend. "I don't know. A drink might have gotten spilled on her dress, or she forgot something. Who knows?" Mackenzie's breath caught. "Or maybe a drink doused her hair, not her dress. She would need to redo her hairstyle, right? And the police couldn't find her hair dryer, remember?"

Angie sat straight up, her eyes wide. "That's right. Okay, she's home. Now what?"

"Greg sees or hears her come home. All of a sudden, he gets the idea that this is his perfect opportunity—a great time to declare his love for Jasmine. His employer and mother are out of the picture, you're in the nursery with Elise. So he leaves the apartment and finds his way to her bedroom, where she is in the midst of redoing her hair. Once she detects his presence, she lays the dryer aside and demands to know what he's doing there."

"I can see her doing just that," Angie said, nodding. "Go on."

"That's when he tells her how much he loves her. Perhaps she laughs at him or threatens to tell Mr. Huntington, but whatever she says, it makes Greg so angry that he picks up the dryer, slams it against her head, jerking the plug out of the wall socket at the same time. She falls to the floor, the blow stunning her—you recall the autopsy revealed a head injury, right?"

Angie nods, her eyes round.

"So with hatred pushing him onward, he cuts the cord with a knife or some other sharp instrument and wraps the cord around her neck, strangling her to death. Now that she's dead, he has to get her away from Park House and dispose of the body."

Angie's face brightened. "That's when Greg somehow got Jasmine's body out of the house and into the limo. And, when he left the property, Mrs. Baxter witnessed his departure. After he dumped her body into the river, he must have realized he had to get rid of her car, so he returned to the house, and then drove the Mercedes to the boat ramp, where he plunged it into the water. How Greg got back to Park House, who knows? A friend maybe?"

Mackenzie laughed. "Nothing wrong with your hammer. You didn't miss a lick—drove the nail straight home."

Sadness filled Angie's eyes. "Do you really think it happened that way? Captain Sprinsky said they didn't find any evidence that she'd been killed in the house. And what about Mr. Crane? Maybe she was at his house, they had a lovers' quarrel, and in a fit of rage, he killed her. She could have taken her hair dryer to his house."

Mackenzie sighed. "I know, but how do you explain the limo leaving the grounds in the early morning hours?"

"I can't. You'd think since Mrs. Baxter told the captain about the matter, they would have questioned Greg about it by this time."

"I'm sure they have. Maybe he couldn't sleep and decided to take the limo to one of those all night car wash establishments so it would be clean for Mr. Huntington's trip to the airport the next day. Oh Angie, I know my imagination goes bizarre sometimes. Unable to sleep last night, I kept trying to devise a motive and a killer in Jasmine's case, and the scenario you just heard is my best creation thus far."

"Mackenzie, no matter how skeptical I am, what you contrived is reasonable—so much so that I think you should discuss it with the captain."

"You don't believe he'd die from laughter?"

Angie shook her head. "No. He would see the same caring, compassionate person that I've found you to be."

Mackenzie blinked back the moisture that sprang to her eyes. "How sweet, Angie. Thanks."

She grinned. "Anytime."

They both grew silent. After a moment, a smile tweaked Mackenzie's lips. "Well, what do you say we set aside my theory of the murder and go with yours?"

Angie frowned. "Huh?"

"Mr. Crane. I might be able to sniff out a hint of his guilt when we meet tomorrow. I still haven't come up with a good excuse to see him"—Mackenzie smiled coyly—"but I have a few hours yet. I'll think of something."

"Now, why don't I doubt that?" Angie said, laughing. Staring into space, she tapped her finger against her lips. "If someone had accused me of this before today, I'd have called them a liar. But at this moment, I feel sorry for the guy. He hasn't a clue what he'll have to deal with once you're sitting across from him."

Mackenzie looked doubtful. "Not so sure about that. I've never been face-to-face with an attorney before."

The next afternoon, Mackenzie sat in the waiting room of Jason Crane's office. The plush surroundings pleased her eye. "Maybe I should have become a lawyer," she said, sighing. Mackenzie glanced toward the secretary at the sound of her voice.

"Did you say something, Miss Adams?"

Mackenzie's cheeks colored. "I was just admiring the decor." She read the nameplate on the desk. "Miss Wilkins, do you think Mr. Crane will see me soon? I can't stay much longer." Before Miss Wilkins could answer, Mr. Crane stepped into the reception area.

"Well, Miss Adams, what a pleasure to see you again." He motioned her toward his office. "Come right in."

Standing, she forced a smile and shook his outstretched hand. "And you as well." Mackenzie cringed at the slight smirk forming on his lips. *Well, that proved to be a good start,* she thought. Would he also detect the real reason for her visit to his office? She stepped in front of the man and made her way to one of the comfortable-looking leather chairs in front of his desk.

Jason, once seated in his chair, studied her momentarily and then picked up a pen, ready to scribble notes on the pad at his fingertips. The look in his eyes saddened. "I can't tell you how distressed I am about the kidnapping. Is there still no news?"

Mackenzie shook her head, forcing back the tears that threatened to mar her makeup. "No. The police don't give us any hope that Elise is still in the country or even alive. Over seventy-two hours since her disappearance, the police say the window for hopeful expectation has passed." A tear streaked down her cheek. "I just can't harbor the fact she may have been killed or, worse, sold to a sex-trafficking ring." Mackenzie cringed. "You hear often about that sort of thing—children kidnapped and either hidden in remote areas or sold to criminals in foreign countries." Mackenzie covered her face with her hands. A moment later, she felt a touch on her shoulder. She looked up to see Mr. Crane at her side.

"Miss Adams, I know how rough this must be for you. Even I'm not immune to the suffering everyone at Park House is enduring. Jasmine sometimes brought Elise to see me when we had business to talk over or met downtown for a friendly lunch. She is an adorable baby. As procurator of Jasmine's estate, I'm sure she would approve of my actions on behalf of her child." He stared off into space, nodding. "Jasmine knew I would do anything for Elise."

Mackenzie leaned forward, drying her face with the handkerchief he'd handed her. "I'm sorry. I don't understand."

"Oh. I just assumed Trace told you I unofficially loaned Drew the ransom the kidnappers demanded. Trace came to my office yesterday morning and picked up the money."

Mackenzie frowned. "Forgive me if I'm overstepping my boundaries a bit here, but your generosity to Mr. Huntington seems odd, considering the obvious dislike between the two of you. May I ask why you granted him the loan?"

Jason smiled. "I understand your inquisitiveness, Miss Adams, but now you must forgive me; my reasons are my own and not to be discussed."

"Okay, so what made you think Mr. Patterson would share family business with me, Elise's nanny?"

"Because of the way he kept his eyes trained on you during the celebration of Jasmine's life." Jason glanced toward an eight-by-ten photo of the late Mrs. Huntington and her daughter, which occupied a spot on top of a book-lined credenza a few feet from his desk. Then he turned back to Mackenzie. "His interest is comprehensible. You are quite lovely, Miss Adams." He smiled. "Knowing Trace, I just assumed you and he would be—as the younger generation say—an item by now. If that's the case, it wouldn't be unusual for you to be aware of family matters."

Mackenzie sat back against the contour of the chair, her spine rigid. "Sorry to disappoint you, Mr. Crane—Mr. Patterson and I are not an *item*. But I am curious. What knowledge do you have about Trace that inspired your fallible notion?"

Jason laughed. "I've known Trace a few years now. When he desires something, he goes after it, no words minced when he declares an intention. And from the way he seemed captivated by you that day, I'm sure by now you've been apprised of his feelings. Am I not right, Miss Adams?" When she opened her mouth, he waved away her response. "Don't bother. I can read the answer in your eyes." He smiled at her dubious expression. "With a good eye and ear, one can gain a world of insight."

The color on her face deepened. "Mr. Crane, I didn't come here to talk about Mr. Patterson's interest in me or anyone else."

Sighing, Jason settled against the back of his chair. "Sorry, Miss Adams. Please tell me how I can help you."

Mackenzie dug in her purse and pulled out a notebook. "Well, Mr. Crane, I plan to work on my doctorate after I've taken a sabbatical from education, but before I can pursue that goal, I need to gather information about family relationships in a variety of economic backgrounds.

"I believe a discussion with Mr. Huntington at this time about his late wife would be distressful for him. So I thought you, as her attorney and friend, might be willing to give me some input about her personality, her life as wife to a man with considerable means and notoriety, and how both affected her relationship with Elise. I would be glad to pay you a reasonable fee for any information that would help my endeavor."

Jason swiveled his chair to a position where he could better view Jasmine's photograph. He stared at it for several minutes before he spoke. "I can't remember a time when Jasmine wasn't striking—even as a child. People would stop and stare at her—on the street, in the mall, or anywhere else she might be. Although polite to those who praised her beauty, later she would laugh off their compliments. She never saw herself as others did."

Jason smiled. "When we were young, she preferred climbing trees with me to participating in the numerous teas and social gatherings her mother required Jasmine to attend from the moment she could carry on a conversation with the guests. Propriety was never a big issue with her. She liked to make her own rules. Often she would sneak away from those events and meet me at our special place."

Makenzie nodded. "Someone did say that you two had grown up together."

"Yes. Our parents lived on the same street. We played together, shared our desires and secrets—and later a first kiss. I've never known anyone like her."

Mackenzie straightened. "You were in love with her."

Jason whipped a gaze toward her, surprise in his eyes. After a moment, he relaxed. "You are an intuitive young woman. Does my appreciation for her show that much?"

Makenzie laughed. "'Fraid so. Did she reciprocate your feelings?"

"Yes. But she wouldn't admit it—at least not until a few weeks before she died."

Mackenzie grew more alert. "And why then?"

"She said she was through playing games and wanted a lifetime relationship with the man she loved. Jasmine planned to divorce Drew and marry me. I had the papers ready. But she died before I had a chance to file them in court."

"Had she told Mr. Huntington about this?"

Jason frowned. "I don't think so." He observed Mackenzie's countenance for a moment before he continued. "Yes, the police are aware of our relationship, but Captain Sprinsky said his report about our conversation would be classified material. And I prefer that you remain mum as well. The only common ground Drew and I shared was Jasmine, but a man can just take so much." Jason leaned forward. "I'm sure you recall the unpleasant episode between us at Park House a few days ago."

How could I forget it? The fury she'd seen on Mr. Huntington's face would remain in her mind for a lifetime. Sadness spread across Mackenzie's face. "Yes, I can fathom pain and how it affects a person. You don't have to be concerned. I won't mention our talk to him." *No worry on that score!* At the look of curiosity in his eyes, she focused on her notebook and penned a few lines before she turned her attention back to the lawyer. "Mr. Crane, since you brought it up, may I ask the nature of that quarrel?"

"A personal disagreement."

"Really," she said, a tinge of sarcasm in her voice. "To me, a simple disagreement would hardly call for a threat on your life."

Jason sighed. "Let's just drop it, shall we?"

"Okay. I have another question. Why have you told me, someone you've just recently met, about your relationship with Mrs. Huntington?"

He grew thoughtful. "I can't say for sure. Other than the fact you seem to care a great deal for Elise."

Mackenzie smiled, her irritation with him evaporating. "On that, you can depend."

"And that you give the impression of being interested in her mother."

"From the day I saw Mrs. Huntington's portrait at Park House, I've wanted to know all about her. And—" Mackenzie lowered her eyelashes.

He lifted an eyebrow, clarity filling his eyes. "And to find out who murdered her?"

She jerked up her head, her eyes wide. "How did you know?"

He shrugged. "As I intimated earlier, I'm trained to read my clients' motivations." He held up his hand, palm out. "Now, don't get me wrong. I think your efforts are commendable; however, should you question the wrong person, you could be in substantial danger. Intelligent as I believe you to be, I'm sure you've considered that probability."

Mackenzie nodded. "I'm aware of that, but from the day I arrived at Park House, I've had this desire—no, more like a driving force within me—to discover her killer. It's always in my mind."

Jason smiled. "And you thought a visit with me, a close family friend, might help you with your quest. If you're thinking I murdered her, you're dead wrong. Pardon the pun. I was in Michigan at the time of her murder, working with the CEO of one of her manufacturing entities to straighten out a safety issue in the plant. The police have confirmed my alibi." Mr. Crane paused, taking in his visitor. "Miss Adams, you don't strike me as a person who enjoys speaking untruth, so I trust you are planning to obtain a doctorate degree in the future."

Mackenzie grinned. "Yes, sir, I really am at some point. And I have started research for my thesis." She smiled inwardly. *She just wouldn't mention that it had been less than twenty-four hours ago.*

Jason grew serious. "You will be careful, won't you? You're playing with a lighted match. Is Captain Sprinsky aware of your sleuthing?"

"I spoke with him briefly about it. He suggested I let him and his officers handle the case."

"Good idea."

"The thing is, they've searched the premises without finding any evidence of her murder there. Mr. Crane, I have nothing to substantiate my idea, but somehow I know the key to finding her killer lies within Park House. I just have to keep searching until I discover it." Mackenzie turned a page in her notebook, smiling within as wonderment splattered his features. "Now, Mr. Crane, will you please tell me more about Jasmine, if it's not too difficult for you to discuss her?"

With a slight shake of his head, he smiled. "I don't mind talking about Jasmine at all. She was the light of my life."

Mackenzie nodded. "I can see that. Did she say when she intended to inform Mr. Huntington about the divorce?"

Jason tapped his pen against the top of his desk. "She wanted to wait until an opportunity to move her and Elise out of the house. When she learned about Drew's upcoming trip to Nashville, she thought it the best time to implement her plans, purposing to tell him of the situation sometime after he had arrived in Nashville. I know that sounds cruel, but she thought he might try to prevent her from taking Elise and wanted to avoid that at all costs. I can't see Drew doing that—he always gave her anything she wanted—but Jasmine was adamant about her decision."

"I see."

"You have to understand that Jasmine was a free spirit. Under her mother's thumb for most of her life, Jasmine became determined to be free of her mother's domineering ways. Her accidental meeting with Drew while both were staying at the same hotel in Boston became her chance to escape when he proposed to her a few weeks later after a whirlwind courtship. When her parents died in a boating accident two years later, she insisted I move to Little Rock, where I could better handle her affairs while building up a practice here. So I left my father's firm in the hands of my younger brother, my partner, and moved to Little Rock. And as you can guess, that wasn't a hard decision for me."

"How did Mr. Huntington feel about your relocation?"

"Believe me, he wasn't pleased. They'd been married a little over two years, but troubles in their marriage had already begun. His traditional upbringing warred against Jasmine's need to be free from any type of dominance. My arrival on the scene made it worse. His jealously of the friendship I had with his wife spawned numerous quarrels between them." Jason stood and moved to the credenza. He picked up the photograph and stared at it. After a moment, he sat it down again and shoved his hands into his pockets. "When Jasmine became pregnant with Elise, they called a truce to their volatile relationship." A bitter laugh exploded from Jason's lips. "Drew could hardly wait for his child to be born."

Her eyes filling with confusion, Mackenzie frowned. She glanced toward Elise's image. After a moment, her eyes widened. She threw a look toward Jason and then turned to study the photograph again, her body becoming immoveable as if stapled to the chair. Yes, she *had* seen Mr. Crane before meeting him—in the eyes of the baby girl who might be gone from them forever.

Jason scrutinized Mackenzie's features, a wry smile twisting his lips. "Well, Miss Adams, I believe you have just detected another secret Jasmine and I shared."

Mackenzie nodded. "You are Elise's father, not Mr. Huntington."

The phone on Jason's desk buzzed. After answering the call, he stood from his chair. "I'm sorry, Miss Adams. We'll have to discuss Jasmine's relationship with Elise another time. My next appointment awaits me."

"So you wouldn't mind seeing me again?"

"Not at all. To me, Jasmine and Elise were like sunshine on the brightest summer day. Shall I escort you to the door?" He walked around the desk and held out his arm.

Vacating her chair, Mackenzie gripped the edge of the desk, her legs wobbly. "I admit I'm a bit concerted by all you've shared. But I appreciate the information, and yes, I would like to have another session with you." After a moment, she placed her hand on his arm, grateful for the support. "I'll make the necessary appointment with Miss Wilkins. Thank you for taking time out of your busy schedule to see me."

"My pleasure," he said, his smile wide. "You are a delightful listener." He opened the office door. "Oh, by the way. No charge for our discussion."

Mackenzie smiled. "Thank you." She held up her notebook. "See you soon." Mackenzie turned. "I commend you for your generosity to Mr. Huntington. I'll let you know if we hear any other details about Elise's disappearance."

Jason's eyes grew moist. "How could I have done anything less? Good day, Miss Adams. And thank you."

Pushing the button to send the elevator her way a few minutes later, Mackenzie marveled at the change she'd observed in the attorney once he'd realized she knew his feelings for Jasmine. Had his crass behavior toward other women been an act in order to hide his love for her? Although Mr. Crane had implied only he and Jasmine knew about Elise's birth, had Mr. Huntington suspected the truth? In the discussion she'd overheard between Trace and her employer the day of the kidnapping, had that knowledge been the ace in his pocket he'd mentioned, the catalyst that had spurred his confidence in Mr. Crane's willingness to provide the money for the ransom?

Chapter 14

A couple hours later, Mackenzie pulled into her parking space at Park House. She stepped out of the car, opened the back door, and reached inside to grab the shopping bags. She jumped at the sound of Mr. Huntington's voice and struck her head against the top of the doorframe. She turned in his direction, smiling as she rubbed her head. "I'm afraid you startled me, sir. I didn't see you in the garage."

He raised his brow. "So it seems." He eyed the plastic bags in her hand and car. "I hope you found everything you needed." He pocketed his keys and reached out his hand. "May I help with those?"

"Yes, I did, and thank you," she said, handing him two bags.

Mackenzie moved toward the kitchen entrance, her employer falling into step beside her. *Much more than I anticipated. But you will never hear that from me.* "It looks like we arrived home about the same time."

"Yes. I had an errand to do after work."

"Have the police phoned to give you an update about Elise?"

He looked away. "No. I keep waiting for the call that will tell me she's been found, but my expectations have dimmed. I don't want to give up."

"Oh no, sir," she said, a look of horror spilling onto her face. "You can't give up." Makenzie's eyes misted over. She looked down, gathering her composure as best she could. "We must not lose hope."

He held up his hand. "You're right, Miss Adams. Please forgive my doubt. I'm sure we'll hear something soon, even if—" He seemed to coerce his features into an expression of expectancy. "A good report, no doubt."

Once inside the house, Mackenzie thanked her employer for his help, retrieving the bags he carried. She mumbled what she hoped to be an intelligent greeting to Mrs. Slater and then made her way through the house, hardly breathing until a few minutes later, when she collapsed onto the floor beside Elise's crib. She pounded the carpet with her fists. *No! It can't be!* How could she convince her employer not to lose faith? He hadn't believed the hope he'd uttered. She'd read the truth in his eyes. Mackenzie held the back of her fist against her mouth. The police *would* find Elise—and alive! A sob caught in Mackenzie's throat. "Oh God, please, let someone somewhere report a true sighting of the child."

Mackenzie bent her legs and folded her arms across her knees, resting her forehead on them. "God, I know I've relinquished my rights to ask anything of you—to even talk to you. I doubt you remember who I am."

Mackenzie, I've never left you or forsaken you. You ran away from me.

For once, she had no doubt about the voice she heard inside her heart. "Yes, it's true. I know Zack wasn't a Christian—didn't want anything to do with you, in fact. I loved him, don't you see? I thought I could win him to you, but he wouldn't budge. I couldn't make myself leave him. So I drifted farther and farther from your presence." She raised her head and wiped the tears from the corners of her eyes with her fingers. "I thought he loved me. He had me convinced that his way would be best for our future. When I discovered the real Zack, guilt and shame engulfed me. I couldn't face you. I realize I'm the prime candidate to win the gold medal for the Biggest Fool of the Year. And you don't have much to do with fools."

Only those who are willing to leave their past behind and seek after me with their whole heart.

"You mean—" She lifted her head, darting a glance toward her room. She heard the knock again, louder this time. Standing, Mackenzie plucked a few tissues from a box nearby and dried her face. A moment later, she invited Angie inside, stepping aside so that her friend could set the tray she held on the table.

Mackenzie's brow wrinkled. "Did I miss dinner?" She peeked at her watch. "Guess I did."

"When you didn't show up at the table, Mr. Huntington told Mrs. Slater to send a meal up to you. He thought you might be upset about Elise."

Mackenzie lifted the towel covering the food. "Um, smells good, but I'm not hungry right now. I'll warm it up in the microwave later."

Angie took in the red splotches on Mackenzie's face. "Looks like our boss made a correct call." Angie put her arm around her friend. "I can stay awhile if you want to talk."

Mackenzie flopped onto the sofa. She motioned for Angie to sit down. "It's not just Elise. My whole life is a mess."

"What do you mean?"

"I left Arizona because of my broken engagement and—" Makenzie looked away from the compassionate look in Angie's eyes. "My parents were so proud of my degree, and when I made the decision to accept this position—a glorified babysitting job, my mother tagged it—my decision disappointed them so much she won't write or talk to me on the phone." Mackenzie let out a long sigh. "At least my father is still speaking to me, albeit he can't understand my purpose for leaving Phoenix. And I can't tell them the whole of it. It would break their hearts." Mackenzie glimpsed the expectancy on Angie's face. "Or anyone else, for that matter. It's something I have to work out on my own."

"Don't you think your mother will come around eventually? You're a grown woman now. You should be able to make your own choices in life."

Mackenzie closed her eyes. *That word again!* How she hated it.

"I think she expected me to follow in her footsteps—respectable job, asset to church and community, that sort of life. Not that I don't want to contribute to society, but I want more than a shelf full of awards for Leader of the Year on a bunch of well-meaning projects. I just haven't found my niche yet." Mackenzie sank deeper into the sofa. "And I'm not sure I can now," she said just above a whisper.

Seeing the confusion etched into Angie's features, Mackenzie stood and held out her hands, frustration gnawing her insides. "To make matters worse, I think I've gotten in over my head trying to solve Jasmine's murder. The notion that the answer to her death lies within these walls"—she swept her arm wide—"is embedded in my brain like ore buried in a remote mine shaft. I keep thinking I'll make a strike, but I keep straying into dead-end tunnels. I've always been one to complete whatever I set my mind to do. But after my meeting today—"

"Oh, that's right. Your appointment with Mr. Crane. Did it not go well?"

"It didn't go quite as you thought it would. I left his office shaken. Although you and I had suspected it, I didn't have an inkling I would hear firsthand about the love triangle that swept through this household."

Angie tipped her head as if an idea had just occurred to her. "Did Mr. Crane say anything that made you believe he could be a person of interest in Jasmine's murder?" Glimpsing Mackenzie's bemused look, Angie laughed. "I've been watching crime shows lately."

"Once I fill you in on my conversation with the prestigious attorney, you can judge for yourself. But first, I'll fix us a cup of hot tea."

Angie nodded. "With a teaspoon of honey, please."

Several minutes later, Angie took a sip from her cup, frowning slightly, as if trying to absorb all she'd heard. "It's not hard for me to comprehend Elise's true parentage. All the signs were in front of me all the time. If we can believe all Mr. Crane said, it seems the only crime he's committed in this case has been his love for another man's wife."

Mackenzie nodded. "The late, vivacious Jasmine Huntington."

The next morning, Mackenzie dragged open her eyes and turned toward the clock, which read 8:20. She realized the late-night visit with Angie accounted for the extra hour of sleep. She frowned. Why did she feel troubled? Had something awakened her?

"Come on, Makenzie—wake up," Angie called from outside the apartment after a loud knock.

Mackenzie jumped from the bed and struggled into her robe. "Be right there." She opened the door, and her mouth dropped at the frenzied look of her friend, who stared back at Mackenzie with eyes full of shock shackled by alarm. "What's wrong, Angie?" Makenzie released her hold on the door handle and motioned Angie inside, but her friend didn't move.

"Get dressed—quick. Captain Sprinsky is waiting downstairs in the living room to see you."

Confusion plowed deep furrows in Mackenzie's brow. "To see me? Whatever for?"

"Hurry, Mackenzie. It's important." With that, Angie spun on her heel and marched toward the stairs.

After a quick brush of her teeth and hair, Mackenzie slipped into her clothes and shoved her feet into a pair of sandals. Her hands shaking, she rushed from the room and soon stood in the wide entryway to the front room of Park House. Glancing around, she took in the members of the household seated about the room, their expressions solemn. Noting that Trace sat on the piano bench, surprise lit up her features. Had he changed his mind about his plan to move back to his condo the previous evening? Captain Sprinsky stepped forward, his smile beckoning her into the room. Trace slid a few inches to the left, making room for her beside him.

"Good morning, Miss Adams. Sorry to disturb you, but another murder has occurred, and I need to ask you a few questions. I've already spoken to the others assembled here. They seem oblivious to the situation, but perhaps you will be able to contribute some helpful information."

Makenzie's jaw lowered. She faced the ruddy-faced detective, a blank look in her eyes. "Me, sir?"

"Please take a seat, and I'll explain."

She slid a glimpse toward Mr. Huntington, who didn't seem at all pleased with her. "Yes, by all means," she said, sitting down next to Trace.

"Last night, Jason Crane was murdered."

Mackenzie gasped and grabbed Trace's arm, her eyes wide. "Murdered? Mr. Crane—murdered?" She darted a glance to Angie and then back to Captain Sprinsky, who raised an eyebrow as though he'd witnessed the young women's silent exchange.

The captain nodded. "Miss Adams, we understand you kept an appointment with him yesterday afternoon. And since you were one of the last people to see him alive, we hope he might have stated something that would indicate his plans for last evening. Would you mind sharing the nature of your visit with him?"

Mackenzie moistened her lips, her heartbeat quickening. Lowering her head, she eyed Mr. Huntington's frown beneath her lashes. "No, sir. I don't mind." She drew a long breath and straightened her spine, turning to look the officer square in the eyes. "I made an appointment with Mr. Crane, the visit in conjunction with the doctorate I plan to obtain in the future. My thesis is to be centered on the similarities and differences of family relationships in a variety of economic backgrounds."

"I'm sorry," the officer said, looking puzzled. "I don't understand how Mr. Crane, a single man, could help you in your endeavor."

"I thought Mr. Crane, as the late Mrs. Huntington's lawyer and friend, might be able to help in my research by acquainting me with the relationship she had with her daughter."

Mr. Huntington jumped to his feet. "I'm all for education, Miss Adams, but don't you think you should have discussed that subject with me?"

Mackenzie cowered at his darkened expression. She looked away, welcoming the pressure of Trace's hand on hers; the gesture helped to restore her courage. She focused on her employer.

"Well, sir. I had thought of speaking to you about the matter, but I know how heartbroken you are about her death, and I didn't want to cause you more anguish. You've treated me with kind respect, and it was my desire to reciprocate." Mackenzie glanced toward Mrs. Slater. "Also, I believed Mr. Crane might be less biased in stating his opinions about the information I needed." The house manager, color rising in her cheeks, glared at Mackenzie.

Mackenzie softened her voice. "I'm sorry, sir, if I offended you."

Mr. Huntington returned to his seat on the sofa, sighing. "I suppose no harm has been done, Miss Adams. But should you have further questions, I would be glad to assist you." Anger sparked in his eyes. "The next time you ask for permission to run a so-called errand, I would appreciate a little more straightforwardness."

Mackenzie winced at the reprimand. "Yes, sir. I will remember that." She smiled up at Trace when he squeezed her hand again.

The captain cleared his throat. "Miss Adams, did Mr. Crane give any hint of his evening plans at any time during your session with him?"

"No, sir," she said, shaking her head. "I do know, though, he had another appointment following mine."

"Oh?" the captain said, moving a step toward Mackenzie. "Do you know who he'd scheduled?"

"No," she said, shaking her head. "During our meeting, his phone rang, and I assumed his secretary had called to remind him of another appointment. But when I left his office, I didn't notice anyone sitting in the waiting area."

The captain glanced at his electronic notes. "You met with Mr. Crane a few minutes after four. How long did your meeting last?"

"About forty-five minutes or so. When I stopped by the secretary's desk to schedule another appointment with Mr. Crane, she shut down her computer after typing in the date and time and then took her keys from her purse as though in the process of leaving for the day. So it must have been close to five o'clock or a few minutes after when I left the building."

"You said you saw no one waiting to see Mr. Crane. Could you have been mistaken about him having another appointment?"

Mackenzie frowned. "When he got off the phone, he told me he had another consultation waiting for him, stating he would see me another time." The creases in her brow deepened. "Come to think of it, he didn't actually say the individual was waiting outside his office." She raised her lashes, enlightenment sweeping into her eyes. "I thought he'd spoken to his secretary, but the phone call could have been from someone else. Do you suppose he planned to meet the person at another location?"

Captain Sprinsky smiled. "My thoughts exactly, Miss Adams. His secretary informed me that you were his last appointment for the day." Captain Sprinsky took a moment to study Mackenzie. Then he smiled. "Have you ever considered switching your educational goals to crime investigation?"

Heat coloring her cheeks, she darted a glance toward Angie, who sat on the sofa, threading and rethreading her fingers. "No, sir, I've never considered that in a professional sense."

The officer's smile deepened momentarily before his expression grew serious. "Back to our discussion of Mr. Crane," Captain Sprinsky said, glimpsing his notes. "Did you see anyone when you were leaving the building or in the parking garage?"

"Not that I can recall. Having the need to purchase some items, I had that mission in mind when I walked to my car."

"I see. Well, Miss Adams, if you think of anything else, please notify me as soon as possible."

"I will, sir," she said, turning away from his incessant gaze. How did he do it? A little voice in her head declared that he would soon be back in touch with her to again discuss her meeting with the attorney.

The officer gave Mackenzie a slight bow of his head. "Thank you, Miss Adams, for your time and cooperation. Until another time." He closed his iPad and glanced around the room. "The same to each of you. Please don't hesitate to phone me if you think of anything pertinent to this investigation."

After taking in everyone's nod of consent, Captain Sprinsky exited the room, and the others followed behind him, each to his or her own destination. Mr. Huntington escorted the detective to the door.

Mackenzie stepped into the hall to return to her room but paused at the sound of her name. She looked back to see Trace eyeing her from just inside the living room. She flinched. Her hair was barely combed, and she wore no makeup; she figured she must look pitiful.

Seeming to read her thoughts, he smiled. "You look fine. I wanted to speak with you last night, but I ended up working late, which altered my plans to move back to my home." He sighed, and then glanced at the briefcase in his hand. Normally, I don't work on Saturdays, but things at the office are piling up. I'm glad Uncle Drew is returning to work next week. Up early, I was about to leave for the office, when Captain Sprinsky arrived to inform us of Jason's death. So difficult to believe."

Bewilderment donned her features. "Unfathomable."

Trace laid his hand on her arm. "Will you be okay?"

"Did Captain Sprinsky say how it happened?"

Trace nodded. "His housekeeper found him on the floor of his den when she arrived to work around six o'clock this morning. He'd been shot in the head early last evening, according to the coroner. The murderer gunned him down through one of the glass doors leading to his patio."

Mackenzie blanched when nausea swept through her. She stood unmoving, willing the sensation to pass. After a moment, she breathed deeply. *Could Mr. Huntington have carried out his threat after all? Was that the errand he mentioned when we were unloading my car?* She sighed deeply. Why had she been the lucky one to become involved with first Jasmine's murder, then Elise's kidnapping, and now the murder of Mr. Crane, who, unlike a leopard, had changed his spots right before her eyes the previous day. "Are there any suspects at all?"

"Not according to the captain. At least not yet. Nor a motive. He seemed to regard Uncle Drew as a possible suspect when he learned from Greg about the dissension between Uncle Drew and Jason, but given Uncle Drew's indisputable alibi for last night, Captain Sprinsky seemed to lay his suspicions to rest."

Mackenzie frowned. "May I ask your uncle's whereabouts at the time of Jason's death?"

The space between Trace's eyes puckered. "He stopped by a client's house to have him sign the paperwork for an offer on the man's property. Why do you ask?"

Mackenzie's shoulders relaxed. "He and I arrived home about the same time last night, so we walked into the house together. He said an errand after work had detained him from arriving home at his usual time. You can imagine what I thought when the captain said Mr. Crane had been murdered early last evening. Especially after we witnessed firsthand Mr. Huntington's threat to kill Mr. Crane." She sighed. "However, anger toward a person doesn't always contrive a motive for murder."

"That's true. Uncle Drew can be unmovable in his business dealings, but no one can make me believe he's a killer."

"I agree. He's far too kind a man." An ironic smile twitched her lips. "A disclaimer regarding his kindness toward me could be announced should he broadcast his opinion about my visit with his adversary."

Trace frowned. "I wondered about that too."

Irritation sparked in her eyes. "I'm sorry you don't approve of my meeting with Mr. Crane. But like you, I couldn't just sit around wondering about Elise and her circumstances. Another day of that and I would go insane. So while you concentrated on keeping Huntington Inc. afloat, I chose to utilize the time working toward my future." All at once, she had the uncanny feeling that she could have played the starring role in the movie *Deception* had they cast a female for the part. She turned toward the stairway, a surge of guilt weaving from her head to her toes.

Smiling, Trace held up his hands. "Sorry. Didn't mean to upset you. Maybe my concern had to do with possible competition."

Mackenzie couldn't resist the twinkle in his eyes. Tension uncoiled from her shoulders. "You're forgiven."

He snapped his fingers. "Say, we never got around to that dinner date." He bowed ceremoniously. "Miss Adams, would you consider allowing me the privilege of dining with you this evening?" Upright again, he sobered. "With Elise still missing, I realize it won't be the joyful occasion I desire, but time away from the house might help take our mind off her dilemma, at least for a little while."

Mackenzie's feelings warred within her. "I don't know, Trace. Perhaps we should wait. I would hate not to be here if the police found her and brought her home." *So now the child becomes your scapegoat. Why don't you just say, "Look, Trace, I know you're a great guy, but I don't want to have anything to do with you?"* Mackenzie focused on the toe of her sandal and then closed her eyes. Deception seemed to have a collage of facets.

Sighing, she raised her head. "I guess we have to eat regardless of the situation we're experiencing."

"I promise it won't be that bad, Mackenzie."

She looked into his eyes, and the wistful plea she saw made the decision for her. Her lips curved slightly. "Sorry. I didn't mean to sound so glum." She gave him her brightest smile. "I would be delighted to have dinner with you, Mr. Patterson."

Trace took her hand in his and held it against his lips momentarily. When he relinquished his hold, he said, "I'll pick you up at six. Okay?"

His gentleness was so unlike anything she'd experienced in the past that she found it hard to breathe. Unable to pry words from her mouth, she nodded. He smiled in a way that told her he understood her discomfiture. Lifting his hand, Trace waved a good-bye before he strode toward the door. "See you later."

After standing immobile until she caught a good breath, she then moved to the foyer window. Trace glanced her way and waved from his car. His grin seemed to indicate he'd known she would be observing his departure.

When she stepped into her apartment shortly thereafter, she heard the sound of her cell phone. She rushed to the bedside table, where she'd parked it the night before. Not recognizing the number, she started not to answer the call, but curiosity won. "Hello?"

"Miss Adams, Captain Sprinsky here. I phoned the residence, and Miss Valencia was kind enough to give me your cell number. I hope you don't mind. I wanted to speak privately with you."

A twinge of fear coursed through her stomach muscles, sympathy clipping her irritation with Angie at the same time. She'd probably had a similar response at hearing the captain's voice. Mackenzie's mouth turned downward. She could just imagine how quickly the smooth-talking detective had wormed the number from Angie's lips. Mackenzie glanced at her wristwatch. He couldn't have driven more than a few blocks before he'd rung the house. "No. How can I help you, sir?" *Like I don't know.*

"I thought we might meet for lunch today. I have some additional questions I believe you can answer for me. How about meeting me at the Pig Pit at twelve sharp?"

"The Pig Pit?"

He chuckled. "Yes, the best barbecue eatery this side of Memphis. A little hole-in-the-wall establishment just down the street from the precinct. I promise you won't go away hungry."

"Okay, sounds good. I do need directions, though."

Mackenzie parked her car and walked the short distance to the café, willing the jitters in her stomach to calm. She'd just entered the door, when the captain stepped up beside her, as if he'd been watching for her. "Right this way, Miss Adams. We have a table right over there," he said, nodding toward the center of the café. Lightly pressing his palm against her back, he wove them through the crowd waiting to be seated.

Mackenzie raised an eyebrow. "We?" she said, tilting back her head to gaze up at him. Before he had time to answer, he pulled out a chair from a table for four and offered it to Mackenzie. She glanced at the policewoman sitting on the opposite side, her bright smile welcoming. The gesture of friendship vanquished the streak of anxiety that slashed across Mackenzie's chest. To her surprise, Captain Sprinsky leaned forward and gave the policewoman a kiss on her cheek. Once seated, he turned to Mackenzie.

"Miss Adams, I'd like to introduce my wife, Officer Laura Sprinsky. Laura, Miss Mackenzie Adams of Park House. Laura is the dispatcher at the station. I hope you don't mind, but I took the liberty of ordering for us, since Laura has to be back at her desk by one. I don't think you'll be disappointed."

Mackenzie reached out to take Laura's outstretched hand; the officer's grip was firm but warm. "If the food is anything like you described on the phone," Mackenzie said, turning to the captain, "I'm sure whatever you've chosen will be superb."

Captain Sprinsky returned Mackenzie's smile, but his expression turned serious seconds later. "Miss Adams, since we don't have a lot of time, I'd like to get straight to the point. When I spoke to Miss Valencia earlier, she indicated that you were indiscreetly investigating Mrs. Huntington's homicide and that she had, in a sense, aided your quest." He eyed Mackenzie with a look of mild disapproval. "Against my warning, I might add."

Mackenzie looked down, her fair complexion turning pink. "Yes, sir. I'm guilty as charged. I seem to have been born with an above-average gene of curiosity, which, in this case, has become an unquenchable thirst to discover the killer."

"Yes, I recall you saying something to that effect when we discussed Mrs. Huntington's death a couple weeks ago." He paused while the waitress placed their plates in front of them.

"Oh my," Mackenzie said when she eyed the sliced brisket sandwich oozing with barbecue sauce. "This looks and smells wonderful."

Laura laughed. "Wait until you taste it."

When the waitress had refilled their tea glasses and departed, Mackenzie bit into her sandwich and brushed her napkin across her lips a moment later. She smiled at Laura. "You're right—it's delicious."

Captain Sprinsky cleared his throat. The two women turned his way.

"Miss Valencia also indicated she'd encouraged you to discuss with me your theory regarding a possible killer in this case , but you'd hesitated because you thought I might, ah"—he smiled—"be unappreciative of your supposition."

Again, Mackenzie colored. *Just wait, Angie. When I get home, you will get an earful from me.* "Yes, sir."

Captain Sprinsky eyed Mackenzie. She wanted to sink into the floor at his next words. "Please don't be upset with your friend. I think I intimidate her. Unintentionally, I assure you." He paused to take a breath. "I promise, Miss Adams, I will take into consideration everything you can tell me with the highest respect."

Mackenzie glanced at the officers—first at Laura, who nodded an encouragement, and then at Captain Sprinsky. She sighed, wonderment encircling her features. Never in her wildest imaginings had she thought she would be in central Arkansas, sitting with two police officers in a café named the Pig Pit, about to disclose her hypothesis in a murder case. She could just imagine what her parents would say if they could see her now.

Chapter 15

*A*fter Mackenzie supplied Captain Sprinsky with the details that led her to believe that Greg Martin had killed Jasmine, the captain drummed his fingers on the plastic red-and-white checkered tablecloth. "Your summation has merit, Miss Adams. Especially since I hadn't been informed about his interest in the deceased. Do you believe she sanctioned his regard for her?"

"No. Not after Mr. Crane—" Mackenzie's eyes widened. She lowered her eyelashes, unable to bear the captain's scrutiny.

"What about Mr. Crane, Miss Adams?" he asked, frowning.

Mackenzie eyed her half-eaten sandwich. She started to take another bite but took a drink of her tea instead. "Well, sir," she said after dabbing the corners of her mouth with her napkin, "Mr. Crane and I didn't have time to discuss the late Mrs. Huntington's relationship with her daughter, because the conversation took a turn, and our discussion was more about *his* relationship with the deceased. Just before I left, he stated that we could talk about Mrs. Huntington's relationship with Elise another time, suggesting I schedule another appointment."

"I see. And what did you learn about the relationship between the two adults?"

"Mr. Crane couldn't seem to stop talking about Mrs. Huntington—so much so that it didn't take me long to discern his love for her. When I questioned his feelings, he admitted they'd loved each other." The space between Mackenzie's eyebrows narrowed. "It's my understanding Mr. Crane voiced this to you."

Captain Sprinsky nodded. "He did."

"It wasn't until later—after studying a photograph of Mrs. Huntington and Elise placed near his desk—that I realized the resemblance between Mr. Crane and the baby. Observing my shocked expression, he became aware I'd perceived that Elise's father could not be Mr. Huntington."

Both the captain and his wife leaned forward, surprise written on their faces. "Are you saying, Miss Adams," Laura said, "that Mr. Crane declared himself to be the father of Mrs. Huntington's child?"

"Yes. He laughed and said that my intuitiveness had uncovered another of his and Jasmine's secrets." Mackenzie's eyes widened. "I had no idea Mr. Crane withheld that information from you."

The captain leaned back in his chair and cupped his chin between the thumb and forefinger of his hand. "It's definitely a meal for thought."

Laura glanced at her watch and stood from her chair. "Sorry, dear, but I have to get back to the station." She smiled at Mackenzie. "Great to have met you. I'm sorry your first time to this part of the country has been so traumatic for you." She gave her husband a quick kiss. "See you this evening. Try not to be too late."

Captain Sprinsky said, "Will do my best, but you know what it's like sometimes."

Laura's expression turned sad. "Afraid I do." Giving Mackenzie a wave, Laura strode toward the door.

Captain Sprinsky observed his wife's exit from the café and then surveyed his dining partner. "So, Miss Adams, do you have any thoughts on who kidnapped the Huntington child?"

Mackenzie's eyes narrowed with thought. "Lacey Carmichael had come to my mind in the beginning, but when you said she'd moved to Tennessee before Elise disappeared, I dropped the notion. To be honest, after meeting her, I didn't perceive her as the aggressive type." Mackenzie frowned. "Although she was adamant about her innocence regarding the theft of Mrs. Huntington's missing necklace." Mackenzie noted the surprise on the detective's face. Her expression turned scornful. "Mr. Martin wasted no time in telling me the reason for Lacey's dismissal the day I arrived at Park House."

"You don't seem to care much for Mr. Martin," the captain said, smiling.

"That's putting it mildly, sir. Back to Lacey. Do you think she might have kidnapped Elise for revenge?"

"I've considered the possibility."

A moment later, Mackenzie waved away the thought. "She just didn't strike me as having the initiative to come up with the idea." Inspiration ignited Mackenzie's features, her eyes dancing. "Unless ..."

Captain Sprinsky settled back against his chair. "Unless?"

"She had help. And as of today, the one person I can think of who had the most interest, plus the ways and means to pull off a kidnapping, would have been Jason Crane. If I recall, Greg stated the day of the kidnapping that he and Lacey were no longer seeing each other, implying she had someone else. What if the new boyfriend had been Jason Crane? He could have worn a disguise and been the kidnapper who drove the car in their getaway." Mackenzie stared at the detective, her gaze hopeful. "Lacey could have lied to her landlady, the move nothing more than a ruse. Maybe she's right here in Little Rock, hiding Elise."

Captain Sprinsky sighed. "Believe me, Miss Adams, your theory about Mr. Crane is plausible, one that I've already checked out, having been aware of the dissension between him and Mr. Huntington. And even more so now that I know his connection to the child. But when I questioned his secretary, she collaborated Mr. Crane's story—that he'd been in his office, conferring with a client, at the time of the kidnapping."

"Well, talk about the fish that ran off with the bait, line, and the pole to boot," Mackenzie said, her shoulders slumping inward. "Guess that leaves me back at square one."

An ironic smile captured the captain's lips. "I find myself in that position often. In police business, that's the name of the game. We just keep theorizing and digging for evidence until we come up with a conclusive answer to the crime."

She began to pleat the corner of her napkin. "We all keep hoping against hope that you will find Elise soon. Sometimes I think it would be better to face the fact that she didn't survive the kidnapping rather than deal with the ongoing question of her whereabouts."

"But if the former were true, Miss Adams, there would be no room for expectation. Hope is the predecessor to faith. Without hope, we cannot trust. Remember that, Miss Adams."

Mackenzie lifted her eyelashes to scan his features, desiring to partake of the wisdom she'd heard in his voice. "Thank you, sir. I believe I will."

Captain Sprinsky shifted his weight in the chair and reached for his tea glass. "What about Mr. Crane? Got any ideas about his murder?"

Starting to reach for her handbag, she paused, a deep frown marring her countenance. So caught up in Jason's disclosure about his relationship with the deceased, she'd forgotten to ask if he'd been the elusive eavesdropper she'd heard skittering away from the office door following her meeting with Mr. Huntington on the day she arrived at Park House. And now she would never know for certain. Mackenzie sighed. "It's difficult to comprehend that less than twenty-four hours ago, I sat face-to-face with him—a man I'd considered a possible killer has instead been killed. To answer your question, no, not at all." She lifted her chin and smiled at the detective, her eyes twinkling with mischief. "But given time, I might come up with something."

The captain stared momentarily at Mackenzie, a hint of admiration mingled with frustration in his eyes. "Miss Adams, again, I caution you. It's not that we don't appreciate your efforts to aid our investigations, but you're venturing into dangerous territory. Should you question the wrong person in this real-life drama, that scene, along with one of the actors, might end up on the cutting-room floor."

As she took in the officer's expression, Mackenzie's eyes widened. For once, words escaped her.

Captain Sprinsky tilted his head sideways, eyeing her reaction, and then lifted an eyebrow. "I see my meaning is clear."

She nodded. "Yes, perfectly." Mackenzie unstrapped her purse from the back of the chair and pointed to the meal check. "What do I owe for my sandwich and drink?"

Captain Sprinsky waved away her offer. "Lunch is on me."

"Thanks, sir." Setting aside his statement to contemplate later, Mackenzie glanced around the café and grinned. "Wait until I text my friends. They'll never believe I ate in a place called the Pig Pit."

He laughed. "Can't argue about the cuisine, though." Seeming to realize that she had nothing further to contribute to their discussion, he stood from his chair. "Thank you, Miss Adams, for your help."

She shook his outstretched hand. "My pleasure. If I discover anything else, I'll phone you," she said, her eyes glittering with laughter.

"Please do. And, Miss Adams," he said, laying his hand on her arm, "do be careful."

She tossed him a look of appreciation. "Yes, sir. I will." She observed the change in his expression, which switched from concern to doubt housed in a slight smile. She grinned. "I promise."

Late that afternoon, Mackenzie took one last look in her dresser mirror to admire the simple black dress she'd purchased that afternoon following her lunch with Captain Sprinsky and his wife, noting that the extra pounds she'd gained before her arrival at Park House had started to disappear. She glanced toward the nursery door. There was no way could she rejoice, considering the cause for her loss of appetite. She hoped Trace wouldn't think he'd wasted his money on her once their evening had ended. A knock interrupted her thoughts. She looked down to read the time on her watch. Had he arrived early for their date? She opened the door to find Mr. Huntington standing in the hallway. She moved aside to invite him in her room, but he stood transfixed.

"I wonder if I might have a word with you, Miss Adams."

Mackenzie motioned toward the other side of the room. "Of course, won't you come in?"

"I'd rather speak with you in my office, if you don't mind."

"Sure, just give me a second." She stepped over to her dresser and picked up her evening bag, her heart beginning to pound. Had Mr. Huntington, who oozed with tradition, found out about her dinner date with Trace and decided to reprimand her for crossing the line of protocol between her—a mere servant in his household—and his nephew? Or worse, had he heard of Elise's demise? She swallowed hard. *Oh, please. Anything but that.* Maybe he intended to fire her for the meeting with Mr. Crane. Closing the door to follow her employer down the staircase, another thought carrying both sadness and relief entered her mind. If so, her worries about an involvement with Trace Patterson would not be a concern.

Once they were seated in the office, Mr. Huntington turned to Mackenzie. "Miss Adams, I'd like to apologize for my outburst this morning when Captain Sprinsky met with all of us. Just because I despised

Crane didn't give me cause to embarrass you. I understand that at this moment in time, all of us need to focus on something that will help keep us sane in an insane situation. It seems in your case, you've chosen to do research for a future degree." His eyes narrowed with curiosity. "So your doctorate will be about relationships between mothers and daughters?"

Mackenzie held her hands against her lap to still her trembling fingers. "Actually, my study will include different types of family relationships in different settings, a subject I've been interested in for several years. And, sir, no need to apologize. I should have come to you first for answers to my questions regarding your family. But you heard my reasoning earlier for this mistake."

He bowed his head. "Yes. Thank you for your consideration. May I ask how Mr. Crane described Jasmine's relationship with our daughter?"

"We didn't get around to that, actually. Mr. Crane talked for the most part about his friendship with Mrs. Huntington, their close relationship beginning when they were children."

"Yes. Quite chummy," Mr. Huntington muttered, his eyes darkening.

Mackenzie sat up straighter, catching the slight sneer that twisted the corners of his mouth. "Sorry, sir, I didn't catch that."

He looked surprised and then grew impassive. "Nothing important, Miss Adams. So in essence, your visit with Jason proved to be insubstantial where your studies are concerned."

"Yes, sir. We ran out of time before we could talk about mother and daughter. But he did say wonderful things about your wife. He seemed to value her as both friend and client."

Mr. Huntington grew quiet momentarily. "We both valued her." He took in Mackenzie's rapt attention. "In different ways, of course." He buried his face in his hands and then lifted his head to stare across the room, a strange glint in his narrowed eyes. "Jasmine meant more to me than anyone will ever know. Only death could have separated us."

Mackenzie studied her employer, compassion filling her soul. What a burden of grief this man had been forced to bear! She lowered her eyelashes to hide the sheen of moisture in her eyes. Could it be he'd not been aware of the true relationship between his wife and Mr. Crane? Had all his allegations in the arguments that Angie had overheard been instead just jealous accusations?

Although he'd loved his wife, perhaps their age difference had been an obstacle in their lack of closeness. And her husband had resented her friendship with Jason for that reason. Makenzie sighed. Maybe Jason had been correct in his assumption that Jasmine hadn't told Mr. Huntington her intentions to leave him. Observing the sorrow in Mr. Huntington's eyes, she hoped that had been the case.

At that moment, he seemed to notice Mackenzie's appearance. "Why, Miss Adams, how elegant you look. I'm so sorry. I had forgotten this was the weekend. I seem to lose track of days lately." He smiled. "You must have a date."

They both turned at the sound of someone entering the open doorway. "Yes, she does, Uncle Drew." Trace grinned. "With yours truly." He walked over to Mackenzie and took her hand to help her from the chair. He ignored the surprised look on his uncle's face. "And now, if you'll excuse us, we'll be on our way. Don't want to be late for our reservations." Trace winked at his uncle. "I'm sure you understand. See you later, Uncle Drew."

Mackenzie barely had time for a quick wave to her openmouthed employer before Trace ushered her through the door.

"Oh great, Trace. Nice way to let me know you hadn't told your uncle about our dinner engagement," she said, sliding into the passenger seat of the Lexus. She narrowed her eyes at him before he closed her door. "You'd better pray I still have a job when we get home."

Trace laughed. "Now, Mackenzie, don't be miffed. I thought it a perfect opportunity to brief him about our plans. Uncle Drew may be stodgy at times with his old-style logic, but he's bendable." He read the misgiving in her eyes. "Just trust me, okay?"

Mackenzie wilted, the little boy pleading in his eyes breaching her irritation. A smile touched her lips. "Okay. I'll trust you, just this one time."

Later, the two of them seated at a table in what Mackenzie believed to be a five-star restaurant, she glanced around wondering if it were the same location where Angie had witnessed the romantic exchange between Jasmine and Mr. Crane. Once the waiter had taken their orders, she smiled at Trace.

"This place is lovely. That chandelier over there is exquisite. I've never seen one like it."

Trace glanced toward the entryway of the restaurant. "I agree. This hotel was built around the turn of the century. A few years ago, several investors bought the place, the renovation taking it back to resemble its original state."

Again, Mackenzie took in her surroundings. "Well, they did an awesome job. Was Huntington Inc. involved in the transaction?"

"Yes. In fact, Uncle Drew let me handle the sale from beginning to end. He must have thought I did well, because a few weeks later, he made me vice president of the company."

"Do you enjoy that position?"

"It's a lot of responsibility, but yeah, I'm happy with my job. With all that's happening lately, my shoulders are weighted down at the moment, but once Elise is found and Uncle Drew has recovered more from Jasmine's death, hopefully things at the office will be better. A boost in the economy would help too. But who knows how soon we'll see that become a reality. In this part of the country, land-development sales have slowed to a snail's pace. If the trend continues, I don't know how long the company will survive."

Recalling her conversation with Captain Sprinsky, Mackenzie smiled. "All a person can do is hope for the best."

Trace nodded. "And pray."

"That too," she said, thankful that the waiter approached their table at that moment. She eyed his careful placement of their food.

About halfway through her chateaubriand and various small talk, Mackenzie could hold back her curiosity no longer. "Trace, would you tell me about Mrs. Huntington? I know I have no right to ask, but the thought of her intrigues me."

Trace smiled. "Is your interest strictly curiosity, or does it have to do with your research on family relationships?"

"A bit of both," she said, smiling. "On the day of her funeral, I saw and heard Mrs. Slater's hatred for Mrs. Huntington, but Angie has a different view—said she'd been treated well by the deceased. With such conflicting views rolling around in my head, I thought a third opinion would help me better understand your uncle's wife. Did you have a good rapport with her?"

Trace stared into space. "Once I got to know her, I decided Uncle Drew had made a mistake in marrying her. Too much age difference, for one thing, and totally opposite in personality."

"I've heard it said those types of relationships are the best. The couple spends their lives celebrating each other's uniqueness—or something of that nature."

Trace laughed, but the sound held no mirth. "Not in their case. Uncle Drew had his ideas of how their marriage should be, and she had hers—never did the twain meet, in my estimation. When Elise came along, I think they both tried to come to terms for her sake, but after a while, Jasmine seemed to renege on her part of the bargain. One time, when I'd stopped by for a visit, I heard her tell Uncle Drew that he expected her to live like a caged animal, and she gave her refusal to abide with him in those circumstances"—Trace grinned—"in words I refuse to ever repeat."

"Did you form any kind of friendship at all?"

"Our paths didn't cross often, mostly at business functions and holiday events at the house. When we did have a chance to talk, our conversations were superficial at best. We didn't have much in common. And I seldom found her at home when I had occasion to drop by for a visit with Uncle Drew."

"Angie told me she played a lot of golf with Mr. Crane." Mackenzie straightened her posture, watching, waiting to see how Trace would respond to her statement. Did he know about their affair?

Trace pulled a long breath. "Yes, in spite of opposition from Uncle Drew. Just before Jasmine disappeared, he told me he intended to put a stop to their frequent outings. When I suggested he take up the game and play with Jasmine in place of Jason, he rejected the idea, saying he had no time to dillydally on a golf course—he had a business to run."

Shadows of pain and sadness dimmed the brightness in Trace's eyes. "Uncle Drew acted as if he'd found the pot of gold at the end of the rainbow when he brought Jasmine to Park House. But a few months prior to her death, I noticed a change in him; his zest for life had dwindled to a large degree. I wouldn't have been surprised at all had I heard one or the other had filed for a divorce."

Mackenzie put down her fork and reached for her water glass. "That surprises me. Mr. Huntington seems to have been devoted to her."

"Yes, I believe he loved her. But being the proud man he is, I think rather than admit to a loveless marriage, he transferred most of the devotion he'd held for his wife to his child."

"That's certainly not questionable. Your uncle adores Elise. I'm sorry his marriage didn't work."

"Same here. Everyone deserves a chance at happiness."

At that moment, the waiter approached their table to take their plates. He returned shortly to place the dessert menu in front of them. After choosing a decadent chocolate confection they could share, Mackenzie studied Trace from beneath her lowered eyelashes while she added cream and sugar to her decaf coffee. She decided to turn the conversation in another direction.

"Speaking of devotion, I saw that in you when you talked about your sister."

Trace looked puzzled. "My sister?"

"Yes, during the get-together at the house following Jasmine's funeral, you started to tell me about her, but we got interrupted."

Trace allowed her to take the first bite of the brownie topped with chocolate-covered ice cream before he spoke. "She always referred to me as Brat, but I knew she loved me." Trace grinned. "Guess I deserved the name. I was the typical ornery little brother. When Dad deserted us, she became my surrogate mother. Mom's despair over his leaving kept her in bed most days—that and her addiction to alcohol. Therefore, Natalie, seven years older than me, took it upon herself to see to my care."

"This was before you came to live with Mr. Huntington, right?"

"Yes. I moved to Park House following my mother's death. She overdosed on sleeping pills a few weeks after I found my sister hanging from a rope inside our garage."

Makenzie gasped. "Oh Trace. I'm so sorry."

He reached across the table and placed his hand over hers. "Thank you."

"Do you know why she took her life?"

"The coroner's report stated that she'd recently aborted a baby." Trace shook his head. "Just barely sixteen and pregnant. The police believed she killed herself because her boyfriend refused to marry her. I'm sure that played a part, but having the sole care of a drunken mother and a younger brother, I think the thought of another responsibility was too overwhelming for her. So she had the abortion and then couldn't live with what she'd done. I'm told suicide is common among those who've had abortions.

"After I grew older and understood the reality of what she'd done, not only did I suffer guilt for not coming home sooner, but I seethed with anger for a long time. A brutal, selfish act had stolen my sister, my mother, and a niece or nephew I would never know. When I turned my life over to God, I was at last able to forgive my sister for her senseless deed, although the guilt and anger hung on for quite some time. But thank God, it's no longer a problem."

Nausea gripped Mackenzie's stomach. She rose from the table. "Excuse me," she said, hurrying to find the ladies' room. A moment later, she held a wet paper towel against her face, keeping back the dry heaves that surged to her throat. A few minutes later, her composure once again intact, she returned to their table and saw concern darkening the usual brilliance in Trace's eyes.

"Mackenzie, please forgive me," he said, surveying her pale complexion. "I didn't realize the story of my sister's death would upset you."

"I'm okay, Trace. Really." She rubbed her hand across her forehead. "All of a sudden, I seemed to be locked in a room with death all around me. Your statement regarding the reason for your sister's death, well, to use your word, overwhelmed me briefly. I had to escape for a few moments. And then there's Elise. I try to curb my thoughts about her, but I keep seeing her face, wondering if she's been harmed in any way or ..." Mackenzie bit her lip.

Trace reached for her hand and held it tightly in his. "We just have to keep praying and trusting that God is watching over her." Trace ran his other hand through his hair, exasperation tightening the muscles in his face. "At this point, that's all we can do.

"Mackenzie, enough about my family. Let's talk about you. Other than the information on your résumé"—he grinned—"some of which I've seen in action with your care of Elise, and the fact that you have the loveliest eyes I've ever seen on a woman, I don't know much about you. In fact, I'm definitely interested in who or what has caused the pain I see too often in your eyes."

Mackenzie eyed her plate. "There's really not much to tell. Until three weeks ago, I'd lived in Arizona my entire life, growing up in a middle-class home—my dad is over a group of IT engineers in a technology plant, and my mom is a teacher. As you know, I graduated from a master's program at Arizona State, and"—she smiled—"here I am."

"Aren't you leaving something out—like the reason you left your family and friends to take a job halfway across the United States? Or maybe I should ask his name?"

Mackenzie recoiled at the question. How could she tell Trace about her involvement with Zack? He'd probably usher her out of the restaurant and out of his life the moment she finished sharing the ugly details. Seeing the determination in Trace's eyes, she tucked a stray lock of hair behind her ear.

"Zack. His name is Zachary Gilbert. I met him in my junior year at college. For me, it was love at first sight. I thought he loved me too. After dating the rest of the year, we decided to live together while we completed our education, his a doctorate degree. We planned to marry in the spring following graduation. Last Christmas, he presented me with an engagement ring. No girl could have been happier than me. A few months later, something happened that challenged our love. Later, when I discovered he'd been seeing someone else while I worked to help get him through school, I broke off the engagement." Mackenzie closed her eyes, allowing a tear to escape. "My trust in men is nil to none."

"Are you still in love with him?" Trace said, massaging the back of her hand with his thumb.

Mackenzie shook her head. "Not on your life. In fact, I hate him—and myself. I allowed him to destroy everything good within me." Violent sobs she couldn't control shook her body from head to toe. Aware that people were staring at them, she opened her bag, her hands trembling so badly that she had difficulty undoing the clasp. Unable to find a tissue, she took the handkerchief Trace offered to her. A moment later, she stood. "Please take me home now, Trace," she said, glancing around. "Please! Get me out of here."

Once inside her room, Mackenzie flung off her shoes and fell onto her bed. How could she have thought she could make a new life away from the bitterness and pain she'd endured? The effects of her mistakes had trailed right along with her like a string of cans tied to a bumper. But these cans, unlike those found on a car to celebrate a wedding, were filthy, stained with the garbage she longed to leave behind her.

On their way home, Trace had been considerate of her feelings, offering a kind ear to her. But she had eluded his questions. No way could she tell him the whole truth. It would destroy any affection he held for her, just as the selfish act he'd referred to earlier had destroyed his sister. The slight ray of hope she'd had for true love in her future had been blotted out by a few spoken words. How could she continue to live with the deed she'd committed?

Mackenzie, my compassions fail not. My mercies are new every morning. Great is my faithfulness. Hope in me.

Mackenzie's breath caught. She raised her head from the wet pillow and sat up, pushing aside her dampened hair from her face. Those words— she'd read them before. She stood, made her way to the dresser, and opened the top drawer. She pulled the worn copy of her Bible from among her clothing. It had been more than five years since she'd held it in her hands for any length of time.

When she'd unpacked her belongings the day she arrived in Arkansas, she'd found the Bible, surprised that she had brought it with her. Turning to the book of Lamentations, she scanned the chapters for the passage of Scripture she'd recalled. Once she had the verses in sight, she strolled to the sofa and curled her legs under her as she sat down to read from the New Living Translation.

Yet I still dare to hope when I remember this;

The faithful love of the Lord never ends; His mercies never cease.

Great is his faithfulness; his mercies begin afresh each morning.

I say to myself, "The Lord is my inheritance; therefore, I will hope in him!"

The Lord is good to those who depend on him, to those who search for him.

So it is good to wait quietly for salvation from the Lord.

Mackenzie closed her Bible and set it next to her on the sofa. Tears of a different breed started to scud down her cheeks—not tears of remorse, but refreshing tears. Tears of hope. Could it be that God had not abandoned her after all?

Chapter 16

The next morning, a scent of lilac in the air, Mackenzie stood across the street from the modest, whitewashed church that had intrigued her from the first day she'd strolled Elise to the park. She tilted her head to better hear the crescendo of the organ music, the sound of the notes wafting through the walls to entice those who happened by to step inside and experience spiritual rejuvenation. The melody tugged at her heart, drawing her back to a time and place when she had uttered without reservation, "It is well with my soul."

But other thoughts warred within her, causing her to question her early morning decision to visit the quaint church. How could she dare think a simple act of faith and a few spoken words could erase the ugliness that had brought her several times of late just short of the point Trace's sister had been unable to transcend? Mackenzie closed her eyes. How often she had stood with the ever-ready bottle of sleeping pills in her hand when the pain of her sin seemed too great to bear. Even now, it sat on a shelf in her bathroom, waiting to bring relief to the guilt and shame she endured. But thus far, she'd resisted the strong urge to end her life; the thought of the heartbreak her parents would suffer had kept the temptation at bay.

She glanced over her shoulder. Perhaps she should just forget the whole idea and return to Park House. But the words of the song the organist played kept her at a standstill.

"Amazing grace, how sweet the sound that saved a wretch like me." Grace—oh, how she needed the heavenly Father's unmerited favor. Would He be willing to bestow His grace on her once again?

Eyeing the last of the stragglers as they entered the church, she glanced at the time on her watch. Ten minutes and the service would begin. She bit her lip. What should she do? The notes of the familiar hymn trailed into silence. Tightening her lips, she stepped across the pavement, refusing to hesitate another moment, lest her courage fail her altogether. Once inside the foyer, she stopped cold, her eyes widening.

No other person in sight, Mackenzie observed the approach of a tall, trim woman who appeared to be in her mid-to-late seventies. She reached to shake Mackenzie's hand, distributing a service bulletin at the same time. *Good heavens,* Mackenzie thought, staring at the lady dressed in hot pink from her head to the shoes on her feet. On another person, the coordinates might not have been unattractive, but the brassy red-gray curls that streaked in all directions from beneath the pillbox hat, a style made popular in the sixties by Jacquelyn Kennedy, caused Mackenzie to do a double take. Recovering her aplomb quickly, she returned the woman's wide smile that began in her hazel eyes and traveled to her lips.

"Hello there, miss."

"Mackenzie Adams."

"Welcome to Mt. Zion Community Church. It's great to have you here." The woman peeked toward the open door. "Lovely morning, isn't it?" A slight frown appeared on her face as she studied Mackenzie.

"Yes. It is," she said, realizing the woman's friendliness downplayed her questionable taste in apparel. Mackenzie produced a mental shrug. As the young character in a popular sitcom several years back used to say, "Different strokes for different folks."

The elderly woman's breath caught. "Oh, I'm sorry. I forgot to introduce myself. I'm Zelda Simpson." She laughed. "I'm practically a fixture in this place. I've been attending this church for more years than I care to remember." She gently wrapped her freckled hand around Mackenzie's arm. "Let me direct you to a nice seat."

Mackenzie followed Zelda through the door leading into the sanctuary. About halfway down the aisle, she paused and motioned for her charge to slide into a shiny wooden pew; the young couple seated in the middle of the pew smiled their welcome. Seeing the music minister had made his way to the podium, Zelda leaned forward and whispered in Mackenzie's ear. "I'll introduce you to some of the members after church."

Before Mackenzie could respond, Zelda moved forward to take a seat close to the front of the church. Mackenzie settled into the pew, a taut smile hovering about her lips. She would squelch that plan. Not that she desired to be rude, but it had been a number of years since she'd been inside a church, and she didn't want to be swarmed by a bunch of friendly, well-meaning parishioners asking questions she wasn't ready to answer. Her smile widened at the alternate blueprint forming in her mind. She would slip out the door during the dismissal prayer, before anyone could notice her.

Mackenzie looked around at the hundred or so members. Their neighbor, Mrs. Baxter, caught Mackenzie's eye and smiled. Returning the gesture, Mackenzie noted that the congregation of all ages had expressions of anticipation, as if they looked forward to the next couple of hours. Guilt warmed her face. She hadn't experienced that feeling for some time.

The music minister invited the people to stand. A moment later, the words and music of a worship chorus filled the sanctuary. Aware that someone had stopped at the end of her pew, she glanced up to see who stood there, and a look of surprise grabbed her features. She moved to the right to make room for Trace, who smiled down at her. Within a few seconds, he lifted his voice in song, his deep bass in perfect harmony with the music.

She lowered her eyelashes, surveying him from the corners of her eyes. Had he been driving past and seen her enter the church? Or did he attend here on a regular basis? Whatever the case, something about his presence beside her seemed germane, like the satisfaction one experienced when he snapped a last puzzle piece into place, the view of the picture no longer fragmented but complete.

A slight frown touched her brow. To chase the dream of his permanency at her side would be a useless pursuit. She closed her eyes, the droop to her shoulders revealing the disappointment that weighed heavily in her mind. Their dinner the previous evening had been a bust. The anger she'd observed in Trace's eyes for his sister's deed had shattered her miniscule belief that a relationship between them beyond friendship could exist.

Besides, her medical records revealed the slim chance of her capability to give him the large family he desired in his future. The thought too disturbing, she cast it aside to concentrate on the words of the next song. In doing so, her gaze fell on a decorative plaque hanging from a sidewall of the stage at the front of the church: "All things are possible with God." *Only if one has the faith to believe it,* she thought.

Later, during the minister's message, Mackenzie's heartbeat roared. It seemed as if he'd prepared his sermon just for her. The Scriptures he read were buried deep in her memory, but hearing them again seemed to bring newness of life like a breath of fresh air. In her mind, she repeated the biblical words he'd read from Hebrews 4:16: "Let us therefore, come boldly unto the throne of grace that we may obtain mercy, and find grace to help in time of need."

Recalling her earlier mind-set just before she'd entered the church, she couldn't think of anyone at the moment who needed God's grace more than she, her allotted portion needing to spill over the rim of the container. She'd grown up believing God's grace sufficient in all things, but that was before she'd chosen to rebel against everything she'd been taught about God and His ways. How easy it had been in the past to spout those divine words when she'd encouraged her young friends in their troubles. She hadn't understood then that to walk the walk of faith required more than a simple discussion on the subject. She sighed. Even if she could trust God to forgive her, how could she find the strength to forgive herself?

Ask, Mackenzie—all you need do is ask. Does not my Word declare, "Ask and you shall receive"?

Mackenzie started at the small voice speaking to her heart. She studied her hands, which guarded her lap, the pastor's voice echoing in the room. "If we confess our sins, He is faithful and just and will forgive our sins and purify us from all unrighteousness."

First John 1:9, she thought. Not so long ago—or had it been a lifetime?—she'd quoted it often when witnessing to her peers about the love of God. Mackenzie's eyes filled with tears. How had she gotten so far away from her Savior? As if in answer to her question, one by one, she began to recall the incidents that had molded her life since high school, each taking precedence over her spiritual relationship with Christ.

When she was in college, the only job available on campus had been the coffeehouse, with just two Sundays off a month. That, along with carrying a full load of classes, had left little time for anything else. Although she'd visited a few churches in the area, none had appealed to her. The issue had become less important to her in the days to come, and she'd developed the habit of sleeping in on Sunday mornings. By the time her sophomore year had passed, the subject of spiritual education had been scratched from her thoughts.

And then she'd met Zachery Gilbert, whose debonair good looks and Irish charm had stolen her heart. Once she'd agreed to his desire for their living arrangements, she'd drifted further away from Christ in the coming months until her own ultimate despicable act had severed her from His love and grace.

But a few weeks after they'd moved in together, their fairy-tale romance began to crumble, and it ended following—

A strangled sob erupted from her throat. She held the back of her fist against her lips, hoping others nearby hadn't heard the noise. Memories of the last months with Zack barreled into her thoughts. She closed her eyes, recalling the fights, his rejection of her, and, finally, her promise to do what he asked, because she knew she could never bear living without him.

She sensed Trace's gaze toward her, but she kept her head down. A moment later, she gripped the handkerchief he wove into her hand, hardly aware of the pressure his arm made on her shoulders. She held her eyelashes tightly against her cheeks, trying to think of anything but the one recollection she desired to erase forever. Yet the memory crashed into her mind like two trains colliding on a single track. Mackenzie began to shake, every detail of the vivid event clear, the words she'd uttered forever engraved in her mind.

"No! Stop! Please stop. I've changed my mind." The words had sounded slurred in her ears. The nurse's expression hard like stone, she'd grabbed Mackenzie's shoulders and pushed downward until Mackenzie had again rested against the cold surgical table, hardly aware of the prick the syringe needle made in her arm a moment later, the anesthesia prohibiting further resistance.

Cold dampness formed on Mackenzie's arms; nausea burned in her throat. Her breath quickened. She had to get out of the church before she suffocated—or worse. She glanced around from beneath her eyelashes. No one other than Trace seemed to be aware of her discomfiture; everyone focused on the pastor and his sermon. She stood, ignoring Trace's startled look. Thankful he allowed her to enter the aisle, she hurried to the back of the church. An usher, noting her approach, opened the door that closed off the foyer. The Scripture the minister read as she made her way to the exit rang in her ears like the sound of tolling bells. "'Therefore being justified by faith, we have peace with God through our Lord Jesus Christ.' And now, dear friends, let us stand to sing our closing hymn."

Peace? How she yearned for it. But instead, she was cursed—cursed by the memory of that fateful moment when her life had been destroyed all because of her selfish love for Zack. If all of a sudden the oceans of the world became one body of water filled to overflowing with forgiveness, it would not be enough to atone for her sins, even if she drowned in it.

Once outside the church, she ran down the steps and across the street. She slowed her stride once on the sidewalk leading to Park House. She glanced over her shoulder when she heard Trace calling her name. She wadded his handkerchief, now drenched, in the ball of her fist. *Why can't he just leave me alone?*

Catching up to her, he stepped in front of Mackenzie and clasped her shoulders in his hands. "Mackenzie, please tell me what's wrong. I know it's more than a broken engagement."

She wrenched out of his grasp and turned aside. "Believe me, it's nothing you want to hear," she muttered.

Sighing deeply, Trace shoved his hands in his pockets. "I can't help you, Mackenzie, unless—"

"Oh Miss Adams! Miss Adams!"

They both turned to see Zelda Simpson among other members spilling out of the church. She walked toward them, swinging a purse in her hand. "Miss Adams, I believe this belongs to you," she said, holding up the shoulder bag.

Mackenzie glanced at her side and frowned. Lifting her eyelashes, she smiled, a look of gratitude in her eyes. "Thank you. I didn't realize I'd left it." She reached for the handbag and strapped it on her shoulder, turning away from the wise assessment she read in Zelda's eyes. Queasiness again formed in the pit of Mackenzie's stomach. Had her thoughts been discerned by the kind woman?

"Yes, thank you, Mrs. Simpson. So kind of you," Trace said. He scanned the sky, pointing upward at the sun. "But you must get out of this heat." A teasing glint appeared in his eyes. "Our life group would be mortified should you become ill and not be able to bring your delicious chocolate cake to our meeting next week."

She laughed, waving away his banter. "Well, now. We can't let that happen, can we?" She turned to Mackenzie. "Would you like to walk me home? I just live a few houses down from the park. And please stay for lunch. I have a small roast and vegetables in the Crock-Pot. And I hate to eat alone."

"Uh, I—"

Trace moved forward a step. "I'd be glad to escort you home, Mrs. Simpson."

She threw him a discouraging glance. "Thank you, Trace, but I prefer Miss Adams's company today. I'd love to have you another time, though." She laid a hand on his arm. "You need to be with your uncle today." She moved her head back and forth, the pink feather in her hat swaying in sync with her movements. "He must be near to inconsolable. I keep praying his troubles will cause him to seek a relationship with God. So sad to think a person would reject such healing love."

Mackenzie looked away, her insides knotting. She gritted her teeth. Why did she feel all of a sudden that she had no control over her own life? She observed the stream of understanding that flowed between the two, the subject of which Mackenzie failed to decipher. She gave herself a mental scolding. It was probably nothing more than Mrs. Simpson letting him know she desired to show hospitality to a stranger. Her parents had often given similar invitations to visitors at their church.

Trace turned to Mackenzie. "You can't go wrong. Mrs. Simpson is one of the best cooks I know."

Mackenzie frowned. "But I—"

Zelda took Mackenzie's arm. "Do come along, dear. The temperature is rising by the minute. I believe you said your name is Mackenzie?"

She nodded and then threw Trace a glance over her shoulder. He just smiled and waved her forward. "Yes, it is. My parents named me after a Scottish ancestor's surname."

"Interesting. I once tried to trace my ancestral history but couldn't seem to get past my great-grandparents' lineage on both sides. I lost interest after a while. Too time consuming."

"I can see how it could be," Mackenzie said, eyeing the swings as they walked past the entrance to the park. "From your conversation with Trace, I guess you've heard about the kidnapping."

Zelda nodded. "I keep praying someone will see her and report it to the police. Such a lovely child. Trace would bring her to church with him now and again."

"So he's a regular attendee at the church?"

"Yes, since his high school days. Reverend Forester was the youth pastor back then. The members took to the boy right away, fostering him spiritually. He grew into a fine young man." Zelda chuckled, a smug expression on her face. "We are quite pleased with ourselves." She turned toward Mackenzie and winked. "And quite handsome as well." Zelda's face lit up with understanding. "It just occurred to me that you must be Elise's new caregiver. Mrs. Baxter informed me that the Huntingtons had hired a new nanny."

A sudden feeling of affection for the oddly dressed, warm-hearted woman swept over Mackenzie. "Yes. I've been here a few weeks now. When I accepted the position, I had no idea I'd find myself involved in such a tragic situation. Did you know Mrs. Huntington?"

Zelda shook her head. "Our paths never crossed." She paused and swung her arm toward a two-story house on her left, the structure built similar in design to the other Victorian homes in the area. "Well, here we are." She took a hankie from her handbag and wiped the moisture from her brow. "I think a glass of iced tea is just what we need at the moment. I've got a pitcher cooling in the fridge."

Momentarily, the two climbed the wooden steps to the wide wraparound porch encircling the house. Mackenzie eyed the white wicker furniture complete with bright, colorful cushions, arranged to draw one's eye to the wide, ornate wooden door gracing the entryway to the house.

The beauty of the stained-glass window in the door caught and held her attention. Seeming to notice Mackenzie's interest, Zelda smiled.

"My grandfather built this house and designed that window, creating the panes himself. A few years ago, I had to replace the original deteriorated door with a custom-designed one that would hold this window. I lost quite a bit of sleep over that project, praying the panes would survive the transition to the new door."

Mackenzie nodded. "I totally understand. I'm sure it's hard to find that kind of craftsmanship today."

Once inside and sipping her tea, Mackenzie waited in the living room while Mrs. Simpson changed her clothes. Her hostess soon reappeared in designer capris and a matching top. Somehow the outfit, although chic, seemed out of place amid the out-of-date decor that covered several decades. Mackenzie smiled within. Her new friend certainly couldn't be classed as conventional.

When they'd cooled a bit, Mackenzie helped Mrs. Simpson get lunch on the table, and Zelda filled their glasses again with the refreshing sweet tea. Mackenzie relished the meal, grateful that her hostess had kept the conversation light. After the kitchen had been restored to order a short time later, Mrs. Simpson suggested a tour of her house. "With your interest in the door earlier, I thought you might wish to see more of my grandfather's work. He could have been a notable artist, but his first love was investments, so his paintings and such were a sideline mostly for relaxation."

"Yes, I would enjoy that," Mackenzie said, removing the apron Zelda had loaned for the cleanup.

Following the delightful excursion back through time, Mrs. Simpson again offered Mackenzie the dessert she'd declined earlier. Enjoying the older woman's company, Mackenzie decided to accept a slice of the coconut cream pie just to extend the visit awhile longer.

"Delicious," Mackenzie said between bites. She took a sip of her hot tea from the delicate china cup. "Thank you for your hospitality, Mrs. Simpson. It's been a rough week for all of us at Park House. I ache so much for Elise."

Mackenzie smiled sadly. "From the moment I saw the child, I was smitten, my heart captured by her toothless grin even before I knew her name." A look of helplessness raked across Mackenzie's expression. "I'm destitute as to how I can aid in the search for her." Mackenzie glanced toward the ceiling. "I can only imagine how it must be for Mr. Huntington and Trace." She leaned forward, a look of appreciation overriding the sadness in her eyes. "But your kindness toward me today has proven to be a welcome distraction."

Zelda grew thoughtful. She set the remains of her dessert on the table next to her chair and then sent a straightforward gaze toward Mackenzie. "Were thoughts of Elise the reason for your untimely exit from the service today?"

Mackenzie's heartbeat revved up a notch. She looked away from Mrs. Simpson's penetrating scrutiny.

"I thought not," Zelda said, folding her hands across her lap. "Mackenzie, do you mind if I share a story with you?"

Mackenzie's fingers starting to shake, she darted a glance toward her hostess. "Of course not."

"Good. Because I think it's just what you need to hear."

Tensing, Mackenzie tried to think of an excuse to leave quickly, but all of a sudden, her mind seemed to be padlocked with the key nowhere in sight. She took a drink of her now-lukewarm tea to moisten her parched lips. "Oh?" she said, her voice strained.

"Yes. In 1943, a young girl close to eight years old lived in New York City. The child—a daughter of an affluent family, her father a stockbroker on Wall Street—was abducted near her home late one winter evening and taken to a remote area where the kidnapper held her captive for several days before he sold her into white slavery. Escape impossible, she realized after a few years her only hope of surviving the horrors she endured would be to help her assailants in their evil ventures. By the time she reached her twenties, she'd been promoted to a lofty position in the criminal organization, residing in a luxury penthouse in San Francisco, California."

"How horrible," Mackenzie said, staring at Zelda with wide eyes. "Had the girl been a friend of yours?"

"The only true friend I had for many years. I knew her well."

Mackenzie's brows knitted together. What purpose did Mrs. Simpson have in mind that she desired to share such bizarre events with her guest? Mackenzie leaned forward slightly. "My instinct tells me there's more to this story."

"Oh yes. Much more. During this time, the woman learned she was with child. Aware the baby would be hidden from society until old enough to be forced into the same despicable life of its mother, the young woman grew desperate to save her baby from the clutches of the underworld. One night, she escaped by climbing into the hotel laundry chute, finding sanctuary in a nearby church. The kind pastor contacted her parents, who welcomed her home with loving arms until—"

Mackenzie held up her hand. "Let me guess. Until they discovered her pregnancy and the circumstances surrounding it."

Zelda nodded. "Afraid their friends would discover the sordid lifestyle their daughter had been compelled to live, they placed her in a home for unwed mothers, the child to be adopted out to a good home. Not having the courage to defy their wishes, the daughter moved to the home right away. Her father said he would pay for her education once the child had been born, stating to his daughter that it would be best for her not to return to her childhood home, suggesting that she should make her own way in the world. At first she wanted to decline his offer, but with no place to go and afraid she'd have to return to prostitution for support, she decided it would be foolish to defy him. In those days, few jobs were available for a woman expecting a child.

"But the administrator of the unwed mother's home allowed the young woman to live and work there until she could obtain her GED. Later, she attended a nearby university. While in her junior year, she met the love of her life, and the two married upon her graduation. Although happily married, she could never get over the loss of her child."

Mackenzie's breath slowed. "Did the woman ever find out who'd adopted the baby?"

"Yes. Her husband hired a private detective to search for the child, discovering that the baby boy had died from pneumonia when but two years old."

Mackenzie gripped the arms of the chair. "So sad."

Dabbing at the corners of her eyes with her fingertips, Zelda nodded. "Depression overcame my friend. She withdrew from everyone. For months, her husband tried to persuade her to get the treatment she needed for her recovery, but she refused all his efforts, wallowing day after day in the mire of guilt and shame, her relationship with her husband growing colder each day. One morning, she couldn't handle the torture any longer. Her husband found her collapsed on the floor from an overdose of sleeping pills."

"Oh no!" Mackenzie said, gasping. She looked down, taking in her trembling fingers. Entwining them, she glanced up to see Mrs. Simpson taking in her reaction. "How terrible it must have been for the man to discover his wife's body."

Zelda looked confused momentarily and then smiled. "Oh, she didn't die. He got her to the hospital in time for the doctors to save her life." Mrs. Simpson stood and poured them another cup of tea.

"Did your friend overcome her despondency after that?"

Mrs. Simpson placed the pot on the warmer, her eyes narrowing with thought. "Not for several weeks," she said, rearranging the pillow in her chair before she sat down. "But one morning, a neighbor my friend had only met a time or two stopped by with a plate of muffins fresh out of the oven. Over tea, they became acquainted, and the neighbor invited my friend to church. Reluctant at first but desiring to repay the neighbor for her kindness, my friend accepted the invitation.

"The following Sunday, she and her husband visited the neighbor's church, and their lives changed forever that morning when, at the close of the service, they accepted the plan of salvation God has freely given to all those willing to ask His Son to dwell in their hearts and lives. Within a short time, both my friend's peace of mind and her marriage had been restored. She'll always miss the child she never had a chance to know, but now she has hope of being reunited with him one day in heaven."

Mackenzie could no longer fight the moisture that had been gathering in her eyes within the last few minutes. The tears rained onto her cheeks. Mrs. Simpson stood and lowered her posture to kneel on the rug in front of Mackenzie's chair. Zelda took hold of her guest's unsteady hands.

"Don't you see, my dear? I recognize that anguish in your eyes—the naked agony that is revealed when one loses a child. And God wants to heal you of that pain, Mackenzie, but you have to be willing to let go of it along with all the guilt and shame you are suffering."

Mackenzie raised her head to stare at her hostess; the unruly curls of Zelda's auburn-spiked hair were now pulled to the side of her head and contained beneath a large baroque hair clip. All of a sudden, Mackenzie's eyes grew wider, the tears slowing at the truth revealed in her hostess's eyes. The young woman in the story had been Mrs. Simpson.

"I do so want to believe you, but you don't understand. It's my fault I lost my child. It wasn't the same as that of your friend."

Zelda, seeming to comprehend that Mackenzie had guessed the truth, began to study her fingers still tightly wrapped around Mackenzie's hands. "But I could have forsaken all the advice I received about the proper welfare for my son and raised him on my own." Zelda drew a long sigh. "Although I'm sure my life would have been quite different. Had I chosen that path, who knows if I would have met my darling husband? Or had two other wonderful children?"

Mackenzie pulled her hands free and reached into her purse to draw out several tissues she'd stuffed into the handbag before leaving Park House. She cleaned her face the best she could. "But at least you gave a childless couple the opportunity to experience the love between a parent and child even though they only had him a short time." Mackenzie looked away. "And my parents—" A look of horror saturated her features. "It would put them into an early grave if they knew I'd deprived them of their grandchild. You see, my mother wasn't able to carry another child after my birth. I just can't see how God can forgive me for my decisions."

Mrs. Simpson stood and seated herself, taking a sip of tea before she spoke. "You'll never be able to perceive it, Mackenzie. No human can. God's forgiveness is based on divine mercy and faithfulness to His unconditional love. All we have to do is ask Him to forgive us and then accept that we've been forgiven."

Mackenzie recalled the words she'd heard in her heart while in the service that morning. "But I don't deserve to be forgiven."

"There's not a person alive who does merit God's grace. But it's ours when we believe in Him and His Word. Pastor said it best this morning when he quoted Romans 5:1: 'Therefore being justified by faith, we have peace with God through our Lord Jesus Christ.' No matter what sin we've committed, Mackenzie, when we ask for forgiveness, we are justified when we take that step of faith. Our sins are wiped away. We stand clean like the purest of snow before our Father God. *Justification* simply means 'just as if it never happened.'"

Mackenzie closed her eyes. "If only I had the courage to ask," she said softly.

Compassion flooded Zelda's face. "Would you like me to help you?"

Mackenzie nodded.

"Then just repeat what I say: 'Father God, I know I have sinned. Please forgive me. Thank you for your peace. In Jesus' name, amen.'"

As the last of the simple prayer flowed from Mackenzie's lips, an overwhelming joy filled her innermost being. It seemed an inexplicable amount of weight lifted from her shoulders. She started to laugh—an inward mirth that rolled upward to escape in Mrs. Simpson's living room. Tears of gladness fell onto her hands. Mrs. Simpson smiled and then began to laugh with Mackenzie, the two doubling over after a moment.

Once their laughter had subsided, Mackenzie sat staring into space, wonderment like a light shining on her face. She couldn't recall when she had been so carefree. Why had she waited so long to experience such divine love?

Zelda stood and began to gather their dishes. Mackenzie jumped up to assist. She paused, her teacup and saucer in her hand. "Mrs. Simpson, I have to ask. How did you know? About me, I mean."

She smiled. "When you first walked into the church this morning," she said as a sad look penetrated her features, "I saw in your eyes the agony I once wore wrapped around myself like a heavy metal garment. I knew immediately that God wanted me to help you shed your suffering. I just didn't realize it would be this soon. But thank God for His awesome ways." She laid her hand on Mackenzie's shoulder. "You will still have times the pain will return.

"But remember, you are forgiven. God's grace and your trust in Him will give you the strength to withstand the temptation to fall back into guilt and shame. Before you leave, I will give you my phone number. And, Mackenzie, do feel free to stop by anytime you need to talk." A faraway look filled her eyes. "Mrs. Townsend, the neighbor I spoke of earlier, God rest her soul, was a lighthouse on my stormy sea many a time."

Chapter 17

$\mathcal{A}$fter waving a last good-bye to Mrs. Simpson, who stood on her porch, her face a portrait of joy, Mackenzie walked along the sidewalk, desiring to skip like a kindergartener. Although Mackenzie's secret had been partially disclosed, Zelda had stated that no one would hear of it from her lips, and Mackenzie believed she could trust the elderly saint to keep her word. She hadn't questioned Mackenzie about the birth of her child, for which Mackenzie had been grateful. Most likely, Mrs. Simpson assumed Mackenzie had given her child up for adoption.

Mackenzie paused outside the door to Park House, other thoughts impairing her newly found elation. She sighed. Mr. Huntington would have to decide soon the feasibility of her employment. It might be weeks or months, even years, as in Zelda's case, before the police would find Elise—Mackenzie shuddered—if they ever did. She rubbed her chest as if the gesture could reduce the sudden pain that surged through her.

It had been six days now, and there had been no enlightenment as to Elise's whereabouts. Mackenzie frowned, considering her options. One, she could return to Arizona. *No! Unthinkable.* The wounds in her heart had yet to heal. Thank God for the marvelous spiritual experience she'd had less than an hour ago—the foundation on which restoration could build. Two, she could start a search for a new nanny position in case her job ended in the near future. Perhaps another family in Mr. Huntington's circle of friends and acquaintances desired to employ a nanny for their children. Mackenzie cringed. A future without Elise? How bleak the thought.

Three, she could begin a quest to find the university that would offer the best online program for a doctorate in her field of study. Option two coincided with three, as she would have to work to finance the degree. A nanny position would offset the cost of room and board elsewhere. She glanced toward the sun, its rays penetrating her skin. She wiped the moisture from her brow and opened the door. But should she have to decide her future anytime soon, she now had an assurance that God would sustain her no matter what circumstances would befall her in the days to come.

Mackenzie entered the foyer and started to climb the stairs, but sensing she wasn't alone, she turned to see Trace leave the living room to make his way toward her, his smile bright with pleasure. Her breath caught at the flip-flop motion inside her chest. Taking in his features, she felt as if she'd just laid eyes on him for the first time. Mrs. Simpson had been correct in her assumption. Trace Patterson was indeed handsome—not just in looks, but in his heart and soul as well. She'd understood that in part, but now it was as if the realization had become full-blown in her mind. She smiled within. *At present, I believe he's the best-looking man I've ever known.*

Trace frowned. He reached up and touched his brow, the confusion in his eyes sprinkled with teasing laughter. "Did I just grow horns or something more grotesque?"

Mackenzie laughed. "Why would you ask that?"

"Well, the way you were eyeballing me, what else could I believe?"

"Oh, sorry, didn't realize I was staring," she said, a stroke of pink highlighting her cheeks.

He took her hand in his and caressed her fingers. "I have no objection to your scrutiny at all. Now, tell me—did you enjoy your afternoon with Mrs. Simpson?"

"Very much. The simple fare was delicious, and after lunch, she showed me her house, along with the different works of art her grandfather had created."

"I've seen them also. She takes great pride in them." Trace led her to the wooden bench stationed adjacent to the entryway. Once they were seated, they were quiet momentarily, each captivated by his or her own thoughts. After a moment, he turned to her, his gaze taking in every inch of her face. "Something is different about you, Mackenzie. Do I dare believe the change in you is what I've been praying for since we met?"

She smiled. "I think God has answered your prayers. Mrs. Simpson helped me rededicate my life back to God. I served Him in my childhood and youth, but I drifted away from His presence when I entered college, allowing my own desires to rule my life. I still have some issues to work out, but I haven't felt this free for a long time."

He cupped her chin with his hand. "That's wonderful news. And as far as those issues are concerned, if I can help in any way, let me know."

Mackenzie averted her gaze. *If only you could!* "Thanks, Trace. I appreciate it."

Hearing a footstep, they both looked up to see Mr. Huntington descending the stairs. An idea popped into Mackenzie's mind. Maybe she should understand where she stood with him before she made any plans.

"Good afternoon, sir," she said, standing. "Would it be possible for me to speak with you for a few moments?"

"Certainly, Miss Adams." He motioned her forward toward his office.

She threw Trace a smile over her shoulder. "Catch up with you later, Trace."

Shortly thereafter, she settled into one of the two chairs in front of Mr. Huntington's desk. "Thank you for taking time to see me on short notice."

"Quite all right, Miss Adams," he said once seated in his desk chair. "How can I be of service to you?"

"Well, sir, I don't want to take advantage of your generosity. It might be some time before we have Elise back, and I thought you might want me to seek employment elsewhere."

He smiled. "That's commendable of you, but unless that's your desire, I'd much prefer you remain at Park House for now." He looked toward the window. "Should anything happen that would alter that plan, we can discuss your employment at that time."

"Thank you, Mr. Huntington. I very much desire to be here when Elise is returned."

"I thought so. Now run along, Miss Adams, and enjoy the rest of the day."

"Yes, sir, I will," she said, her expression turning sad. "As much as any of us can."

When Mackenzie left Mr. Huntington's office, she found Trace waiting for her on the bench where they'd been sitting earlier. She quelled her surprise behind a smile.

"That was fast," he said, concern etched on his brow. "Don't mean to be nosy, but is everything okay?"

She nodded. "I didn't want your uncle to feel like he had to keep me on as Elise's nanny, since he's paying for services not rendered. The nursery and my room are spotless. I can't imagine what I can do to earn my keep this next week." She grinned. "I offered my aid to Mrs. Slater, but I think I insulted her." Mackenzie brightened. "I'll ask Angie if she'd like some help."

"I'm sure she would. You two seem to have become good friends."

"Yes. Also, she's been assisting my—" Panic seized Mackenzie. She glanced away. The curiosity in Trace's eyes begged for an explanation. She turned aside, biting down hard on her lip. What could she say now? Nothing about her sleuthing attempts—that was a given, considering he might inform his uncle about her snooping into affairs in which she had no right to delve. An image of her living on the street popped into her mind. Mackenzie caught and held the grin that lurked at the corners of her mouth. She forced cheerfulness into her voice. "I mean, we ..." *Oh God, help me think of something truthful.* "Angie has been helping me with my research project. You know, the thesis for my doctorate?" Circles of pink formed on Makenzie's cheeks. *Well, she did ask Angie about Jasmine's relationship with her daughter.*

Trace narrowed his vision slightly. "Oh yes, the doctorate. How's that coming along?"

Mackenzie glanced away, noting the hint of disbelief written on his face. "Okay, I suppose. But I've just been working on it a short time." Maybe you could share some information that would contribute to the project," she said, smiling, her eyes wide with feigned innocence.

He nodded slowly. "Yeah, maybe so." He took her arm. "Why don't we go for a drive and talk about it?"

Mackenzie held back momentarily. Then she smiled. "Why not? Just let me freshen up a bit and grab my notebook."

"Sounds good. I'll be waiting in my car. Take your time. I need to make a phone call before we go."

Less than an hour later, Trace drove them into downtown Little Rock. Soon they were in the center of the city, where Makenzie took in the Capitol Building and the Old Statehouse. Their talk along the way had nothing to do with her project, she'd noted with interest. Had he thought she'd been less than truthful with him? Mackenzie squirmed inside, guilt overshadowing her. Well, hadn't she? She breathed a sigh of relief when, a few moments later, they drove into an obvious historic district and Trace began to share the history of the area.

"This is known as the Quapaw Quarter," he explained to Mackenzie. "It covers a nine-square-mile radius, some of the homes dating back to pre–Civil War." Driving down Center Street, he slowed the car to let her get a good view of the Governor's Mansion. Using her phone, she snapped another picture.

"Wow," she said, taking in the beauty of the Georgian colonial mansion. "It looks as if it could be a substitute for the White House in Washington, DC."

Trace laughed. "Yeah. It's that big. People that call Little Rock home are proud of that fact." He drove through the neighborhoods one by one, giving her tidbits about several of the homes, slowing to point out one particular house. "That's the Villa Marre. It was often featured in the television series *Designing Women*."

Mackenzie feasted her eyes on the home. "I thought it looked familiar. Just couldn't remember where I'd seen a likeness of it."

At the end of their tour a few minutes later, Mackenzie found herself gazing upon the Arkansas River as Trace drove them down Riverfront Road. When he pulled into a parking lot, she turned to see a steamboat, paddle wheel and all, docked at the edge of the river. He got out of the car and, within a few seconds, opened the passenger door. He smiled at the question in her eyes.

"Have you ever had dinner on a steamboat before?" He placed the palm of his hand on her back and guided her toward the boat. "I made reservations for us just before we left Park House. We were lucky. They only had three seats left."

"No. Nor have I ridden on one." She smoothed the outer edges of her dress. She glanced around, happy to note that other embarking passengers had on attire similar to hers.

Later, following their dinner, they left their table to go to the top deck to observe the grand scenery along the waterfront. Leaning against the railing of the boat, Trace seemed preoccupied with something other than their adventure, although he pointed out the sights as they passed them, giving her a short history lesson on the settling of the delta area and pointing out the monument that held the little rock that had given the city its name. After a few moments, he turned to Mackenzie, his expression grim.

"Captain Sprinsky phoned me while you were at Mrs. Simpson's house."

As she read the look in his eyes, alarm coated Mackenzie's thoughts. Had the captain phoned to give bad news about Elise? "Oh?"

Trace ran the back of his hand down Mackenzie's cheek. "The officer is worried about you."

She stepped back. "Me?" The noise from a speeding motorboat a short distance from the steamboat caught their attention, and Mackenzie was thankful for the momentary distraction. "Did he give a reason for his concern?"

"He did mention that he'd spoken to you about it already."

"Oh, that." She rested her elbows on the railing and held the backs of her hands against her lips, refusing to look his way. *Busted*—there was no other word for it. At least it excluded her need to devise a plan in how to gently break the news of her deceit.

"Mackenzie, look at me." He lowered his voice when he noticed the gaping stares of passengers nearby. "You and Angie may think it's exciting to play amateur detective, but if the killer or killers find out about your little project, your lives won't be worth the cost of a one-cent postage stamp. And all you can say is 'Oh, that?'"

The corners of her mouth twitched in response to the twinkle in her eyes. "That much, huh?" The look on his face squelched her humor.

With an exasperated sigh, Trace pushed his hands inside the pockets of his trousers. "If you hurry, maybe the producers will hire you as an additional artist for the comedy show scheduled for this evening." He smiled wanly at the perturbed look on her face before he sent an apologetic look her way. "Sorry, Mackenzie. I shouldn't have said that. But we need to be serious about this."

Gripped by remorse, Mackenzie turned away from him. "Look, Trace, I appreciate the apprehension you and Captain Sprinsky have about my probing into matters that are none of my concern. And please believe me—Angie has done nothing but relay to me a few tidbits of conversation she's accidently overheard.

"Yes, I've asked questions about the murder, the reason being that after I heard about Jasmine's death, I've had this intuitive knowledge that the answer to her death lies within the house—whether literally or figuratively or both, I'm not sure. Also, I believe Elise's kidnapping may be connected in some way. And just so you know, I'm not playing a game. I will keep asking and keep looking until this urge within me is mollified."

Trace rubbed his hand across his jawline and then faced Mackenzie. "To be honest, I've had a similar inclination. But I haven't had time to pursue it. Please be careful, Mackenzie." He reached out and smoothed a lock of her hair that the breeze had blown out of place. "Now that I've met you, it would grieve me considerably should you get hurt—or worse." He cupped his hand around the back of her neck and pulled her close to him. His lips were on hers a second later. He broke the kiss when the sound of music floated up from the lower deck. "Guess we should return to our table before we miss the entire show."

Mesmerized by the feel of his lips, Mackenzie stood in place, while her legs quivered like jelled gravy. She opened her eyes and looked around, realizing they were alone save for one other couple on the opposite side of the deck. "I suppose so." A moment later, Trace took her arm, and they walked toward the deck stairs.

Mackenzie's mind whirled. How was she going to deal with him now? Noticing Trace was engrossed in the comedian's jokes, she touched her lips with her fingertips, recalling the feel of his mouth on hers. She closed her eyes, the memory of the gentle yet passionate embrace rocking her emotions. A moment later, she sensed Trace's scrutiny. Her face blazed. He lifted an eyebrow as if he'd read her thoughts, his gaze drifting to her mouth. Her stomach seemed to fall to her feet.

She faced the stage, centering her attention on the show, but didn't pull away when he slipped her hand into his palm. A feeling like warm honey poured over her. She frowned. How could she allow their relationship to advance? The pain ahead would be too hard to endure—for both of them.

Soon the act ended. They listened to the MC's announcement that the boat had docked and then stood to follow the crowd toward the exit. When they reached Trace's car, they paused to eye the captivating glow of the setting sun over the water. Mackenzie grew troubled. *It would be best to speak now,* she thought when Trace opened the door for her. *Just end it once and for all.* But she couldn't find the words she'd planned to say. Losing her courage, she opted for appreciation versus annihilation of his affection. *And what about your affection for him?* Mackenzie shrugged off the thought. No way would she go there.

"Thank you, Trace, for the entertaining afternoon," she said once they were back on the road.

"My pleasure, Mackenzie." He reached across the car, took her hand, and drew it to his lips. Averting his gaze back to the road, he smiled. "We'll plan another excursion soon."

She sighed. "Trace, I—" His cell phone rang, breaking off her words.

"Excuse me," he said, pulling the device from the clip on his belt.

"Hello? Oh hi, Uncle Drew. Yes. We're on our way home now."

Mackenzie turned to take in the landscape from the side window. Would Mr. Huntington approve of Trace's time with her? She closed her eyes, mentally kicking herself. Why had she agreed to the outing? She could still taste the sweetness of his lips. She couldn't let that happen again. Building a relationship on lies would be like constructing a house on sand. It could never withstand the storms of life. She'd already crossed one bridge of deception today and didn't desire to encounter another.

Before they arrived at Park House, she would inform Trace she desired only friendship with him, not a romantic involvement. She cringed at the thought of the hurt she would see in his eyes, not to mention the torture her intention wielded within her own heart. Better, though, to observe the pain of her rejection than the disgust she would see should he discover the truth that lay within her, she decided. She clasped her hands together to still the trembling in her fingers. She would collapse under the weight of that cross. She took a deep breath and then exhaled slowly. Yes, a clean break would be best for both of them. But how could she get her sentiments across to him without destroying their camaraderie?

"So did Captain Sprinsky find anything in the car that gave a clue to Elise's location?" Trace said into his phone.

Mackenzie whipped a gaze in Trace's direction. Had the blue van been found? She caught his eye but couldn't discern the answer. She traced the geometric pattern in her dress, waiting not so patiently until the call ended.

"I see. Thanks for letting me know. See you shortly."

Her eyes full of questions, she eyed his thoughtful expression. She held her breath. At last, he looked her way.

"Someone called in to report an abandoned car at the end of a dead-end street in North Little Rock. When the police investigated, they found it to be a blue older-model Ford Escape. Once the van had been towed to the police yard, the forensic team found a baby bottle under the seat, partially filled with the same type of formula used for Elise. They also discovered a long blonde hair they later determined to be from the wig the policewoman found in the bathroom at the bus station. And to top that off, the car had been stolen."

Mackenzie brushed her hair back from her face, cynicism creeping into her features. "Now, why is that not surprising? First, a car rented with a false ID, and now a stolen van." Mackenzie shook her head. "Such ingenuity."

Trace grinned. "Well, a suspected female kidnapper did manage to cart a million dollars past the watchful eyes of half a dozen or more police officers and out the bus terminal door, disappearing without a trace of her destination."

"Touché," Mackenzie said, returning his smile. "Do the police believe the kidnappers used the abandoned van to transport Elise to that section of the city?"

"Captain Sprinsky is certain the kidnappers used that vehicle."

"What proof does he have?"

"Although they tried to wipe the vehicle clean of all prints, the kidnappers missed a tiny fingerprint on the back side window that matches Elise's forefinger print."

Mackenzie shot him a skeptical look. "How could the police have known that?"

"According to Uncle Drew, a few weeks before Jasmine died, she'd seen a child-protection ad in the newspaper urging parents to have their children fingerprinted. He'd wanted to wait until Elise grew older, but

Jasmine insisted that they do it right away, in case a situation occurred such as we have now."

"Do you think Mrs. Huntington had some kind of premonition about Elise's kidnapping?"

Trace shrugged. "Who knows?"

Deep lines formed on Mackenzie's brow. "Did the person say how long the vehicle had been parked on the street?"

"The gentleman calling in noticed it late Thursday afternoon when he returned home from work but couldn't say how long it had been there. At first, he thought his neighbor had a visitor, but discovering this morning there was no truth to his notion, the man decided to report the situation to the police.

"My guess is, the kidnappers dropped it there not long before they drove to the bus station in another vehicle to pick up the ransom money. I wouldn't think they'd take a chance on the car being spotted near the terminal since the story of the kidnapping has been broadcast on every media source available."

"I agree. I don't suppose the police found anyone who might have seen the occupants of the van."

Trace lifted a shoulder. "No one of whom I'm aware."

Mackenzie sighed deeply. "So the police still have no idea of Elise's location."

"That's correct," Trace said sadly.

Desiring to change the subject, she pulled the notebook she'd placed in the side pocket of her handbag just before they left the house earlier that afternoon. "Trace, you indicated you might give me some information that would help with my case study. Would you tell me from your perspective the kind of relationship Mrs. Huntington shared with her daughter?"

Trace grew pensive, his thumbs lightly tapping the center column of the steering wheel. "I can't say that Jasmine was the most nurturing of women, but she loved Elise. Just didn't show it in conventional ways. Jasmine made sure her daughter had everything necessary to provide the best for all facets of her young life. Before Elise was born, Jasmine supervised the renovation of the nursery and nanny room."

"She did a marvelous job. I was astounded when I saw the nursery for the first time—every tool available for play and the best of educational material from birth through the toddler stage. And my room—oh my word—it's, why, I or any other caregiver couldn't ask for anything better."

"Uncle Drew said Jasmine had hoped that Elise wouldn't have a barrage of nannies, but one who would make a career of caring for her child. That's why she desired to make the nanny room as attractive as possible." Trace took his eyes off the road momentarily to glance at Mackenzie. "Expressing her disappointment in Miss Carmichael to me one morning, Jasmine shared her hope you would fit that criteria." Laughter glittered in his eyes. "But I can't see that happening. Some Prince Charming will snatch you away in due time. Your beauty and charm have turned the heads of two men in the Huntington kingdom already." His expression turning serious, Trace squeezed her hand. "I'm not a knight in shining armor, Mackenzie, but I sure would like to win this race for your affection."

Mackenzie glanced away, tears blurring her vision. She blinked them away quickly. "Trace, there's something I need to discuss," she said, her words barely audible.

"Well, here we are," he said, pulling into the driveway. "I'm sorry, Mackenzie. What did you say?"

She'd been so absorbed in their conversation that she hadn't realized they'd arrived at Park House. "Well, I—" A movement caught her eye. She glanced toward the porch and then frowned. "Mr. Huntington is pacing back and forth across the porch." She took in his features. "He looks upset."

Trace narrowed his vision to better view his uncle. "You're right. I wonder what's wrong." A moment later, he helped Mackenzie out of the car, and they both hurried to Mr. Huntington's side.

"Uncle Drew, is everything okay?"

"Not by any means. Just got a call from Cranston. He just found out the property we sold him last month is in a flood zone."

Trace looked stunned. "How could he not have known that? The contract stated that fact."

"Not his copy." Mr. Huntington's eyes widened as if he'd just realized Mackenzie stood nearby. "Oh, Miss Adams. Please excuse us. I need to talk to Trace."

"Of course." She turned to Trace. "Thanks again for the tour of the city. Now, if you two will excuse me." Smiling at the two men, Mackenzie closed the door behind her, leaving them to sort out whatever current crisis had occurred. About to climb the stairs, she started at the sound of Greg's voice.

"Good evening, Miss Adams."

Tensing, she turned to see Greg striding toward her from the hallway. "Hello, Greg," she said, her smile tight.

Raising his brow, he nodded toward the porch. "Trace seems to be spending a lot of time at Park House lately." The familiar smirk appeared in his eyes.

Heat spreading across her face, Mackenzie turned her back on him and took a step upward. "I'm sure having his nephew around during this awful time is a great comfort to Mr. Huntington."

"And what about you? Is Trace a great comfort to you as well?"

Although she couldn't see his features, she could hear the sneer in his voice. She turned around, her eyes piercing. "As a matter of fact, he has become a good friend. Do you have a problem with that?" Facing the stairwell once again, she climbed to the upper floor, leaving her adversary staring up at her, his mouth wide open. *Oh, the nerve of the incorrigible cad. Trying to bait me like that.*

Once in her room, she raised her eyes toward the ceiling, the corners of her mouth turned upward with a wry smile. "Thanks for helping me. Had I said to Greg the words in my mind, I'd be asking both you and him to forgive me. And he'd probably gloat about it from now until eternity."

Speaking of eternity, Mackenzie, Greg needs to hear the good news. Now that you've rededicated your life to me, are you willing to lay aside your grievances against him to be the witness he needs?

"Oh Father, please send someone else. You know I can hardly bear to be in the same room with Greg."

Don't you think he knows that? All the more reason to plant seeds of my love in his heart.

Mackenzie sighed. "Okay, Father. You give the opportunity, and I will share the good news of Christ's love with Greg Martin—that he too might come to know the riches of your love, mercy, and grace."

Actions of love will pave the way for him to hear the gospel with his heart.

She sighed. "That too, Father, even if it kills me."

Remember, Mackenzie, no love is greater than the love of one who is willing to lay down his life for another.

"Yes, Father. I understand. It won't be easy, but I will treat him with kindness no matter how much ridicule or sarcasm he throws back at me."

Well said, beloved. All I ask for is a willing and obedient heart.

Following her shower, Mackenzie curled up on the sofa and reached for the book on the corner table, but she held it in her hands unopened. The memory of the look in Trace's eyes just before they'd kissed sent wave after wave of heat throughout her body. No way could she be alone with him again; her resistance to his unprecedented charm was, at present, near the bottom of the scale. If he kissed her again, her heart would become like water-softened clay to be molded at his will. She just couldn't take the chance.

A moment later, she sat down at the table and opened her laptop to catch up on her friends' lives. Just the distraction she needed to keep her thoughts of Trace in check. About to answer an e-mail from Kari, her cell phone rang. Recognizing the distinctive ring tone, she swiped the screen, a bittersweet smile clinging to her lips.

"Hello, Dad. How are you and Mom?" Mackenzie listened, a flood of homesickness washing over her at the sound of her father's voice. "I'm doing well. I've got great news. I visited a church just down the street from Park House this morning, and with the encouragement from a new friend, I decided this afternoon to turn my life back to God. My heart is overflowing again with His peace and praise for my Savior's love." Hearing her father's expression of joy, she smiled. Perhaps her news would somehow allay the disappointment she'd caused her parents.

"Thanks for all the prayers you and Mom have prayed for me. Do you think she would let me tell her about it? Oh, I see. Please mention it when she gets home. Okay? Maybe she'll phone me later." Mackenzie's voice began to crack. "I know patience is my strength, Dad. You might let her know I've begun to work on my doctorate—at least the research for my thesis. She should be pleased about that. Okay, Dad, I will. You take care too. I love you, and as always, tell Mom I love her."

Mackenzie pushed the end button on the phone. Would her mom be interested enough in her daughter's spiritual experience to make the call? Drawing a tearful breath, Mackenzie padded over to her bed and readied it for the night. Only if she hadn't been disowned in her mother's heart.

Chapter 18

"**G**ood morning," Mackenzie chirped, entering the kitchen the next day. She glanced out the window. "Looks like we may get some rain today. Personally, I wouldn't mind. We could use a break from the heat." She took in the other three members of household staff seated at the table. Mrs. Slater, her usual cheery self, grunted a greeting, while Greg, taking a sip of his coffee, frowned at her behind his cup. Angie lifted her hand in a wave, her sunny smile a godsend to Mackenzie. Otherwise, she would have done an about-face and retreated to a less hostile setting.

"Good morning to you." Angie motioned Mackenzie to the chair across from her.

Mackenzie eyed the breakfast fare. "This looks delicious." She caught Mrs. Slater's eye. "But any food you prepare is great," Mackenzie said, spooning gravy over the fluffy biscuit she'd taken from the breadbasket.

Mrs. Slater held her fork in midair, a smile cracking her solemn expression. "Thank you, Miss Adams," she said with a slight shake of her head. "You seem full of good spirits today."

Mackenzie laughed. *Yeah, the Holy Spirit.* "Well, at least one anyway." She chuckled within at the confused look on the house manager's face. She glanced Angie's way at the sound of her voice.

"Did you hear that the police located the blue van the kidnappers used after they ditched the rental car?"

"Yes." She cut a quick glimpse toward Greg and then lifted her chin slightly, again focusing on her friend. "Trace told me everything he knows about the discovery. Any news concerning Elise?"

Angie shook her head. "Not that I've heard." She took in mother and son. "How about you all?"

"I did overhear Captain Sprinsky tell Mr. Huntington that the chief of police has now called in the FBI to help with the investigation," Mrs. Slater said, forking a bite of egg.

"Oh, it must be the FBI's Child Rapid Abduction Deployment Team he mentioned," Angie said, grinning at the shock on her companions' faces. "Since Elise was taken, I've been doing a lot of research on kidnapping crimes—so much so that I've decided to attend college this fall, eventually securing a degree in criminology. I've found the subject to be fascinating." Her expression saddened. "I'll be able to take just a few courses at a time"—she shrugged—"but it takes a start to bring an end."

Mackenzie clapped her hands. "Oh Angie, I'm so proud of you. I'm positive you'll be one of the brightest students on campus."

A humph sounded at the other end of the table. Mackenzie glared at Greg and then smiled sweetly. "Did you want to add a congratulatory remark as well?"

Greg pushed back his plate and stood from the table without a word. A moment later, he exited the kitchen, slamming the door behind him. Eyeing her son's departure, Mrs. Slater pursed her lips, her expression etched with disapproval.

"Don't pay any attention to him, Miss Valencia. He had his chance to better himself but didn't accept it. However, I, on the other hand, approve of your decision heartily." She stared off into space. "Education will take you wherever you wish to go." A look of sadness crossed her countenance. "Don't let the opportunity slip from your fingers. Or you will regret it for the rest of your life."

A ripple of compassion moved in Mackenzie's heart. "Did that happen to you, Mrs. Slater? A missed opportunity when you were near our age?"

The house manager studied the young women's expressions and then drew a long sigh. "When I was a young teenager, I began work at Park House as a nanny. Mr. Huntington was my charge; his older sister was away at boarding school. As he grew, his father employed the best tutors the city had to offer. Unknown to his teachers, I learned right along with him, studying his textbooks after I'd put him to bed.

"When Mr. Huntington enrolled in prep school, I took it upon myself to obtain a GED from the adult education center in Little Rock. After receiving my diploma, I applied and was accepted to an African American college in another state. But I let my mother talk me out of it. She didn't want me to leave her alone, so I stayed on at Park House and later married the chauffeur at the time, working my way up from housemaid to house manager within a few years. When my husband abandoned me, I thought again about pursuing a career, but having to care for my mother, who'd discovered she had terminal cancer, I gave up the idea. I've often wondered how different my life would have been had I pursued my dream to become the lead chef in a five-star restaurant."

Silence filled the room. A moment or so later, Mrs. Slater stood from the table and began to gather the dishes, breaking the reflective interlude. Mackenzie and Angie rushed to help.

"Say, Angie," Mackenzie said once the dishwasher began to sing its usual song, "would you like some help today? I don't relish another day of staring at the walls in my room."

"Sure. That way, we can chat at the same time." Angie turned to the house manager. "You don't mind, do you, Mrs. Slater?"

"No." She waved them out of the kitchen. "Run along, and stop bothering me. I have work to do."

Mackenzie and Angie exchanged looks, both seeming to read each other's thoughts. No way were they going to pass up this break. Mackenzie followed Angie out of the room, stifling a giggle until they reached the cleaning closet in the laundry room.

Handing dustcloths and spray to Mackenzie, Angie moved back a step to study her friend. "What's happened to you, Mackenzie? I've never seen you this giddy. And your face is shining like new silk. Come on—out with it."

"It's really simple—honest. Yesterday I decided to stop trying to manage my own life and problems, releasing all of them along with my heart and soul into the hands of God. Growing up, I had a good relationship with Him, but I rejected His love and grace to do my own thing."

Angie's eyes widened. "Oh, *mi amiga*—my friend," she said, her eyes dewy with moisture. "I am so happy for you. Each time I saw sadness in your eyes, I prayed you would turn to our Savior for comfort." She smiled.

"But now all I see is joy." She reached out and hugged Mackenzie. "My mother and father will be glad to hear this news." Laughing, she dragged the vacuum cleaner from the closet, and the two hurried to begin the daily chore of tidying Park House.

Later, while they worked in the den, Mackenzie, dusting the books and shelves, paused momentarily, her gaze wandering toward the ceiling.

Angie pressed the power button on the vacuum, quieting the machine. "Is something bothering you, Mackenzie?"

"I just find it interesting that this morning is the first time Mrs. Slater has been civil toward me. Do you think she's finally ready to accept me into her domain?"

"I don't know. If she has, it will sure ease the tension in the house."

"You've got that right." Mackenzie pulled several books from the next shelf and wiped them free of dust. "I couldn't help but feel sorry for her. It's a shame she didn't get to pursue her dream." Mackenzie smiled. "I bet she would have made it too, the way she can cook. I wonder if she's thought about publishing her recipes in a cookbook."

"I'm not certain she's ready to divulge them. One night some time ago, I asked for her recipe for fettuccine Alfredo. But she declined, declaring her recipes were not for public use. Why don't you suggest the cookbook idea to Mrs. Slater? She might go for it."

"Maybe I will."

Following the noon meal, Mackenzie and Angie made the climb up the stairs to finish the work for the day. Entering the master suite, Mackenzie, with a critical eye, surveyed the elaborate furnishings set in a decor of burgundy and gold. "Kind of creepy knowing that a possible murder occurred in this room, isn't it?"

Angie nodded. "Yeah. I always get the strangest feeling when I walk in here, like I'm intruding or something."

Mackenzie shivered. "I see what you mean. Do you think Jasmine died here?"

"If not, then why do we feel this way?"

"Would it be all right if I poked around a bit?" She frowned at Angie's wary look. "You know it's *possible* the police overlooked something."

"I suppose. But just remember, Mr. Huntington is downstairs. He might decide he needs something from his room and come in unexpectedly. That's what happened when Lacey Carmichael got caught snooping in Mrs. Huntington's things."

Mackenzie nodded. "Yeah, Greg told me that. Don't worry, Angie. I'll keep a dustcloth in my hand in case he walks in unannounced." Mackenzie walked across the room and opened the door to a large walk-in closet. "That's odd."

"What is?" Angie said, straightening a stack of magazines.

"Aren't these Jasmine's clothes?"

Angie peaked around the closet door, surveying the two long racks of garments. "Yeah. I recognize some of them. Why?"

"Strange that Mr. Huntington hasn't found a new home for them by now."

Angie shrugged. "Maybe it's comforting for him to keep them for a time."

"Perhaps." Not noting anything that seemed important to a murder case, Mackenzie closed the door and made her way into the dressing room, where the vanity piqued her interest. Discovering nothing of importance, she retraced her steps and picked up the bathroom cleaning supplies. At that moment, the door opened. Mackenzie froze, the supplies tight against her chest.

"Hello, girls," Mr. Huntington said, easing into the room. "Sorry to disturb you, but I think I left—oh, there it is." He strode over to the nightstand and picked up a legal-looking document. "You all are doing a great job in the house today. Why don't you plan to swim for a while when you're finished? I'll tell Mrs. Slater to prepare you some snacks."

"Thanks, Mr. Huntington," Mackenzie said. Had her voice just squeaked? "We'll plan on it." She swallowed hard once he closed the door behind him. Weak in the knees, she sat down on the edge of the bed, waiting momentarily while color returned to her face. "I swear, Angie. I thought my heart had stopped"—she pointed toward the door—"when Mr. Huntington walked into this room."

Angie grinned. "I told you it could happen."

Mackenzie threw a cleaning rag at her friend. "Yes, you did. I guess I'm a little crazy to think I could outdo the investigators. What do you say we hurry and get this suite in shape? The hallway won't take long with both of us working on it. We'll be ready to dive into the pool by then."

"But I don't have a swimsuit with me."

"I've got an extra one. It's a little small for me. It should fit you fine."

Angie smiled. "Then I guess I'm along for the ride."

A few hours later, the two sat beside the pool, sipping their peach tea following a vigorous swim. Grinning, Mackenzie held up her glass. "You know, I just might make the South my permanent place of residence."

"We've found it to be a hospitable place," Angie said, leaning back in her lounge chair. "My grandparents crossed the border illegally but were able to get citizenship after a time. I'm proud of my Hispanic heritage, but I'm glad I was born and raised in this country." She faced her friend. "Have you any plans for the upcoming Fourth of July?"

Mackenzie shook her head. "What about you?"

"My boyfriend is taking me to dinner on the riverboat. Then we'll watch the fantastic fireworks show the city puts on every year at the river from the top deck of the boat. We've had our tickets for months."

"The *Mark Twain*?"

"Yes. How did you know about the steamboat?"

"Trace took me on it last night after he gave me a tour of your city."

Angie scooted to a sitting position. "And you're just now sharing this?" She pretended to pout, a grin tweaking the corners of her mouth. "Some friend you are. So tell me about your date."

Mackenzie moved her sunglasses from the top of her head to cover her eyes. "It wasn't a date really. Just two friends together on a pleasant outing."

"You can't fool me, girlfriend. I've seen the way you look at Trace when you think he doesn't notice."

Mackenzie frowned. "You don't understand, Angie. It wouldn't ever work out for us. Too much baggage on my part."

"What was that I heard earlier from you—something about trusting God to take care of your problems?"

"It would have to be a miracle in this situation."

"From what I hear now and then, I believe He's still creating them."

Mackenzie laid her hand on Angie's arm. "Please, I'd rather not discuss it. Okay?"

Angie sighed. "So be it. But I've never seen two people more gone on each other than you and Trace Patterson." Angie held up her hand at the look in her friend's eyes. "All right. I won't say another word."

"About that fireworks display," Mackenzie said, relaxing against the back of the chaise lounge, glad that the sun had decided to shine after the good rain earlier in the day. "Where did you say it takes place? It sounds like an event I might enjoy."

"Remind me when we go back inside, and I'll jot down the details for you."

"Good as done."

The Fourth of July dawned clear, the temperature sizzling by late afternoon. Mackenzie dressed in her coolest outfit, the white shorts and filmy top overlaying a cotton tank showing off her tan to perfection. With little to do since the kidnapping, she'd spent more time beside the pool, a pleasure she'd savored during her lifetime. She'd been a champion swimmer by age twelve.

She brushed back her hair and secured it with a trendy hair clip, believing the style would keep her cooler during her time at the waterfront. She looked forward to the entertainment that included a live concert performed by the Arkansas Symphonic Orchestra prior to the fireworks display.

Pulling a small purse from her closet shelf, she tucked her keys and phone in the two zippered outside compartments and then placed her wallet inside the handbag. She hoped the experience of the next few hours would shade her mind from the tragedies that permeated Park House, at least for the duration of the evening. Stepping into her sandals, she tried to ward off the despondency that threatened to spoil the evening ahead. It had begun two days ago after seeing the crushed look and confusion in Trace's eyes when she'd declined his invitation to attend the city's annual Pops on the River celebration.

How difficult it had been to walk away from him. She'd told him she planned to be at the event but hadn't mentioned her intention to go alone. Drawing a deep sigh, she placed the long purse strap over her head, adjusting the handbag to ride at her side. Dabbing away the moisture from her eyes, she closed the door behind her, determined to enjoy the festivities.

A couple hours later, she climbed the steps in the amphitheater overlooking Riverfront Park and took an empty seat near the aisle, excitement dispelling some of her gloom as the orchestra began tuning up for the grand performance. She smiled. Angie hadn't exaggerated a bit.

The vendors at the River Market held enough variety to make the experience a treat. Sadness filled her eyes. It was just the kind of shopping atmosphere she and her mother loved to plod through, examining together each unique item that caught their interest. Mackenzie drew a ragged breath. "Oh God," she breathed, "please restore the relationship I once had with my mother. I know I'm more to blame than she, but how can I ask her to forgive me if she won't talk to me?"

Noting that the amphitheater had filled to overflowing, Mackenzie turned her attention to the crowd that had gathered in the river park. While some relaxed in lawn chairs, others, along with their children, sat on blankets that had been spread on the grass, all waiting for the orchestra to play its first selection. Tears welled in her eyes. For all the thousands of people in her sight, she had never before felt more alone than she did at that moment.

A short time later, she seemed to be drawn to the small group standing off to the side near the entrance to the theater. Her breath caught as her heartbeat picked a rhythm not quite in keeping with the Strass waltz the maestro conducted. Standing off a few feet from the others, Trace stood with his hands in his pockets, glancing upward as if searching for someone among those seated in the outdoor arena. Catching her eye a moment or so later, he smiled.

Mackenzie tried to turn away, but his look held her gaze. *Why can't I be free of you?* He shook his head as if he'd read her thoughts. She closed her eyes momentarily, refusing to look his way again, determined to concentrate on the program.

An hour later, just as the fireworks show was about to begin, she glanced downward, breathing a sigh of relief that Trace was no longer in sight. Needing to use the facilities, she descended the stairs and hurried toward them, hoping she wouldn't miss any of the action. When she returned to the theater, she noticed that someone had taken her seat. Exhaling a sigh of irritation, she moved a short distance away to mingle with the crowd, waiting in anticipation for the magic to begin. About halfway through the show, she felt a gentle grip on her elbow.

"Hello, Mackenzie."

A shudder of delight traveled through her body at the voice close to her ear. She cut a glance toward Trace, sighing with frustration at her reaction to him. *Will the man never give up?*

"Pleasant evening all around, isn't it?" he said, watching the sky explode with a kaleidoscope of colors from a round of fireworks. He smiled at Mackenzie and then leaned close to her. "I need to talk to you when this is over."

She frowned. Had they heard something about Elise or the murder of Jason Crane or Jasmine? Mackenzie nodded, relaxing for the moment. Obviously, it wasn't urgent. However, just as soon as the last spark died from the grand finale, Trace took hold of her arm and guided her through the parting crowd, keeping her at his side. Mackenzie pointed the direction to her car the moment they stepped onto the parking lot. By the time they reached the Camry, her stomach shook as if she'd been caught in a mischievous deed. He'd hardly uttered a word during their walk across the grounds.

After unlocking the car with the remote, she started to open the door, when Trace put his arms on her shoulders, blocking her purpose. He took a step, backing her up against the side of the car. He stood momentarily eyeing her in the light from the departing vehicles and then lowered his head and placed his lips on hers. She tried to break the kiss, but he took her face in his hands, gently holding her in place. No longer able to resist, she gave in to the embrace, sliding her arms around his waist. He grasped the back of her neck, pulling her closer, deepening his kiss. When he finally let her go, they both stood there, trembling beneath the canopy of stars, his arms tightly around her.

Able to breathe normally again, she lifted her head from his shoulder. "Trace, what did you need to say to me?"

He released his hold on her but placed his palms against the side roof of the car, pinning her between his arms. "Mackenzie, I followed you tonight because I wanted to see what competition I might have. I must say it took me by surprise when I saw that you had come to the celebration alone. It would take a thousand years to describe how happy that made me."

He paused momentarily, his gaze searching as he took in her expression, her features growing softer in the glow from the streetlamps illuminating the now-deserted parking lot. "I know we've only known each other less than a month, but from the first moment I met you in Uncle Drew's office, I've known you are special."

"Trace, I—"

He held up his hand. "Mackenzie, hear me out, please. I think about you all the time." He laughed. "My feelings for you are so obvious my secretary wanted to know who I was seeing and if we had set a date for the wedding. The thing is, Mackenzie, I know you're struggling with similar feelings for me. Our kiss just now proved it. What I don't understand is why you can't seem to give in to the attraction between us. I've prayed for years that God would bring someone like you into my life, and now I believe He's answered my prayers."

Mackenzie ducked from beneath his arms and moved a few feet away. "Trace, stop. Don't say any more. Believe me, I am not the girl for you. I can't deny I have feelings for you too, but a relationship between us is impossible."

"Are you trying to tell me you're still in love with your ex-fiancé?"

She looked away, her face contorted with disgust. "No! Not in the least."

He took a step, reached out, and placed his hands on her arms, shaking her slightly. "So tell me, Mackenzie—what could possibly keep us apart?"

A sob tore from her throat. She knotted her hands into fists, her expression a sea of desperation. As hard as it would be, she had to tell him the truth—the ugly reality that an irresponsible decision had guaranteed she might never carry another child and that she could never be the one to birth the children he so desired. He would never wish to see her again once she spoke the words.

"I saw the repulsion on your face that night at the restaurant when you told me about your sister's death, the look of loathing when you talked about her abortion."

Trace dropped his hands, his brow lined in confusion. "Yes, that's true. I hated it then; I hate it now, but what does my sister's death have to do—"

His eyes widened, and he moved backward a step as if to better glimpse her face. "Are you trying to say—?"

Mackenzie watched as the truth dawned in his eyes. She gritted her teeth. "Yes!" she screamed. "I had an abortion! I didn't desire it—I despise myself for letting it happen. But I can't change the fact—oh dear God— that I murdered my child. Ever!" Her legs wobbly and weak, she leaned against her car and slid to the pavement. She covered her face with her hands, the sobs pouring from the deepest part of her tortured soul and shaking her entire body.

Several minutes later, when it seemed she hadn't another tear left to shed, she glanced upward, and her mouth dropped in surprise that Trace still stood nearby. His shoulders slumped forward as if he carried the weight of the world on his back. Silence now hanging in the air, he turned and came to her side, helping her to her feet.

"Do you think you're able to drive?" he said, opening the car door, his voice wooden.

Her throat too raw to speak, Mackenzie nodded and slipped into the driver's seat a moment later. She grabbed several sheets from the ever-ready box of tissues beneath the dash of the car and scrubbed away the residue from her confession. She put the car in reverse, backed out of the parking space, and waited while Trace walked the short distance to his car. As she observed him in the rearview mirror, a single tear dripped onto her hand. She lowered her torso to rest her cheek against her hands, which gripped the steering wheel as if it somehow could sustain her sanity. For all the lights that had lit up the ebony sky less than an hour earlier, she believed it was the blackest night she'd ever seen.

You're a fool, Mackenzie Adams. If you'd just kept quiet, Trace would never have known your transgression. So what if the two of you had decided to marry at some point in the future and he'd learned of your possible incapability to bear his children? You could always adopt.

Mackenzie shook her head, refusing to listen to the voice in her head. She could never do that to Trace or any other man. "Oh God," she said, swiping at the fresh tears clouding her vision. "I knew better than to let my feelings for Trace surface." She lifted her head to again glance in the mirror. Seeing the lights of his car, she drove forward. Would she have to endure the repercussions of her horrendous mistake the rest of her life?

Trace is a good man. And there is—or was—something special between us. Mackenzie drew a tattered sigh. Any chance of a relationship with him now seemed as remote as the most distant country in the world. Any affection he'd previously held for her had been destroyed by the foulness of the burden she'd carried inside her for months. She'd read the bitter truth of it in his eyes.

Mackenzie winced, recalling the shock on his face. Maybe it would be best to just pack her bags and leave Park House. She wasn't needed there anyway. Besides, Trace would probably welcome her exit from the estate. If she stayed, it was inevitable they'd run into one another. It would mangle her heart anew to see the hurt and anger in his eyes again, should he even look her way.

Mackenzie pulled into the driveway of Park House, holding her breath. A moment later, she allowed a sigh of relief to brush across her lips. Trace's car was nowhere in sight. After closing the garage door behind her car, she soon entered the kitchen. Making her way across the house, each step seemed laden, like one trying to drag log beams soaked in water.

Shortly thereafter, she opened the mirrored cabinet in her bathroom and took out the tube of toothpaste housed there. Her gaze fell on the bottle of sleeping pills her doctor had prescribed a few weeks before she graduated. He'd thought her sleeplessness had been due to finals anxiety. She opened the bottle and shook the pills into her hand. How many would it take to end all her heartache? She looked into the mirror, eyeing her swollen face. All she had to do was stuff them in her mouth, take a drink of water, and swallow. She raised the hand holding the pills to her lips.

Mackenzie jumped at the sound of her cell phone. Reading the name on the screen, she frowned. *Angie? At this time of night?*

"Hi, Angie. Are you okay?"

"Yes, I am. But what about you? I just got in from my date and found Mom awake. She thought I should phone you. Said she woke up earlier with a strong urge to pray for you."

Mackenzie opened her fist and stared at the sleeping pills. What had she been thinking? *Dear God. What chaos that would have been.* "A little depressed, but yeah, I'm fine. Thinking a little straighter now."

"You want to chat about it?"

"Thanks, but no. I'm extremely tired. Maybe another time. Angie, please tell your mom thank you for her prayers. They were a gift from heaven." Mackenzie closed her eyes. *How could I give enough praise to God for this second chance at life?*

"Sure," Angie said, hesitating momentarily. "Mackenzie, you do know we're here for you anytime you need us. Oh, and Mom says to please come see us. You're welcome anytime."

"Thank you—I will. And, Angie, thanks for listening to your mom. It was a life-changing moment for me."

"I assume you'll explain all that to me later."

Mackenzie heard the grin in her friend's voice. "Maybe. Good night, Angie. See you Monday."

"Dear Father God, forgive me. How could I have considered the deplorable act of taking my own life? Thank you for telling Mrs. Valencia to pray for me. How great is your mercy and love! I desire to serve you. But sometimes the remorse of what I did overwhelms me. I know you've forgiven me; please help me forgive myself. Also, show me what to do. Am I to stay or go?"

I have a plan for you, Mackenzie—a plan that will give you hope and peace. Just trust in me, beloved. I will make the crooked paths straight. Seek after me, for my thoughts and ways are not your thoughts and ways. Be still, and know that I am your God. Remember, I reward those who trust solely in me.

Mackenzie uncurled her fingers, flung the capsules into the toilet bowl, and tossed the container that had held them into the trash. *Yes, God, I will do my best to trust in you.* All at once, an image of Zelda Simpson filled her mind. Maybe she'd be willing to teach a new convert how to better build her faith in Christ.

Mackenzie stepped into the shower and stood beneath the calming stream of water, doing her best to scrub the effects of her confrontation with Trace from both body and mind. How things would play out for them, she hadn't a clue. But now, she could depend on God and his faithfulness to map out the journey for her life. She just had to be patient and trust him. And she believed a talk with Mrs. Simpson would be a step in the right direction. Her spirits lifting, Mackenzie decided she'd phone Zelda the next morning to arrange a visit with her as soon as possible.

Chapter 19

"Come in, dear child. Come in," Zelda said, holding the door of her house wide open. "I've made us a fresh pot of tea and some raspberry scones."

"You didn't have to go to that much trouble for me, Mrs. Simpson."

"Nonsense. I've looked forward to our visit from the moment you phoned this morning." She motioned Mackenzie toward the spacious living room. "I hope you're not in a big hurry. I don't often get to chat with members of the younger generation."

"Nor I the older." Mackenzie grinned. "But I think we've managed to bridge the gap, don't you?"

Zelda laughed. "Yes, quite well. Please have a seat while I get our refreshments."

"Let me help you."

"No, no. You just sit right there," Zelda said, pointing to a chair across the room. "I'm sure you need to cool a mite after the walk to my house. It's as hot as hades today." She smiled. "Well, not exactly, but that one-hundred-five-degree temperature out there could sure be an appetizer for the main meal."

Mackenzie giggled. "Mrs. Simpson, you're the bomb."

Zelda looked confused. "A bomb?"

"Yeah. You know, someone who's cool or the best—that sort of thing."

"Oh, I see." The timer on the oven dinged. "Excuse me, dear. The scones are ready. I'll be right back." She walked toward the kitchen, muttering. "A bomb. Of all things."

Observing Mrs. Simpson's exit from the room, Mackenzie smiled. Today, her new friend had on zebra-striped capris and a bright red sleeveless shirt that clashed with the smattering of red-orange in her hair, which she'd pulled to the back of her neck, held in place by a large red-and-black leopard-print clip.

"Is there any new word about the baby's disappearance?" Zelda said once she'd placed the tea tray on the table between matching Queen Anne chairs, one of which Mackenzie now occupied.

Mackenzie's features wilted into sadness. She waited until Zelda had filled their cups before answering her host's question. "Nothing more than the fact that one of the vehicles the kidnappers drove is now in the hands of the police."

"Yes. I heard that on the news." Zelda shook her head. "Such a tragic affair." She brightened after a moment. "And how is that nice young man Trace Patterson getting along?"

At the mention of his name, Mackenzie's eyes smarted. She reached for a scone from the platter and took a moment to butter it. She compelled her lips into a smile. "I really can't say for sure."

Setting her teacup aside, Mrs. Simpson leaned toward Mackenzie and patted her knee. "You look as if your heart is broken. What has happened, dear?"

A soft moan escaped Mackenzie's mouth. She lowered her lashes, unable to face her friend; she didn't deserve the compassion she'd read in Mrs. Simpson's eyes. Mackenzie tried to hold back her tears, but they trickled down her cheeks one by one. "Mrs. Simpson, I committed a horrible sin a few months ago. You said you discerned that I'd had a child, but the truth is, I had an abortion.

"My fiancé threatened to break off our engagement if I didn't. He said, 'Get rid of the inconvenience or it's curtains for us.' I loved him so much I bowed to his will. But soon afterward, I discovered he'd been unfaithful to me for several months. I broke our engagement and moved back to my parents' home. No one but Zack knew I had aborted our child. At the clinic, I tried to stop it, but the nurse drugged me. When I woke up, my baby was dead." Tears gushed from Mackenzie's eyes.

Mrs. Simpson rushed from the room and returned a moment later, handing Mackenzie a handkerchief. When she'd calmed a bit, Mackenzie took a drink of the hot tea. "I kept that knowledge buried inside me all these months until last night. I knew that Trace and I were attracted to one another, but I couldn't let it continue. You see, the doctor that took my baby's life told me I would probably never have another child. He didn't explain why, just walked out of the room as quickly as he could." Mackenzie shrugged. "I suppose something must have happened during the abortion.

"From the start of our friendship, I knew Trace desired a large family. That's why I tried to ignore the attraction between us, doing my utmost to discourage his attentions. Last night, he declared his feelings for me."

"That's wonderful, dear. Trace is a godly man."

"No. You don't understand. That's the last thing I wanted to hear from him. In one of our discussions, he mentioned his hatred of abortions, and realizing he wasn't going to accept my excuses for not seeing him, I told him the whole sordid story, including the repercussions." Mackenzie blew her nose. "I don't think Trace will ever speak to me again. And I can't blame him."

Mrs. Simpson lowered her head and placed her folded hands in her lap, seemingly engrossed in the pattern of the age spots on her skin. After a few moments, she raised her eyelashes. "You do know that when you accepted Christ back into your life, God forgave you," she said, surveying her guest.

Mackenzie nodded. "Yes, I do. If I didn't, I think I would go crazy. The reason I wanted to see you is … Please tell me, Mrs. Simpson—how can I forgive myself? How can I get rid of the guilt and shame? Not only have I made a disaster of my life, but now I've destroyed Trace's faith in me. Not to mention the anguish I've caused my parents because I couldn't face up to what I had done. Instead, I chose to run. I couldn't bear to look into their trusting eyes, knowing I had killed their grandchild."

"Mackenzie, you're not the first woman who's suffered from this sin. Nor will you be the last, I'm sorry to say. At least not until Christ's return to this earth. Do you not think your parents love you enough to help you through this?"

"Are you kidding me? My parents participate every year in the annual pro-life march sponsored by a number of churches in Phoenix. I could never make them understand how their child could go against everything she'd been taught. How could I possibly tell them, Mrs. Simpson? At this moment, my mother won't talk to me, because I left Arizona to take the nanny job at the Huntingtons'. I can just imagine her reaction if I told her about this."

"Well, dear, having never known your mother, I can't answer that, nor can I tell you what to do. That is something you'll have to work out with the heavenly Father. For now, though, I suggest you keep loving God with all your heart, soul, mind, and strength; keep seeking His will for your life; and keep asking Him to heal your hurts of the past. The salvation Christ bought for us by His death on the cross and resurrection from the dead gave us not only forgiveness for sin but also freedom from all guilt, shame, and condemnation. But it's up to us to accept that precious gift.

"The Scripture tells us to think on things that are good, holy, and upright. Mackenzie, don't dwell on the past, but consider how God has brought you out of darkness and into His marvelous light. If you do these things, you'll soon experience in reality the freedom you desire. Above all, you must trust God and believe that He will complete the good work that He's begun in you, His design for your life according to His will and purpose.

"In Psalm 119, we find that His Word is a lamp to our feet and a light to our path. You'll find all the answers to your questions in His Word. And, Mackenzie, give your mother some space. I'm sure she's just disappointed that her dreams for you took a turn she didn't expect. A mother's love never dies for her children, no matter the direction they take in life. She'll forgive you in time and welcome you back into her arms."

"You really think so, Mrs. Simpson?"

"I do. Trust is the key, Mackenzie—trust in our Savior's love." Zelda smiled, a teasing glint in her eyes. "I haven't lived all these years without learning something about the subject of trust." She glanced at Mackenzie's plate. "Now eat up, child, before your scone gets any colder."

An hour or so later, Mackenzie lumbered toward Park House, mulling over Mrs. Simpson's encouragement, realizing the words she'd heard in her heart the previous evening were similar to the ones spoken by Zelda. Mackenzie shuddered, recalling how close she'd been to snuffing out her life.

All at once, the memory of the only time she'd met her great-grandmother Louise Adams waltzed into Mackenzie's mind. Her great-grandmother had traveled from Mississippi with Mackenzie's grandparents to Arizona for a visit. Mackenzie recalled how she had sat at the woman's feet, enthralled with the stories she told of life growing up on the family farm in Mississippi. Her great-grandmother had said that trust in God's love and grace had carried them through the hard times. The chorus of an old song Mackenzie had heard Grandmother Louise sing floated into Mackenzie's mind.

> Trust and obey,
> For there's no other way
> To be happy in Jesus
> But to trust and obey.

Mackenzie smiled. "Guess I won't hear it any straighter than that," she said, glancing toward the hazy sky. *Thank you, Father, for the grace I need to trust you. Thank you for healing me from my sinful past and helping me to become the person you desire me to be.*

Nearing the house, she noticed Trace's car parked in the drive. She groaned. *Oh please, God, let me make it to my room without encountering him.* Stepping onto the porch shortly thereafter, Mackenzie opened the door as quietly as possible, but her heart sank when she saw him come out of his uncle's office. She glanced at him and then at the stairs but realized she'd never make the climb before he noticed her presence. As she observed his approach, her insides began to quake. He had his head lowered and a troubled look on his face. He lifted his chin, and his eyes brightened with pleasure momentarily until a look of sorrow passed across his features.

"Hello, Mackenzie. Did you enjoy your visit with Mrs. Simpson?" Trace smiled at the surprise lighting up her expression. "Uncle Drew told me where you were."

"Oh," she said, lowering her eyelashes.

Victoria Burks

He reached out to her and then dropped his hand. "Mackenzie, could we go somewhere? I need to speak with you."

She started to shake her head, but a look in his eye she couldn't define halted her intention. She moistened her lips. "I suppose. Is something wrong, Trace?"

He glanced over his shoulder. "Not here, Mackenzie. Let's take a ride, shall we?"

"Okay," she said, frowning. "Just let me grab my purse."

"I'll wait outside."

She nodded and then hurried up the stairs. Trace opened the car door for her a few minutes later. She wanted to question him, but her intuition directed her otherwise. It seemed a thousand thoughts jangled in her head as to what might have upset him. They soon sat parked in a semiprivate pull-off overlooking the Arkansas River.

Mackenzie couldn't wait any longer. The silence during the drive had been maddening, Trace's preoccupation with his thoughts fraying her nerves. She could stand it no longer. "Trace, what's wrong? Is it Elise?"

He faced her, looking confused momentarily. "Elise?" Seeming to take note of the panic in her eyes, he reached out and touched her arm. "No, not Elise."

"Then what? Why are you so distressed?"

Trace rubbed his hand across his face. "First of all, Mackenzie, I want to apologize for my horrid behavior last night. I had a different ending planned for the evening." A woeful smile turned up one corner of his mouth. "Things didn't turn out quite like I expected."

"I'm sorry, Trace."

"No," he said, shaking his head. "I'm the one who's sorry—a million times sorry. I realize now why you've discouraged our, ah, friendship. I believe it had to do with what I shared about my sister. Correct?"

Mackenzie turned away from his gaze. "Yes, to a large degree. But also, my trust in men is on the negative side of the number line at this point in time. Don't get me wrong. Zack and I were both responsible for the mur— uh, death—of our child. I blame myself more than Zack. The bottom line is, I didn't refuse his demands. I made the wrong choice—a senseless decision that will plague me the rest of my life. I didn't understand the

234

heartbreak I would suffer or how it might affect my family or a future husband should I ever decide to marry."

"I admit you shocked me," Trace said, taking her hand. "And yes, I hate the act of abortion. In the case of my sister's suicide, three lives were destroyed, leaving behind a homeless child." He ran his free hand through his hair.

"Don't get me wrong—I've had a good life at Park House. But it can never replace what I lost early in my life." He reached out and ran the back of his hand along Mackenzie's cheekbone, tenderness filling his eyes. "Yes, I despise abortion but not those who've been victimized by the horror. Especially you, Mackenzie." He released Mackenzie's hand and stared out the car window, drumming his fingers on the steering wheel. "God and I had a long talk last night." He again faced Mackenzie. "Please forgive me for my judgmental behavior. That privilege belongs to God alone."

Mackenzie placed her hand on his arm. "With what you had gone through with your sister and mother, your reaction to my confession is understandable. Trace, I'm sorry I hurt you. I just felt I had to be honest with you, make you see that there's a very real possibility I could never have children."

"Mackenzie, there are more ways than one to have children." He grinned. "Or haven't you heard of adoption or"—he paused, noting the heightened color in her cheeks—"other ways?"

She laughed and then sobered. "Trace, I'm just saying please don't expect more of me than I can give at the moment. The wounds in my heart are still open and raw. I know that God is in the process of healing me, but it will take time. Right now, I need to concentrate on my relationship with God until I feel my life is on a more solid foundation. I'm just asking for some space."

Trace smiled. "I suppose I *have* been a bit pushy in relaying my admiration for you."

"Maybe a little," she said, unable to withhold a grin at his boyish demeanor. "Trace?"

"Yes?"

"I couldn't help but notice how upset you were earlier when you came out of your uncle's office. Since you didn't elaborate any further about

Elise, I can't help but wonder if a new development has occurred in either Jasmine's or Jason's murder."

"No, not that I've been told." He ran his fingers through his hair again, his eyes narrowing. "We have a buyer by the name of Cranston who believes we defrauded him in a land purchase. Uncle Drew tried to tell the buyer the statement got deleted from the contract by accident, but he refuses to accept the explanation."

"The statement?"

"Yes, a clause stating the land is in a flood zone, although it is quite a distance from the river. And it is true that particular property hasn't flooded for many years, but the buyer talked to an older gentleman who owed one of the adjoining properties, discovering that our buyer's land had been badly flooded about thirty-five years ago."

"Oh my. I can understand why Mr. Cranston would be disgruntled." Noting a strange look that suddenly appeared in Trace's eyes, Mackenzie frowned. "Is this the same situation Mr. Huntington was concerned about when we came home last Sunday evening?"

"Yes. I read the contract after the secretary typed it. The clause about the flood zone was definitely in the paperwork."

"So what do you think happened?"

A sigh of anger gushed from his lips. "My thoughts about that right now are too ugly to expose. I plan to look more into the matter as soon as I get to the office Monday morning"—he frowned—"or maybe sooner."

As much as Mackenzie desired to question him further, the look on his face silenced her. At that moment, Trace keyed the engine of the Lexus to life, backed out of the overlook, and drove toward Park House, his thoughts seemingly on something other than the girl at his side. Just before they arrived at their destination, he turned to her, a smile smoothing the worry lines from his brow. "Mackenzie, I promise I won't crowd you. All I'm asking for now is friendship. Can you at least allow me that?"

She smiled. "Friendship it is." She held out her hand. "Can we shake on it?"

Trace laughed. "You bet."

"Good morning," Mrs. Simpson said to Mackenzie the next day, drawing her to a vacant corner of the church foyer. I'm not the assigned greeter today, but I waited for you because I want to introduce you to the teachers of the college-and-career class that meets at ten o'clock on Sunday mornings."

"Sounds great. I would like to become more involved in the church."

"Good. The class should have ended a few minutes ago. Oh," Zelda said, glancing toward the staircase descending to the classrooms on the lower floor of the church. "Here are the leaders now." She took hold of Mackenzie's arm and led her toward an attractive couple in their forties who'd stopped to speak to a young woman about Mackenzie's age. Upon their approach, the couple turned to smile at Zelda.

"Good morning, Mrs. Simpson," the gentleman said, taking in Mackenzie as he reached to shake Zelda's hand.

"Yes, it is a lovely morning. Mackenzie, I'd like you to meet Mike and Gretchen Carter, leaders of the class I mentioned." Zelda turned to the young woman at their side. "And this is Darcy Evans, one of the class members."

"How do you do?" Mackenzie said, extending her arm to shake their hands. "I'm Mackenzie Adams. I've just recently moved here from Arizona."

Gretchen took hold of Mackenzie's hand. "So glad to make your acquaintance. What brings you to our city—school, job?"

"She came here to become nanny to the Huntingtons' baby daughter—you know, the child down the street that was kidnapped about two weeks ago, the one our church is praying for daily that she will be returned home safe?" Zelda said before Mackenzie could utter a sound.

Gretchen nodded. "So sad. Mike and I are following the story on the news. Trace Patterson, Mr. Huntington's nephew, is in our class. Well, speak of angels," Gretchen said, grinning. "Missed you in class, Trace."

"Hi, everyone," Trace said, his gaze centering on Mackenzie's face after a brief nod and handshakes all around. "Sorry I missed it. Had a bit of business to attend to before coming to church. Mackenzie, did you make it to Sunday school?"

"Not today. But I plan on being here for the class next week."

"Good. I'll drop by Park House and pick you up."

From the corners of her eyes, Mackenzie caught the look that passed between Zelda and the Carters, a knowing smile on each of their faces.

She also noticed the sudden you-light-up-my-life expression hovering over Darcy's features after Trace greeted her. The young woman seemed spellbound, unable to tear her gaze away from him. Mackenzie moved a half step closer to Trace.

"Thank you. I appreciate the kindness," she said, doing her best to ignore the realization that without thinking about it, she'd just marked her territory. The look of disappointment that appeared on Darcy's face revealed the truth. *Now, why did I do that?* Remorse nipping at her, Mackenzie reached out and touched Darcy's arm.

"So nice to have met you."

Darcy straightened her posture. "Same to you." She bounced a glance toward Trace and then back to Mackenzie, a look of resignation filling her blue eyes. She smiled. "Maybe we can get together sometime—take in a movie or something."

"I'd like that," Mackenzie said, noticing the worship service was about to begin. "Let's exchange phone numbers after church."

"Great. I'll see you then," Darcy said, turning to follow the Carters into the sanctuary.

Trace offered Zelda his arm to do likewise, Mackenzie at his side. Sitting beside her after escorting Mrs. Simpson to her pew, Trace spoke softly to Mackenzie. "I've asked Mrs. Simpson to have lunch with me today. Would you like to come with us?" His look sharpened when Mackenzie seemed reluctant to answer. "Just a *friendly* lunch—nothing more," he said, grinning.

Mackenzie smiled back at him. "I'd be glad to tag along. I'd intended to ask Mrs. Simpson the same thing today after the service."

"If you don't mind, we'll go someplace where we don't have to wait long. That business I mentioned to you yesterday requires my attention this afternoon, and I want to complete it before church this evening. The pastor has scheduled a missionary I don't want to miss."

Nodding her agreement, Mackenzie stood with the rest of the congregation at the worship minister's cue. She began to sing with the people, her mind turning to something more important: extolling praise to her Savior, the King of Kings and Lord of Lords.

Early that afternoon, Mackenzie hid a smile at the shocked glances from those stationed in the lobby of the restaurant, waiting to be seated. She hoped the promised fifteen-minute wait from the hostess would be just that. Although Zelda didn't seem to notice, Mackenzie couldn't argue with the probable thoughts of the onlookers as they tried not to stare at Mrs. Simpson's costume.

Today Zelda was decked out in royal blue, from her turban hat to her sparkly midheel pumps; the lapels and pocket flaps on the jacket of her summer suit were dotted with blue sequins. While Mrs. Simpson carried on a conversation with a woman she'd introduced to her companions as a longtime friend, Mackenzie eyed the blue sapphires set in sterling silver that dangled from her elderly friend's ears; she had a matching necklace draped around her neck. Unable to keep her lips poised, Mackenzie smiled. She had to admit Mrs. Simpson struck quite a pose.

Mackenzie stole a glance around the crowd, her eyes narrowing at the two woman who stood across from them taking in Zelda's apparel and tittering behind their hands. They caught Mackenzie's gaze and turned away, sheepish looks on their faces. *Okay, so Zelda's style in fashion tends to be a bit eccentric, but those nearby have no idea the kindness that dwells in the woman's soul,* Mackenzie thought. At that moment, the hostess called Trace's name. The three were soon ordering their meals.

Eyeing Trace's departure from Park House after he'd dropped his lunch companions off at their respective abodes, Mackenzie couldn't help but wonder what Trace would find concerning the Cranston affair when he arrived at his office. Had Mr. Huntington or his secretary deleted the flood clause from the contract before Mr. Cranston could sign the document?

Mackenzie shook her head. She couldn't believe her employer would deliberately do something so underhanded. She frowned. Hadn't she overheard him say he'd do anything to keep his company secure? But surely he hadn't meant anything unethical or illegal. She sighed. To her, he didn't fit that paradigm at all. Had Trace considered the possibility as well? Was that the "ugly" he'd referred to when they'd discussed the matter the previous day? *Oh God, please, for Trace's sake, let him find someone at fault other than his uncle.*

Chapter 20

*D*isappointed that Trace hadn't made it to the service that evening, Mackenzie walked toward home, curious about the why of his absence, speculating that he hadn't completed his search for his answers to the Cranston error. Knowing of his desire to hear the visiting missionary, she'd asked Zelda for an introduction to the church secretary so that a tape of the service could be ordered for him. That accomplished, Mackenzie had promised Zelda a visit later in the upcoming week before the two had parted company.

Stepping into the entryway of Park House, Mackenzie heard shouting. Making her way cautiously down the hall, she realized the voices came from Mr. Huntington's office. Her curiosity winning over decorum, she paused to listen.

"Uncle Drew, how could you be so uncouth as to do such a thing?"

"Who says I did?"

"I say so. I talked to your secretary, and she swears the flood clause was in the contract when I gave it to her to prepare a copy to be mailed to Mr. Cranston the next day for his approval. We now know that his initial copy and the one he signed in our office that day were different from the original one. Only you, Uncle Drew, could have deleted that clause. Is that why you told her you would mail the contract after you had gone over it?

"You just couldn't stand the thought that Mr. Cranston might not buy the land, could you? So you decided to misrepresent it. I don't even have to ask why. All for the company and the name behind it, right? You'd better hope that you can talk Cranston into forfeiting his purchase."

Silence filled the air momentarily. Mackenzie edged closer to the office door so that she could hear Mr. Huntington's softer, intense tone. "Huntington Incorporated means everything to me, as it did to my father and his. Sometimes I believe it's the air I breathe. I can't risk seeing it dwindle and die. It's your future as well, Trace. And Elise's too, should she be returned to us. Have you even considered that?"

"That doesn't alter the fact that should Cranston take us to court, we have no chance of winning. I won't lie, Uncle Drew, not even for you."

"Enough said, Trace. Go home now. I have to figure a way to get us out of this mess. It's obvious your sanctimonious input won't suffice."

"I'm sorry you feel that way. Good night, Uncle Drew."

Mackenzie retreated to the stairs as quietly as possible and rushed up the steps. She made it around the corner of the upper hallway just as the front door opened. She hugged the wall until she heard the door close and then hurried to her room, feeling as if all of a sudden her breath had been yanked from her body.

Could Trace be wrong about his uncle? Mr. Huntington hadn't admitted he'd committed the fraud. But he'd never stated his innocence either. So what was she to believe? Mackenzie took a bottle of water from the fridge and put it to her mouth, her eyes widening. Mr. Huntington had talked as though Elise might not be returned to him. Could it be possible? Had everyone's prayers in the past days that had now turned into weeks been in vain?

Mackenzie changed out of her church apparel into a comfortable pair of jeans and a T-shirt and then walked into the nursery, where she moved about the room, touching first one toy and then another. With her fingers, she traced the titles of the children's books that sat between a pair of wooden bookends on the top shelf of the toy cubby. Could it be that Elise hadn't been killed after all? Would she be able to enjoy her things once again?

All at once, Mackenzie frowned. *That's odd,* she thought eyeing the open space between the pages of a pop-up book she hadn't yet read to

Elise. Mackenzie pulled it from the shelf, and it fell open at the center of the book. At once, she discovered the reason the book didn't close properly.

The story was about pirates and gold. She lifted the lid of the lumpy pop-up treasure chest and pulled out what appeared to be a page of scented stationery folded to fit inside the envelope-like compartment. Mackenzie's heart began to pound. She'd smelled the same perfume another time—in the master suite when she'd opened the door to Jasmine's closet.

Mackenzie carefully unfolded the stationery to see a handwritten letter in flowery script, dated a few days before she'd arrived at Park House. She took a drink from the bottle of water to moisten her suddenly parched lips. Sitting down in the rocking chair, she began to read the contents of the letter.

To Whom It May Concern:

I must hurry and write this before Drew returns upstairs from his meeting with an unexpected visitor. I fear for my life. Drew and I got into a bitter argument over Jason. I blurted out that I'd decided to file for divorce days ago—that we were too incompatible to live together any longer. When he refused to accept my decision, I stated the real purpose for my decision: to marry Jason Crane, Elise's true father and that I intended to leave tonight, taking Elise with me. I've never seen him so angry. He grabbed my throat and squeezed. He said if I tried to leave, I would never make it out of the house alive. When the doorbell rang, he let me go. During the quarrel Drew shouted that he would see me dead before he'd allow Jason Crane to have me or Elise.

He said he'd known about our ongoing affair for more than a year. He even showed me the results of the paternity test that proved he was not Elise's father.

Aware that my husband is a vicious and vindictive man beneath all his solemnity and virtuous ways, I know his threat is not just idle words. He will kill me. He will find a way that will exonerate him of any connection to my murder, conniving man that he is. I fear for Jason as well. Although Drew knows Elise will inherit my estate, he'll do everything in his power to get his hands on my inheritance.

I'm so afraid. I have no doubt that I will die. So please, whoever is reading this, take this letter to the police. I don't want Drew to get away with murder. I must go to Elise now. I may never get to see her again.

Jasmine Huntington

Mackenzie stared at the letter, surveying the words once again. Not realizing she'd been holding her breath, she let it out slowly. Taking in a large gulp of air, she read Jasmine's proclamation a third time. Mackenzie moved her head back and forth. Mr. Huntington—a vicious man? A murderer? The image she'd seen of his hands around Jason's throat in the foyer of Park House materialized in her mind. Was it possible? Had his kindness to her been nothing more than a facade? She glanced toward the empty crib. Could he have murdered both mother and child? A sob caught in Mackenzie's throat. Had the love he'd exemplified toward Elise been an act? No. She couldn't believe it. His emotions had been too real in love shown to her and his devastation over her kidnapping.

She rubbed her hand back and forth across her brow. She had to think. *Dear God, please show me what to do.* Mackenzie jumped to her feet and dashed into her room. She glanced around, grasping the letter tightly in her hand. Catching a glimpse of her cell phone, she grabbed it from the desk seconds later, and punched the symbol for her contact list. Scrolling down the names, she quickly found Angie's number. Her hands trembled so much that she missed the call symbol pictogram and pushed the message icon instead. Frowning, she slowly backtracked her movements. She breathed a sigh of relief when she heard Angie's upbeat greeting.

"Angie, you'll never guess what I found."

"Mackenzie," Angie said, her voice barely audible after she'd heard the details of the discovery. "You have to phone Captain Sprinsky."

"Yes. I know. I now understand your feelings of disloyalty toward the Huntingtons."

"But this is evidence in a murder case. You can't withhold it from the police."

"That's what I keep telling myself. But what if someone else killed her and made her write that letter, wanting to blame Mr. Huntington for her death? As you know, we've found possible motives for Mrs. Slater, Greg, and even Mr. Crane. His death may not be related at all. As an attorney, he could have had any number of enemies."

"True, but who would think to put the letter in one of Elise's storybooks? She must have been afraid to hide it anywhere else in the house, knowing it would be destroyed by Mr. Huntington or Mrs. Slater if found by either of them. It's my guess she hoped the new nanny would find it eventually and turn it over to the police."

"I'm surprised they didn't find it when they searched the nursery."

"Probably just didn't catch the difference between that book and the others."

"I bet you're right. Listen, Angie, thanks. Even though this is all too surreal to be sane, you've helped me understand what I must do. I will phone the captain right away. Do you think I should inform Trace about this?"

Angie hesitated a moment before answering. "Maybe you should let the police handle that."

"I agree. He might say something to his uncle before Captain Sprinsky has time to investigate the matter. Maybe Mr. Huntington thought he had reason to kill Jasmine, but I just can't fathom his murdering Elise." Mackenzie's eyes widened at her next thought. "Do you think he might have staged the kidnapping and then murdered Jason Crane to keep from paying back the million he loaned to Mr. Huntington?"

Mackenzie heard Angie's sigh. "Sounds a little far out. But if he's as conniving as Jasmine suggested, it's possible."

"You're right. The theory is a little out there. Guess I'd better phone Captain Sprinsky. And, Angie, pray that nothing comes of this. I really like Mr. Huntington."

"Gotcha covered, girl. See you tomorrow."

Ending the call, Mackenzie returned to the nursery and picked up the storybook from the floor, where it had fallen from her hands earlier. *The captain will need this as well,* she decided. *If they find Jasmine's fingerprints, it will prove she placed the letter inside the book.* Mackenzie refolded the sheet of stationery, placed it inside the simulated treasure chest, and smoothed the lid over the tiny strip of Velcro that kept it shut. She closed the book and pulled her cell phone from the back pocket of her jeans to key in the officer's number. Taking a seat in the rocker, she turned toward the crib, eyeing Elise's handmade blanket. *Above all, dear God, please save the child if it's still possible.*

"Captain Sprinsky," Mackenzie said, disappointment cloaking her features at having to leave a message, "this is Mackenzie Adams. I've found something at Park House you need to see. It has to do with Jasmine Huntington's murder. Please phone me as soon as you get this message."

As she pocketed her cell phone, this time in the front pocket of her jeans, all of a sudden, an artic sensation gripped the back of her neck. She glanced upward. Mr. Huntington stood just inside the nursery door. Her eyes widened at the look on his face. "Oh, Mr. Huntington. I didn't realize you were there."

"I guess you didn't hear my knock. Thinking you weren't in the nursery, I came on inside. The longing for my daughter today is overwhelming, and I thought a trip to the nursery would in some way help me feel close to her. Sorry to have barged in like this." He took a step forward. "But at hearing your message to Captain Sprinsky, I can see it's important that I did."

She shrank back; the gleam in his eyes turned from friendly to eerie, like the look of a caged animal trying to escape.

"What did you find that had to do with my wife's murder, Miss Adams?"

She stood from the chair. *God, help me. The man looks insane.* If she could just get out the door, she could run. She pushed words from her tightened throat. "Really, it wasn't anything, sir. Just some silly notion I had." She held the storybook close to her chest, hoping he hadn't noticed her trembling body.

"Would it have something to do with that book clutched in your hands?"

Mackenzie started to speak, but before she could say a word, he jerked the storybook from her fingers.

"Let's just take a look, shall we?" He opened the book and flipped through the pages, keeping an eye on her at the same time. About halfway through the book, he paused.

Mackenzie felt as if her stomach dropped to her toes. She knew without a doubt he was looking at the protruding treasure chest. The tearing sound of the lid pulling away from its fastener seemed to coincide with the thought that her life could be ripped from her at any moment.

"Well now. What do we have here?"

She observed his movements as he drew the sheet of stationery from its hiding place, glancing at Mackenzie every few minutes while he read Jasmine's letter. The image of her parents' faces flashed in her mind. Would she ever see them again? She closed her eyes. And Trace. If only she could have denounced her fear and told him how much she cared for him.

A look of disgust flickered across her employer's features. "Leave it to Jasmine to have the last word." He focused his full attention on Mackenzie. "I assume this is what you intended to give to Captain Sprinsky."

Unable to speak a word, she lowered her eyelashes, giving him a slight nod.

"I'm sure you realize I can't let you do that. It would destroy all my plans. I believe you need to come with me now, Miss Adams." He folded the letter to its original state, placed it inside his sports jacket, and tossed the book onto the child's table nearby.

All at once, she found her voice. "Where are we going?" she said, her eyes wide with fright when she saw the small-caliber gun he pulled from the side pocket of his coat.

"Not far. In a little while, it won't matter to you anyway," he said, giving her a cool smile. He grabbed her arm with a viselike grip, the cold, hard look in his eyes warming somewhat as he took in her countenance. "I'm really sorry about this, Miss Adams. You are a credit to your peerage. But surely you understand my position here. Too bad you had to become a victim of circumstance." He lifted the barrel of the gun toward her face. "Shall we go?"

She tried to yank free, but he tightened his hold. She winced from the pain. Terror rained down from the dark cloud of despair that loomed over her. If her intuition was correct, she would be as dead as the former mistress of Park House within a few moments. *Oh God, please help me.*

Her eyes bright with alarm, she moved toward the door when he released her arm, the barrel of his gun positioned in the middle of her back, prodding her steps. Once on the main floor, she glanced toward the front door.

"I wouldn't even think about that, Miss Adams. You'd never make it out the door." He waved the gun toward the hall. "Shall we continue?"

Her gaze straying from his face to the gun, she walked toward the back of the house, realizing every step she took might be her last. At the end of the hallway, he held up his hand, signaling her to stop. He reached out and touched what Makenzie thought was a knot of wood in the paneling. With eyes rounding in surprise, she grew more astonished when a portion of the narrow wall before them opened to reveal a cement staircase descending to what she believed to be a basement. Flipping a switch on the back side of the wall, he motioned with his gun for her to step down into the concrete abyss.

Halfway down the steps, she realized they were in not a room but a tunnel-like corridor that seemed to stretch for several yards. Shortly thereafter, they stepped into a large room lined with wooden shelves; several old mason jars were stationed here and there atop the planking. A sofa several decades past its prime occupied the one wall free of shelving. A table and four chairs were situated a few feet from the sofa. Had Jasmine been killed here rather than in her room before her body and car were dumped into the river?

A stack of old, dusty ledgers sat atop the table, as if the person who'd been working in them had left his job temporarily but would return at any moment to finish his ciphering. She darted a glance around the room. This had to be the old headquarters of the illegal alcohol transport business whereby Mr. Huntington's grandfather had made his fortune in the thirties. What was the term Trace had used to describe the alcohol when he'd told the story? Oh yes—*moonshine.*

At the sound of Mr. Huntington's voice, she turned toward him, noting he held his cell phone to his ear. She touched the right front pocket of her jeans. A glimmer of hope rose within her. If she could get a message to Angie to phone the police, she might have a chance for survival. She just had to think of a way without Mr. Huntington being aware of it. While he waited for a response from the person he'd called, she moved toward the table. She jumped when he said her name.

"Yes, Miss Adams. Make yourself comfortable while you can." After a moment, he spoke into the phone. "Where are you? Come to the cellar. And make it quick! We've got a problem." Ending the call, he stared at her, a glazed look in his eyes. "Greg will be here soon, and we can solve the situation at hand," he said as though speaking to himself.

Mackenzie had a hard time swallowing past the lump in her throat. Her knees were trembling so hard that she thought she would collapse onto the concrete floor. She grabbed the back of the nearest chair and took a deep breath. A moment later, she sat down and scooted the chair close to the table. She darted a glance toward her adversary. *God, please help me think of a way to divert his attention long enough to send Angie a text.* She leaned back against the chair, a sudden calmness settling over her. As she glimpsed the ledgers, an idea formed in her mind. She closed her eyes momentarily. *Thank you, Father.*

In her peripheral vision, she watched Mr. Huntington pace back and forth across the room. She glimpsed the gun he kept aimed in her direction. Her stomach lurched. Never had she seen him this agitated. Angry, yes, but panicky like a female cat about to have her first litter of kittens? No. She opened one of the ledgers. When he turned his head away from her momentarily, she quickly slid the phone from the front pocket of her jeans and hid it between the pages of the ledger near her.

"May I ask you something, sir?" she said, pretending to read the handwritten numbers in front of her, the fingers of her right hand moving among the icons on her phone.

He stopped pacing to scrutinize her. "What is it?" he said abruptly.

"Since you knew Elise wasn't your child, why didn't you just let Mrs. Huntington have her divorce?"

His gaze seemed to drift to another time, another place. "When I married Jasmine, I knew I couldn't have children. Since she didn't seem interested in having a baby, I never bothered to mention my inability.

"When the economy collapsed a couple years ago, Huntington Inc. had a drastic downturn in sales. I tried to talk Jasmine into parting with some of her fortune to boost the cash flow of the company, but she wouldn't even consider my request. When she became pregnant, at first it grieved me to know she'd been unfaithful to me. But knowing she'd leave her inheritance to her child, I thought of a way to eventually get a permanent financial backing for Huntington Inc. I didn't realize at the time that I would come to love Elise like my own daughter." His voice cracked.

Mackenzie's lips curled in disgust, her stomach growing queasy. She'd lost all her sympathy for the man. While he seemed to be pondering his words, she peeked at her phone, scrolling down to Angie's number, the pages of the ledger shielding her actions. "I think I understand. In order to have custody of Elise and power of attorney over the fortune, her mother would have to die."

"You are a very perceptive young lady, Miss Adams," he said.

"Speaking of Mr. Crane, would you please tell me the reason for the brutal argument Trace and I witnessed between the two of you a few days ago?"

"He came to the house to inform me that Elise was his child and that he intended to pursue his parental rights through the court system. I couldn't let that happen. Now that Crane is dead, Elise's parentage is no longer an issue, is it, Miss Adams?"

They both turned at the sound of footsteps on a second set of stairs at the far end of the room. Greg entered the cellar. A look of shock clambered over his features when he saw Mackenzie seated at the narrow table.

"What's going on here?" Greg said, eyeing the pistol trained on Mackenzie. Mr. Huntington slid his hand beneath his coat, pulled out Jasmine's note, and handed it to Greg.

While Mr. Huntington explained his intention to Greg after he'd read the letter, Mackenzie grasped her window of opportunity, typing her message with one finger as quickly as she could: *Mr. H is going to kill me. Phone Capt. S then Trace. Tell him cellar with mason jars.*

She punched the send button and then eased the phone back into her pocket, again shielding her movements with the ledger. But if they didn't arrive before she died, would her body be taken from Park House and tossed into the river? She shuddered, her mind switching to thoughts of her parents. *Oh Mother, Father, I'm so sorry I disappointed you.*

Tears gathered in her eyes. She wiped them away with her hands, determined not to allow her captors the privilege of seeing her cry. She glanced around the room, taking in the few items sitting on the shelves. Suddenly, she gasped. Both men turned toward her at the sound and then looked in the direction that held her attention.

Mr. Huntington strode across the room and picked up the cordless dryer that had caught her attention; he held it up for her to better see it. He stroked the frayed three or so inches of cord sticking out of the end of the dryer. She took in the open gash on the side of the dryer and the dark hairs that dangled from it. Mackenzie turned away, unable to bear his manic expression or the hideous laugh that escaped his throat. Her theory of Jasmine's death had been closer to the truth than she could have imagined.

"Andrew!"

Startled, the three turned toward the corridor. Mrs. Slater stood at the entrance to the room, her hands on her hips. A low growl erupted from Mr. Huntington's throat. "What are you doing here?"

She eyed the gun and hair dryer in his hands. "When I saw Greg's face turn white like paste after he received a phone call a few minutes ago, I knew something was wrong. Surmising the call came from you, I followed him, not surprised at all to see him enter the old carriage house. I knew exactly where I would find the two of you." She faced Mackenzie. "However, you're a surprise, Miss Adams."

"Cut the chitchat, Lois. Miss Adams has discovered a piece of incriminating evidence against me in Jasmine's murder. I'm afraid she'll have to pay for that." He aimed the gun at Mackenzie's head.

Mrs. Slater stepped farther into the room. "What evidence?"

"Show her, Greg."

Greg handed the letter to his mother. She returned it to him a moment later. That's not any kind of proof, only Jasmine's word against yours."

"You're forgetting this," he said, throwing the hair dryer to the floor. "Now that Miss Adams has seen this, I wouldn't stand a chance in court. My fingerprints are all over it."

Mrs. Slater moved close to Mackenzie. "Are you so bloodthirsty you're willing to add another victim to your list? You've gone insane, Andrew. Our father ruined you with his constant droning about your obligation to keep Huntington Incorporated a success. And now you're a murderer. First Jasmine, most likely Mr. Crane, and the child?" Mrs. Slater's voice cracked. "The only beautiful and innocent being, along with Trace, that's lived in this house for decades. Heartbreak visible in her eyes, Mrs. Slater took in her son. "And it's my guess, Greg assisted you in your evil deeds."

Mr. Huntington lifted his chin, defiance written in his eyes. "What makes you think I murdered Jason and Elise?"

"Because I know you better than anyone. You could never stand someone to best you. Not when you were a boy or now." She glanced at the letter still in her son's hand. "Jasmine and Mr. Crane died the moment you discovered their affair—at least in your mind—and their child became nothing more than a monetary stake in your hands from that moment forward."

Mr. Huntington's shoulders slumped forward. "I love my daughter," he said, his voice breaking. All at once, his spine grew straighter, and his eyes narrowed into thin slits. "My father's legacy will never expire. It will continue to be passed down from generation to generation, as my father and grandfather intended it to be. If Elise is never found, Trace will be my soul heir. I will see to it no matter how many obstacles I have to eliminate along the way." He raised the gun and moved toward Mackenzie.

"No, Andrew!" Mrs. Slater shouted, stepping in front of Mackenzie. "I won't let you kill Miss Adams. She doesn't deserve to die."

Greg, a look of horror on his face, moved a step forward, his arm outstretched toward his employer. "Mr. Huntington, take it easy. You need to think about what you're doing."

A wicked laugh pealed from his throat. "Oh, I know what I'm doing all right. And if you know what's good for you, you'll keep quiet. Now stand aside, Lois."

"No. I can't do that."

At that moment, he raised his gun and fired; the sound reverberated throughout the chamber. Mrs. Slater slumped to the cold floor in front of Mackenzie. She stood there stunned, unable to focus on anything but the red blood pouring from Mrs. Slater's chest. She heard Greg yell as he dropped to his knees beside Mrs. Slater.

"Mother, no!"

Mr. Huntington stood immobile momentarily, staring at the scene, and then lifted the gun again. Just before he fired, Mackenzie thought she heard Trace call out her name.

Chapter 21

ackenzie tried to rouse from the black chasm that surrounded her, but her eyelids wouldn't cooperate. All at once, she became aware of excruciating pain in her chest. She heard voices. *Mother, Dad?* She tried to speak, but something in her throat blocked her words.

"Look, Steve. Mackenzie just moved her fingers. I think she's trying to come out of the coma. Ring for the nurse."

Nurse? Coma? What did she mean? What happened? Where am I?

"Miss Adams, can you open your eyes?"

Mackenzie labored to lift her eyelids, straining against her body's natural instinct to float back into oblivion. At last, she succeeded.

"Good girl," the nurse said lightly, patting Mackenzie's arm. "You're going to be just fine. I bet you'd like to say hello to your parents." Smiling, the nurse pointed to the other side of the bed. After reading the monitor, she reached up and adjusted the flow of the IV tube attached to Mackenzie's hand. "You'll feel better in a few moments—I promise."

Mackenzie slowly turned her head. The breathing tube in her throat made it difficult to move. She took in her parents' smiling faces. Reagan reached out and picked up her daughter's free hand. "Oh Mackenzie, thank God you're alive."

Steve nodded, his eyes reddening. "Yes, child. Hundreds of people are praying for you."

The nurse straightened the bedclothes, securing the blanket around her patient. "I think we need to let Miss Adams rest now. She'll be able to respond better in the morning. The doctor will be in shortly. He'll be pleased to know she's awake."

When Makenzie awoke the next day, the whole scenario of her date with death crashed into her mind. How she'd survived, she had no clue. Only God could have spared her. She turned her head, and her mother stood at Mackenzie's bedside seconds later.

"Good morning, Mackenzie."

A groan emitted from her lips. She lifted her hand to point at the tube.

Her mother smiled. "Yes, I understand. The doctor just left. He said you're progressing as expected. He's talking with your father outside the door right now. The nurse will take you off the ventilator in a few minutes to see if you can breathe on your own. But I have no doubt of that. You're going to be up and around before you know it. God is on our side, Mackenzie." Her mother paused momentarily. "Your dad told me about your rededication to Christ. I'm so proud of you."

Reagan lowered her eyelashes, sadness overwhelming her countenance. "I'm so sorry for the way I've treated you." She ran her hand across Mackenzie's brow. "But we'll talk about that another day. All we have to think about now is getting you well."

Mackenzie nodded. At the swish of the door, she looked up and saw her dad walk into the room. He leaned forward, kissed her cheek, and then grasped her fingers between his palms. "Welcome back to our world, Mackenzie. Dr. Vanders said all signs point to a full recovery."

Mackenzie frowned. She wanted to ask what had taken place after she'd been shot. Had she dreamed that Trace had spoken her name just before Mr. Huntington pulled the trigger? And what about Mrs. Slater? Had she lived as well? Had Mr. Huntington killed Elise? Mackenzie closed her eyes, the thought too hard to bear. She couldn't think about that now. All she desired to do was drown the memories of that horrific day in sleep—blessed sleep.

Early that evening, she glanced up to see Trace and Angie enter the room. The breathing tube removed by the nurse earlier, Mackenzie tried to say hello, but her voice wouldn't cooperate. She waved instead.

"No more than fifteen minutes," the nurse said as she recorded Mackenzie's vitals.

After greeting the newcomers, Steve stood from one of the chairs near the hospital bed. "Mackenzie, your mother and I will take a trip to the cafeteria while you visit with your friends. We won't be gone long."

Mackenzie nodded. Smiling, she waved them toward the door, positive they needed the break. No one had mentioned how many days she'd been in the hospital, but maybe she'd find out in a few minutes. Her eyes saturated with expectation, Mackenzie turned toward her friends. Her stomach danced inside her when Trace kissed her cheek. She gazed at him, amazed at her response to him in spite of the seriousness of her injuries.

She motioned for him to come closer. "What happened after Mr. Huntington shot me?" she whispered. "How long have I been here?"

Trace straightened, turning to Angie. "She wants to know the details following Uncle Drew's attempt on her life and how long she's been in the hospital."

Angie stepped forward and smiled at her friend. "You gave us quite a scare, Mackenzie. You were unconscious for five days. But God has answered our prayers. Trace and I have been keeping tabs on you via your parents. The nurses wouldn't let you have visitors until today."

Trace nodded. "I've practically been living at this hospital." He grinned. "I've threatened, cajoled, and even tried a bribe or two, but the nurses refused to let me see you until tonight."

Mackenzie returned his smile. She opened her mouth to speak, and her friends leaned forward to catch her words. "Are you saying your persuasive powers only work on me?"

He took her hand in his. "I certainly hope so."

After a moment, her expression sobered. "Trace, please tell me about Mrs. Slater."

Trace looked at Angie, who nodded at the question in his eyes. "I'm sorry. Mrs. Slater died before the ambulance could get there."

Tears sprang to her eyes. *Why did Mrs. Slater have to die when we were just beginning to reach an understanding with one another?*

Angie curled her fingers around Mackenzie's hand. "Please try not to take it too hard, Mackenzie."

"Trace, when did you find me?"

"Captain Sprinsky and I reached the cellar just before Uncle Drew fired his gun. I called your name, and you looked toward me, but we couldn't get to you or him in time." He blinked several times. "I'm so sorry. The captain said just that fraction of a movement helped save your life. According to the doctor, the bullet stopped within an inch of your heart."

Mackenzie took a moment to turn his words over in her mind. "Are Greg and Mr. Huntington in jail?"

Trace nodded. "Locked up tighter than a rusty bolt on a tire wheel."

Mackenzie laid her hand on Trace's arm. "I can't imagine how hard this has been on you."

Sorrow gripped his features. "It's difficult to grasp the idea that Uncle Drew is a murderer. The police now know he killed Jason; the bullets taken from his body were fired from Uncle Drew's gun. Greg swears he knows nothing about Crane's death, but he did confess to aiding and abetting in the murder of Jasmine."

Mackenzie frowned. "How could Mr. Huntington have been so nonchalant about Jason's murder?"

Confusion filled Angie's eyes. "What do you mean, Mackenzie?"

"Mr. Huntington and I arrived home about the same time following my trip to the store after my appointment with Mr. Crane. Expressing my surprise at his lateness, he explained that an errand after work had delayed him. Apparently, Mr. Crane's murder had been his mission."

Angie nodded. "At least the time coincides. Mackenzie, our theory about Mrs. Huntington being murdered in her bedroom proved to be true. We just had the wrong suspect. After Mr. Huntington killed Jasmine, Greg helped load the body into her car, and Mr. Huntington drove the vehicle to the boat ramp, where he pushed the car into the river. When Mrs. Baxter saw the limo leaving Park House, Greg was behind the wheel, his assignment to pick up Mr. Huntington at a remote spot a short distance from the boat ramp.

"Captain Sprinsky believes Mr. Huntington lost his billfold in Jasmine's car when he drove her body to the pier. You may recall that when we were told about the police discovering Mr. Huntington's wallet in her car after they dragged it from the river, the captain failed to mention that the wallet had been lodged between the driver's seat and the console, not the passenger side. In the statement Mr. Huntington gave to the police early on, he had said that Jasmine had driven them home from the restaurant. According to Captain Sprinsky, Mr. Huntington became a prime suspect after they found the wallet, but they had no other evidence to back it up."

"What about Elise? Did he murder her as well?"

Before Trace could answer, the nurse walked into the room with Mackenzie's parents in tow. "Sorry, but you must go now," the nurse said to the visitors. "Miss Adams needs to call it a night."

Mackenzie yawned. "I guess I am a little tired," she said, her voice a bit stronger. "Thank you so much for coming."

"So glad we finally got to see you," Angie said. "We'll be back tomorrow. Right, Trace?"

"You can count on it, Mackenzie," he said with a gentle squeeze to her hand.

Giving the others a parting nod, Angie and Trace walked out the door.

"So tell me about Mr. Patterson," Reagan said to Mackenzie the next afternoon when she awoke from a nap. "When we met him the night we arrived at the hospital, he advised us of his relationship to Mr. Huntington."

Mackenzie, now able to speak in a more normal tone, chose her words with care. "Also, he's the vice president of Huntington Inc."

"He seems to care a great deal for you."

"We've become good friends since I've been in Arkansas."

Reagan smiled. "From what I've noticed, his interest in you is more than just friendly. And I understand he's a Christian."

"Yes, he is." Her cheeks warming, Makenzie tossed a glance around the room. "Where's Dad?"

"At the hotel, working on a problem at work. He said he would make it back here as soon as possible."

"I see. Mom, who notified you about me?"

"Your friend Angie. She found our phone numbers in your room and phoned your dad to tell him you were in surgery. We boarded the first available flight to Little Rock. By the way, I let Kari know about your situation, and she gave me instructions to tell you to pay her a visit once you've recuperated."

"I might do that."

Reagan folded and refolded her hands, moistening her lips before she spoke again. "Mackenzie, I need to ask your forgiveness. My efforts to control your life were unfair. You're not a child but a grown woman—a daughter I'm proud to call my own. I love you, Mackenzie."

"I've missed you, Mom."

"We've missed you too, more than I can say."

"I need some forgiveness from you as well. I'm sorry I hurt you and Dad, but I had to get away. Too many people and places to remind me of Zack and the problems that occurred in our relationship."

Mackenzie surveyed her mother's countenance. Could she reveal the main reason for leaving her home state? At once, Mackenzie knew the answer. No way could she put that burden of knowledge on her parents' shoulders. It would destroy every ounce of their faith in her. She could not, would not hurt them more than she had already. She loved them too much. And in time, with God's help and strength, her pain would lessen, and she'd be able to live with joy the life God had in mind for her, to fear Him and obey His commands—she smiled inwardly—the whole duty of mankind according to the biblical book of Ecclesiastes.

"I can understand that. Sometimes a new environment does help us put everything into perspective and brings healing, especially if we allow God to hold the reins. I just wish I had realized that a few weeks ago." Reagan stood to give her daughter a kiss.

"Because God's love and mercy is so prevalent in our lives, we can now put all our mistakes in the past, Mackenzie. This is a new beginning for us. And I will respect whatever decision you make for your life. If you desire to come home when you're able, so be it. But if you choose to stay in Arkansas, we won't interfere."

"Thanks, Mom. I really appreciate that." Mackenzie frowned. "I have no clue what I will do as yet."

"You don't have to make any kind of decision right away. The most important thing for you to do is concentrate on getting over this. Dad will have to fly back in a few days to go back to work, but I'm here for as long as you need me."

"I love you, Mom."

A couple of days later, the nurses moved Mackenzie from the ICU floor to her own private room. All settled in and about to eat her first real meal, she looked up to see Captain Sprinsky standing in the doorway. "Come in, Captain."

"I see you've had an upgrade," he said, grinning.

She smiled back at him. "Yes, my room in ICU was a little cramped with all the machinery stacked in there." She glanced at her mom and then motioned toward her. "Sir, this is my mother, Reagan Adams. Mom, this is Captain Sprinsky of the Little Rock Police Department.

Reagan smiled. "Yes, we met our first night here. How are you, Captain?"

"Fine, thank you. I just stopped by to see how my favorite amateur detective is doing."

"Amateur detective?" Reagan said, frowning.

Mackenzie bit her lip, fear leaping into her eyes. She gave the captain a slight shake of her head. Evidently, he didn't get the message she tried to portray.

"Yes, Mrs. Adams. Your daughter was my top spy in the Huntington household."

Mackenzie groaned inside and sank deeper into the pillow at the look on her mother's face.

"Mackenzie," Reagan said, her features lined with disapproval, "what have you been up to with this spy thing?"

"Really, Mom. It—" Mackenzie glimpsed the laughter in Captain Sprinsky's eyes. "It wasn't anything special. I was just curious about Mrs. Huntington's death.

Reagan drew a long sigh. "Knowing you, I can just imagine what that entailed."

The detective laughed. "Don't be too hard on her, Mrs. Adams. She actually was a big help to our investigation. She discovered the hard pieces of evidence we needed to convict Mr. Huntington of killing his wife. He's been a person of interest since the onset of the investigation into his wife's murder, but we could find nothing concrete to make an arrest. Mr. Patterson and I arrived on the scene mere seconds before he shot your daughter."

Mackenzie observed his change in demeanor. The humor in his eyes dwindled, sadness mingled with compassion taking its place. He turned to Mackenzie.

"I'm truly sorry, Miss Adams, that we didn't get there in time to prevent this from happening to you."

"Please don't feel bad, sir. I'm still alive, and that counts for something, doesn't it?"

"You bet it does. God certainly had His hand on you."

"Yes, He did. By the way, Captain, I assume Angie received my text and phoned you."

He nodded. "But having heard your phone message, I had arrived at Park House and was ringing the doorbell when she phoned. Mr. Patterson drove into the driveway while I was talking to her. He rushed to my side, instructing me to follow him as he unlocked the door, explaining later that Miss Valencia had phoned him as well, giving him your message. I received quite a shock when he tripped the lock on that hidden door. Just as we were about to enter the tunnel, Miss Valencia entered the house. Seeing us, she rushed down the hall, her expression mirroring my astonishment. When I saw the look of determination on her face, I just said, 'Follow us.'"

Mackenzie's chin dropped. "You mean Angie saw the whole thing?"

He nodded. "When Mr. Huntington saw the three of us standing there after he shot you, he just wilted, dropping the gun to the floor. Getting my set of handcuffs on him, I phoned for backup and an ambulance while Miss Valencia held her hands on your chest, keeping the blood flow at bay as much as possible. In the meantime, Mr. Patterson kept Mr. Martin in check. Sorry to say it was too late for Mrs. Slater."

"I didn't know—about Angie, I mean. She's a true friend."

"Yes. The medics declared she had helped save your life, along with the slight turn you made when Trace called to you. But I believe divine intervention was the greatest factor involved."

Mackenzie sighed. "I agree, sir." Mackenzie ran her hand along her brow. Reagan stepped to her daughter's side.

"I believe Mackenzie should rest now, Captain. If you don't mind."

"Just one more thing. I also wanted to let you know that Mr. Martin has made a full confession to his part in Mrs. Huntington's murder. When you get out of the hospital, I would ask that you not leave town until after the arraignments. We'll need your testimony at both hearings."

"I understand. Thank you, sir, for helping me get a clearer picture of everything."

"You're welcome. You take care now."

"Yes, sir, I will."

Once the captain had exited the room, Mackenzie glanced at her mom. Her mother's expression caused a tremor of alarm to ripple down Mackenzie's spine.

"Please, Mom, not now."

A hint of a smile touched Reagan's lips at Mackenzie's apprehensive expression. "Okay, but don't think I'm going to dismiss this sleuthing notion of yours. Once you're up and around, you can be assured it will be a matter of discussion between us."

Mackenzie nodded and then closed her eyes, the scheduled dose of pain medicine dripping into her veins doing its work. *A perfect time to take a long rest,* she decided as drowsiness stilled her thoughts.

A few days later, Mackenzie sat in Trace's car, gazing toward Park House. Angie stood on the porch, waving to them. Mackenzie smiled at her friend's eagerness to welcome them home.

"Are you sure you want to stay here, considering the bad memories you have of this place?" Reagan said, eyeing the house from the backseat. "Your dad would have found us temporary housing."

"I know, but there's good memories too, Mom. I've thought it over, and I can't leave until I know one way or the other about Elise—and Trace agrees that I should stay."

Reagan laughed. "Of course he would. I'm not blind. He's got it bad for you. And if I know my daughter, I'd say the feelings are mutual."

"We're just friends."

"Sure. And horses fly."

"What about Pegasus, the winged horse?"

"Just as mythical as your friend statement."

At that moment, Trace opened both their doors, aiding Mackenzie's walk to the house.

"Welcome home, Miss Adams."

Mackenzie turned at the sound of the greeting from across the street. "Thank you, Mrs. Baxter."

"I just finished making a fresh batch of cookies. I'll bring them over later."

Mackenzie and Trace exchanged glances. "Don't worry, Mackenzie. Either I or your mom will run interference for you. You don't have to tell her a thing."

"A nosy neighbor?" Reagan asked in a soft tone.

Mackenzie nodded. "But with a golden heart. She supervises the Neighborhood Watch program in our area."

Reagan grinned. "Well, that should make you feel safe."

"Thanks, Mrs. Baxter," Trace said. "No one makes cookies like you do. I'm sure we'll enjoy them."

Once inside the house, Mackenzie determined that her decision to remain at Park House for now had been wise, in spite of the reservations she'd had earlier. She received Angie's hug, giving her friend one in return. "Captain Sprinsky told me what you did for me after I was shot. I owe you one."

"*Mi amiga*, that's what friends do."

Tears welled in Mackenzie's eyes. "Like I said, I owe you one."

"Well now, let's get you upstairs and settled." Angie glanced over her shoulder. "Mrs. Adams, I have a room all prepared for you just down the hall from Mackenzie."

"Thank you, Angie."

"Not a problem. Mackenzie, you be careful on those stairs."

"Oh, great. Now I have to put up with two mothering fowl," she said, grinning.

"And one take-charge rooster." That said, Trace carefully scooped Mackenzie into his arms and climbed toward the upper floor. Too startled to say a word, she winced at the sound of Angie and her mother's laughter at the bottom of the stairs.

When they reached the door to her room, Trace eased her from his arms until she stood sure-footed on the hallway floor. When she turned to thank him, her breath caught. He held her in his gaze momentarily, his eyes full of feelings that far exceeded the affection of a friend. Her energy seemed to melt away. He reached around her and opened the door. "I'll bring your things up in a few minutes," he said, his voice husky.

Mackenzie straightened and moved back a step at the sound of her mother's voice complimenting the decor of the guest room near the top of the stairs. "Thanks, Trace," she said, speaking softly. She heard his sharp intake of breath.

"I'll be back shortly."

Nodding, she entered her room. It shined with Angie's touch. Not a dust particle could be seen. She walked over to the window and looked down; the sight of the sparkling pool soothed her as if she were experiencing a fresh breath of spring. Yes, newness of life. God had granted her a new beginning and by His strength she would be able to endure living at Park House, regardless of all that had happened?

She hadn't asked, but she'd supposed now that Mr. Huntington had made Trace power of attorney, he would oversee both the business and the house. Angie had stated on one of her visits to the hospital that he'd hired her to be the live-in house manager until he decided what to do with the property. Mackenzie relished the idea. She wouldn't be alone in the house when her mother had to leave to begin the new school term in a few weeks.

A knock on the doorjamb broke her musing. Trace entered the room, his arms encircling a couple plants and the vase of flowers she'd desired to bring from the hospital. She'd given the other expressions of kindness to patients who hadn't received like gifts of thoughtfulness. She took the bouquet of roses from him and took a whiff of their fragrance before she deposited the container in the middle of her small kitchen table.

"You shouldn't have indulged in such extravagance," she said as she adjusted the flowers. She grinned. "But I'm glad you did. They're beautiful."

"Indeed they are," her mother said, sweeping into the room. Angie filed in behind Reagan.

Angie's eyes widened. "I'd say so." She crossed the room, read the card, and turned to give Mackenzie a wink. "I told you so."

Mackenzie turned from her guests, her cheeks flaming. "What do you say to our ordering a pizza? I'm starved. Hospital food is not my idea of a gourmet meal."

"Well, maybe I can remedy that if Angie will let me help out in the kitchen while I'm here."

Angie brightened. "Oh, would you? I can cook, but Mackenzie might get tired of Hispanic food every day."

"Well, that settles it. Show me the way to the kitchen, and I'll get started."

Angie held up her hand. "Not today. Several ladies in Mackenzie's church have brought in food. Mrs. Simpson is in the kitchen organizing everything. The smells are heavenly."

Mackenzie's eyes widened. "Mrs. Simpson? How gracious of her. Mom, I bet she could use your assistance, if you don't mind."

"Glad to help. Come on, Angie—point me in the right direction."

Mackenzie recalled the day Mrs. Simpson had paid a visit to the hospital. Her parents' difficulty at hiding their astonishment when Zelda walked into the room had been amusing. That day, her new friend had been dressed in bright orange, looking as if she were on her way to a southern-belle tea party. It had taken several minutes to convince her parents that Mrs. Simpson did not suffer from insanity.

Trace grinned. "I think I'll journey downstairs and check out that delectable fare. Would you like to eat downstairs with us or have a tray sent to your room?"

"I'll eat with you. I don't want to be confined any longer. But, Trace, you don't have to carry me down the stairs. If I take it slow, I'll make it just fine."

"Are you sure?" he said, reaching out to stroke her cheek. "I thought you rather enjoyed my arms around you earlier. I know I did." He backed up a step at seeing the frustration build on her face. He held up his hands. "Okay, I remember. Friends—just friends."

A few mornings later, Mackenzie, after returning from having her stitches removed, sat in the den with her mother, enjoying a glass of sweet tea. She couldn't contain her pleasure when Trace walked into the room.

"I have a surprise for you, Mackenzie."

"Oh?" she said, her eyes brightening.

He turned toward the doorway. "Okay, Angie."

The hint of confusion in her expression changed to utter delight when Angie walked into the room with Elise in her arms. Tears of joy fell from beneath her eyelashes. She stood, hurried across the room as quickly as her body would allow, and took the child into her arms.

Mackenzie glanced from her mom to Angie and then shifted her gaze to Trace; all of their eyes shimmered with tears. Elise smiled widely, and Mackenzie saw that the baby had grown another tooth.

"When? Where?" Mackenzie asked Trace when they had somewhat regained their composure. She couldn't seem to hold Elise close enough or give her enough kisses. After a moment, Mackenzie returned to the sofa and sat down; Trace took a seat next to her. Angie joined Reagan on the love seat.

"Talk to us, Trace," Mackenzie said. "The suspense is killing me."

"Captain Sprinsky phoned me early this morning to let me know Elise had been found and was at the hospital. As her godfather and now her guardian, I had to sign the papers for her to be examined by a physician."

"Hospital?" Mackenzie checked Elise for signs of illness but didn't discern a problem.

"Just normal police procedure for a child that's been kidnapped for a time. While we were waiting for the nurse to bring Elise to me, Captain Sprinsky filled me in on her rescue."

"And?" Angie said, scooting to the edge of the love seat.

"The kidnappers took Elise to a remote backwoods area near Mountain View, a town northeast of here. Known as a tourist area, the townspeople wouldn't pay much attention to another stranger or two. But the kidnappers weren't taking any chances. They held her in a home belonging to the grandmother of one of Greg's former street buddies."

"Greg!" the girls said in unison. Reagan sat quietly, her eyes glowing with confusion.

Trace sighed. "Yes, my dear cousin instigated the whole plan. His way, he said, of getting a share of the Huntington inheritance, aware that he probably wouldn't be named in Uncle Drew's will."

"So you're saying that Greg drove the car when Elise was taken?" Mackenzie said.

Trace shook his head. "He couldn't take the risk. Several years ago, Greg and some friends stole a car and sold it to a hack shop. Greg, the only one of them who hadn't been in trouble with law enforcement previously, received a suspended sentence, compelled to do community service for a year. The other two did prison time.

"When Greg learned that one of his former partners in crime, Nate Ingles, had been released from prison, Greg looked him up, offering to give part of the ransom to his friend if he would help with the kidnapping scheme."

"What a jerk!" Angie said, reaching for Elise's hand. "And the woman involved?"

"Think about it. Who would Greg desire most to participate in the conspiracy?"

Mackenzie brightened. "Lacey Carmichael, without a doubt. I'm guessing that the temptation of a share of the money, revenge against Mr. Huntington, and her fondness for Elise helped spur her motivation."

"What about the grandmother?" Reagan said. "Was she in on the plot as well?"

"No, she and Elise were the only innocent parties. Nate had told his grandmother that Lacey and he were married but that she needed protection from an ex-husband who'd threatened to kill Lacey and her child, asking his grandmother to house them until he could get enough money together to settle his little family out of the state."

Deep lines formed on Reagan's brow. "I don't understand. How could the grandmother not be aware of the kidnapping when it's been broadcast on every news media available?"

"I questioned the captain about that as well. The woman didn't have much in the way of material possessions—no media devices except a radio."

Angie drew a long sigh. "I suppose Greg finally confessed all this."

Trace shook his head. "It was Lacey who notified the police of Elise's location."

"Oh my word! The woman has a conscience after all."

Trace laughed. "Maybe. But actually, she'd gone into Mountain View to get some supplies for Elise and decided to have lunch in town. While dining, she saw the broadcast of Greg's and Uncle Drew's arrests on the public television in the restaurant. Thinking Greg would eventually confess to their crime, she opted to phone Captain Sprinsky, hoping the court would give her a lighter sentence for revealing the plot."

Angie held up her hand. "Wait a minute. I thought she and Greg were no longer seeing each other."

"All part of the scam. He even promised Lacey they would get married when the heat died down, telling her they would travel the world on the ransom money."

"After Lacey saw his arrest on TV, she must have decided to expose their con in hopes that his future—a prison cell—would be deleted from her environment," Angie said, grinning.

"Once Greg knew Lacey had notified the captain about the crime, he confessed, giving the location where they'd stashed the money. Once the court no longer needs what's left of the ransom for evidence, it will be returned to Jason's estate, which, by the way, is now in the hands of Jason's brother. He phoned me a few days ago to inform me that Jason had set up a large trust fund for Elise to be given to her when she becomes twenty-five years in age.

"Nate is now in jail as well. Since he broke his probation, he'll be taken back to prison soon. The grandmother, of course, was not arrested when Lacey shared the woman's innocence in the situation. She'll have to testify as a witness at the trial, but that's all."

"Well, the important thing," Mackenzie said, again hugging her charge, "is that Elise is home now and safe. For all that he's done, I'm glad Mr. Huntington didn't have anything to do with the kidnapping, his concern for Elise genuine. I guess he did love his daughter."

Everyone nodded.

Late that evening, Mackenzie sat on the nursery floor next to the crib, observing Elise's slumber, wondering if she had dreamed the whole nightmarish event. She reached out and touched the baby, so thankful that Elise had survived the ordeal. *Thank you, God, for answering our prayers.*

A light tap on the hall door startled her. Angie and Reagan had retired earlier in the evening. When she opened the door, her eyes widened. Trace peeked inside the room over Mackenzie's shoulder and then motioned for her to step into the hall. A moment later, she closed the door behind her.

"I thought you'd gone home."

"No, I started the task of sorting the paperwork in Uncle Drew's office. Mackenzie, it's difficult to understand my uncle's actions. I think he truly loved Jasmine. When he found out about her affair with Jason, I believe both her indiscretion and his need for revenge against Jason drove him insane. Captain Sprinsky said he won't talk at all, just sits in his cell, staring at the wall. I never saw the side of him Jasmine portrayed in her note. Brutal in business when needed but never with me. I know he'll die for his crimes eventually. I just want him to give his heart to Christ before that happens."

"Trace, we'll just have to keep praying for him."

"Yes. I will continue to do that." He ran his hand through his hair. "Mackenzie, I know you'd thought about going back to Arizona once we discovered Elise's fate, but I'm asking you to stay on as her nanny. I'm responsible for her, and I can't see anyone in that position but you. I know you love her."

"With all my heart."

"And, Mackenzie, I'm not asking just for her. I need you to stay too. I'm in love with you. I know you have feelings for me too, even though it's hard for you to trust them. I'm sorry. I don't want to be just friends with you. My desire is to love and protect you, provide for you, and maybe someday not too far down the road, you will allow me to win your heart."

All of a sudden, the mistrust inside her seemed to vanish. She took a step toward him, and Trace opened his arms wide. She moved into them without question, savoring the feel of them around her. She lifted her lips to receive his kiss. At that moment, Mackenzie, her heart overflowing with joy, realized that she, like Elise, had finally come home.

Epilogue

Two Years Later

At the sound of her name, Mackenzie stepped onto the platform of the auditorium and marched across the stage, her head held high, cords of success hanging around her neck. She received the well-wishes and her doctorate diploma from the president of the university with grace.

On her way back to her seat, she waved toward the area in the stands where she believed her family sat, having heard whistles and cheers from that section when she'd crossed the platform a moment ago. Soon she would watch Angie take the same journey to receive her associate's degree in criminology.

Once seated, Mackenzie placed her hand on her stomach. It thrilled her every time the baby moved inside her. In a few months, she would give Trace a son, a prayer of thanks on her lips that God had pardoned not only her sins but also her bareness. A simple procedure a few months following her marriage to Trace had corrected the problem.

Recalling her wedding in Arizona in the autumn of last year, she smiled. Kari had flown in from California to be her maid of honor, while Angie had arrived, along with her family, by car to be Mackenzie's first bridesmaid of the three she'd chosen to precede her down the aisle.

Although modest, everything regarding the wedding had been done to perfection; her mother had been in charge of the whole affair.

Trace had surprised his bride-to-be by bringing Mrs. Simpson with him when he flew out with his best man and groomsmen a few days before the wedding. As usual, Zelda had stood out among the other guests, but by the end of the reception, she'd done such a marvelous job of charming everyone that no one paid attention to her apparel.

The only blight on the day was the sentencing of Trace's uncle a few days prior to the groom's arrival in Arizona. Mr. Huntington would die by lethal injection. To date, he was still on death row, awaiting his scheduled time. Greg had been sentenced to several years in prison a few months later, while Lacey had been given a suspended sentence for turning state's evidence, along with her responsible care of Elise, a plus in her case.

A few weeks before their wedding, Trace had sold Park House and bought a home near Huntington Inc. He said he didn't want to start their marriage in a home that had too much sadness in its history.

Elise had made the transition just fine. Almost three now, she was looking forward to her baby brother. Mr. Huntington had given up his rights to her soon after Mackenzie and Trace had married. They'd started adoption proceedings immediately. She was now Elise Patterson.

The realty market had increased in the last year, and Huntington Inc. was holding its own. The last time Trace had visited his uncle, he'd inquired about the plan of salvation. He hadn't accepted Christ as his Savior that day, but she and her husband were praying daily that the next visit would find Mr. Huntington at peace with God and hopefully himself.

So all in all, things are going well for the Pattersons, she thought. She never ceased to give God the glory for all He had done in their lives. As the recessional began, Mackenzie stood with her fellow classmates. Along with them, she waited patiently until she could begin her journey into the future.

Once outside on the lawn, she eagerly waited for her family to find her, and she soon collected hugs and congratulations from her parents and Trace. Elise clapped her hands, enjoying the excitement all around her.

Angie and her family joined them a few minutes later, and Mrs. Valencia made sure Mackenzie and her family would be attending the graduation celebration Rosa had planned for Angie late that afternoon.

"Don't worry," Angie said, laughing, seeming to read her friend's mind. "Yes, tons of my relatives will come, but we're having the party in our backyard. Plenty of space for everyone. See you later," she said as the Valencias began the walk to the parking lot.

Once seated in the minivan they now owned, Mackenzie rolled down the window to take in the odors of spring, observing the new life spread before her. She turned to smile at her parents and her daughter. Elise sat in the car seat between her grandparents, chattering about her expected brother.

After a moment, Mackenzie glanced at her husband, who smiled lovingly at her. Yes, she had much for which she could be thankful. *And, God, please help me not to forget a single one of your benefits all the days of my life.*